A SHOT OF LOVE

By

Jesse Myrow

Artwork by Elena Pintilii

Acknowledgements

I would like to say a big, heartfelt thank you to Elena Pintilii, the CEO of "Ana's Stories," for yet another amazing book cover.

Looking at Elena's wonderfully creative work on the covers of both "The Bridge" and "A Shot of Love," you truly realize that you really can judge a book by its cover!

Prologue

July 2032, Little Alamo Compound, Texas

Tex Pemberton cut a striking figure as he staggered toward the small, wooden bench with both hands clasped to his stomach. At six-five with a linebacker's physique, he was a man not easily ignored. Beneath his wide-brimmed hat, his thick mop of silver-gray hair was plastered to his head with sweat as he fought against the pain threatening to take him to the ground. Hot, sticky blood pumped through Tex's fingers with each step he took, each thud of his struggling heart, to turn his shirt and faded 501s a dark red that looked almost black in the fading light.

The raucous noise of the victory celebrations going on in full swing in the compound's square behind Tex had drowned out the sound of the gunshot that had punched a hole through his guts; it felt good to hear such joy, such happiness, even as Tex knew he was dying.

Flopping down on the little bench with a loud grunt of pain and exertion, Tex watched with dismay as his blood ran in thick, viscous rivulets over the seat's roughly hewn wooden slats. Being there brought Tex comfort in what he knew were his final moments, for it was the special place he'd shared with Victoria over their years together at Little Alamo.

Perched by the side of the small green, the bench overlooked the weed-choked pond once home to a dozen or so loud, greedy ducks who would pester anyone who happened by for a morsel of bread. The ducks were long gone, of course. They'd been eaten by the compound's increasingly hungry and desperate citizens as food became scarce, and there was little room left for sentimentality. All that remained was Lonesome Georgina, the last remaining swan; she was old and bad-tempered, and nobody had the heart—or stomach— to eat her. The compound's kids had named her after the famous Galapagos tortoise, Lonesome George, who was the last of his kind on one of those remote islands.

It kinda suited the old girl.

Tex hoped, with the victory he'd secured that day, there would be ducks—and swan company for Georgina—once more on the Little Alamo Pond.

It was a peaceful, tranquil place for Tex Pemberton, a place filled with happy memories and love.

It was a good place to die.

"What the hell happened?!" A voice jarred Tex's focus from thoughts of colorful ducks and nipping beaks. *"Tex?"*

It took great effort and a white-hot flash of pain to turn his head to see the owner of the voice, although he'd recognized it straight away.

"Howdy, Lump." Tex heard his own voice slurring like he'd been at the compound's homemade moonshine.

John "Lump" Christie sat himself down next to Tex, not seeming to care he'd just sat in the spreading pool of his best friend's blood. "Shit, we need to get you to Doc Barker." There was panic, alarm, etched in his voice.

Leaning over, Lump teased Tex's hand away from his blood-soaked belly, then cringed as a fresh gout of bright-red blood gushed out from the gaping hole there.

"Leave me." Tex brushed Lump's hand away with a flap of his own. "I'm dying here."

Lump stripped of his shirt and pressed it hard against Tex's midsection; a fresh wave of agony ripped through Tex's body and made him cry out.

"I'm going to get Andy," Lump told Tex. "If I try moving you, you'll bleed out before we get you to the infirmary."

"I told you to leave me," Tex growled, blood frothing from the corners of his mouth. "Just let me fucking die, here, Lump. I don't want to go staring at Doc Barker's ugly face."

"Who did this to you, Tex?" Lump demanded as he stood up from the bench, his pants soaked through and glistening with blood.

Tex gave his friend a dismissive wave with a bloodied hand. "It really doesn't matter, Lump," he said. "It was just my time, is all."

"I'll be right back," Lump told him. "Doc Barker will have you patched up in no time."

"Yeah." The word came out pained, breathy, and created a dull, gnawing pain deep in Tex's gut. His head felt light, his vision swam as dark gray crept in from the sides. "I'm sure he will do just that."

So, this's what dying feels like. Tex thought it actually didn't feel so bad, and it sure as hell was far better than facing a lifetime with the pain of betrayal and lost love.

"Okay, go get the doc," Tex said as he watched his friend dash away from the bench. "I'm sure he'll fix me up just fine." Tex knew, of course, he'd be dead long before Lump found the doctor amid the Little Alamo's revelry and brought him back to the bench.

That pleased Tex, as it meant he could die alone and in peace with his memories.

THE BEFORE TIMES

Chapter One

November 2028, Fort Worth, Texas

The whole thing was just a wretched, unbelievable mess. It had gotten so bad that Tex dreaded switching on the TV each morning, but he knew the importance of staying informed with what was going on in the world—it would literally mean the difference between life and death when it came down to the wire.

War played out on the screen above the refrigerator: tanks rolled through shell-damaged towns, homes burned, civilians fled on foot clutching what few belongings they could while stepping over the corpses of those far less fortunate than even themselves.

"I don't know why you insist on watching the news, Jonah, it's so depressing," Krista moaned at him from across the breakfast table. She'd always refused to call him Tex—that was a nickname reserved for his ex-Army buddies. They'd saddled him with the moniker back in basic training because he'd been the only new recruit there from the Lone Star State.

"Just keeping up with current events, babe." Tex offered his wife a smile. She was very much a head-in-the-sand kinda gal, which Tex figured he ought to find annoying given the circumstances, but he actually found it wonderfully innocent and endearing in troubled times. Krista had made the excuse of wanting to shield their son from all the bad things going on, even though, at thirteen, Lee was on the cusp of becoming a man.

She'd even flat refused to let the kid watch the Reuters news coverage of Russia marching into Ukraine just like they had six years before, only this time, they had no intention of bowing to international and NATO pressure, and their actions had sparked a nasty war across Europe.

Having said that, Tex had not stopped Lee watching the coverage of China finally making good on its threat to take back Taiwan or North Korea taking full advantage of the global chaos to let loose its missiles onto its southern neighbor's soil. The mêlée resulting from that action kicked off a full-blown, spectacularly bloody war between the two, while the world stood by and waited for the inevitable escalation into nuclear conflict.

"Why don't we help those people, Dad?" Lee had asked Tex late one night. He'd let the boy stay up to watch the world descend into chaos, while they talked about the compound Tex and his friends were building way beyond the outskirts of their small suburb.

"Because we can't," Tex had told him. "We have enough troubles of our own without getting involved in other peoples'."

"But we're *America.*" The purity of his son's innocence brought tears to Tex's eyes. The kid's blind faith and unerring confidence in his country was evocative of the patriotism that had once made the United States great, a world leader.

But that was before.

Before the police were defunded to such an extent they were no longer able to maintain even basic law and order. Before things had been made all the more difficult due to ongoing COVID restrictions throughout the country; they'd been in place since 2020 and strengthened with each new variant of the virus. Although the restrictions varied state to state, the overriding interpretation was one of suppression of the masses, which served well to fan the flames of rebellion.

And, once gas prices went through the roof and food shortages swept the country, the predictable repercussion was a country at war with itself. The once mighty USA drifted recklessly into another civil war as rioters hit the streets with murderous intent, looters took what they wanted because the police had little power to stop them, and all across the country, the cities burned.

Only, unlike in the eighteen-sixties, the war was not North versus South, but everyone against everyone; every man for himself, and to hell with the rest. It saddened Tex to see the country he'd fought for in Afghanistan and Iraq plunged into such terrible disarray. Even harder was the heartbreaking realization there would be no coming back from this one until the United States was razed to the dirt and given the opportunity to build itself back up again.

"What ya watching?" Lee asked, walking into the kitchen. Behind him padded Winnie, the family's dog; Krista had named the dog when Tex brought him home for the kid's eleventh birthday—she thought the white, curly-haired thing that never grew higher than Tex's knee looked like a "Winnie" and the name was cute. In the two years since then, boy and dog had been inseparable.

"Nothing for nosy people," Krista said with a frosty smile. She grabbed the TV remote from the countertop and switched channels at the prod of an immaculately manicured finger.

"Spongebob?" Lee exchanged smirks with his father. "Really, Mom?"

"The boy's too old for cartoons, Krista," Tex said. "He needs to know what's going on in the world."

"What he needs is to focus on his Texas history test today—or did you forget that?"

Lee rolled his eyes at his mother and grabbed the orange juice from the refrigerator. "I didn't forget," he told her, then took a hearty swig straight from the carton just like he'd seen his father do a thousand times before.

"Eww!" Krista visibly recoiled, which had Tex smiling. "What have I told you about doing that, Lee?"

"Not to do that," Lee replied with a cheeky grin and took another swig.

"Jonah!" Krista snapped at Tex. "Will you tell your son to quit doing that?!"

Tex shrugged and tipped Lee a sly wink. "I think with all that's happening right now, drinking juice from the carton is the last thing we have to worry about."

Krista let out a long, loud sigh of defeat and stood up from the table. "You two are as bad as each other," she grumbled. "I hope you both catch cooties."

It took all Tex had to not laugh out loud at that; he knew it would have seriously hurt his sweet wife's feelings and likely lead to a full-on, stand-up row. And that's something he really didn't want to have to face.

"There was more trouble in Fort Worth last night," Tex told his son.

"More riots?" Lee sat himself down opposite Tex and fed the dog Krista's leftover toast—in all the years she and Tex had been together, he'd not once seen her eat the crusts.

"Looting, too," Tex said.

"Maybe we should go sometime—I could use a new flat screen in my room." Lee grinned at his own joke.

Tex high-fived his son, much to the chagrin of his wife, who stomped out of the kitchen muttering something under her breath about laundry and how Jonah was corrupting her dear, sweet little boy.

Tex picked up the remote and flicked back to the news channel. There, images of the smoldering Fort Worth streets were being compared with those of Dallas, San Antonio, and Houston—those cities were all but lawless wrecks run by the gangs and crazies.

"Looks like we're next, Dad?" Lee's boyish countenance slipped as he took in the destruction and ticker tape tally of the night's dead that ran beneath the stern-faced reporter as she read monotonously from her autocue.

Tex nodded.

As much as he wanted to tell his son there was nothing for him to worry about and everything was going to be okay, that their sleepy little suburb on the outskirts of Forth Worth would be safe from the madness taking over the world outside their door, Tex couldn't bring himself to do it. He knew full well what was coming—he'd spent most of the past ten years planning for it—and that the Texas history Lee had been up late cramming for was about to be rewritten along with that of the rest of the world.

"When will we go to the Little Alamo?" Lee was straight to the point as usual; he'd spent a whole lot of weekends at the compound Tex and his buddies were building and seemed to be genuinely looking forward to being there.

Tex and his friends had spent a long time picking out just the perfect place for the Little Alamo; it had to be someplace remote, strategically located to garner protection from the natural cover of trees and mountains. It also had to have a good, reliable water source and plenty of hunting—there'd be a lot of hungry mouths to feed once things went south in the outside world and the carefully selected residents took their places in the compound.

After countless hours of studying maps and taking

long reconnaissance trips to check out each and every possible location, they'd finally decided upon a place in East Texas, deep in pine tree country, Lilly Creek Bottoms, which sat a good two-and-a-half hours east of Fort Worth. Secluded, surrounded by dense forest, and with a natural spring running beneath, it was perfect.

"When we *need* to go," Tex told his son. "We're not quite ready just yet." His eyes flicked to the death and destruction on the TV screen, and he wondered if they actually had time to make the final finishing touches to their refuge.

"Will you quit filling the boy's head with your prepper crap, Jonah?" Krista appeared back in the kitchen as if she'd made the effort simply to chastise her husband.

"It's not crap." Tex's retort was met with an angry stare. He hated that she referred to him as a *prepper*—she threw the word around like a cussword when she was mad at him—had steadfastly refused to visit the Little Alamo for as long as he'd been working on the project.

"It's all you ever talk about these days," Krista snapped back, and Tex knew his wife was angling for a fight—she knew precisely where his buttons were and which ones to press. "It's just you and your old army buddy playing Wild West at the expense of spending time with your family—Lump Christie's wife left him because of it… took the kids with her, too."

"Have you *seen* anything of what's going on out there?" Tex took the bait, much against his better judgment; Krista was evidently itching for a fight. "The whole country is just one step away from complete chaos—how long before the power goes out, the Internet quits working, and the army turns on what's left of the government? Then we'll really be back in the Wild West."

"And you'd just *love* that, wouldn't you?" Krista spat. "Then you can all go play cowboys and Indians like a bunch of little kids."

Lee couldn't help but smirk at his mother's use of the word *Indian*. Even he knew it was politically incorrect to refer to Native Americans that way—no matter how badly society was circling the drain.

"You think this is all one big game, don't you?" Krista rounded on her son. "You father is filling your head with all his end of the world bullcrap and telling you school doesn't matter anymore and you're failing everything! He's ruining your damn life, Lee, and you're too young to see it."

Tex stood up from the table, his hackles up. "I am not ruining the boy's life!" He felt the need to defend himself; had Lee not been there, he'd have let Krista's words wash over him—he knew she knew more about the world's events than she was prepared to admit, and it terrified her. Lashing out that way was simply his wife's way of coping. "Preparing for this all these years may just save his life, Krista—*our* lives. We'll be safe at the Little Alamo with all the other families, and we can ride out whatever the fuck is going on."

"Safe?" Krista hit back. "How can you call living in the desert with a bunch of lunatic preppers *safe*?"

"We'll be away from the cities, Krista, I've explained that before—"

"Away from civilization and any kind of law enforcement." Krista snatched up the remote and switched off the TV as if to emphasize her point. "What makes you think I want to live in some lawless wasteland waiting to be raped and murdered in my sleep by some crazy ass with a gun?"

"They're all good people, Krista, John and me picked them all personally."

"They're people *you two* know." Krista raised her voice a tad more. "And that hardly makes them upstanding, stable citizens I'd want me and my son to live with in some dumb little fort in the middle of nowhere."

"You know Victoria..." Tex ventured; Krista was right, of course, she'd had no say in which families he and John had invited to live in the Little Alamo when the day finally came, but that had only been because of her refusal to have any involvement other than castigate Tex over it.

"Only because she's another army buddy's widow and lives three doors down the street," Krista replied. "I really wouldn't use her as a prime example, if I were you."

Tex refused to take his wife on with the subject of Victoria Hyatt and the death of her husband and his best friend, Rusty; it was a cruel low blow, and she knew it.

"You'll be happy enough to be at the compound when you need to be," Tex told Krista. "Jed Timothy and his clan are already living at theirs and he says it's a relief to be away from all the crazy stuff."

"Jed's been looking forward to dropping off the grid for years," Krista said. "And that hick wife of his is as loony-tunes as him."

There was a definite ring of truth in Krista's accusation: Jed had been the archetypal prepper a long time before Tex and John spotted the writing on the wall. The guy had amassed an impressive array of guns and ammunition, which he'd kept in his homemade underground fallout shelter until his compound was ready. Jed had once shown Tex the mountains of canned goods and chemical toilets he'd collected, along with stacks of solar panels and water purifiers—now, those had been a terrific idea.

"Best place for Jed and Kath Timothy is out of civilization, if you ask me." Krista clearly wasn't about to let the discussion go. Tex was pleased to see his wife's misplaced anger toward him, and his fellow *preppers*, wasn't upsetting Lee any. If anything, he thought he saw a hint of amusement on his son's face—the kid was only just a teen, and he could already see through his mother's rhetoric.

But, for as crazy as Krista sounded, Tex loved the woman as much then as he did the first time they'd met back in high school—with every fiber of his being—if not more so with each passing day.

She was scared, that much he knew, and lashing out against him and those like him who she thought were actually looking forward to the inevitable collapse of human society was simply a way to deal with her fear. Naturally, Krista's maternal instinct was to protect her son at all costs, no matter what might be happening around them. It was why she insisted he still get up and go to school every morning despite a large proportion of his classmates no longer attending—traditional education was of no use in a world at war. So, she had Lee finish up his homework each evening and restricted his TV and Internet time—Tex reckoned it was Krista's way of thinking everything was normal, and all would be okay if only she kept up the pretense.

Tex's heart ached for his beloved wife. He couldn't help but wonder how her growing detachment from reality would serve once they were ensconced in the Little Alamo. Lee would be perfectly fine—the kid had a level, mature head on his shoulders and Tex had taught him how to shoot, hunt, fish, and live off the land. Their weekends together supervising the compound's construction had been put to very good use.

"I'm hoping it doesn't come to it." Tex tried to placate his wife. "There's still time for the government to get a handle on things and restore law and order in the cities." Even as the lie left his mouth, Tex felt ashamed for having said it. Krista wasn't dumb, and she knew him too well to swallow his hollow words. The government had lost control months ago, in line with governments in Europe, Asia, and China—the end was inevitable and fast approaching.

"I really think you're right." Krista put her hands on Lee's shoulders and Tex saw in her eyes she didn't believe a word of it. "We've lived through so much these last few years, I'm sure we'll survive this latest hiccup."

Lee shrugged off his mother's hands and stood up. "I guess I should be going…" he left it hanging there, hoping as he did every morning either of his parents would tell him it was okay, he didn't have to go to school that day. The kid was an optimist, Tex had to give him that, but they'd made him go even after the school bus quit coming by.

"I'll drive him," Tex told Krista—it would do them both good for him to get out of the house, even for a short while.

"Please yourself," Krista grumped and turned to leave the kitchen. "Have a great day, Lee." With that, she was gone; the silence between father and son was broken only by sound of the dog crunching toast crusts under the table.

Chapter Two

"You could always drop me off at the arcade." Lee sounded hopeful. "That's where *everybody* hangs out anyways."

Tex laughed—he certainly couldn't fault the boy for trying. "And face more of your mother's bad mood?" he said. "You really think I'm *that* crazy, Lee?"

"I think you're the cool parent," Lee replied with a cheeky grin. "C'mon, Dad, nobody's going to school anymore."

"There's enough to make it worth your while, son," Tex told him, although he was painfully aware of how class sizes had diminished in the past few months, as well as the number of teachers abandoning their posts. Still, those who remained, along with a handful of stalwart substitutes and classroom assistants, were providing at least the rudiments of an education while maintaining the appearance of near normality. "You never know, you might just learn something useful today."

Tex said that *every* day.

"I'd learn more at the Little Alamo," Lee clearly wasn't about to give up. "You promised to let me have a go with the longbows."

"That can wait 'til the weekend," Tex said as he

pulled the car onto the main drag that led to Pioneer Heritage Intermediary School—just one more semester to go and the kid would be a high-schooler.

"When will we be moving there, Dad?" There was a sadness in his son's tone that tugged hard at Tex's heart.

"No idea," he replied honestly. "Could be soon—may be never if things get sorted out."

"It looks like Jed Timothy doesn't think things are going back to normal," Lee said. "I was in a chatroom with Jeb, and he said his old man reckons it's only a matter of time before the Russians or Chinese start flinging nukes around—what happens then, Dad?"

It was a question Tex really didn't want to answer; how the hell do you tell a kid teetering on the cusp of manhood with the rest of his life stretching before him that the world could very well be ending? "It won't come to that," Tex said with some conviction.

There was still some part of him that truly believed common sense would prevail; surely no one would want global annihilation, no matter how badly they were losing a war? But Tex's deep-down fear was economic collapse; its resulting destruction of society's norms would be far more devastating even than nuclear warheads.

"If it comes to that, we'll be safe at the Little Alamo," Tex said. "We have everything we need there and will be self-sustainable for as long as we need to be—the soil's good out there for growing crops, and we have the pigs and chickens for breeding."

"Jeb says all the pigs and chickens and solar panels in the world won't matter a shit if the bombs start falling." There was no humor in Lee's voice, his face a picture of worry.

"That Jeb Timothy's as blockheaded as his father," Tex snapped. "If—and it's a *big* if, son—the Russians or Chinese start firing missiles at us, they're going to go for the strategic targets. Houston, for definite, because of the oil industry and space center, Dallas because it's finance, and maybe Austin because it's too full of hippy liberals for even the communists to stomach." His attempt at levity fell woefully flat. "Nobody's gonna want to nuke the middle of nowhere miles away from any small town, let alone a city. We'll be perfectly safe at the Little Alamo, son."

Tex knew there were more families than Jed Timothy's heading out to the compounds and bunkers that the so-called preppers had been diligently constructing for a long time—some dated as far back as the first Cold War in the seventies and eighties. From there, they hunkered down and prepared themselves to watch the world go to hell in a handbasket.

Along with his buddy, John, Tex had kept abreast of everything going on across the country, and they figured all those heading for the hills—literally in some cases—were being more than a tad premature.

Although, as things looked to Tex that morning, he was beginning to have his doubts.

The roads were uncharacteristically quiet, given it was the middle of the school run—Tex even checked his car's clock to make sure he'd not set off stupidly early or too late. Sure, the amount of traffic on the roads had declined, but there'd still been enough soccer-mom mobiles and crappy drivers to annoy Tex on the mornings he drove Lee to school. But, other than the occasional trucks, beat-up sedans, and police cruisers, it was quiet—eerily so.

It was like a portent to something brewing only Tex knew nothing about.

"Where is everybody?" Lee voiced his father's niggling worry.

Tex shrugged. "Maybe they're all at the arcade with your schoolmates," he ventured with a wry smile.

"Now you're talking!" Lee chirped, ever the optimist.

"I said no, and I meant no." Tex was firm. "If Mom ever found out, I'd be mincemeat."

"She'd never find out from me."

"Your mother has her ways, son," Tex told him. "I don't know how she does it, but she finds out about *everything*."

Like the time he'd gotten drunk and wrecked the car—then brazenly reported it stolen to the cops. Or when he'd lied to her about how Rusty Hyatt died over in Iraq.

Tex was just about to offer Lee the suggestion his mother was some kind of clairvoyant when it came to the men in her life when his cell phone rang—the tinny rendition of *The Star-Spangled Banner* sparking up in the center console's cup holder made him jump.

Picking up the phone, Tex thumbed its screen to take John Christie's call. "Hey."

"Hey, Tex." His friend sounded a tad more subdued than was normal for such an early hour—Christie was definitely a morning person, a throwback to their Army training days that Tex had managed to shake off a year or so after being discharged.

"You okay, John?" Tex's heart upped its beat as a trickle of adrenalin seeped into his system; they rarely communicated by cell phone anymore, as there was no way of knowing who was listening in. The same went for the Internet, as both Tex and Christie—along with the majority of the prepper community—believed the government and other, more powerful, agencies were monitoring every goddamn keystroke. The theory even stretched so far as the Deep Web, which was supposed to be ultra-secure, but could just as easily be a government trap to catch the subversives.

And that's how Tex saw himself and the prepper community—subversives against the global regime that was crumbling around them—even though it did little to alleviate their reputation for being overzealous lunatics.

"Did you see the news already?" Christie pressed.

"Yeah—looks like Fort Worth is going down."

"It's worse than that, Tex. The city's trashed and there's mobs heading our way—the news reports are hours behind."

Tex's heart weighed heavy in his chest, and a dull pain gnawed away at the pit of his stomach; surely things weren't kicking off so soon? What the hell happened to the powers that be resolving the volatile situation?

"How far away, John?"

Tex heard his friend's labored breathing. As if he, too, was fighting down a nauseating wave of panic. "Not far enough—I'm hearing reports they've already reached some of the 'burbs."

"Shit," Tex growled between gritted teeth. Mentally, he kicked himself for not giving in to Lee's arcade request—it was much closer to home. "Everything looks okay here, John," Tex said. "The roads are quiet, but that's pretty much it."

Pressing the phone to his ear with his shoulder, Tex flicked the blinker and rounded the corner onto the street that led to Pioneer Heritage Intermediary.

"Dad…" Lee's face drained of color, and he pointed out through the windshield, toward his school.

Tex stomped on the brakes, bringing the car to a sudden stop—he jerked forward, and his seatbelt snapped into place to catch him.

The entrance was smashed beyond recognition, along with its surrounding windows. Shattered safety glass was strewn all along the paved walkway, which was dotted with the lifeless, bloodied bodies of what Tex assumed to be administrative staff and early-riser teachers.

The grass easement in front of the school was

festooned with cars, trucks, and vans, as was the staff parking lot, which was full for the first time in a long time. As Tex looked on, more vehicles were arriving, streaming in from the side streets and across the sports fields.

Dark, gray smoke curled out from the ruined doorway and the broken second-story windows above it. Dozens upon dozens of wild-eyed people ran out from the building clutching computers, arms full of chemistry-lab chemicals, and anything else they deemed valuable. Some carried guns, others, axes and machetes, and every single man, woman, and child among them looked angry and ready to kill anyone who stood in their path; it was like watching a swarm of marauding ants picking over a carcass.

"They're robbing my school, Dad." Lee's voice trembled as he spoke, and for as much as he'd wanted to avoid the place that morning, he sounded protective and pissed at the desecration of the school by hooligan looters.

"What's going on over there?" Christic sounded concerned.

"The school," Tex replied quietly, as if a raised voice would alert the mob and send them his way. "They're destroying it."

"You need to get the fuck away from there, Tex." Christie raised his voice so much, Tex had to hold it away from his ear and Lee heard him shout, "*Now*!"

"Dad…"

A sudden movement to the left.

Tex twisted his head to see, and his cell phone fell from his hand and landed in the narrow gap between the car's seat and door. "*Dammit*!" Tex growled, and in the heartbeat it took him to glance down to see where his cell had fallen, the car was surrounded.

There were six, maybe seven of them, all wielding guns, all thumping at the windows trying to break them to get at Tex and Lee. One of them, a young woman no older than nineteen with blood-matted hair and long streaks of black eye shadow down her cheeks, leapt onto the hood and began bashing at the windshield with the butt of her shiny silver Glock.

Tex froze, his body refusing to do what his racing brain demanded of it and sat there with his hands glued to the steering wheel while Christie's voice strained up from beside the seat.

"Tex?! You there? *What the fuck is going on*?!"

The young woman screeched something indiscernible at the top of her lungs—so loud, so shrill, it physically *hurt* Tex's ears and had them ringing—and doubled down on her attempt to smash her way through the windshield.

Tex's eyes fixed on the fine spread of spider-web cracks in his windshield and figured the woman would break through in a few more blows. But he still couldn't move, even as the woman's compatriots pounded on the car and howled like uncaged animals to bring the mob running from the school and toward the car.

A sharp report split the air as the young woman's gun went off.

Her head snapped back as the bullet blew away the top of her head and sprayed the fast-approaching rioters with a fine red mist, clumps of splintered skull, and gray-pink brains.

The gunshot jolted Tex out of his stupor and, as the woman's limp body slithered from the hood, he slammed the car into reverse and floored the gas pedal.

Lee cried out and screwed his eyes tight shut as Tex pulled away from the mob. They yelled obscenities and vile threats as the car retreated; a few even let off a few shots in its direction, which dinged off the hood and blew out the left headlight.

Tex clenched his jaw as the wheels bumped over what were unmistakably two, possibly three, of the mob who'd been trying their damnedest to break into the car through the trunk. The sickening sensation of soft, yielding flesh and the wet crunch of bones conjured vivid images in his mind of his last tour of duty—only, that time, his son hadn't been there to experience it with him.

"We're okay, John!" Tex yelled and hoped his buddy heard him. At the end of the street, and with some distance between them and the mob, Tex spun the car around and pulled back onto the main drag; had the traffic been at its normal volume, he'd definitely have hit something.

Behind him, the mob followed, baying for blood as some trampled over their fallen brethren, hungry for revenge, and others scrambled to their vehicles and made ready to give chase.

"It's Code Black, Tex, *Code Black*!" John Christie's faint voice echoed from somewhere beneath Tex's seat as he raced through red lights and on toward home.

"What does Uncle John mean?" Lee asked, and Tex caught the ammonia whiff off pee coming from his son—that made him angry at the mob and he fought against the instinct to turn the car around and run down every single one of them until they were nothing more than red smears on the road.

"He means we need to be ready to leave, Lee," Tex told his son. "The shit just hit the fan."

Chapter Three

Tex screeched to a halt outside the house, his car leaving black tire marks along half the length of the double driveway.

"You know what to do, Lee—go do it now!" he barked at his son, who had fallen quiet with shock; it wasn't everyday he got to see some random crazy lady blow her brains out in full technicolor mere inches from his face or feel his dad run over people like they were nothing more than roadkill armadillos and possums. Tex wanted nothing more than to take the kid in his arms, hold him, and tell him everything was going to be alright.

Only, it wasn't.

The best Tex could hope for was the kid would have time to change his pants before they had to leave.

"Krista?" Tex hollered as he ran into the house. "Where the fuck are you, woman?" he mumbled beneath his breath as he reached the bottom of the stairs—he'd scanned the shoe rack on his way in and saw his wife's running shoes there. Thankfully, she was not on her morning run. *"Krista!"*

"What the hell, Jonah?" Krista appeared at the top of the stairs in her maroon sweats, her hair wrapped in a high towel turban.

"We gotta go, babe." Tex was out of breath; his face felt flushed red.

"Go where?"

"Go, *go*."

"I'm not going anywhere." Krista scowled down the stairs at Tex. "I'm meeting up with Victoria at nine—we're going to the park for our mile run."

Shit, Victoria—she was part of the Pembertons' escape plan, too. "You need to call her and get her round here right now, Krista," Tex ordered. "We all have to go."

"You're scaring me, Jonah."

Good.

"Things are happening, baby, and they're happening right now. We need to go—just like we practiced." Tex had made his family rehearse for the very moment they were facing, often in the middle of the night. Somehow, he'd always figured they'd flee the collapse of civilization under cover of darkness, not first thing in the morning and in broad daylight.

Lee scooted by his father and took the stairs two at a time with Winnie hot on his heels, tongue lolling, tail wagging. Tex had no time to worry about what effect their confrontation with the mob outside the school might be having on the boy—there would be plenty of time for that later, when they were all safe within the walls of the Little Alamo.

"Get dressed, Krista." Tex tried to instill some sense of urgency in his wife, but she remained rooted at the top of the stairs like some stunned deer in the headlights of the car about to kill it.

"If this is one of your stupid drills, Jonah…"

Tex bit his tongue—literally—and tasted blood. It was not the time to antagonize Krista by snapping at her; it was crucial she kept a level head and followed instructions—otherwise they might not make it out of the house alive, let alone to the damn compound. "It's not a drill, Krista," Tex told her, his voice calm, collected. "I promise. The school was… *destroyed*, and the mob that did it are heading this way. Lump called—"

Krista rolled her eyes at him. "What the hell does John Christie ever know?" she spat. "I wish you'd think for yourself, Jonah, and not let your Army buddy do it for you."

"I saw it with my own eyes, baby." Tex fought hard to keep his temper; there *really* wasn't time for any of this. "They attacked the car at the school and…" Did he really want to tell his wife their son had just watched someone blow off the top of their own head and his father reverse over real-life people? "Can you just please get yourself ready to go?"

To emphasize his point, Tex pulled open the top drawer of the antique credenza that stood in the hallway and pulled out the old Colt .45 Grandfather Rocky had given him shortly before he died. It had been passed down to him from his own father and the old man wanted it to go to a fellow military man. Rocky had never hidden his disdain that Tex's father had refused to enlist, and not giving him the Colt had been the man's final say on the matter.

As Krista finally got the message, she huffed and turned toward their bedroom door. Tex felt a sharp pang in his chest as the realization hit him that it may well be the last time either of them went in there. He watched his wife disappear into the room, slamming the door in her wake, and hoped he'd managed to get across just how urgent their situation was.

"I'll go round up Victoria," Tex shouted after Krista and didn't hang around to listen for her reply. It would no doubt be something sardonic—Krista had a bee in her bonnet about her theory of her husband being attracted to his old friend's widow that she simply wouldn't let go.

And all because of something she *thought* she'd seen a lifetime ago.

"We'll be in the garage!" Lee panted as he raced back down the stairs clutching his bulging backpack. He shot by Tex and off down the hallway. The dog followed on, his nails click-clacking on the laminate floor as he ran as fast as his stumpy legs would carry him.

Tex had his second car all loaded up and ready to go in the garage. It was a Toyota Land Cruiser—top of the range—no matter what they might say about the Japanese vehicles versus good ol' American models, the Cruiser was by far the best four-wheel-drive off-roader there was. The thing was just perfect for the rugged terrain they'd be facing on their way to the compound, and Tex had it converted to take liquid petroleum gas six months before in preparation for the times ahead. Liquid petroleum gas, also more commonly known as LPG, didn't deteriorate like gasoline and diesel and gave far more mileage than electric, which made it the perfect fuel for sitting in the vehicle, waiting for the right time to flee.

Lee had christened the Cruiser their *Getaway Car*, like they were a family of criminal fugitives just waiting for the knock on the door from the FBI—Tex liked how the kid embraced the whole thing and hadn't once questioned or considered him to be some lunatic conspiracy theorist. Maybe the boy understood more about what was happening in the world than Tex had given him credit for?

Making his way to the front door, Tex pulled up Victoria's number and thumbed his cell phone's screen to call.

"Hello, this is Victoria. I'm sorry I can't get to the phone—"

Cursing beneath his breath, Tex upped his step and

set off along the street; the Hyatt house was less than a hundred yards away but knowing danger was on the way made it feel like a hundred miles to Tex.

A thick plume of black smoke swirled high into the morning sky from the neighboring subdivision; screams cut short by gunfire carried in the still air, which had Tex's adrenaline pumping once more.

Slipping his phone back into his back pocket, he broke into a jog.

"Victoria?!" Tex thumped on his neighbor's door and waggled the handle.

It was locked.

"It's me, Tex!"

"Gimme a minute!"

Tex let out the breath he'd been holding; it was a relief to hear Victoria's voice. Had she not been home, there'd have been nothing he could have done. There was no time to go hunting for the woman, especially if she wasn't picking up her phone calls.

The door opened and Victoria squinted out at Tex, shielding her eyes from the harsh Texas morning sunshine. She was dressed in dark-purple running gear, which clung to her gym-toned body like a second skin and was the perfect complement to her flame-red hair. Of course, she'd arranged to go for a pleasant jog around the park with Krista.

"Grab your prep' bag," Tex told her. "We gotta go."

"Now?" Victoria's cordial smile dropped from her full, rosebud lips; even without makeup, she was a striking woman. Craning her neck through the doorway, Victoria saw the smoke, heard the screams and gun shots, and she looked terrified.

"Now," Tex reiterated; he was fully prepared to carry her to the Cruiser if necessary—there was no way he'd let Rusty down.

Not again.

"You sure, Tex?" Victoria cast a glance back into the house she'd lived in since she and Rusty got married, the house she'd refused to leave after he came home from the Middle East in a wooden box.

"As sure as I'll ever be, Vicky," Tex said. "Lee and Krista are waiting for you—it's time we got to someplace safe."

"The Little Alamo?" She ventured a half-smile.

"One and the same," Tex returned the smile, and for the briefest moment, he felt *something* flow between them.

A deafening, resonant *bang* split the air. Tex twisted around in time to see an orange and black fireball mushroom from one of the ranch-style houses at the end of the street—somebody's car had just gone up in flames. Even more alarming than that were the stampeding horde of rioters followed by the hodge-podge of vehicles Tex recognized from the school.

"I'll get the bag," Victoria said as she ducked back into the house and into the downstairs restroom—Tex had advised her to keep her prep' bag as close to the front door as possible for a quick getaway. The bag, just as those he'd had Lee and Krista put together, contained a change of clothes, water, a handgun and ammunition, a small first aid kit, and enough dried and dehydrated survivalist food to last at least a week. It wouldn't take them that long to get to the Little Alamo, but Tex wanted to leave nothing to chance. In such times, there was no predicting the unpredictable.

Tex and Victoria ran back to Tex's house—he'd offered to carry the bag, but she'd shook her head and slung it over her shoulder. That stubborn independence was something Tex admired about Victoria—Krista would have plopped the prep' bag into her husband's hands and expected him to lug the thing.

The garage door was open and the Cruiser running when Tex and Victoria got there. Lee sat in the driver's seat peering out through the windshield Tex had reinforced with black steel bars. Beside him, Krista, her face set in a grim scowl, wet hair plastered to her forehead.

"Scoot!" Tex said to Lee as he pulled open the Cruiser's door. Beside him, Victoria opened the back door and clambered in beside Winnie, who proceeded to lick her face.

Lee climbed between the seats to join Victoria and the dog as Tex pulled the Cruiser out of the garage and maneuvered around the car he'd left in the driveway—the hood was smeared with a thin film of drying blood and there were clumps of bloodied hair clinging to the exhaust pipes.

Down along the street, Tex saw the mob and murderous motorcade making their way house to house; the sound of their shouts and gunfire pierced the air.

A scream caught Tex's attention and instinct had his foot hit the brakes. The Cruiser jolted to a stop at the end of the driveway. Heart pounding, Tex peered through the side window and saw the single-story house on the corner of their street had flames flickering through the front picture window. The owners—a sweet newlywed couple Tex only knew as Chuck and Veronica—were being dragged out onto the front lawn. Chuck, a tall, skinny African American guy was putting up one hell of a fight as a half dozen of the mob shoved him to the ground and pounded his body with baseball bats, hunks of two-by-four, and rifle butts. Chuck lashed out with his feet, catching one of his assailants square in the balls, the other hard in the knee—both went down howling, only to be replaced by others. Chuck cried out his wife's name as the mob stripped her naked and closed in, ignoring her screams and pleas for mercy.

Everything within Tex's psyche screamed at him to help those people, to help all his neighbors who were being brutally killed in their own homes—there was a time it had been his job, his *duty*, to go to their aid, and to hell with the danger. He had weapons in the Cruiser, but nowhere near enough to take on the mob streaming down his street, and he had his family to think about. He also had the Little Alamo to get to—there'd be a hundred thirty people relying on him there—providing all the selected families made it out of the towns and cities in one piece.

"Oh shit!" Krista's exclamation jarred Tex's already jangled nerves. He turned around in his seat, expecting to see his wife's horrified face and wide eyes as the full horror of their neighbors' predicament hit her.

Instead, she had the door's handle in her hand and was unclipping her seat belt.

"What the hell are you doing?" Tex growled as Krista pushed open the Cruiser's door.

"I forgot our wedding album!" Krista's retort caught Tex completely by surprise. He'd seen the results of extreme shock in combat situations before and knew disassociation was common but seeing it in his own wife hit him hard.

"You can't—" Before Tex could finish, Krista was out of the Cruiser and heading back to the house.

"*Mom*!" Lee's shout filled the car and Winnie yapped as Krista slammed the door shut behind her.

Victoria reached for the handle by her side.

"Don't!" Tex snapped at the woman, and she visibly recoiled, shocked into inactivity; her eyes followed Krista as she disappeared into the house.

Tex's mind raced ahead as he fought every instinct to chase after his wife, angry she'd put them in danger by delaying their flight. The mob was closing in fast, and Tex saw the six-foot fence to the rear of the house shaking.

Experience told him that could mean only one thing: the bloodthirsty rioters were either trying to climb over or break the thing down.

Krista wouldn't stand a chance if the mob trapped her in the house, and if Tex didn't get her out, no one else would. It was obvious societal norms had broken down—collapsed, even—and calling the cops would be a waste of precious time. Even if there were any police still prepared to attend a call, Tex knew they'd never get there in time. He also figured it was highly unlikely any of the emergency services would be working, and the authorities that commanded them were probably dead or running for the proverbial hills.

It was just as he and Lump and all the other preppers had predicted—he was completely alone, and if he wanted to prevent his wife being torn apart by the baying mob, it was in his hands.

But Tex had his son's safety to think about—and Victoria. Back in the day, he and Rusty had made a solemn pact back to always look out for one another's families should the worse happen.

And the worse *had* happened.

Tex had pushed the events of that fateful day way down into the darkest recesses of his mind. But seeing Krista dash back to the house, and the rising panic he felt in his gut as the mob closed in, brought it all flooding back.

Tex and Rusty were on their second deployment to Iraq, ostensibly to help win over the hearts and minds of the populace. The general idea was that by keeping law and order in the towns, training up the local military and police forces to deal with the insurgents, and handing out American chocolate to the children, the Iraqis would welcome the armed forces with open arms.

Only, it didn't quite work out like that.

***

As Tex and Rusty found out very early on in their first trip, many of the Iraqi people they were supposed to be helping didn't take kindly to Western interference and the destabilization of their country. And so, lethal danger lurked behind every door, down every street, and behind the eyes of the outwardly friendly people—not even women and children could be trusted.

And, the insurgents would strap suicide vests to willing women and children in order to ambush the wary American soldiers—Tex could never fathom how the hell they were supposed to even begin to take on an enemy who were prepared to do that.

"Sir. Yessir!" Rusty barked back as Tex handed out his orders; Tex had been given a promotion shortly before they headed back to Iraq, and Rusty took every opportunity to rib him about it—respectfully in front of the platoon, of course.

They were in Tikrit, 140 kilometers northwest of Baghdad and hometown of Saddam Hussein himself—that alone made the town key to the entire hearts and minds strategy.

"All we need to do is sweep the streets leading up to the mosque." Tex pointed out the towering minarets of the imposing building up ahead. He raised his voice above the muezzin's wailing call to prayer that resounded throughout the streets and bounced between the sandstone buildings; Tex had deliberately picked the time to brief his men to minimize the risk of being overheard—the general populace would be too busy praying to Allah, and anyone in the immediate vicinity would struggle to make out what he was saying above the cacophonous noise.

"You three take the square." Tex indicated the direction with an outstretched arm. "Rusty, you head down to the bazaar—take Jed with you."

Rusty gave his commanding officer another *Sir, yessir* and fist-bumped Jed Hawkins, who towered a good six, seven inches above everyone in the squad and built like the proverbial brick outhouse. Jed and Rusty made a formidable team, but Tex knew their camaraderie would never come even close to what he'd shared with Rusty before the promotion.

Tex had an uneasy feeling about the bazaar: it seemed a tad too quiet, even before the call to prayer, and there was a definite air of anticipation hanging over it.

Tex put it down to the presence of Americans in the heart of the town—he'd experienced the quiet hostility before—and decided to get on with the job they'd gone there to do.

"You guys," he nodded to the two soldiers behind Jed, "you're coming with me—we'll take the main street down to the mosque." Tex calculated the muezzin would have wrapped up his wailing by the time they got there, and long before Rusty and Jed made it to the bazaar.

As the squad split up and went their separate ways, Tex glanced over his shoulder at Rusty; his friend was all but obscured by Jed's bulk, and Tex couldn't quite shake the over-protective feeling he had toward the guy. He had a pregnant wife he had to get back to after the tour; Victoria was four months gone, which coincided with the end of the last leave, and Tex had promised her he'd get Rusty home in one piece.

As predicted, the wailing stopped, although it seemed to echo about the hot, dusty streets awhile, then all fell silent. Tex's mouth felt dry, his heart thumped in his chest, and his eyes darted everywhere: A rustle of paper on the ground, a lizard scurrying along a wall, a glint of light from a window high above. Nothing escaped his attention because all it took was one moment of distraction and it could be all over.

They kept to the middle of the street and away from parked-up cars, trash cans, and piles of wind-blown litter that accumulated in corners between the houses. Anyone of those could harbor an improvised explosive device—the dreaded IEDs that could wipe out a unit with one blast—left lying in wait by the insurgents or the sympathizers in Tikrit who remained loyal to Hussein even after he was dragged out of his foxhole like some cowardly animal.

A movement.

A doorway up ahead; dark figure and concealed face.

In unison, Tex and his comrades swung their guns toward the doorway. Tex held up a hand and the three stopped dead in their tracks.

The figure, a woman, stepped out of the house and onto the street, her black jilbab stirring the fine dust around her concealed feet. She stared down the street at the American soldiers with horror and hatred in her eyes.

Tex stood firm; it wasn't the first time he'd seen that look on an Iraqi's face, and he reckoned it wouldn't be the last. And, while he felt empathy for the people who'd been forced to endure the invasion of their country, he was wary of what they were capable of. He'd lost good friends to suicide bombers in the past and knew no one out there could really be trusted not to be a walking claymore mine.

Then, a deafening bang pressed in on Tex's ears and a whirling cloud of red dust raced down the street behind him.

At first, in his confusion, Tex assumed the woman had detonated an explosive belt secreted beneath her flowing robe. Instinctively, he dropped down to the ground and rolled to the side of the street; often, a second device would be set to catch those going to the aid of the fallen.

Looking up, Tex saw the woman was still there and

all in one piece. She scurried back into her home and pulled the peeling wooden door firmly shut in her wake.

If the blast hadn't come from the woman in front, Tex knew that could mean only one thing.

It had come from the bazaar behind him.

Rusty.

Ignoring his training and the very real danger of a secondary IED, Tex scrambled to his feet and set off in the direction of the bazaar; he'd disappeared into the thick cloud of dust and smoke before his two comrades were even up on their feet.

Tex found Jed first. Or, at least what was left of the big guy. It looked like he'd taken the brunt of the explosion and the majority of his midsection from sternum to hips was gone, his guts spread across the ruined bazaar in glistening, tiny pieces. Jed's face was gone, too, his raw, bloodied skull grinning up at the clear blue sky above like some grim portent. Tex snorted as he stepped over Jed's remains and experienced a pang on behalf of the soldier's family, who wouldn't even have the comfort of an open coffin. There wasn't a mortician alive who'd be able to patch Jed up, and his loved ones would have to say their goodbyes to a wooden box and folded flag.

Tears filled his eyes as Tex made his way through the fragments of splintered wood and scattered, ruined merchandise that covered the ground.

"That you, Tex?" Rusty's voice drifted out through the air, thick with dust. For a heartbeat, Tex dared hope his old friend had survived the explosion relatively unscathed, and they'd be back at the barracks by the end of the day.

Rusty was a mess.

He lay in a corner of what remained of the small marketplace, propped up with his back against the wall as if he were just sitting awhile to take a load off and soak in the sights. But his left arm and both legs were gone, and it looked to Tex like the bomb had robbed Rusty of his dick and balls, too. His face, miraculously, had only a few abrasions and spatters of blood, and his eyes were still very much alert—Tex guessed Jed's wide, muscular body had somehow shielded Rusty's head when the IED went off.

"What the fuck, man?" Tex grunted, swallowing down the tears in a hard lump that scoured his throat. He knelt down beside his friend and immediately the knees of his fatigues were soaked through with blood. He heard footsteps running up behind him; instinct told him it was the rest of the squad. He heard Zip calling for backup.

"Didn't even see it coming," Rusty said, his voice weak, labored. "One minute Jed and me were checking out a coupla fancy bowls, the next…" He made an explosion noise at the back of his throat and coughed up a fat clot of dark blood.

"Suicide bomber?" Tex's mind spun back to the woman in the doorway.

Rusty shook his head. "Must have been under one of the tables, or in a trash can—you know how they are with their trash cans." As he spoke, Rusty's body slid sideways a little against the wall and a gush of blood pumped out from the stump of what had once been his left leg.

"Shit!" Tex growled and, without thinking, thrust his hand into the gnarled mess to squeeze shut the femoral artery. Perversely, he was thankful the blast had sealed shut the main artery in Rusty's other leg—the flesh there looked like badly cooked steak.

"Leave it." It took some effort, but Rusty managed to grab Tex's hand and pull it away from the wound.

Tex fought against his friend, determined not to lose him. "Medivac is on the way, buddy," he said. "You just need to hang on 'til then."

Rusty laughed at him.

Actually *laughed.*

"You're fucking joking, right?" Rusty wheezed.

Tex shook his head and twisted his arm from his friend's hand; had circumstances been different and Rusty not so badly messed up, that wouldn't have been possible—Rusty had an iron grip second to none. "You got this, Rusty," he said as he felt around in the raw meat of Rusty's thigh, his fingers homing in on the source of the blood flow. "I just need you to stay with me."

"I lost my fucking balls, Tex," Rusty said. "Look at me… I don't wanna live like this."

"Think about Victoria—and the baby. You don't want the kid growing up without a dad."

"I don't want him growing up with half a dad." Rusty gasped as Tex's fingers clamped down on the artery in his leg. "What kind of life is that for a kid—pushing his old man around in a wheelchair?"

"You still got a hell of a lot to offer, buddy." Even as the words left Tex's mouth, he knew how hollow they sounded. Had the tables been turned and it was him lying there in the dirt with half his body—and genitals—blown away, he was sure he wouldn't want to carry on, either.

"Please, Tex. Leave it." Rusty laid his hand on Tex's wrist again, but there was no strength left to pull him away. "Just let me go—just promise me you'll look out for V"

And so, Tex made the hardest decision of his life to that point and took his hand away. Guarded by the platoon, he cradled Rusty's head against his shoulder as his lifeblood pumped out and soaked into the parched ground beneath them.

Rusty was gone ten, fifteen minutes before backup arrived. Tex felt the burden of guilt weigh down upon him like some great, leaden albatross he knew would stay with him until the day he was reunited with his old friend; he knew in his heart he should have sent Rusty to the mosque and taken on the bazaar himself.

They sent Tex back home to Texas to deal with the PTSD and the loss of his friend. His first port of call was to Victoria, who was in the hospital—she'd been admitted the day she'd received the visit to tell her that Rusty had been killed in action. Tex heard poor Victoria collapsed right in front of the general and his assistant.

She'd lost the baby later that day—the shock of the terrible news had simply been too much for her body to handle and when Tex called in on her at the infirmary, she was without the one remaining part of Rusty she had left.

Tex told Victoria everything: his decision to send her husband to scope out the bazaar that day, his honoring Rusty's final wish to be allowed to die with some dignity—if bleeding to death in some God-forsaken desert hellhole could ever be dignified—and his promise to look out for Victoria for as long as he was able.

"I don't need looking after," Victoria had told him with a forced smile. "I'm a big girl, Tex, you know that."

And, through the brave words, Tex saw a terrified, hurting little girl. "I'm so sorry, V," he said. "I should have been looking out for him, not sending him out to be killed like that."

"It's not your fault," Victoria soothed. "You did your job. Rusty did his job, too, and he always knew the risks. I'm just pleased you were there for him when… when he needed you the most."

Victoria's words jabbed at Tex's heart like hot knives; had he been there when Rusty truly needed him, they wouldn't be flying home half of her husband in a body bag.

The guilt of his friend's death had stuck in Tex's psyche from that day in Tikrit; never diminishing, never rationalized, and never showing any signs of leaving him be. Even after he was honorably discharged and started a family with Krista, even as he kept his promise to look out for Victoria—he and Krista helped her move two doors down—and even when he told her of his plans to include her in the Little Alamo should the inevitable happen.

None of it assuaged Tex's guilt, but at least he knew Victoria would be safe and he was keeping his vow to Rusty.

Chapter Four

A shrill scream rang out from across the street. Snapping Tex from his reverie, he was jarred back to the Landcruiser and Lee and Victoria. The mob had smashed its way into the white fascia house catty-corner from Tex's and were dragging out the young single mother who lived there. Tex heard the smashing of glass, a cry cut short, and hoped to hell the mob hadn't thrown the poor woman's kid from an upstairs window.

Krista was still in the house.

Jolted into action, Tex dropped open the glove compartment and plucked out the Glock he'd secreted there; the Colt was a terrific gun, but it only held six shots. With the Glock, he'd have sixteen and he figured that would be enough if he got to the house straight away. Any more delaying and the mob would be finished beating on his young neighbor and move on to his house.

"Stay here!" Tex ordered his son and Victoria as he pushed open the car door. "Lock it!" he barked, and with that, he raced off with his focus on the front door of the house.

Tex made it to the house at full pelt. "Krista?" He called out as loud as he dared—he'd pulled the door to behind him to avoid attracting the attention of the mob;

their shouts and angry screams followed him into the hallway. "Where are you?"

"I'll be down in a minute!" Krista's voice carried no sense or urgency, which worried Tex: she sounded like she was just running a little late for date night. Tex knew his wife well—she could be incredibly dissociative when she felt things were getting out of control. Hence her jumping out of the car to go find the wedding album.

"We really need to go, Krista," Tex shouted up the stairs.

"Did you move it?"

"Move *what*?" Tex let out an exasperated sigh and headed for the stairs. They'd not so much as glanced at their wedding photographs since their first anniversary what felt like a lifetime ago, so why the hell he'd have moved the thing made no sense.

"I left it in the closet on the top shelf," Krista's reply was alarmingly calm. "Can you come help me look?"

Tex took the stairs two, three at a time. "We really don't have time for this!" he barked at his wife as he ran into their bedroom.

Krista emerged from the closet with the white leather-bound wedding album clasped tight to her chest; Tex made out their names in fancy gold calligraphy on the front, and saw the detached calm in Krista's eyes. His heart went out to her at that moment; he was angry at her for delaying their escape for the dumb photos but in reality, she was just terrified and desperately clinging to some semblance of normality.

"You found it." Tex gave his wife the best smile he could muster. From the corner of his eye, he saw a portion of the mob—a hundred or so of them—making its way along the easement behind the fence that separated the subdivision's houses from the empty land behind. Some clambered over the six-foot high fence, while others kicked and punched and shook it. "We *really* gotta go, babe." Tex put some urgency into his voice—the fence was at the very bottom of their third-acre plot, but it was still too close for comfort should the mob start climbing over it.

"It was in the closet. On the top shelf." Krista sounded distant, like she was having a bad dream.

Tex took his wife's hand and led her down the stairs—he hoped to dear God she'd be content with the wedding album and wouldn't suddenly decide she *had* to take something else from the house. But, if he had to pick the woman up and carry her kicking and screaming to the Landcruiser, Tex was fully prepared to do so.

"*Shit*," Tex growled under his breath as they reached the bottom of the stairs and pulled open the front door. The mob was spreading out along the street and a half-dozen of them were making their way over to the house.

"What do they want?" Finally, there was some fear in Krista's tone, and she squeezed Tex's hand so tight he felt the small bones grind against one another.

"Get in the car, Krista." Tex pulled the Colt from the waistband of his jeans and pointed toward the Landcruiser with it; Lee peered out through the window at them, his face a mask of fear, Winnie perched on his lap. *"Now!"*

Tex swung the gun around and took aim at the bunch of people heading straight toward them. Krista let go of his hand and Tex pulled out the Glock and took aim with that, too.

Krista hurried over to the car as the people upped their pace and let out bloodthirsty yells as they homed in on their new prey.

Krista screamed.

The mob broke into a run, and yet more of them turned on their heels and headed in Tex's direction.

Tex's first shot took down a short, skinny guy at the

front of the pack. The Colt's slug punched straight through his ribs on the left-hand side and he hit the ground face-first. It was a calculated risk Tex thought would deter the mob, or at the very least slow them down a little. Instead, the resonant sound of the gunshot and the fall of one of their own seemed to incite them all the more and they herded toward the house, the car, and Krista.

A couple of scruffy young men, both shirtless and wearing faded, oil-stained Levis, ran full pelt along the driveway—their sights were set firmly on Krista as she bustled to the Landcruiser. Tex set off after his wife, and as he ran, he let off another couple of shots from his grandfather's gun.

One of the young men yelped as a bullet tore through his arm, spraying the guy beside him with blood and gobbets of flesh. He stayed on his feet, though, his pace barely slowing, and Tex's second bullet missed its mark and ripped a hole through the garage door.

Krista screamed again and took a panicked glance over her shoulder. Her eyes widened as she saw the mob hurtling toward her and, instead of pulling open the car door and getting herself safely inside, she veered off to the right and made for the gate that led to the backyard.

"*Krista*! *No*!" Tex's voice rang loud and shrill above the baying of the mob and stirred them up even more. Heart pounding, Tex ran after his wife. He gunned down a handful of people at the front of the mob—those closest to Krista—only to have them replaced by more.

Krista was through the old wooden gate before Tex got to her. Scooting around the side of the Landcruiser closest to the house to get ahead of the mob, he caught sight of Victoria. She had Lee in her arms, his head pressed tight against her shoulder.

Tex followed Krista into the backyard; he figured his plan to throw her over his shoulder and carry her to the car might well be his best bet. She seemed in a daze, as if she'd blocked out all of the mayhem going on around her and was unaware of the danger she was putting herself and her family in. Finally, Tex caught up to Krista. He tucked the Glock into his pants and grabbed her. He spun her around and saw she still had their wedding album clutched tight to her chest. "Krista, please—"

At that moment, the fence at the very back of Tex's yard crashed inward, three entire sections toppled by the sheer weight of the mob; it was like something from a Romero movie, only these were not rotting, lumbering undead—they were very much alive and in control of their murderous faculties. The mob yowled in triumph and hurtled toward Tex and Krista.

"*Ow*!" Krista squealed as Tex pulled on her arm to all but drag her across their neatly manicured lawn. It took a few seconds or so, but Krista's legs managed to catch up to Tex's pace and she ran along close behind him, wedding album held tight in one hand.

Tex took down a couple of people—a middle-aged man with dried blood caked on his face and a heavyset teen boy in the school's track uniform—as they pushed through the gate. He then twisted around and fired his last bullet from the Colt into the mob racing behind him and Krista.

With the Colt empty, Tex suddenly felt incredibly vulnerable. He let go of Krista's hand to pull out the Glock while at the same time sticking the revolver into the waistband of his pants—the old trope of throwing an empty weapon at the enemy was bullshit to anyone who'd ever served.

And then, Krista wasn't running behind him anymore.

"Oh, Krista, no…" Tex stopped dead, his heart in his mouth.

Somehow, the album had slipped from Krista's hand, and she'd stopped to retrieve it from the lawn.

Tex set off toward her and opened his mouth to scream *run*, but the first of the mob were upon her.

Mentally keeping count of how many times he fired the Glock—an old Army trick that had saved lives countless times—Tex dropped three of the youths who dragged Krista to the ground and were setting about her with fists and feet.

"Jonah!" Krista's voice, filled with pain and terror, punched at Tex's heart as hard as the mob punched at his wife. He got to Krista at the same time as another dozen or so of the mob and, as they stared down at the Glock pointing at them and at their fallen brethren, there was a moment's standoff.

Krista struggled to her feet, her legs wobbly, her face smeared with blood from her split lips and a nasty wound above her left eye.

"Leave us the fuck alone," Tex snarled at the mob as they stared him down with pure hate in their eyes. Tex wondered just what the hell had happened to those people to turn them from everyday, law-abiding citizens to thugs and killers—sure, the world was in disarray, but surely the complete disintegration of decency wouldn't occur in a heartbeat like that?

A movement within the mob, and a burly, grim-faced woman pushed her way through. In her hand, she carried a four-foot-long strip of metal rebar. She elbowed aside her fellow rioters and swung the bar at Krista before Tex could pull the trigger.

Krista lurched to her right when the bar connected with her skull; a loud, wet, *crunch* rang out and blood poured from her split scalp. And, somehow, she managed to stay on her feel and hold on to the dammed wedding album.

"*No*!" Tex's anguished cry was drowned out by the Glock.

The slug made a neat hole in the rebar lady's cheek and punched out most of the back of her head. As she went down, the mob surged forward and swarmed over Krista with bats, hunks of wood, fists, and feet.

Tex leapt forward as Krista screamed and vanished amid the flurry of cruel, kicking feet. He pulled some of the mob away, shot others point-blank in the face, and punched away the grasping hands that sought to drag him down alongside his wife.

Three bullets left in the Glock.

Tex knew in his heart it was already too late for his wife; she lay lifeless and covered in blood only a few feet away from him—it may as well have been a thousand feet for all the good he'd been able to help her—her head was twisted at an unnatural angle and there was an ugly knot of broken bone bulging out at the back of her neck.

Rage and pain filled Tex's heart, and all he wanted to do was shoot and punch and break bones until he lay limp and lifeless next to his beloved wife and the wedding photographs scattered around her broken body.

But he had Lee to think about.

Tex knew if he succumbed to the mob in the name of anger and retribution, Lee would surely perish. Victoria may have been a tough cookie, but she lacked the skills to get herself and Lee away from the danger in the suburbs and all the way to Little Alamo.

"You fuckers!"

Tex fired off his last bullets into the people closest to him and was halfway across the backyard before the mob mobilized after him.

Yanking the gate closed, Tex ran to the Landcruiser; the gate wouldn't hold the mob, he knew that much, but at least it could buy him a few vital seconds. The empty Glock was still in his hand, useless as a firearm, but still a hefty chunk of metal.

Tex put it to good use getting through the crowd of rioters surrounding the car. They were beating on it with bare fists and pulling at the locked doors in their attempts to get to Lee and Victoria inside. As the two cowered, Winnie leapt up and down, jumping from the front seats to the back and back again, all the while yapping at the angry mob through the windows.

The Glock proved most effective clearing through the mob. Paired with Tex's fist, it knocked people down and out of his way in a blur of pained faces and split skin.

Tex took a hard blow to the temple, which made his vision blur and his head spin, but he steadfastly refused to lose his footing. Instead, he spun around and smashed the gun sideways-on into his assailant's face, a handsome older man in a smart, thousand-dollar blue suit. As the man crumpled, his nose smashed flat across his face, Tex reached the Landcruiser's door.

"Open the damn door!" he yelled at Victoria who, for one heart-stopping moment looked like she didn't want to do that—as if leaving Tex outside and at the mercy of the mob was a safer option for her.

Tex banged an open palm onto the window, which stirred Victoria from her inaction. And, as she leaned across the driver's seat to pop the door lock, a thick, strong arm snaked around Tex's throat.

Gasping for air, Tex felt his feet leave the ground as he was lifted up from behind. He clawed at the bare arm with his free hand, tearing away thick clods of black hair; the assailant's grip tightened until he couldn't draw even a thin trickle of air into his lungs.

In his rapidly fading peripheral vision, Tex espied an elderly man approaching with an aluminum baseball bat raised high above his head with both hands. There was murderous intent in the old man's rheumy eyes and Tex knew he had to act fast or die right there on his own driveway.

Despite his lungs' desperate ache for air, Tex's training kicked in. He'd always aced hand-to-hand combat and had relished its use in the field on the odd occasion he'd gotten to use it. Fighting against his instinct to keep on clawing at the arm choking him, Tex raised up his hand and jabbed his stiffened fingers at where he guessed his attacker's eyes to be.

The guy let out a loud, pained grunt that Tex *felt* more than heard. The arm loosened just a tad, but enough for Tex to gulp in a lungful of air and, as his feet touched ground, he delivered a hard, backward stomp onto the top of his would-be killer's foot.

The arm was no longer around Tex's neck as the huge guy behind him staggered back on his broken foot; Tex had felt the small bones crush under his heel and knew he'd effectively disabled the man from further attack.

Tex grabbed at the Landcruiser's handle and yanked open the door. Just as he did so, the old man brought the baseball bat down.

A reflexive duck to the side spared Tex a smashed skull, but the bat connected with his shoulder. Tex felt the muscle there squash beneath the hard metal; white-hot pain flared up along his arm, and Tex lost contact with the door handle.

The old man dropped the bat and thrust his arm through the half-opened car door to grab at Victoria and Lee. At that same moment, the garden gate crashed open, and the other half of the mob poured out onto the driveway. Distracted by the sudden movement, the old man glanced across at the new arrivals with a puzzled expression.

Seizing his opportunity, Tex rammed his shoulder against the door, which slammed shut on the old man's arm. The man screamed out in agony as the door all-but severed his arm and, when Tex pulled the door open again, he collapsed unconscious to the ground.

Tex stepped on the old man's body and scrambled into the driver's seat. Ignoring his shell-shocked son and best friend's widow, he closed and locked the door before gunning the engine and pulling the shift into *drive*.

"Where's Mom?" Lee asked, his voice quiet, quivering.

All Tex could do was shake his head and hit the gas pedal; there'd be plenty of time for explanations when they were safely ensconced in Little Alamo, and plenty of time for them both to heal.

The Landcruiser lurched forward into the mob. They refused to move out of the way, some even launching themselves at the car as it plowed through them. Tex ground his teeth together as, for the second time that day, he experienced the sickening *bump-bump-bump* and yielding crunch of human bodies beneath the wheels of his car.

As he drove away, the mob chasing on foot along the quiet, suburban street that had been his home for so many years, Tex refused himself the pain of looking back. Krista was back there, life beaten from her because she'd wanted to hang on to just one memento of how life used to be, happy memories of normality and love Tex knew in his heart he'd never feel again.

Chapter Five

It was getting late by the time they finally set eyes on the Little Alamo. The sun was sinking, fat and bloated, toward the horizon; it painted the Texas evening sky a vivid salmon pink, hazy with smoke from the burning cities.

Taking the largely off-road route to avoid the already clogged roads had added hours onto the journey from the Fort Worth suburbs. But, having attempted the 161 frontage road, Tex knew going off-road was the safest thing to do; the frontage road had trees laying across it—all freshly cut down—by means of trapping unwary travelers. Luckily, whoever had laid the traps were rookies who'd not prepared for off-road vehicles and had left the dry ditch on one side completely free.

As Tex maneuvered the Cruiser through the ditch, he saw the rapid flash of a scope trying to get to get a lock on them, and told Lee to hold Winnie down and keep his head out of sight of the window. Then came the harsh crack of a shot, which missed the Cruiser and dug up a small clod of dirt off to the left.

Poor Lee was panicking and crying, and Tex's heart ached for the boy; he'd just witness his mother's death and had people shooting at him.

As Tex left the frontage road ditch and sped off across the rough terrain, he couldn't help but notice the multitude of burning cars on either side of the road—he, Lee, and Victoria had definitely been the lucky ones.

Once well away from of the city, Tex had headed onward to the east and into the hidden depths of pine tree country.

It was a long haul, but at least Tex had gotten them all there safely.

All except Krista, of course.

He'd done his best to push all thoughts of his wife and how she'd died right there in front of him to the farthest corners of his mind, but as he drove, those cruel memories kept on creeping back to haunt him. The guilt gnawed at him, too, but Tex knew there was nothing he'd be able to do about that. Not even telling himself he'd done the best thing for Lee by not taking on the mob once he realized it was too late to save Krista managed to assuage his conscience. He was an ex-soldier, for Christ's sake; there *must* have been something he could have done to prevent Krista dying like that…

"We're here," Tex placed a hand on Victoria's shoulder and gently rocked her awake. She and Lee had been asleep for the last hour or so of the journey, which had made for a lonely, introspective time for Tex. He really didn't want to be left alone with his broken heart and guilt-ridden thoughts for any length of time, but Tex figured it best to let the two of them sleep—they'd been through a hell of a lot since that morning and deserved some respite.

So, Tex had searched through the few radio stations still operating—the majority were off the air and silent—and managed to find nothing but emergency broadcasts and grim news broadcasts delivering up-to-the-minute bulletins from around the state as the towns and cities were laid waste and vicious mobs plundered and killed everything and everyone in their path. Tex did happen upon a handful of hellfire-and-brimstone preachers citing lengthy Bible passages about the End of Times and how man's wickedness and greed had brought it all about; he wasn't a particularly God-fearing man, but Tex couldn't help but think they might have been onto something.

Tex had spent the majority of the trip in silence.

"Huh?" Victoria groaned as she stirred from her deep sleep. Blinking against the light from the low-slung sun, she stared out through the windshield at the towering pine trees that surrounded them like an army of green-topped giants just waiting to pounce.

"Little Alamo," Tex explained. "It's just around this bend."

"Oh." Victoria poked the sleep from the corner of her eyes and leaned forward to peer ahead.

Of course, there was nothing to see at that point—Tex, Lump, and the other Little Alamo founders had planned that detail with great care. They'd deliberately built the dirt road leading up to the fort from the south with a sharp 45-degree bend. The idea was the bend would conceal the Little Alamo until the very last moment, slow down any potential attackers, and buy its inhabitants time to prepare should an attack ever happen. They'd done the same on the northern road in, too, and the trees provided concealment and protection from the east and west.

"Lee," Tex reached a hand to the back seat, where his son lay sprawled out and dead to the world. Winnie perked up at the sound of Tex's voice and jumped up onto Lee's belly from the footwell.

In the rearview, Tex saw Lee awaken with a start, and just for a second, there was a spark of excitement in the boy's eyes as he recognized where he was. Tex envied his son that: forgetting the loss of his mother, even if it was only for a brief moment.

And then the sadness returned to Lee's young face and Tex felt guilty all over again.

Tex tapped the brake, steered the Landcruiser around the bend, and was immediately greeted by the Little Alamo's tall outer wall and wide steel gate. The spire of the compound's church, which sat dead center of the fort, towered high into the dusk sky. The pristine, white-painted wooden cross at its top looked for all the world like friendly, open arms welcoming Tex to the safety of the small town he'd built piece by piece over the years.

Little Alamo was a town he'd designed and helped build along with dozens of others who'd all hoped they'd never need it; that it would be little more than a grandiose hobby for him and his fellow preppers. Maybe, at most, it would be used as a weekend getaway for hunting trips and family vacations. And, even as Tex watched the world crumble around him, he'd still hoped against hope it would never come to this.

"We're here, buddy," Tex said. Of course, the boy could see for himself where they were, but Tex just wanted to split the silence between them. There was a time, back in the day, when the two of them would take the trip out to spend long weekends constructing the buildings within the compound's walls or clearing patches of the surrounding pine trees in anticipation of crops and animals, and Lee would be beside himself with excitement. It had always been their happy place; somewhere father and son called their own and where they could build bonds Tex had hoped would never be broken.

But, looking at his son's slack face and dull eyes at that moment, Tex had begun to question if that was possible anymore.

Just a little.

"This is amazing, Tex," Victoria said, craning her neck to take in the impressive view. "You *built* all this?"

"We did have some help," Tex forced a smile as he eased the Cruiser to a stop six yards or so from the compound's gate. "Ain't that right, Lee?"

Lee nodded quietly and stroked Winnie's ears.

"I had no idea," Victoria continued. "When Krista used to tell me about what you guys were up to out here, I was expecting a bunch of wooden shacks and a homemade distillery."

Tex's gut knotted at the sound of his wife's name; he wasn't ready to hear it spoken aloud, especially by Victoria. The truth was, Krista had never visited the Little Alamo—not once. She'd poo-pooed the whole idea as crazy prepper nonsense and only put up with Tex spending so much time there because it made for a happier home life. It also got him and Lee out of the house and gave Krista some of her much-needed alone time. Exactly what she got up to during those times, Tex had never asked. He trusted his wife enough to know she'd not be out screwing around on him.

Swallowing down the thick lump at the back of his throat and fighting back bitter tears, Tex gave the horn three swift taps followed by a longer burst of precisely three seconds. The signal was Lump's idea, although, as they'd debated it over Coors Lite and barbecue ribs, Tex had thought it was a tad over the top; a little too cloak and dagger for his liking.

A face appeared from one of the sentry boxes Tex recalled building at the left-hand corner at the top of the wall. There was a narrow walkway on the inside of the wall that connected each of the four boxes—one in each corner—and the whole thing gave the Little Alamo a pioneer look, just like in the old Western movies Tex had grown up watching.

"Howdy! Stay right there!" A voice boomed down from the wall. Tex recognized it as TJ, a fellow founder, and it sure as hell felt good to see the guy again.

Tex got out of the car as the compound's gate swung slowly open; the massive, handmade hinges squeaked loudly as metal ground against metal, and Tex made a mental note to make sure somebody applied a little oil.

A solitary figure stepped out from the shadows behind the half-open gate.

"Howdy," Tex greeted the guy with his arms outstretched and feet apart. He kinda knew the man from the selection process the founders had gone through, but not personally. His name was Cory Mulgrew, and he was one of Lump's old friends. The guy was handy with a hunting rifle and a veterinarian to boot—he'd been a definite shoe-in.

"Mr. Pemberton," Mulgrew said with a smile and lowered the 12-guage he had pointed at Tex's chest. "It's good to see you."

"Good to see you, too, Cory," Tex returned the smile. "I don't think you're supposed to take that off me until you've secured the vehicle."

Tex knew the protocol by heart—he ought to—because he was the one who'd co-written it with TJ, the ex-Marine who'd been designated the fort's Head of Security.

"Yessir, Mr. Pemberton." The shotgun was once more aimed at Tex's heart, although Mulgrew did appear more than a little embarrassed to be pointing a firearm at the Little Alamo's founding father.

"I think you can call me Tex—given the present circumstances an' all." Tex lowered his arms; he'd made it clear he was friend, not foe. "You gonna check the vehicle?" He knew the guy had no such intention, but it was important that he do so—anyone could be lurking inside the Landcruiser, holding Tex's loved ones hostage so they could gain entry to the Little Alamo.

Again, it was all in the protocol, and that protocol would keep all the Little Alamo's inhabitants safe.

Mulgrew very quickly slipped back into military mode and did a thorough sweep of the car. He pulled open each one of the doors, along with the back, and checked beneath with his flashlight; the light was fading fast as the sun disappeared behind the tree line.

"All clear, Mr.—*Tex*," Mulgrew declared with a friendly grin as he shouldered the shotgun. "Welcome to Little Alamo." He waved a hand above his head, and the gate lurched open all the way.

"Thank you, Cory," Tex replied as he clambered back into the car. He pulled the door closed, fired up the engine, and drove slowly through the gate and into the main square of the compound.

Lump was there to greet them.

Tex brought the Landcruiser to a rolling stop outside the John Wayne bar he'd helped put together with his own bare hands. The name had been Lump's idea because he was a huge Wayne fan, and he reckoned the bar looked so much like the countless saloons in which the movie star had enjoyed beautifully choreographed bar fights. Tex and Lump had known each other from their Army days—Lump was originally from Carlyle, Illinois and had settled in Texas after his discharge—and he'd been a good friend after Rusty died. Had it not been for Lump, Tex was convinced he'd have gone completely off the rails at that time, so the least he could do was allow the guy to give their compound's bar a stupid name.

"You made it!" Lump gave Tex a rib-crushing bear hug the second he was out of the car. "We've been hearing a lot of bad things about the Fort Worth area, and I have to say I was getting worried."

"It wasn't pretty, Lump," Tex told him with a heavy sigh. Behind him, Victoria and Lee got out of the Cruiser, followed by Winnie, who proceeded to cock a leg and pee right by Lump's foot.

"Krista?" Lump peered over his old friend's shoulder, puzzled at Tex having only the two passengers.

Tex gave him a shake of the head, downturn of the eyes, and a barely perceptible nod toward Lee—it was all it took to have the subject quickly changed.

"You won't get that to work here, miss. No signal," Lump informed Victoria, who was holding her cell phone up to the heavens as if offering the thing as sacrifice.

"There aren't any towers for miles," Tex explained. "Even Lily Creek doesn't have one, and we're in a valley bottom surrounded by forests. We decided against putting up one of our own because we reckon the networks will quit working soon enough and it would be best not to be relying on them."

Victoria looked annoyed, like the end of civilization wasn't bad enough for her without having to give up her cell. "I suppose there's no internet, either?"

"Same argument," Lump chipped in. "As things progress, electricity will be hard to come by, and with no power or folks to maintain the servers, the World Wide Web will cease to exist before too long."

"So, we're totally isolated here?"

"No, ma'am." Lump offered Victoria a smile Tex figured was meant to reassure, but which he thought came across as a touch condescending. "We have short-wave radios all over the compound. That way, we can stay in touch with other forts around the country—and we have regular radio, of course, to listen in on the news stations while they're still going."

"Perfect," Victoria grumbled and tucked her phone back into her pocket.

Lump ignored her and gave a sharp whistle to a stocky, shaven-headed guy standing by the bar's main doors and nursing a bottle of beer. "Hey, Rhino! Over here!"

The guy looked up and made his way across the square.

"This is Steve Wazowski—we call him Rhino—Rhino, this is Tex Pemberton." Lump made with the introductions.

"Good to meet you, sir." Rhino stuck out his free hand for Tex to shake.

"Rhino is one of our lieutenants—ex-Navy SEAL, damn good with a gun and too good at hand to hand." Lump gave the guy a hearty slap on the back.

Shaking hands with Rhino, Tex couldn't help but think how things could have turned out different that morning if he'd had somebody like the Navy SEAL by his side. Maybe they could have saved Krista, maybe she'd be there at the Little Alamo with her family instead of…

Maybes weren't going to bring Krista back, Tex admonished himself. He had Lee to think about, along with the one hundred and thirty-four other inhabitants of the small community he'd planned and built, and didn't have the luxury of time to wallow in self-pity and guilt.

There'd be plenty time for that later, Tex knew, in the darkness of the small hours as he lay alone and sleepless in his new bed in Little Alamo.

"Take Tex's car to the lot," Lump ordered. "We'll unload and have your stuff taken over to your house, Tex."

"It's okay, I can do that." Tex's protest fell on deaf ears.

"You guys have had a long trip," Lump said. "What say we go grab a beer and a bite while you relax a little? The John Wayne does some awesome wings, and there's no dumb twenty-one-year-old age limit, neither." He winked at Lee and the boy returned a sad half-smile.

"I guess I could eat," Tex said. "The keys are still in,"

he told Rhino, and watched as the guy climbed into the Cruiser.

"I just want to go to bed," Victoria said. "I'm not really hungry."

"Rhino can drop you off at your designated house," Lump told her. "It's over on the west side, overlooking the duck pond."

Victoria shrugged and got back in the car.

"We'll give her the grand tour in the morning," Lump said as he ushered Tex and Lee in the direction of the bar. Voices and music drifted out into the cooling night air, which gave the place a soothing air of normality.

"Maybe you'd like to show Victoria around tomorrow?" Tex suggested to Lee.

"Yeah," the boy replied, shuffling his feet alongside his father; Winnie scampered along behind them, eyes wide, tongue lolling from the side of his mouth—it was just all one big adventure for the dog.

Tex rested a hand on his son's shoulder as they walked in silence. He knew from hard experience the kid had not even begun to process the reality of what happened to his mom. It was a small mercy he'd not seen what the angry mob had done, but he'd lost her, nonetheless. Tex wished he could somehow just take the pain and grief away from his son, spare him the agony and confusion he knew was waiting for him in the weeks, months, even years ahead. Tex been through all of that after Rusty, and he wouldn't wish it on his worst enemy, let alone his own flesh and blood.

As for Victoria… well, Tex reckoned she'd get over herself once she realized just how lucky she was he'd kept the promise to her dying husband to make sure there was a place for her at the Little Alamo. She'd also come to terms with the relatively minor inconvenience of living without a cell phone and the Internet—by Tex's thinking, it would be a small price to pay for surviving the end of the civilized world.

Just as Victoria had lost her husband to one of Tex's decisions all those years before in Tikrit, Tex had lost his beloved Krista, and now he was alone, too.

Perhaps, in some perverse way in Tex's mind, it made him and his best friend's widow even?

Chapter Six

Morning came, and Tex was awakened by one of the compound's cocks crowing what sounded to be just outside his bedroom window. Of course, he knew that was impossible, since the chickens—along with the cattle, pigs, sheep, and horses—were corralled at the north side of Little Alamo, adjacent to the garage and fuel dump and well away from the housing.

Even so, the bird was damn loud.

Tex heard Lee stirring in the room next to his and hoped the kid had managed to sleep some. They'd stayed out late at the bar with Lump, his son, Gabriel, and wife, Shannon. Gabe was a couple years and change older than Lee, but the two had become friends over the long weekends they'd spent mucking in with the compound's build. Tex had high hopes of the kid helping Lee get through the difficult times he had coming.

"It's seven already," Lee called through the bedroom door. "You agreed to do the rounds this morning, remember?"

Tex groaned to himself; yeah, he remembered promising Lump he'd take the new influx of families around the compound and give them their assigned roles. There were only a couple newbies from the day before—

pretty much everyone who had a place at the Little Alamo had arrived before Tex and were settling in.

As far as he knew, there were only a handful left, including Gordon Oliver, his wife, and three daughters. Gordon was to be Little Alamo's resident doctor—he'd been a field medic back in Iraq and was one of the best in the business.

"Gimme five," Tex replied, as he swung his legs over the side of the bed and sat for a moment in the single bright shaft of sunlight that snuck between the blackout curtains of his small bedroom. It felt pleasant, warm on his bare skin, and helped pull Tex into the present and away from the haunting memories of the nightmare he'd had about Krista.

Tex let out a long, heavy sigh; he knew in his broken heart it would be a long, long time before the nightmares of losing his wife would dissipate and a long time before he'd quit waking up in the darkest hours of the night expecting to find her asleep beside him. The images of her dying at the hands of the blood-crazed mob—their bloodied wedding album clutched to her chest—were indelibly etched into his mind, where Tex knew they'd stay.

He smelled pancakes.

Lee was cooking breakfast and, by the sounds of clattering and singing drifting through the small house, he was making a meal of it—literally. Of course, Tex had taught the boy the basics of how to cook for himself—including the preparation of fish and game for the table—but it was something Lee only ever did on special occasions such as his parents' birthdays. It was a treat Krista always cherished.

Tex rubbed at his stubbled chin with both hands; it rasped loudly, and he couldn't quite recall the last time he'd run a razor over it. Lee was cooking, he sounded happy, and that greatly concerned Tex. It meant the kid wasn't processing the loss of his mother and was most likely in some state of deep denial. The night before, at the saloon, he'd chatted on to Gabe about his mother in the present tense, as if she was alive and well and would be joining them for wings any minute. Tex had let it go—he was unsure as to the proper thing to say, for one, and he figured Lee would process when he was good and ready.

But, in the cold, harsh reality of the morning, Tex was left wondering just what the hell he was supposed to say to the boy, or how he was meant to broach the subject to get Lee facing up to what had happened back at the house.

Tex pulled on his 501s and a T-shirt and made a mental note to maybe get Lee to talk to Doc. Oliver when he finally got to the Little Alamo. The guy had talked Tex and his squad's survivors down after Rusty bought it in Tikrit—he'd know how to handle the boy.

"Smells good, son." Tex padded down the stairs barefoot.

"You want three strips of bacon, or four?" Lee greeted him with a broad grin.

"Four for me," Tex replied and returned the smile as best he could; he saw Lee had laid the table for three. "It's gonna be a busy day, and I reckon I'll need all the fortitude I can get."

"Four it is then." Lee set to laying thick strips of bacon in the skillet, and the tiny kitchen filled with the mouth-wateringly aromatic smell.

They ate breakfast together, and all the while Lee chatted excitedly about finally getting to live at the Little Alamo. He didn't mention once the chaos going on in the world beyond the fortified walls that meant that was their life now, nor did he refer to Krista in any way. That came as some relief to Tex because it meant not having to break the illusion of a happy family morning, but it also worried him to see his son carrying on as if it was just another day at the compound helping his dad with the construction—just like the good ol' days.

"It's time I wasn't here." Tex broke through Lee's chatter. A glance at the wall clock told him it was getting close to eight, and the new families would be gathering outside the John Wayne for their orienteering.

"Is it okay if I come along?" Lee asked through a mouthful of almost-burned pancake doused in syrup.

Tex cast a wary eye across the clutter of dirty pots and dishes his son had generated cooking breakfast and contemplated telling him to stay home and do the washing up. It was a habit he'd picked up over the years—not leaving the kitchen until everything was clean and put away. It was one Krista had instilled in him from the early days of their marriage.

"As long as this lot gets done when we're done." Tex waved a hand toward the dirty dishes. He was going to have to get used to life without a dishwasher—it was one of the luxury items Tex and the Little Alamo founders had agreed they could all do without. The things gobbled water and electricity and, while both resources were in abundance at the compound, there was no guarantee they would be years down the line.

"I promise," Lee replied with a cheeky grin. "You can help me, Dad—it'll be some great father-son bonding time."

Tex got up from the table to put on his boots. "At least see if you can get most of it into the sink,"

Lee polished off what remained of his breakfast and went about his chore with a smile and humming some rap song Tex thought he recognized. It most definitely had the type of obnoxious lyrics Krista would never have approved of.

There were two families waiting for them outside the John Wayne, neither of which Tex knew personally. They were invites from the other founders—Tex recognized them from their pictures in the compound's personnel files.

There were the Johnsons, an African American family of five from Madisonville, and the Mims, a family of three, soon to be four, from Galveston. Susan Mims was almost eight months gone and was already wilting in the Texas morning heat.

Around them, the streets were beginning to fill with people, all of whom bustled about to get to where they needed to be to start their day. Some had been at the compound a week or two and already had their routines worked out; everything had been meticulously planned out to ensure the Little Alamo's smooth running—there was no deadwood, no free rides.

Tex waited a few minutes for Victoria to join the group, but she was nowhere to be seen. She'd visited the Little Alamo a couple times during its construction and had even bummed a ride from Tex and Lee, much to Krista's chagrin. Even though the two had been good friends, Krista had never totally trusted Victoria around her husband.

Victoria already knew her allocated job, so Tex reckoned it wasn't the end of the world for her to miss the orientation—she'd volunteered a while back to manage the greenhouses and had taken classes on beekeeping so she could oversee the apiaries. Tex was disappointed to not see her that morning and reminded himself to drop in on her later in the day.

"Welcome to the Little Alamo, folks," Tex greeted the Johnsons and Mims with a warm smile. "Since we're all gonna be neighbors for the foreseeable future, I think it's good we get off on the right footing." He then shook hands with each and every one of the new folks—including Al Mims' three-year-old son, Petey—and had them all follow suit until everybody had shaken hands with everybody else.

Ice duly broken, Tex said, "Okay, folks, if you'll follow me. We'll start at the living areas, then onto the farm and the outer areas."

"We're going outside the wall?" Joe Johnson looked horrified at the prospect.

Tex nodded. "You'll be just fine, Joe," he reassured. "The arable fields and solar farm are surrounded by razor wire, and we have the lookouts." He pointed toward the matching pair of sentry towers that overlooked the area that had been cleared from the forest beyond the compound wall; they were manned night and day by armed guards and, along with the taller one in the middle of the compound that stood ten-feet higher than the wall and was manned day and night by a sniper, they had been strategically placed to spot anything out of the ordinary for miles around.

Joe Johnson shrugged and looked uncomfortable despite Tex's confidence in the Little Alamo's security. If only he'd known the hours of discussion and attention to detail Tex, Lump, and the other founders had put into ensuring the compound was safe for all the families, he'd have relaxed a little more.

Tex led the group along the main street with Lee at his side. "We cleared the entire ten-acre site over a six-month period," Tex told them. "And we used every single tree in the construct of the compound's buildings." It made perfect sense, of course, to utilize the abundant natural resources on the land the founders had carefully purchased for the Little Alamo. Even with the ten acres cleared for the compound and the fields for the crops, animals, and solar panels, there were more than enough trees surrounding the plot to provide building materials, firewood, and concealment for decades.

Tex ushered the families through the narrow streets

between the two- and three-story buildings that comprised the small rustic city. He was proud of the place they'd call home until whatever madness was going on in the world beyond its fortified gates came to an end—one way or another.

"You'll see we've put solar panels on every roof." Tex was doing his best not to sound too much like some second-rate tour guide. Speaking to strangers wasn't exactly his forte—Lump, on the other hand, loved it, but was doing something in the communications room that morning—but he figured it was a necessary evil in the cause of building strong community relations. And he was one of the leaders, after all.

Each roof of each building in the Little Alamo was entirely covered with black, glinting solar panels. Designed to take full advantage of Texas' abundance of sunshine, the panels, along with those taking up an acre or so outside the walls, generated more than enough power to run the Little Alamo, charge up the electric vehicles they'd stockpiled for when the diesel and LPG ran short, and still store plenty in the huge capacitors secreted away in the storage sheds near the corrals and barns.

"We have plenty of wood to keep the furnaces going for a long time," Tex explained, "But having plenty of juice means we can utilize the surrounding trees at a more sustainable rate."

"What about water?" One of the Johnson kids piped up. A pretty girl, Clara looked to be seventeen, maybe eighteen, and had a smart, bookish air to her.

"There's an underground stream that runs directly under the compound," Lee told her. "It comes straight from the hills and is filtered by the rocks."

"Don't forget the well." Tex rested a fatherly hand on the boy's shoulder, delighted to see how proud he was of the community he'd had a hand in building. Heck, Lee had helped dig the well!

"Yeah, there's the well, too." Lee blushed a little as Clara smiled at him.

"It took some digging, but it taps deep into the water table," Tex said. "For just in case the stream runs dry."

"Is that likely?" Susan Mims asked, rubbing her distended belly.

Tex shook his head no. "It would have to be a really, *really*, hot, dry summer for that to happen. But this *is* Texas, and I figured it best to be safe than sorry."

With that, Tex led the group around the duck pond. There, the small flock of ducks stirred from their slumber and began making their way over with a hungry look in their little eyes.

"I guess they think we've brought breakfast." Tex laughed. "Sometimes it's nice to just sit on one of the benches and throw them a few crumbs—it's a great way to spend a little downtime."

"Be careful of those guys, though." Lee pointed across the pond at the quartet of majestic swans; behind one pair swam a string of eight gray, fluffy cygnets.

"Yeah, Lee found out what happens when you get too close, and they have babies to protect." Tex couldn't help but smile. Less than six months before, what seemed a lifetime ago now, Lee had gotten a hard peck to the backside that left him bruised and unable to sit down for a day or two.

Krista had been less than impressed when they'd returned home.

Momentarily distracted by thoughts of his beloved wife, Tex gazed across the pond at the neat row of wooden houses opposite. The end house, a sweet two-story cottage, was Victoria's. There was no sign of life, the curtains all closed, and Tex assumed she'd still be sleeping off the trauma of the previous day.

By the time Tex maneuvered the small group to the rear of the compound, the animals were being let out into the fields for the day. A dozen people—men, women, and a couple older kids—were busy guiding the cows, horses, and sheep out through the rear gate and into the electric-wire fenced pastures beyond. The pigs, already in place and snorting happily, had their own mud patch immediately to the left of the gate, which was watched over by a surly pair of armed guards. While Tex was confident in his security measures, he knew well enough the Little Alamo was at its most vulnerable with those back gates open.

And it paid to not take unnecessary risks with so many lives depending upon him.

Tex took the group out through the gates—Johnson *still* looked uncomfortable being outside—and between the pasture fields.

"This is our solar farm." Tex stated the obvious. They were standing dead center of an acre and a half of waist-height solar panels, which all faced in the same direction. Lump had supervised their placement, along with Phil Cross, the supply manager; Cross had worked for a solar company sometime in his past and, although he'd been nothing grander than a salesman, it made him the compound's resident expert. "If there's one thing the Little Alamo is going to have, it's plenty of electricity," Tex said with pride.

"Does that mean we have Internet and Wifi?" Clara asked.

Tex fought the urge to laugh; it never ceased to amaze him how kids just naturally assumed there was always Internet everywhere. Did it never occur to them to think *where* it actually came from.

"The Internet will be gone within the next few weeks," Tex told her. "So, there's little point in us relying on it. We do have short wave radio to keep in touch with the other compounds and the outside world, though—"

"And our own telephone system," Lee added.

"Yeah, all the buildings are hooked up to an internal telephone system—the digital exchange is in the comm's room."

"Which is where?" Al Mims asked. The guy had a background in telecoms, and he'd been assigned to communications under Lump.

"Right this way." Tex swept out a hand to indicate the group should all make their way back through the gate and into the compound, much to Joe Johnson's visible relief.

The communication room was compact, little more than fifteen feet square, with a low ceiling and a whole array of radio equipment and backup batteries. It also housed the brain of the compound's telephone system and had been constructed of double-thick walls reinforced with steel bars. Lump had insisted the room be the Little Alamo's most secure after the weapons and ammunition silo. Tex and the other founders had not argued with the guy's logic; they understood it would be imperative to maintain contact with as much of the outside world in the After Times. Even after the collapse of society as they knew it, cooperation between the survivors would be key to survival.

"Hey, Lump," Tex greeted his old friend with a clap on the shoulder; he sat hunched over one of the short-wave radio sets with bulky headphones covering his ears.

"Oh, hey, Tex." Lump started a little at the interruption but put on a warm smile for the impromptu visitors. He pulled off the headphones, unplugged them from the radio receiver, and set them down on the table.

"You know these guys, right?" Tex pointed at the two families who'd followed him in.

"Yeah." Lump nodded at the Johnsons and Mims. "Good to see you all here." And, as he smiled at the families, Lump's eyes didn't once leave the array of illuminated dials on the receiver.

"What's going on, Lump?" Concerned, Tex leaned over his friend's shoulder.

"It's the Olivers." Lump spoke quietly, casting a furtive glance at the visitors. "They hit some trouble at Fort Hood, and I lost communication with them."

Tex swore beneath his breath. Doc. Oliver and his family were supposed to be traveling overnight from Killeen—they were due at the compound literally any minute. "They're still at Hood?"

Lump nodded just as the radio squawked back to life.

"You there, John? Are you receiving me?" The doctor's voice sounded strained, as if the guy was fighting a losing battle against blind panic. In the background, Tex heard shouts, gunfire, and what could well have been explosions.

"Receiving, Gordon." Lump leaned into the microphone. "What is your location?"

"Twenty miles due south of Fort Hood. We are under attack."

"Shit," Lump growled and shot a look over Tex's shoulder at the two families who'd only popped in for a look-see.

"The café across the plaza does terrific coffee and donuts," Tex told them. "What say I catch up with you guys there?" And, so saying, he began maneuvering them toward the comms room door.

"Is there anything I can do to help?" Al Mims held back as his wife waddled out into the sunshine, practically dragged out by Petey in his excitement at the prospect of donuts.

"You can try reaching one of the compounds close to

Fort Hood." Lump pointed at one of the other shortwave receivers with his chin. "See if they can go help the doc."

Mims sat himself down at the desk adjacent to Lump and brought the receiver to life.

"*We're going to make a run for it*!" The doctor's voice was close to breaking; Tex heard the unmistakable sound of crying, and his heart went out to the guy's wife and daughters.

"No!" Lump barked into the mic. "Lay low—we're trying to get help to you!"

"Try Jed Timothy," Tex said to Mims. "He's just East of Gilmer and has contacts all over that area—maybe someone will be willing to leave their bunker to go help Gordon."

Mims got straight to it.

"Are they gonna be okay, Dad?" Lee's voice startled Tex; he'd been so preoccupied with Doc. Oliver's predicament, he didn't realize the boy hadn't left with the others.

"Of course, they are," Tex told him. "They need to go to ground 'til we can rustle up some help or things die down over there.

Lump's radio blasted out the sound of a car engine firing up and Tex's heart sank.

"We gotta go! They're coming!"

"Stay where you are!" Lump yelled into the microphone. "Do not move! I repeat—*do not move*!"

Tex knew it was already too late before the words left his friend's mouth. The doctor had allowed panic to overcome him, and he was making a break from whatever hiding place had kept him and his family safe all night.

The raucous sound of angry, bloodthirsty voices boomed from the radio's speaker and in an instant, Tex was transported back to facing the mob in his own backyard.

From Lump's radio, a scream.

Lump jumped back in his chair like the equipment had bitten him.

Another scream, high-pitched, terrified, along with the smashing of glass and those blood-curdling voices.

"*They're in the car*!" Oliver yelled through the speaker. "*They're in the fucking car*!"

Gunshots cracked and cries of pain filled the comms room. For a split second, Tex allowed himself to believe the doctor and his family would get away safely from the murderous mob despite what his own experience had taught him. He'd only gotten away with his life because he'd been more than prepared to shoot and mow down anyone who stood in his way.

Another scream—Doc. Oliver's—and the radio fell silent.

"You didn't save them!" Lee howled. "Just like you didn't save Mom!"

Before Tex could say a word to his son, Lee had hightailed it from the communications room and across the plaza like the devil was on his heels.

"You need to go after him," Lump said with a weary sigh. "There's nothing you can do here now."

"I'm sorry." Tex rested a comforting hand on his friend's arm. The doctor and his family had been closer to Lump and his, and Tex understood his loss meant more to him than the Little Alamo losing its doctor—although that posed a pretty big problem in itself. But, for as much as Tex knew Lump was hurting, it was Lee who needed him the most at that moment in time.

Tex found Lee by the duck pond, sitting alone on one of the roughly hewn wooden benches he'd helped to build only a month or so before. It wrenched at Tex's heart to see his son in so much pain—his sweet, innocent face was wet with tears and his shoulder heaved with each loud, heavy sob.

"Lee…"

"Go away!" Lee spat. "You said you'd keep us all safe!"

Tex cringed at the boy's angry words; it was true, of course—he'd promised Lee time and time again they'd all be safe when they came to live at the Little Alamo, and he'd allowed the kid's mother to die before they'd even set off. And for Lee to hear the obvious demise of Doc. Oliver and his young family was unforgivable.

"I'm sorry, son—" Tex sat down on the bench.

Lee shrugged off his father's comforting arm and turned to face Tex with so much hurt and venom in his eyes Tex barely recognized him. "You let them die!" He snarled. "Just like you let them kill my mom—*you don't fucking care*!"

"There was nothing I could do, son…"

"Bullshit."

A fleeting thought crossed Tex's mind: Krista would never chastise Lee for the potty mouth he'd picked up from his father, nor would she give Tex that shaming *look* whenever the boy accidentally let an expletive slip.

And boy, that *really* hurt.

"The doctor decided to go against orders," Tex told his son. "If they'd stayed put—"

"You were there," Lee cut him off, his voice thick with tears. "You could have shot them."

Of course, Lee's grief was for his own mother, not a family he only knew in passing from the occasional times they'd spent together during the compound's construction. The Olivers' fate played out over the short wave had served as a trigger, which had unleashed all of Lee's pain from losing his mom the day before. In some ways, Tex was grateful Lee was no longer bottling it all up and carrying on as if Krista would be joining them at the Little

Alamo at any moment, but it still killed him to see his son hurting so damn much and knowing there was very little he could do to ease that pain.

"Hey." A soft voice from behind broke Tex's reverie. Twisting around, his eyes met Victoria's.

"Hi." Tex could think of nothing else to say to the woman.

"Hey, Lee," Victoria said as she sat herself down on the opposite side of Lee and snaked an arm around his shoulders. "It's all going to be okay."

Instead of shrugging off Victoria's arm, Lee leaned in and rested his head against her shoulder. It stung Tex a little to feel his son's obvious rejection, but in the same instant, he was happy the boy had *someone* to comfort him; someone he didn't feel had let him down in the worse way possible.

"She's dead," Lee sobbed. "He let them kill her."

"Your dad did everything he could, Lee," Victoria said quietly, all the while stroking the boy's hair. "I promise you that—there's no way he'd have left if there'd been even the slightest chance of saving her. He had you to think about, too, remember—if it wasn't for him, you wouldn't be here right now… none of us would be." She looked over Lee's head at Tex, her eyes seeking his, and Tex knew her soothing words were as much for his benefit as his son's.

Lee said nothing more after that. Instead, he pressed himself close to Victoria and cried his heart out.

"Thank you, Vic," Tex said as, absently, he watched the ducks and swans go about their business on the pond—life going on as usual for them. "I didn't know what to say…"

"There's nothing you *could* say, Tex," Victoria reassured him. "There are no words that can make any of this right, nothing you can do to take away the pain—

you're hurting too, and you'll have to face your own reality in your own time."

She spoke from bitter experience, of course, and Tex knew the pain of losing a loved one in such an abrupt, terrible way would never truly leave. There had been many times since Rusty's death that he'd seen a faraway look in Victoria's eyes and suspected she was reliving the moment she was told he was gone for good.

"I know," Tex said with a sad smile. "But thank you for coming over. Thank you for being here for Lee." He rested a hand on his son's knee and wished he had some idea of what to say to make everything better. But as his own grandmother always used to say: time was the great healer.

And that was something they had plenty of now they were safe within the Little Alamo's walls.

THE AFTER TIMES

Chapter Seven

April 2029, Little Alamo, Texas

"Another beer, guys?" Lump stood up from the table and made his way over to the bar. Tex had commandeered the John Wayne for the afternoon for the monthly founders' meeting. He'd never been one for round table meetings back in the Before Times but Lump and the others had persuaded him—they were vital to the smooth running of the Little Alamo. At Tex's feet, Winnie lay curled up and fast asleep; the little dog had rarely left his side since they'd arrived at the compound six months before—he even seemed to prefer Tex to Lee.

"I'll take another, thanks," Heather Johnson threw in. As head of the compound's school program, she'd proven invaluable in getting all the kids back on track with their education in some semblance of normality. Of course, lessons had to fit around the kids' chores and obligations—even the small ones were given things to do around the fort—and there was a heavy emphasis on learning practical skills that were very much needed in the new society. So, the youngsters were taught motor maintenance, farming, animal husbandry, hunting, culinary skills, and everything else that would help them become valued contributors to the Little Alamo and ensure their survival and that of everyone around them.

"Make it a full round—on me," Tex told his friend; they'd all had one hell of a long week and he reckoned they deserved another beer each.

Around the table, along with Tex, Heather Johnson, and Lump, were Phil Cross the supplies manager, Rhino, and TJ. Lump had requested the latter two's attendance because he had a plan he intended to float and wanted the soldiers there for their input.

"You gonna spill, Lump?" Tex prompted the guy. "Or is it some big secret you're not gonna share?"

Lump laughed and asked the barkeep for another round of beers—it was the first batch of Little Alamo's micro-brewed IPA, which had been rather unimaginatively christened *Batch One*. But, despite the name, it tasted good and was a credit to Jesus Menendez, the bar's manager and head brewer.

"I think it's time we ventured outside," Lump said upon his return to the table. "Take a look at what's left out there."

"We *know* what's out there," Rhino said.

"We know what we've been *told* is out there, Rhino," Lump countered.

"I think we can trust what the other compounds and preppers are telling us," TJ added. "It's not like they're Fox News or something."

A nervous laugh rippled around the table. Tex joined in, fighting the creeping sensation of unease that nestled in the pit of his stomach. No one had ventured beyond the Little Alamo's boundaries since the last of the families arrived a couple days or so after what happened to Doc. Oliver and his family and that suited him just fine. They had everything they needed within the compound—winter had been mild and kind to them, the crops were coming along nicely, the animals were beginning to breed, and supplies of food, water, and medicines were running high—what possible reason could Lump have for wanting to go out into whatever was left out there?

"The cities are all burned out," Tex said. "You've heard the reports as well as I have, Lump."

"What's not burned to the ground are just lawless hellholes crawling with nomads," Rhino said. "We've been lucky enough to have kept off their radar so far—I don't see why we should draw attention to ourselves just for the sake of it."

"There were reports of nomads close to the Timothy compound," Heather joined in. "Joe was talking to Jed a couple days ago, and he said they'd seen them circling out in the desert."

When the nomads first began appearing, Tex had dismissed them as rag-tag groups of what was left of the mobs that ransacked the cities and murdered everyone who crossed their path in cold blood. It hadn't taken too long for the mobs to clash with one another in days-long battles that laid waste to entire towns and suburbs as they vented their anger and frustrations upon one another. Then, when resources began running out—less than a month after society's total collapse and the absence of law enforcement in the form of the police and the Army—the mobs had turned on their fellow mobsters and all but a handful had survived that.

They, along with a few pockets of isolated people who'd survived the apocalypse only by sheer luck, had taken to roaming the countryside and banding together with others amongst society's stragglers. They'd pick off the less-prepared preppers and loot what they could from the remains of the towns and cities but had been sensible enough to leave the compounds alone; every single one of the forts Tex knew of was more than well-equipped to fend off an attack by the nomads, and he reckoned they knew it.

But, if the nomads ever got themselves organized in larger numbers and better armed, Tex thought they might just present a threat. As it was, with the intel Lump and Joe Johnson had gathered over the months, Tex reckoned that scenario was highly unlikely.

"I say it's worth a recce, at the very least," TJ spoke up. He was a man of very few words, but one hell of a soldier—nothing ever fazed the guy. "There's gonna be resources out there we could use."

"Such as what?" Rhino asked him.

TJ shrugged. "Food, medicine."

"We have *plenty* of food and medicine," Cross said. "We don't need to be risking lives to get more."

"We'd be stupid to wait 'til we need it to go looking." TJ eased his muscular bulk back into his seat and scratched at the long, snaking scar that ran along the side of his neck—a souvenir he'd brought back from his final tour of Afghanistan.

"That's a good point." Lump nodded as he watched the barkeep making his way across the bar with the fresh beers. "There's bound to be stuff still out there we could use—it's only been six months. I was talking to Cory yesterday, and he said they could always use more antibiotics at the infirmary."

Cory Mulgrew, the resident veterinarian, had stepped in to fill Doc. Oliver's shoes—not that he'd had much choice in the matter since the Little Alamo needed someone to head up the infirmary. It was obvious to everyone the guy much preferred dealing with four-legged patients, though, as he made very little attempt to hide the fact. Nonetheless, Cory had managed to deliver Susan Mims' baby just before Christmas with very little difficulty—he'd likened the poor woman to one of the heifers he'd helped give birth a couple days before.

"Then we should definitely go," TJ said with an air of finality.

"Won't Chrissy have something to say about that," Rhino threw in; he made a whipping action with his hand, accompanied by the appropriate noise.

Everyone around the table laughed—including TJ. It was a running joke the guy, as badass as he made himself out to be, was decidedly under his girlfriend's thumb—especially so since giving birth to the twins just a year or so before having to move to the Little Alamo.

"Screw you, guys," TJ said with a broad grin. Chrissy was the love of his life, the hottest gal in the compound, and never failed to turn heads; TJ was more than happy to put up with a little nagging for that.

"TJ's right." Lump sipped at his ice-cold beer. "We should put a posse together and take a trip out to Briar Creek—we can be there and back in a day."

Tex snorted at his friend's choice of word. "It's only been six months, Lump." He laughed. "I realize everything's gone to hell in a handbasket out there, but I didn't think we'd regress to the Wild West quite so soon."

"What?" Lump was nonplussed, not quite getting the joke.

"*Posse*—makes you sound like Gary Cooper or John Wayne," Tex explained. "You'll be saying *varmint* and *gulch* next."

Lump cracked a smile. "I figured it'd happen sooner rather than later," he said. "It won't be too long before we're relying on the horses to get around, which is about as cowboy as it's possible to get."

"We're running out of gas already?" Rhino looked concerned.

Phil Cross shook his head. "Not even close," he told Rhino. "We have gasoline for at least twelve months, and

LPG for twenty-four. And don't forget we have the all-electric trucks, too—and I can't see the Texas sun running out any day soon."

Rhino let out a relieved chuckle; Tex had known the guy long enough to know he was one heck of a forward planner, which had the unfortunate side effect of him being a bit of a pessimistic worrywart.

"We'll take one of the hybrid trucks," Lump said; he'd never been entirely comfortable with purely electric vehicles—he was definitely an old-school gas lover when it came to his transport. But, as with Tex and the others, he was smart enough to realize the day would come when they had to rely on electricity alone—hence the abundance of solar panels about the Little Alamo.

"Sounds good," Tex agreed. "All we need to decide now is who's going to be part of Lump's *posse*."

"I'd say the four of us," Lump pointed at Tex, TJ, and Rhino.

"Isn't that risky?" Rhino asked. "Four of the founders leaving the compound together? What if something happened?"

"Nothing's gonna happen," Lump said with the same bravado Tex had become used to back in Iraq. Sometimes, he thought Lump truly believed himself to be untouchable—*immortal*, even.

"You don't know that," Rhino countered. "There's no way of us knowing for sure what's out there—and you've all heard the reports on the nomads."

"Relax, Rhino," Tex told him. "We've not seen or heard anyone even close to us since we got here and closed the gates. The nomads are sticking mostly around the cities, and the other compounds that have reported them say they're in small groups and badly armed."

"And we'll take enough firepower with us to wipe out a small army," Lump threw in. "Plus, we'll take two vehicles—for just in case, Rhino."

That appeared to placate Rhino. The guy was a born soldier and, no doubt, the thought of tooling up with a choice of highly effective weapons from the Little Alamo armory more than countered his reticence at venturing out into whatever remained of the world they'd all left behind a half year ago.

"I say we head out this morning." Tex checked his watch. It was already after nine, and if they wanted enough time to recce the town for anything of use, they would need to head out before eleven a.m. to make it back before sundown.

Everyone nodded their agreement—including Heather, although she did seem to be uneasy about Lump's proposed excursion—and drained their beer glasses.

"If there's no other business…" Tex got to his feet; a familiar face had passed by the window, someone he'd not spoken to in a while. "I have things to get done before we head out into the great unknown." And, with that, he made his way out of the bar.

"Hey, Vic!" Tex jogged to catch up with Victoria, Winnie scampering along behind him. Carrying a large, plain, brown cardboard box, Victoria was making her way along the main street toward the general store. Of course, none of the Little Alamo's residents had to pay for any goods or services—the work they all put into the collective was their currency—but it was nice for everyone to have the familiarity of the small store to visit, which added to the social nuance of the compound.

"Oh, hi, Tex." Victoria smiled, her beautiful face caught in the morning sunlight. She quit walking and placed her box on the ground.

"Need a hand?" Tex nodded down at the box.

Victoria shook her head no. "I think I can manage a couple dozen jars of honey, thank you."

The gal was as independent as ever—Tex admired that. “I haven’t seen much of you these past few weeks,” he said.

“It’s been a busy time,” Victoria offered. “As you can see.” She nudged the box with her foot. “Managing the bees and the greenhouses is more taxing than you’d think.”

“I can imagine,” Tex said, although he couldn’t. Surely, the bees did all the hard work and the plants just kinda grew under the glass.

“I’ve seen Lee more than a few times.” Victoria looked a little awkward. “Did he tell you?”

“He doesn’t tell me much about any of that stuff,” Tex admitted. “I figured he was off to see you when he disappears in the evenings.”

“Hope you don’t mind,” Victoria said. “He says he can talk to me about… about what happened. He doesn’t like to bring the subject up to you because he doesn’t want to hurt your feelings.”

Tex shrugged. While it hurt his heart that his own son felt he couldn’t open up to him about losing his mother, Tex was happy Lee had *someone* he could share with; it was important the kid had someone to offer him the emotional support he needed after losing a parent. And Tex was pleased that someone was Victoria, and she’d more than willingly allowed herself to become Lee’s mother figure—not that she’d ever attempted to replace Krista.

Since that day on the bench by the duck pond, when Victoria had appeared as if out of nowhere to comfort his son as he broke down, Tex had owed the woman a huge debt of gratitude. Lee was certainly coping with the changes in his life thanks to Victoria. She had kept her distance from Tex since that day, though, but he reckoned that was just her way of giving him the space he needed to process his own loss and throw himself into running the Little Alamo.

"Thank you, for being there for Lee," Tex said. "I know it means a lot to him, and I think it's really helping the boy."

"It *always* helps to talk, Tex." Victoria's statement was a loaded one. "If you ever need to talk about Krista, about anything, I'm here for you as well."

"I appreciate that." Tex stole a glance into Victoria's eyes; he saw the warmth in there as she met his gaze, and, just for a heartbeat, he imagined something more.

"Rebecca Smithson has been asking after you." Averting her eyes from Tex's, Victoria broke the spell. "I think she's interested…"

Tex grimaced. Rebecca was a nice enough lady—she'd lost her husband to the mob when Dallas was trashed—but she just didn't appeal to Tex in that way. He'd noticed a few of the compound's single ladies giving him the eye and being more than cordially friendly of late, although he'd done nothing at all to encourage them. And, besides, it had only been a touch over six months since he'd watched Krista die. Tex was still grieving and wasn't ready to spark up any sort of new relationship with anyone.

Except, perhaps…

Victoria gave Tex a sweet smile. "I know it's too soon, Tex." Reaching out, she held his arm.

"It's okay." Tex's skin tingled at Victoria's touch; her skin was soft, warm, and Tex realized it had been a long time since he'd felt a woman's touch. "I'm sure I'll get back on that horse when the time feels right."

Victoria let out a loud chortle. "I'll be sure to let Rebecca know you called her a horse."

"No…" Tex stammered; his face suddenly felt hot, flushed. "I didn't mean…"

"Relax, Tex, I promise I won't." Victoria laughed at Tex's embarrassment and stepped back a tad; people were looking in their direction and it seemed to make her uncomfortable.

"You got me there." Tex laughed along; had it been so long that he'd forgotten how to take a little gentle teasing? The spot where Victoria's hand had rested on Tex's bare arm felt a little cool with it gone, although he imagined he still felt her fingertips there.

And he missed them.

"Maybe we could get a drink sometime?" Victoria said with a glance toward the John Wayne. "Catch up a little?"

Tex studied her as she bent over to pick up her box of honey; she'd always been a fine-looking lady, and time had done nothing to diminish that in his eyes.

"Yeah," Tex replied, aware his heartbeat had quickened some. "I'd really like that, Vic."

Chapter Eight

April 2029, Little Alamo, Texas

It was eleven on the dot when the Little Alamo's front gates swung open. They'd remained steadfastly closed for the better part of six months, and the huge steel hinges squealed their protest.

"A little WD-40 wouldn't go amiss," Tex grumbled as he drove slowly out through the wide wooden gates. Riding shotgun beside him, TJ remained silent and peered out through the side window like he'd never seen trees before. The hybrid 4x4 Jeep moved silently along the grass-festooned dirt road leading away from the compound and out into the pine forest beyond. It hadn't taken Mother Nature too long to begin reclaiming the unused road Tex and the others had carved out of the forest prior to the Little Alamo's construction—there were even foot-high pine saplings sprouting up among the clumps of fresh, verdant grass and weeds.

"You reading me, Lump?" Tex said.

"Loud and clear," Lump's voice boomed through the radio they'd hooked up in both of the Jeeps to stay in constant contact with each other and Joe Johnson back in the compound's comms room. Tex glanced in the rearview mirror and saw Lump and Rhino in the identical black Jeep behind them. As he watched, the gates swung closed behind Lump's vehicle, and Tex experienced the same weird churning in his gut that was all too commonplace back Iraq: that adrenaline-fueled feeling of being entirely alone and at the mercy of whatever lay beyond the safety of those gates.

"You gonna step on it, Tex?" Lump chastised, his voice strained and tinny over the radio. "Or are we sightseeing here?"

Taking the hint, Tex pressed his foot on the gas; the Jeep lurched forward, and the convoy of two set off along the bumpy road into the unknown.

In the two hours and some it took to get to Briar Creek, Tex saw no signs of human life. Sure, there were abandoned, burned-out cars dotted here and there along the roads leading to the small town, and a handful of small farmhouses, none of which appeared occupied. Some of the latter had been burned down to their chimney stacks and foundations with only a couple having been spared that ignominy by the rampaging mobs.

Around them, the fields had grown wild and small herds of longhorn cattle roamed free. The animals, it seemed, had truly lucked out with the end of society: they no longer had the inevitable final trip to the slaughterhouse looming over them. Tex made a mental note of the cattle—his next trip out of the Little Alamo would be with hunting rifles and a low-loader. There were more than enough cows wandering around wild to feed the compound's citizens for quite some time.

Briar Creek, the closest town to the Little Alamo, appeared deserted. There were a few burned out cars and trucks on the main streets and all the stores on both sides had been gutted by fire. Driving slowly, his senses on red alert, Tex espied random bundles of rags dotted here and there, which, upon closer inspection, turned out to be the remains of the town's people who hadn't made it out alive.

Their corpses had been picked clean—the local coyotes, raccoons, and buzzards had eaten well—and odd bones were scattered across the road; they made a sickening, dry *crunch* when the Jeep's wheels ran over them.

"You getting all this, Lump?" Tex asked.

"Yeah. The place looks deserted."

"The pharmacy is gone." Looking ahead, Tex saw what remained of the Briar Creek CVS—it was little more than a charred shell. "I don't think there's much point even stopping by."

"Agreed." Lump sounded as deflated as Tex felt. "

"There's a trailer park off to the left," Tex told his buddy; he remembered the Sunny Fields Trailer Park from the times he'd driven through Briar Creek back in the Before Times. "If it's still there, of course."

"I guess it's always worth a look," Lump said. "Might be propane there at least."

In the distance, the sharp, unmistakable sound of a gunshot.

"Shit." TJ jumped in his seat, a hand automatically pulling his sidearm from its holster.

Tex gripped the steering wheel but kept the car moving; his trained ear told him the shot—most likely a high-velocity hunting rifle—was far enough away to not pose an immediate threat. It did let him know, however, there were some people still around the town and they were armed.

"You hear that?" Lump's question was rhetorical, of course.

"Roger that," Tex replied. "Stay close." As he drove slowly by, he eyed every single one of the burned-out storefronts. He was looking out for any signs of movement and listening for the sound of footsteps or another vehicle; running on battery power, the Jeeps made no sound other than the tires against the road's blacktop, and for that, Tex was grateful.

Pulling his vehicle off the main street, Tex drove toward the trailer park, which lay on the periphery of the town. It always felt to him as if the place was an embarrassment to the genteel folk of Briar Creek, its inhabitants were second-class citizens at best. But it appeared Sunny Fields had had the last laugh—most of the trailers were still intact.

As was the supply store.

"Bingo!" Lump's voice sounded brighter. "There's gotta be something here for us."

"Don't get your hopes too high," Tex replied. "The store's had a good going-over by the look of things."

Pulling up alongside the park's general store, Tex peered in through the wide-open doors. Inside the gloomy interior, the shelves were stripped bare, and little more than empty packets and litter adorned the dirt-covered tiled floor.

"I'm gonna take a look in the back," Lump said as he pulled up an inch from Tex's rear fender. "Maybe the storeroom still has something we can grab."

Tex climbed out of the car and grabbed the AK-47 he'd kept on the back seat—it was a little overkill in his mind, but better safe than sorry. "I'll come with," he told Lump. Then, turning to TJ and Rhino, he said, "You guys stay here and keep your eyes peeled."

"Yessir." TJ scanned the double row of single-wide trailers with suspicion; they all appeared deserted, but he knew from experience the enemy rarely make themselves known until it's too late. He cradled his machine gun in his arms with a finger resting on the trigger. Rhino joined him, identically armed, and the two stood sentry by the supply store entrance as Tex and Lump made their way inside.

It was cool inside, even though the AC would have quit working when the power grid went down not long before New Year's. The morning sun hadn't reached its tin roof, although once it did, Tex reckoned the inside of the store would be hot as hell.

Pointing his gun's muzzle into the shadows at the rear of the store, Tex tapped Lump's arm and pointed with two fingers toward the staff only door in the back left-hand corner.

Lump nodded.

The two made their way there slowly, checking behind every possible hiding place—every shadow was a possible assassin, every pile of rags or litter a potential IED.

The door was locked.

An initial, temporary inconvenience, Tex saw it as a positive sign: whoever had looted the store had not made it into the storeroom. It meant there was a good likelihood of them finding supplies still inside.

Taking careful aim, Lump let off a couple rounds into the door's lock. The metal exploded into a bright array of fragments and sparks, along with a fat chunk of the door's thick wood.

"You could have just shouldered it," Tex hissed, his ears ringing.

"Yeah, but where's the fun in that?" Lump grinned like a naughty schoolkid.

Tex shook his head and kicked at the ruined storeroom door with the toe of his boot; it swung open to reveal yet more shadows and gloom lurking within.

A sudden flash of bright, white light from behind startled Tex. "What the f—?"

"Sorry, bud," Lump said, aiming his flashlight away from Tex and into far corners of the storeroom.

Although the shelves in the storeroom were sparsely

populated, at least there was *something* in there. As Tex made his way into the small room, he noted the canned meats and vegetables dotted about the metal racks, a handful of toilet paper multipacks, and the fact that there was no way out of the room other than the doorway they'd come through.

"Let's pack up all this stuff and get the hell out of here," Tex grumbled. The place gave him the creeps, and the fact that he and Lump would be cornered in the cramped storeroom if they came under attack wasn't lost on him.

"I'm not seeing any propane." Lump swept his flashlight's stark beam in a wide arc.

"If there are any tanks left, they'll probably be at the back of the store," Tex offered. "We'll have to go around—there's no way out from in here."

The two backed out and back into the store; TJ and Rhino were exactly where Tex and Lump had left them, looking out over the trailer park, guns at the ready.

"All clear, guys," Tex told them. "Grab a few bags and go load up what's in there." He nodded at the storeroom door. "There's not much, but it's something."

"We're gonna check around the back," Lump added. "Keep your eyes peeled."

As it turned out, there were a half dozen or so propane tanks in an overgrown enclave twenty paces out from the back of the trailer park store. Three of the squat, rusted tanks were full; the others lay empty and useless. Tex kicked at each one in turn to ascertain the contents. "Let's put these three in the Jeep," he said to Lump. "I'm sure they'll come in handy." Slinging his gun over his shoulder, Tex grabbed two of the tanks and made his way back to the vehicles at the front of the general store.

A shot rang out, splitting the warm, still air.

A little way ahead of Tex, the side window of his Jeep

shattered, spilling shards of glass onto the dirt.

Instinctively, Tex dropped the propane tanks and hit the ground with his gun in his hands and ready to return fire. Behind him, Lump followed suit, and the two crawled to the edge of the building.

Another shot ricocheted off the metal façade of the trailer park store; inside, TJ and Rhino hunkered down and took cover behind the counter.

The second shot, Tex's expert eye told him, came from one of the abandoned trailers to his left—it was of a silver, retro design, which put him in mind of the roadside diners he and Lee loved to frequent on their trips to the Little Alamo. Although it had come completely out of the blue and taken him by surprise, Tex reckoned the first shot had originated from somewhere on the right-hand side of the dirt track that split the trailer park in two.

Which meant Tex, Lump, and their comrades were pinned down by at least two snipers, possibly more. He knew from experience that the only way out of such a situation was to take down the snipers—otherwise the four of them would likely be picked off one by one.

"I'm gonna take the right," Tex whispered to Lump. "You go left—I think the second shooter is inside the silver trailer."

"Roger that," Lump said and began crawling after Tex toward the Jeeps. The vehicles would afford some reasonable cover until Lump and Tex could split up and make their way around to either side of the park.

"You guys got our backs in there?" Tex called out to TJ and Rhino once he was safely behind his Jeep's rear wheel.

He *knew* they all ought to have grabbed one of the walkie-talkies before the four of them split up to recce the general store. He'd been complacent because the park looked deserted and his mind was on the potential for a good supply haul; he'd made a dumb, rookie mistake, one that could have gotten them killed.

No doubt Lump would have something to say to him about it once they got themselves out of the situation.

"We got you, Tex," TJ's voice wafted out of the store. Of course, the snipers knew damn well where TJ and Rhino were, so it wasn't as if they were giving anything away there.

"Go," Tex hissed at Lump, and the two of them darted out from behind the Jeep. Gun shots filled the air as TJ and Rhino let loose a controlled volley of fire in the general direction of where they thought the snipers were, safely over their comrade's heads, of course.

Tex made it to the first trailer and was greeted by a flying clod of dirt churned up by one of the sniper's rounds. A plume of dust rose high into the air less than a few feet in front of Tex's face, and he dove for cover among the cool shadows and myriad spider webs beneath the trailer.

The air fell quiet, still, and Tex crawled to a vantage point at the corner of the trailer. There, a panel of broken, peeling trellis offered some cover while allowing him to scan most of the right-hand side of the park.

Nothing.

Not even the slightest movement or the sound of footsteps; their snipers were just sitting, waiting.

Back in Iraq, Tex had been good friends with one of the unit's best snipers, Si Thwaites. The guy could hunker down for days if necessary, sustaining himself on a little water and peeing in the empty bottles. He'd once asked Thwaites what the hell he thought about for all that time on his own, and the guy had told him he didn't think about anything. Apparently, what made a good sniper was the ability to switch off and focus purely on waiting, looking for movement, some little telltale sign that would give the target away. It was very much a war of patience, Thwaites had told Tex, and he who lost that first, more often than not lost their life.

Tex didn't have the luxury of time to wait out his assailants' patience—they had to get back to the Little Alamo before sundown. Tex knew he and the other three had no real option other than to take out the snipers—any attempt on their part to leave the trailer park would most likely end in disaster.

A movement.

Barely noticeable, but Tex caught it in his peripheral vision: the unmistakable puffs of dry, red dust created by running feet between two trailers about a hundred, hundred-fifty yards from where he was laying.

"Gotchya," Tex whispered beneath his breath and, once again, mentally chastised himself for not grabbing the walkie-talkie.

Tex let out a short, sharp whistle, and Lump's head appeared from behind the single-wide on the opposite side of the track. Tex pointed toward the penultimate trailer on the row and indicated he and Lump should advance.

With his senses on high alert, Tex crawled out from beneath the trailer and made his way down its side toward what he could see were definite footprints in the dirt. Only one person had gone that way, but that likely meant the other snipers would also be scanning the park for movement—it was also possible the runner was acting as a decoy to draw Tex and Lump out into the open.

Heart pounding, Tex focused on following the footprints. They kept close to the side of the silver trailer, then disappeared into the sparse array of weeds and flattened the straggly clumps of couch grass by the door of the next trailer, which was badly neglected and had a chunk of its roof ripped off by a high wind.

And there, the footprints stopped.

Catching Lump's eye, Tex pointed at the trailer's

door and motioned that he should provide cover while he approached it; the thought that the other sniper—or snipers—was just waiting for him to break cover chilled Tex to his core. Nonetheless, it was what he was trained to do—take the risks to get his men out of trouble.

Tex stayed close to the ground and the side of the decrepit trailer and took his time getting to the door. With each step he took, Tex braced himself for the sound of a rifle's report and the donkey-kick of a bullet tearing through his body; it certainly was one way to keep the adrenaline pumping.

Pausing by the door to take a deep breath or two—and give his pounding heart the chance to quieten down some—Tex strained his neck to look up for any signs of life inside the trailer; the windows that weren't broken through and covered with moldy boards were so grimy and cracked it made it impossible to make out anything lurking within. It meant going in blind, but Tex really had no choice.

Tex maneuvered himself onto the bottom step of the half-dozen leading up to the trailer's door—a glance down at the state of the rotten wood beneath his feet had him praying they would hold his weight long enough for him to get through the door.

Lump gave Tex the nod to let him know he had good cover, and Tex readied his gun.

In a flash, Tex took the rickety wooden steps two at a time and kicked out at the middle of the trailer's decaying door.

"*Get down*!" Tex yelled as he burst through the door with his gun aimed and ready to take down whoever was hiding inside the trailer.

A high-pitched scream rang out from the gloomy corner to Tex's right. He spun around in an instant, finger already on the trigger.

"Don't shoot me!"

Something stopped Tex squeezing the AK-47's trigger and spraying the far end of the old trailer with enough bullets to cut down anyone hiding there in the shadows. Maybe it was the scream so filled with terror, or the plea for him not to shoot that sounded so painfully young.

Or just simple, gut instinct.

"Show yourself—*Now*!" Tex ordered, his eye not leaving his gun's sights. "Throw down your weapon!"

A heavy clatter of metal hitting the trailer's linoleum floor, and a hunting rifle slid toward Tex.

"Please… don't kill me."

A shape emerged from the gloom with hands raised.

"What the…?" Tex muttered as the young girl stepped forward, her sweet young face etched with terror.

"Please, sir, I wasn't trying to hurt you."

"Where are the others?" Tex demanded, all the while keeping his gun pointed at her center mass

"What others?" The girl spoke quietly, the tremble in her voice all but masking her words. All the way out of the shadows, she stopped walking and stood stock-still a handful of strides away from Tex.

"I don't have time for this bullshit," Tex growled as he eyed the girl down the barrel of his gun; she looked to be a skinny five-feet at the most, with long, straggly hair and a cute, elfin face—the kid was probably no more than a couple years older than Lee. "Call off the others."

The young girl began to cry. "There is no one else," she sniffled. "I'm all alone."

Tex took a step forward, his intention to intimidate the girl to giving up her comrades, or at the very least have them lay down their arms and ensure the safety of the people they'd been taking pot-shots at.

"It's just me, *honest*," the girl insisted. "I took shots

from different places so you'd *think* there was more. I never meant to hurt anyone—I just wanted to scare you away from the store. There's food in there—I found it this morning."

Shooting from multiple locations was a classic ploy for lone snipers, but not one Tex would have attributed to a teenage girl.

"I'm Tex. Who are you?" Tex was edging toward believing the girl, but nonetheless kept his gun trained on her chest.

"Sarah," she replied, her voice a tad stronger.

"From?"

Sara shrugged. "My folks moved around a lot. Last place we lived before we took to the hills was Bear Creek."

"You got family?"

"Not anymore."

Sarah's simple reply broke Tex's heart. "And you're genuinely on your own?" He truly wanted to believe the girl—he didn't have it in him to shoot a hungry, lonely, scared kid.

Nodding, Sarah wiped her snotty nose on her sleeve. "Yeah. I have been since everything went to shit."

Tex almost told the girl to mind her language. "Your folks? Were they… hurt by one of the mobs?"

Sarah gave Tex what could have been construed as a half-smile. "My Mom and Dad *were* one of the mobs," she replied. "They taught me how to shoot and drive and take care of myself before any of it happened. Then, they went crazy and turned on our neighbors. They could have just stayed in the shelter Daddy built 'til it all went back to normal, but they reckoned it was our duty to take what we could from the weaker folks—Mom called it survival of the fittest, like that Darwin fella."

"Why did you leave them?" Tex lowered his gun a touch. "Surely you were safer with them than being out here all alone?"

Sarah shrugged her skinny shoulders again. "I had enough when they murdered our next-door neighbors in cold blood—little kids an' all. I used to go to school with the Matheson twins, and Daddy just shot 'em up on the front lawn like they were just vermin. I waited 'til it got dark, and I took Daddy's truck and left 'em to it."

Tex thought of Lee, and just how easily he could have ended up alone and at the mercy of the crazies and the bloodthirsty in the After Times; it brought him a little comfort at not having been able to save Krista.

"All clear, Lump!" Tex pointed his gun at the trailer floor and saw Sarah visibly relax. "I guess I can trust you," he said to the girl.

"What's going on, Tex?" Lump came in, gun aimed directly at Sarah. "What the hell—?"

"This is Sarah," Tex made the introduction. "She's the one who's had us shitting out pants."

"You gotta be kidding me." Lump eyed Sarah like he'd never seen a teenaged girl before. "You?"

Sarah offered Lump a smile, her eyes flicking from the muzzle of his AK-47 to Tex and back again.

"Says she's on her own," Tex said. "I think we're good."

Lump took Tex's lead and lowered his weapon. "What were you thinking, firing on four soldiers?"

"I only wanted the food that's in the storeroom," Sarah told him. "I was going to take another load to my truck." She looked down at large canvas bag on the stained foldout bed to her left.

"We didn't see any other vehicles." Lump replied, suddenly wary again.

"I hid it in the bushes around the outside of the trailer park," Sarah explained. "Figured it'd be stupid to bring it in and risk getting trapped—and I ain't stupid."

Tex couldn't help but crack a wry smile at that one—the girl was one canny customer, that was for sure.

"You come across anyone else around here?" Lump asked Sarah.

"A couple of folks the next town over. There's a small town that's not on any of the maps—they call it 'Coon's Trail. It's just a few houses and a general store—that was all burned out by the time I got to it, and only a couple of the ranch houses had anyone in them."

"They still there?"

Sarah nodded. "I stayed with Doctor Barker and his wife awhile, until Mrs. Barker passed, that is."

"A doctor?" Lump threw in. "Is he still there?"

"He was a couple weeks ago when I left. It was real sad—him and Mrs. Barker were really looking forward to that baby—it was their first one. After she died, the doctor took to his bed and wouldn't even eat much."

"That must have been hard for you," Tex said.

"It wasn't the worse thing that's happened to me."

"We really gotta be going, Tex," Lump said with a concerned look outside; he clearly wasn't one hundred percent Sarah was telling the truth about being alone—he'd always been the more mistrusting one in the squad.

"You can come with us, Sarah," Tex said, picking the girl's hunting rifle up off the floor. He emptied the chamber and handed it back—it always paid to be safe rather than sorry, and the girl was still spooked. "We have a nice place a couple hours from here. A proper community, with proper houses, stores, kids your age, and plenty of food. You'll never have to worry about being safe again."

"I'm good, thanks." Sarah took the rifle from Tex and set about picking up the handful of rounds he'd emptied onto the floor.

"You won't survive out here on your own—you'll be

far better off around other people."

"I've managed to survive this long." Sarah sounded way beyond her years. "And wasn't it people banding together that caused all these problems in the first place?"

Tex opened his mouth to reply but found he had no comeback to that: the young girl's logic was pretty darn flawless. Maybe she was the one with the right idea—live a nomadic life, trust no one, rely only on yourself; he hoped she was ballsy enough to make it.

"You can have the food."

"It's only fair—I saw it first."

Tex smiled—Sarah was invoking the age-old kids' rule of dibs. "We'll help you carry it to your truck. Unless you'd rather bring it round?"

Sarah shook her head; the wariness was evidently mutual. "I'd appreciate your help getting to my truck. Thank you, Tex."

Tex and Lump escorted Sarah to the park's general store; both men kept a cautious eye out for any movement that would indicate Sarah had been lying to them, and a cynical part of Tex half expected to hear a gunshot at any second.

But Sarah had been entirely honest: she was all alone and only interested in the meagre pickings to be had from the storeroom. TJ and Rhino were nonplussed, too, upon meeting the sniper who'd had them pinned down.

They loaded up the canned goods and propane tanks into the back of Tex's Jeep and drove out of the park to where Sarah had secreted her black F250 truck. She'd made a good job of it, too—Tex and his crew had driven past the thing on the way in and hadn't noticed a thing.

"That's one hell of a big chunk of metal for a little lady." Rhino grinned as he watched Sarah clambering into the cabin; the huge truck swallowed her; she looked positively tiny in the driver's seat. Tex noticed she had blocks of wood strapped to the gas and brake pedals—the girl sure as hell wasn't one to be beaten.

"Are you sure you won't reconsider coming with us?" Tex asked the girl as TJ and Lump loaded the last of the supplies into the back of the truck.

"I'm good, thanks," Sarah replied and pulled the door closed as the window hummed down.

"If you ever find yourself in need of a place," Tex persisted. "There'll always be a place for you at the Little Alamo—drive two and a half hours due east of Fort Worth and head into pine tree country. You'll find us."

Sarah gunned the F250's engine and the hulking vehicle roared to life. "Thank you," she replied with a frown. "I'll be okay—you guys take care of yourselves, though."

Tex watched Sarah drive away, her truck kicking up a cloud of dust in its wake, and offered up a silent prayer to whomever may be watching over her to keep her safe. Her words bounced around in his mind: it was people getting together that caused the whole unholy mess the world had gotten into—all he could hope for was that mankind had learned its lesson.

"We need to head back," Rhino broke the pregnant silence between the four men. "We don't want to be driving around in the dark."

"I'm gonna stay out," Lump said. "Take a look around, see if the doctor she was talking about is still where she left him."

"No," Tex told him. "It's far too risky—we can always head back in a few days."

"It's a good idea," TJ chipped in. "We're not too far from 'Coon's Trail—an hour, maybe less—and it's a hell of a trek to go back to the compound only to come back."

"I'll take TJ with me," Lump gave Tex a reassuring smile. "We'll be just fine, Tex."

Tex knew when he was beat; Lump had made up his mind and nothing he was going to say from that point was going to make a damn bit of difference. Besides which, Lump's idea was a sound one, no matter how risky it would be to stay outside so far from the safety of the Little Alamo overnight. They did need a doctor to replace Doc. Oliver—even if the compound's resident veterinarian was doing a good job of filling the niche left by Oliver's tragic demise. If Sarah's Doctor Barker was still holed up in 'Coon's Trail and of reasonably sound mind, the Little Alamo could certainly use him.

"Take my Jeep," Tex said to Lump. "There's plenty of spare gas and ammo in the back, and I threw in some extra food rations."

"You thought we'd be staying out here?" Lump said with a knowing wink.

"You know me, Lump," Tex laughed. "Always prepared for any eventuality."

"Yeah, I forget you were an Eagle Scout. TJ and me will be just fine—there's nothing out here anywhere close to what we faced in Iraq." He looked around the quiet, tranquil countryside. "And we came out of that in one piece."

Tex stopped himself short of saying *except Rusty*. "Just make sure you bring us back a doctor," he said and clapped his old buddy hard on the shoulder.

"You ready, boss?" Rhino asked.

"Yeah, let's hit the road." Tex turned toward the Jeep. "See you tomorrow, Lump."

"Sure thing, Tex. Have a coupla cold ones for me tonight," Lump called after him.

Chapter Nine

April 2029, Little Alamo, Texas

The light was fading fast when Tex and Rhino rolled up to the Little Alamo gates. The air had turned cooler, the sky was clear with a silver, crescent moon and dotted with bright, twinkling stars.

As they waited for the gates to swing open—someone had taken the hint and applied a goodly amount of oil while Tex had been out, and they eased apart in absolute silence—Tex thought about Lump and TJ. Part of him worried they wouldn't be okay out in whatever the outside world had become, and part of him wished he'd gone with Lump instead of TJ. It would have been just like the old days—him and Lump on some wild adventure into the unknown—but common sense dictated one of them had to return to the Little Alamo.

The ride home had been an uneventful one, for which Tex was grateful. They'd heard the occasional gunshot in the distance, carried across the flat fields on the hot, gentle breeze, and had seen a few columns of smoke rising up against the horizon. Tex figured it would likely be hunters out to take advantage of the abandoned cattle and abundant deer and wild pigs that populated the area.

"Buy you a beer?" Rhino asked as Tex maneuvered the Jeep through the gates and across the compound to the garage.

"Sure," Tex replied—a couple of cold ones sounded like a mighty fine idea at that moment in time; just what he needed to unwind after the stress of the day. "I'll check in with Lee first and meet you at John Wayne's—around eight good for you?"

"Perfect."

***

The bar was busy—it was a Saturday night, after all, and a fair amount of the bar with Rhino, chewing the fat and nursing his second beer of the evening; it felt good to have some down time, and the buzz from the cool, home-brewed beer helping Tex relax rather nicely.

It was Tex who had insisted they build the bar back in the early planning stages of the compound, much to the chagrin of the more God-fearing amongst the founders—their argument was that a church would be a far better focus for the new community than a den of iniquity such as a bar serving alcohol.

Fortunately for Tex, his idea was greeted with much enthusiasm, which was why the Little Alamo was graced with both the magnificent, white-boarded church *and* the John Wayne bar with its fine selection of home-brewed beers.

"Hello, Tex." Victoria sat herself next to him at the bar.

"Oh, hi, Vic." Tex looked over her shoulder to see Rhino had upped and left him and was making his way toward Joe Johnson and Cory Mulgrew; had he deliberately vacated his seat upon seeing Victoria approaching in order to leave Tex alone with her?

"Buy you another?" Victoria glanced down at Tex's glass—he was down to the muddy dregs.

"It should be me buying you a drink," Tex replied with a warm smile.

"Times have changed, Tex Pemberton," Victoria returned the smile with a cheeky glint in her eye. "Or didn't you notice?"

Tex took an exaggerated look around the bar, which resembled an old Wild Werst saloon more than he'd planned it to; all that was missing was an old man plinking away on an old, beat-up piano, spittoons, and a bunch of good time hoochie girls.

"Well, so they have!" He laughed. "I guess time has just rolled by this old soldier."

"You're not that old, Tex," Victoria said as she flagged down one of the barmaids with a friendly wave. "And certainly not too ancient to venture out beyond the walls."

"Ahh, that was nothing much." Tex felt his cheeks burning; the last thing on his mind when he'd agreed to the excursion was to play any kind of hero. It had been a necessary, exploratory mission for the good of the community and nothing more. Even so, it felt good to be on the receiving end of a little admiration.

Victoria ordered two beers and settled herself down on the stool next to Tex. The bar was crowded, the seating close together, and Tex felt the warmth of Victoria's knee as it brushed against his.

"So…" Victoria said with an expectant squint of her eyes.

"So, what?"

"What was it like—out there?"

Tex shrugged and took a gulp of ice-cold beer. "Much the same as it was when we last drove through it, Vic. It's only been six months."

Victoria looked quite disappointed. "I imagined it would be like some terrible wasteland by now."

"It's actually the opposite," Tex said, making a note *not* to tell her about the scattered bones and coyote-ravaged corpses he and his comrades had happened upon in the streets of the small town or the burned-out buildings. "The fields are high with grass, the spring trees more beautiful than ever, and the air is so clean it tastes sweet. If I'd had to pick a way for human civilization to fail, it would have been like it did—so much better than some stupid, retaliatory nuclear war ruining everything."

"I guess Mother Nature does know best after all?"

Tex nodded. "It's weird not hearing traffic or seeing airplanes in the sky, but it's all very… *peaceful* out there."

"Sounds wonderful," Victoria sighed and sipped at her drink. "Perhaps you could take me out to see for myself sometime?"

"Once we can be sure it's safe, I'd be happy to."

"You mean the nomads?" Victoria frowned. "Did you see any? Were you worried you'd be followed back here?"

"We were extra-vigilant and, no, we didn't see any," Tex reassured her.

"I've heard such awful things about them… from other compounds on the radio. They don't care who they kill to take what they want, and then there's all the rumors of cannibalism…"

"I wouldn't believe all you hear on the air waves," Tex said with a weary sigh. Six months without TV or social media and wild rumors *still* found a way of spreading like some malignant disease. It was human nature, he guessed, and had likely been going on since early man first daubed rudimentary pictures on cave walls. "There's no evidence of nomads eating people, Victoria," Tex told her, although he did wonder about those scattered bones. It was always possible something other than coyotes and buzzards had eaten their fill of the fallen.

"They won't bother us," Tex added. "They'd have no reason to think there's anything this far out in the pine forests worth the fuel and effort to take the trip out. It's one of the main reasons we built the compound where we did."

"I hope you're right, Tex." Victoria touched his arm with her fingertips, then pulled them quickly away. Tex couldn't be entirely sure, but it felt like more than an accident.

"Even if I'm not, we're all perfectly safe here. We built a strong fort and have good people—nobody's gonna eat any of us." He said with a broad grin.

"Tex Pemberton!" Victoria chastised, laughing. "You're making fun of me!"

"Guilty as charged." Tex chuckled along with Victoria; he couldn't recall when he'd last enjoyed a woman's company so much—most likely it had been with Krista in the Before Times. And it was the first time since that fateful day he'd not felt guilty talking to another woman, enjoying her company, and that felt good.

"Say, might you fancy taking in a little night air?" Victoria took Tex by surprise. "It's getting a bit too noisy in here, and I get the feeling it's only going to get louder."

She was right, of course, as the beer and liquor flowed, the Little Alamo's residents were becoming increasingly more raucous as folks raised their voices to make themselves heard against the chatter and laughter. It was a wonderful, heady atmosphere; one Tex had envisaged from the very inception of the Little Alamo. Good people, good spirits, all safe and sound in the micro world they'd created to shelter from the crumbling world outside.

"You know, that sounds great." Tex leaned in a little closer so Victoria could better hear him; she smelled of vanilla soap and woman, she smelled good.

The streets outside the bar were all but deserted. A handful of couples strolled along, aimlessly wandering between the wooden buildings with no destination in mind. For young lovers, it was the walk—being together—that was important, not having someplace to be.

Victoria slipped her harm through the crook of Tex's elbow as they walked, the soft curve of her breast pressed into his side. Tex fought every instinct he had to pull away as the old, familiar guilt crept back into his mind and thoughts of Krista came flooding in.

"Is this okay?" Victoria asked, perhaps sensing Tex's reticence or picking up on his body tensing despite his best efforts to relax.

"Yeah, it's fine." Tex struggled to get the words out; just by being close to Victoria, albeit innocently, made him feel like he was being unfaithful to his wife. And it was an emotion he didn't relish feeling again.

They walked along in silence for what felt like an age to Tex, although they only reached the end of the main street before Victoria broke the silence between them. "Rebecca Smithson has been asking after you again," she said with a hint of mischief in her tone.

Tex sighed a heavy sigh; Rebecca had been making more and more of an effort to insinuate herself into his company over the last month or so, and without as much as a grain of encouragement on his part. "Yeah, I've heard," he said.

"Too soon?" Victoria said, gently steering Tex by the arm in the direction of the moonlit duck pond.

"Too Rebecca," Tex laughed. "That woman is relentless."

"She is when she sets her sights on something… or *someone*."

"Tenacity is not a bad trait to have, especially in a

farmer—she's fantastic with the cows and sheep, and she's got the spring crops looking fit and well—but why does she have to point it at me?"

"Who knows the intricacies of love?" Victoria teased. "The heart wants what the heart wants, Tex—surely you know that by now?"

"I've done nothing to encourage Rebecca," Tex protested; they neared the bench upon which, not too long ago, he'd consoled his son after the loss of the mother who had been his entire world.

"You've done nothing to *discourage* her, either, Tex." Victoria unhooked her arm from Tex's and settled herself down on the wooden bench. "She's a fine-looking gal—she's slim, fit, and healthy… she's almost as pretty as me." Victoria let out a light, dancing chuckle.

"If you're gonna tell me she's got good child-bearing hips like one of her prize cows, Victoria, I'm going to leave you right here and go home." Laughing, Tex sat down beside Victoria; his arm felt cold, lonely, without hers nestled against it. "And, besides which, you're not so pretty," he said with a cheeky wink. "There's just *something* about you, though."

"I wouldn't be so crass as to compare Rebecca with the cows." Victoria feigned offense. But her grin let Tex know without uncertainty that phrase, indeed, was going to be the next thing out of her mouth.

"And since when did you become the Little Alamo's resident matchmaker?" Tex smirked and inched a little closer to Victoria; they both gazed out across the dark, glass-smooth water of the pond. It seemed eerily quiet without the cacophony of the ducks and swans and their respective progeny, almost too quiet—like everything was dead. "I didn't think you'd have the time to be meddling in other folks' private business—you never even have the time to stop by and say hello to me and the boy these days."

"It's not that I'm too busy, Tex," Victoria rested a hand on his knee, a friendly gesture. "I figured you and Lee both needed the space and some time to find your place together. He last thing you need is me… *meddling*."

While Tex appreciated Victoria's thoughtful gesture, there had been plenty of times during the past six months he could really have used a familiar shoulder to cry on.

"I think me and the boy have found our common ground now," Tex told her. "He still has the nightmares, and I know he can talk to you when he needs to, so I reckon he's gonna be alright."

"He's a good kid, Tex." Victoria squeezed his knee a little. "You've raised him well."

"It was Krista who raised him, Vic, you know that. I was too busy off fighting a war to have much input into how he's turning out."

"I know how that one goes." There was sadness in Victoria's voice. "There's not a day goes by still I don't think of Rusty and what could have been."

"Victoria… I'm sorry—"

She silenced him with a finger to the lips; the soft touch of Victoria's skin against his had Tex yearning for more.

"Life moves on, Tex," Victoria said after a moment or two. She took her finger away as she spoke and rested her hand back on Tex's knee. "It *has* to—there is only one other way to avoid it, and that's never going to be an option."

Tex nodded. She was right, naturally, and thoughts of putting a gun in his mouth had crossed Tex's mind on more than one occasion after Krista. He'd actually done so on one of his darkest nights; it was only thoughts of leaving Lee all alone in the world and his duty to the Little Alamo and its good citizens that had prevented him from pulling the trigger.

"You sound like one of those soppy love story books Krista used to love reading," Tex snorted. "Those ones where the square-jawed hero is saved by some mousey little gal who turns out to be tougher than he first thought."

Victoria giggled at that. "You should spend some time in the library the next time I'm volunteering, Tex," she said. "It's full of romance books just like that."

"That's what you get when you let the womenfolk choose what books to stock it with." Tex feigned annoyance—the founders had left it to TJ's wife and her friends to decide what books to put on the shelves and, as a result, over half were mushy romances with buxom ladies and impossibly handsome, broad-chested men on the covers.

"Maybe it's not for you, then," Victoria said with a fond smile. "I see you as more of a horror and action thriller kinda guy."

"That's some assumptive profiling there, lady." Tex placed his hand on top of Victoria's and gently squeezed her fingers. "I think you might just be surprised at what reading material takes my fancy." Doing his best to appear enigmatic, Tex doubted very much he'd fooled Victoria. She'd hit the nail pretty much square on the head with her assumption—he wouldn't be caught dead with his nose in such slushy, romantic bull crap and its unrealistic take on love. In Tex's experience, love led to heartache and pain and unbearable loss.

And he was dammed if he was going to go through that all over again—not with Rebecca Smithson and her womanly hips, not even with…

"Victoria…" Tex entwined his fingers with hers

"Tex?" Victoria leaned toward him on the bench, her thigh pressed against his, her chin tilted ever so slightly upward.

Then, they kissed.

Tex couldn't help but close his eyes at the soft, sweet touch of Victoria's lips. There was no urgency, no busy, probing tongues with overtly sexual undertones, just a wonderful connecting of two people on that dark, moonlit night.

"I'm sorry…" Victoria broke the magical spell between them, her lips all too quickly gone from Tex's, and he missed them terribly.

She stood up.

"I think I've had a little too much beer," she offered. "I'm so sorry, Tex."

And, before Tex could tell Victoria she had nothing at all to apologize for, she'd set off running across the green toward her house.

Tex watched her go with a dull ache in his chest; for the first time in a long time, he'd felt the flame of desire, the yearning to be with someone other than himself and his son, and the moment had ended before it began.

Perhaps, Tex consoled himself, he would speak to Victoria in the morning; in the cold light of day and with a clear head, he would be able to tell her how he felt and that maybe they could build something.

But circumstances were joining to conspire against Tex, and he wouldn't get that opportunity

Chapter Ten

April 2029, Little Alamo, Texas

Tex's bedside telephone awakened him from a stifling, panic-riddled dream in which Krista died all over again in front of his eyes; the all-too familiar claustrophobic sensation of helplessness and anguish had him jolting awake among twisted, sweat-dampened bedsheets with a cry in his throat.

Quickly composing himself, Tex grabbed the phone; it was barely dawn on Sunday morning, so he knew the call was not a social one.

"We need you at the gate!" An urgent, raised voice barked in Tex's ear. "It's Lump!"

The sound of his friend's name had Tex fully alert and jumping out of his bed. Quickly, quietly so as not to disturb Lee, Tex dressed and let himself out of the house.

The gates were still closed when Tex arrived; Rhino stood by the gatehouse having a heated conversation with the two guards.

"You can't just open up," his raised voice resounded about the empty street behind him. "Not without following protocol."

"What the fuck is going on, Rhino?"

"Lump and TJ are outside." One of the guards, a middle-aged guy Tex only knew as Burgess, explained. His face was red, his blood pressure likely up, and Tex saw the frustration burning in the guy's eyes. "Lump says they were followed—we have to let them in!"

The thought of Lump and TJ having been followed back to the Little Alamo chilled Tex to his core; it was always inevitable the compound would be discovered one day, but that didn't make the news any easier to swallow.

"They have someone with them," Rhino butted in. "You know we have a set protocol in place for that, Tex."

"We do," Tex agreed. "Who is it?"

"They say he's Doctor Barker from 'Coon's Trail—he doesn't look much like a doctor to me, though."

Tex strode across to the gate and peered through the small metal grate at his friend, TJ, and the guy they'd brought back like some poor, stray animal.

Rhino was correct: the man standing between Lump and TJ more resembled some scruffy hobo than a man of medicine. His clothes were filthy and disheveled, his hair matted, lank, and rested on his scrawny shoulders, and his salt-and-pepper beard straggled all the way down his chest and contained myriad tiny pieces of food.

"You have to let us through, Tex," Lump said through the grate. "There's a pack of nomads on our tail—we can't stay out here."

"We have to follow protocol, Lump, you know that." Tex told him. "We'll have you inside in ten minutes at the most." The protocol for such an occasion had been written up by Tex and Lump and ratified by the rest of the founders. It stated no stranger would be allowed into the Little Alamo without full verification—even if they were accompanied by someone from the fort. With the benefit of hindsight, Tex figured it was not entirely reasonable for anyone in the After Times to have documents and certificates with them, but asking for any ID, papers, and certificates for the guards to look over, bought time for the Little Alamo's scouts to be sent out to ensure the newcomers didn't have murderous associates hidden close by. Of course, all that would take time, which was entirely by design: it gave the soldiers the opportunity to flush out anyone lurking in the forest, or for any wrongdoers to give themselves away.

Lump took a worried glance behind himself. "That'll be too late, Tex. They'll be here long before that."

Tex stepped away from the doors, his mind racing. He and Lump had put the protocols together for the safety of everyone in the Little Alamo and breaking the one pertaining to allowing strangers inside was not one Tex wanted to do. What if the doctor was not a doctor and had designs on wreaking havoc inside the compound? What if he was in cahoots with the nomads and had somehow coerced Lump and TJ into revealing the fort's location? For all Tex knew, the nomads Lump said were on their tail could be hiding among the trees with guns trained on Lump and TJ, just waiting for the gates to swing open.

On the other hand, to leave the three of them on the wrong side of the gates would be tantamount to signing their death warrants; even if the rumors about the nomads Victoria had mentioned were untrue, Tex knew they weren't known for being merciful to anyone who crossed their path.

"You sure he's the doctor the girl told us about, Lump?" Tex asked through the grate.

"Found him in the same house she said she'd left him in—even had a coupla graves dug out in the backyard." Lump's reply was what Tex had been hoping for.

"And you're not under any duress?"

"We will be if you don't let us in!" There was panic in Lump's voice.

Tex eyed the dirt road behind his friend and saw fine red dust rising up between the trees just beyond the bend.

"Open the gates," Tex said.

"Tex!" Rhino squared up to him. "You can't…"

"I trust Lump." Tex refused to back down. "If that guy presented any sort of danger, he'd have been eliminated by now."

From experience, Tex knew Lump would sacrifice his own life before allowing the Little Alamo to come under any serious threat. Thinking with a clear head, Tex was confident Lump and TJ were making the best call—by the looks of the dust cloud, there were a considerable number of nomads on their way to the compound

"I said, open the damn gates!" Tex barked at Burgess. "Now!"

"I hope you know what you're doing, Tex," Rhino said and, as the gates swung silently open, he pointed his ever-present AK-47 toward them.

"I do, Rhino," Tex reassured. "If we leave 'em out there, they'll die for sure. And, besides which, we need a doctor."

Through the expanding gap between the twin gates, Tex aimed his old revolver through the space and watched with heightened caution as TJ, Lump, and the hobo doctor clambered back into the Jeep. The car grumbled to life, and Lump steered it slowly into the compound. While Burgess closed the gates behind the Jeep, the other guard, Tex, and Rhino trained their weapons on it; one suspicious move and they were fully prepared to let loose.

The Jeep jolted to a stop and Lump, TJ, and the doctor climbed out.

"Thanks for that, Tex," Lump said with a wary glance at Rhino's gun, which was aimed squarely at his heart. "I know we should have stuck to protocol, but—"

"How many nomads?" Tex didn't have the time or

patience for small talk. If the compound was about to come under attack, he had to act—and think—fast.

"Ten, maybe twelve," Lump replied. "They picked us up when we left 'Coon's Trail—we didn't have the firepower to take them on, and if we had, we'd have only attracted more. I thought we could outrun them… I'm sorry, Tex."

"It's probable they were staking out the doc's place," Tex said. "They'd know someone would come for him."

"You think the girl set us up?" TJ asked.

"Sarah wouldn't do that," the doctor broke his silence. "She's a good girl—she helped me when Maggie had the baby…"

Tex's heart wrenched at the devastated look that took over Doctor Barker's grimy face. "Take the doc to get cleaned up," he ordered Burgess. "Get him something to eat and a bed. No offense, doc, but you look beat."

Doc Barker gave a weary nod and shuffled off after Burgess, his eyes not once leaving the muzzle of Rhino's gun, which followed him as he walked by.

The sound of vehicles filled the morning air—the sun was finally making an appearance over the treetops to cast its red glow over the compound.

Tex took another look through the door's grate and saw a small fleet of trucks and four-by-fours. Through the dust they stirred up, he counted eight in total, and most of them carried at least two passengers, although it was impossible to be certain because they had blacked out rear windows.

Lump had underestimated the convoy he'd led straight back to the Little Alamo; they approached the gates and spread out around the periphery—they'd be looking for a weak point to gain entry.

"Round up the guys," Tex told TJ and Rhino. He knew once the nomads realized there was no weak point, they'd set about making one—it was what he'd do, after all. "This is gonna get ugly."

Rhino dashed into the guards' room and grabbed the phone. One call to the comms room and every man designated as a Little Alamo soldier would be buzzed by the red alert signal; the walls would be manned in under ten minutes if the drills they'd performed had been accurate.

"Make sure the rear entrance is secured," Tex said. "All the animals will still be inside—make sure Rebecca and the others know to keep it that way. We'll need at least six men on the back wall to guard the fields and solar farm." Tex cursed under his breath at having run out of time to erect a better defense around the panels.

A thick plume of gray-black smoke drifted up from the compound's west wall; it was accompanied by the sound of gunshots—shotgun blasts, to be accurate.

"Shit," TJ snapped. "They're trying to burn their way through." The walls, as thick as they were and reinforced in key places with cinder block, were still made of wood, and they'd burn.

Tex followed TJ across the compound toward the smoke; the acrid reek of kerosene stung at his nostrils as he ran. Another column of smoke rose up from the opposite side of the fort, and shotgun blasts echoed out from the front gates.

The first of the soldiers arrived, running full pelt down the main street. They knew their positions—Tex and Lump's drills had been incredibly thorough—and they climbed the ladders to take their places on the narrow walkway that ran around the top of the entire outer wall. Some carried buckets of sand and water to pour over the fires the nomads were setting below. Tex had insisted they design the walls along the lines of the Roman and Medieval forts he'd researched—sentry boxes at each corner, the walkway to provide the advantage when repelling marauders on the ground below, and narrow gaps in strategic places to give cover to the compound's soldiers.

There came the sound of voices from outside the walls; Tex couldn't make out what they were saying, but they were far from the angry, disjointed shouts and screams of the mobs he'd encountered all those months ago—these nomads were cold, calculating, and had most likely laid siege to compounds like the Little Alamo before.

They knew what they were doing, and Tex had no doubt whatsoever they weren't going to give up until they got what they wanted. Sure, they were outnumbered and outgunned, but they could cause untold damage and casualties if—when—they burned holes in the outer walls.

"We gotta stop them now," Tex said to TJ. "Before any of this goes too far." He glanced over at one of the rising columns of smoke and flinched a little as gunshots filled the morning air. Revolver in hand, Tex climbed the nearest ladder to take a look-see for himself. TJ followed close behind.

"Looks like they're staying close to the walls," TJ said, peering through one of the thin slots in the wooden wall. "It's gonna be hard to take them down."

Tex took a look for himself and was shocked to see a handful of young men setting about lighting a kerosene fire almost directly below where he was standing; they looked to be barely out of short pants. Twenty strides or so from the young men, a trio of young women aimed shotguns upwards, waiting for their chance to pick off any of the compound's soldiers who dared pop their head over the top of the wall.

"We need to take the fight to them," Tex told him. It wasn't an ideal solution as it would put his men in danger, but Tex knew it really was the only thing they could do.

Lump and Rhino were waiting for Tex at the bottom

of the ladder. "They're setting fires everywhere," Lump said before Tex even got to the bottom step. "We have to stop them, Tex."

"I'll take a squad out through the back gate—take them by surprise," Tex told him. "I reckon ten plus me ought to do it."

Lump shook his head. "Can't let you do that, Tex."

"Seriously?"

"Seriously, Tex," Lump said. "We can't risk losing you out there."

Tex gave his old friend a hard stare and tipped his hat up a tad; they were both equally important to the Little Alamo, both were founders and shared responsibility for the compound and its inhabitants. Was it possible Lump thought Tex couldn't handle himself in a combat situation any more?

A volley of gunshots—rifle and shotgun—split the air; everyone ran for cover, heads down.

A soldier fell screaming from the wall, an arcing gush of blood spouting from his neck. He hit the ground with a dull thud and lay silent in the dirt as a bunch of people rushed to his aid; the sound of shots and stink of smoke had dragged the Little Alamo's citizens from their Sunday morning slumber.

More shots rang out, and another fire sprouted up at the eastern corner of the compound.

"I'll head up the squad," TJ offered.

"No," Tex protested. "You have a wife, kids, and one on the way. I can't let you risk that."

"I'm going, Tex." TJ was most firm on the matter. "It has to be done, and done properly. You know we can't allow a single one of those nomads to leave here alive. If we do, there'll be more of them in a few days, maybe even more than we can fight off—you've heard the reports as well as I have."

Tex had listened in on the radio to compound leaders under siege, their walls breached and nomads running riot within. The sound of screaming and shots as innocent citizens were massacred would haunt him for the rest of his days. The nomads were gaining a reputation for being coldhearted, ruthless killers who thought nothing of slaughtering men, women, and children in order to loot a compound's supplies. There'd been reports of widespread rape and kidnapping of younger women and girls and, of course, the so-far unfounded rumors of cannibalism.

"Okay," Tex said to TJ. "Take Rhino and the best guys you can think of."

TJ tapped at his temple with a steady forefinger. "I already have my dream team up here," he said with a confident smile.

"Take the walkie-talkies and keep in contact," Tex ordered. "And make sure there's no survivors."

"Roger that," TJ replied with a salute. "Consider the job done."

Chapter Eleven

April 2029, Little Alamo, Texas

TJ's team made their way through the rear gates of the compound. They'd eased them open just wide enough for him and his squad of nine to slip through—a pair of guards stood by to close them the moment the final soldier was on the outside. Behind TJ, the panicked lowing of the cattle masked the sound of the gate's hinges and his squad's footsteps; the nomads wouldn't know what hit them.

Memories of sneaking around the small towns and farms in Iraq popped up in TJ's mind—he'd done such maneuvers countless times before and taken on far more deadly adversaries than a bunch of kids with kerosene and old 12-gauges. Naturally, he knew all too well it would be a mistake to underestimate the nomads, no matter how young they appeared to be. They were hungry and desperate and determined to get their hands on everything he and the Little Alamo's good people had worked so hard to preserve.

And TJ was damned if he was about to let that happen.

A wave of his hand split TJ's squad into two and each headed in opposite directions with Rhino leading up the other group; the plan was to perform the traditional pincer movement that had proven so effective in Tikrit: each half of the squad would take out the enemy as they came across them and meet in the middle. Knowing the nomads were staying close to the fort's walls to avoid getting shot, the idea was any of them fleeing one squad would run straight into the path of the other.

No survivors.

Rounding a corner of the compound's wall, TJ espied a pair of nomads. Busy preparing yet another fire, they didn't notice the five soldiers slipping into the tall bushes a few feet away from the compound's walls.

Using the brush for cover, TJ led his men closer to the nomads, all the while keeping a watchful eye open for others. He knew his squad well and was comfortable they all had one another's backs, but it always paid to be hypervigilant.

Less than ten yards away, the two nomads still hadn't realized they were being surrounded. They worked diligently, piling dry sticks and old, brown leaves up against the wall and drenching them with kerosene. TJ couldn't help but wonder what would go through their minds once they realized it was the last thing they were ever going to do; it was a thought that always flashed through his brain before he pulled the trigger on someone, a fleeting fragment of conscience—he just couldn't help it.

TJ shoved the thought to the back of his mind and focused on the nomads.

A brief pause to ready his trusty AK-47 and ensure his four comrades were also fully prepared, followed by a subtle nod.

TJ burst from the undergrowth with his squad hot on his heels. Holding his fire until the last possible moment, TJ was all but upon the two nomads before they realized what was happening.

One of the nomads, a young guy with a stubbled, shaven head, made a grab for the hunting rifle he had propped up against a tree stump.

TJ cut the guy down with a short burst of fire; the AK's bullets all but sliced his body in half and he was pretty much dead before he hit the ground. His companion froze, his face slack with terror, eyes wide and staring. One of TJ's squad took the nomad out with just a couple shots to the head; he slumped sideways and died without any fuss.

Voices, shouts of surprise, and gunfire echoed out from the other side of the compound. Rhino and his half of the squad were clearly engaging the nomads they'd found there. TJ figured it was only a matter of moments before he and his squad were under attack by others alerted by the sudden noise of gunfire from the ground.

He also knew from lessons learned that hard way, this was the point at which he'd find out for certain if his enemy had been smart enough to secrete soldiers of their own behind the myriad of trees surrounding the Little Alamo. With one cautious eye on his periphery, TJ made his way slowly forward, pausing only to kick away the kerosene-soaked sticks away from the compound's wall—one less fire to worry about.

Three nomads appeared from the trees to TJ's right. They ran, guns blazing at the soldiers, and sent TJ and his men diving for cover. One of the squad took a hit to the shoulder; the slug knocked him clean off his feet and slammed him against the compound wall.

TJ and his three remaining soldiers returned fire from behind their respective tree stumps and eliminated two of the nomads. The third, a young woman, darted behind the fat trunk of a pine tree and vanished from sight.

TJ crawled on his belly to check out the wounded soldier; he was conscious and very much alive—the bullet was a through-and-through and had punched a hole through the meaty part of his shoulder—but judging by the amount of blood he was losing, the slug had nicked the artery there. The soldier was clearly in agony and trying hard not to show it; he needed patching up before he bled out.

"Get him back inside," TJ ordered another of his squad. "We'll go deal with that." He pointed toward the tree; the nomad girl was still behind it.

"Yessir," the soldier replied, and he helped his fallen comrade to his feet and hurried him back toward the rear gates. TJ fired a couple rounds into the tree to ensure the nomad gal stayed pinned down and didn't decide to take potshots at his retreating men.

More shots rang out from the other side of the compound. It was mainly submachine gunfire, which let TJ know Rhino was rounding off the fight over there

With the wounded safely out of the way, TJ began to advance on the nomad girl. Again, his head swam with thoughts of what he was about to do, and it even crossed his mind that maybe they could have the young woman surrender and welcome her into the bosom of the Little Alamo community.

No.

That was just the type of thinking that got good men like him killed.

The nomads couldn't be trusted, and he had clear orders from Tex.

Absolutely no survivors.

Crouching low, TJ approached the tree. There'd been no movement, no sound of footsteps rustling among the dry pine needles that covered the forest floor—the target was still very much in place.

He motioned for his two soldiers to take the left and right flanks while he continued on in a straight line toward the broad, rough trunk of the pine tree. The tree itself was an ancient one, its gnarled branches and thick canopy stretching out way above the forest floor, blocking out much of the sun's light—the shadows it created provided perfect cover.

Heart thumping hard in his chest, TJ stayed low and took in a couple deep breaths. In the background, the *crack, crack, crack* of single pistol shots signaled the grim end to Rhino's part of the fight: he and his men were finishing off the nomads they'd overpowered.

TJ ran full speed the last ten, fifteen yards toward the tree. Either side, the two soldiers followed suit and closed in. At the last second, TJ rounded the tree and found himself face to face with the nomad who'd survived as her two companions had been mown down in a hail of gunfire. It took TJ a split second to assess the fact she was young—no more than twenty if she was a day—and had a gaping bullet wound to her left thigh; she was noticeably pregnant.

It took another split second for TJ's finger to hesitate on his gun's trigger and for the nomad girl to swing her rifle in his direction.

Shots resonated between the old pine trees, their sound dulled by the thick undergrowth and ancient wood. The girl's body spouted thick fountains of blood as the soldiers' bullets ripped through it, and fat clods of flesh and splintered bone flew in all directions.

TJ hit the forest floor before the girl died, a single, almost perfect hole just below his right cheekbone. At such close proximity, the bullet from the nomad's rifle had blasted out the back of his skull and scattered his brain over the desiccated pine needles behind him.

Chapter Twelve

April 2029, Little Alamo, Texas

It was a grim first day in the Little Alamo infirmary for Doc Barker. He'd barely had the chance to get cleaned up before he'd been called to attend to the soldier who'd taken a nomad bullet to the chest and fallen from the compound's wall, another who'd been shot with a goodly amount of buckshot—most of which was embedded in his face—and TJ.

"I'm sorry, Tex," the doctor addressed Tex, Lump, and Rhino. "He told me how close you guys were."

"Shit it." Tex fought back the tears; he was pleased Victoria was there—she'd volunteered to help with the wounded. "What the fuck happened out there?"

"The nomad was waiting for him," one of the soldiers replied; he was drenched head to toe in TJ's blood.

Tex stared down at his buddy's corpse on the gurney. He'd closed TJ's eyes, and were it not for the small, round, red hole in his cheek, he'd look like he was sleeping peacefully. The doctor had propped TJ's head up on a small pillow to hide the fact the back of it was missing; all ready for the new widow to say her final goodbyes.

"Has somebody told Chrissy yet?" Tex asked.

“I was just about to,” Victoria said. “She’s waiting outside.”

“I’ll do it,” Tex growled. TJ was his Army buddy, and he’d been the one who’d given the order to take on the nomads outside the safety of the compound’s walls. The thought reminded him he’d have to organize a posse to go clear away the bodies scattered around the Little Alamo—give the marauding nomads a halfway decent burial in the forest and avoid attracting wild animals looking for an easy meal.

“You sure, Tex?” Lump said. “I know Chrissy, I could go speak to her.”

Tex shook his head. “It’s my duty,” he said, and he was right. Tex took the responsibilities of leadership seriously, as did all the founders. “It’s the least I can do.”

“Let me come with you.” Victoria placed her hand on Tex’s arm, and he flinched a little.

Tex didn’t have it in his heavy heart to argue, so he left the infirmary with Victoria by his side. Besides, it felt good to have her with him for moral support if nothing else—the touch of her hand on his arm had been incredibly comforting.

Chrissy was all alone in the waiting room; she’d been in there from the moment she’d been told her husband had been wounded—no one had told her he’d been killed outright, so she still had a grain of hope to cling onto.

That hope evaporated the moment she looked up and saw Tex walking slowly toward her.

“Oh no,” Chrissy groaned, and her pretty face crumpled as tears rolled down her cheeks. “No, no, no…”

Victoria rushed over and took Chrissy in her arms.

“I’m so very sorry, Chrissy,” Tex offered, although he knew his words were hollow, cold comfort for his comrade’s grieving widow. But, what else could he say? What else could he do?

"You sent him out there to die!" Chrissy rounded on Tex, her face an ugly mask of contempt. "You sent my husband out there and they fucking killed him!" Shrugging off Victoria's arms, she struggled to her feet and squared up to Tex,

"You bastard!" She pounded his broad chest with her fists. "This is all your fault! Why didn't *you* go out there and fucking die?!"

Tex stood there and took it—what the hell was he supposed to do? Let Chrissy vent her pain; if it helped her to blame him for the decision he'd made, then so be it.

"Chrissy…" Victoria held the woman's shoulders and gently pulled her away from Tex.

"Get off me!" Chrissy snarled and batted Victoria's hands away. "You don't know—!" Chrissy's legs crumpled beneath her, and she hit the waiting room floor with a loud smack. Moaning in pain, she curled into a fetal ball and clutched at her belly.

"Oh shit, the baby!" Victoria cried out and dropped to her knees next to the stricken Chrissy. She gave a worried look at the spreading blood stain on the seat of Chrissy's jeans. "Get the doctor in here!" she barked at Tex.

Jolted into action, Tex turned back toward the infirmary. As he did so, his eyes met Victoria's and he knew at that precise moment she was thinking the exact same thing as he was.

Rusty.

And, in that moment that passed between them, Tex saw the look in Victoria's eyes, and it was one of insurmountable pain and anguish he hoped he'd never have to see again.

As he rushed out to grab Doc Barker, Tex's mind jumped to the kiss he'd shared with Victoria just the evening before, and the wonderful closeness of her warm, soft body next to his.

And along with the memory, the realization he might never experience either again.

Chapter Thirteen

May 2032, Fort Simons, Texas

"Tex Pemberton? Are you receiving me?" Kris Garcia raised his voice as he spoke into the microphone like it would help him get through easier. It was four in the morning, and all he could hope for was the closest community to his would man their communications twenty-four-seven. He could hear the panicked desperation in his own voice, and prayed someone, *anyone*, would be able to help.

"Fort Simons, this is Joe Johnson." Just hearing another voice brought Garcia comfort; it was calm, cool, collected.

"This is Kris Garcia, we haven't spoken before, Joe, but we need help."

"What's going on over there, Joe?" Johnson asked. "I usually speak to Blue, is he there?"

Garcia took in a long, deep breath and leaned into the microphone. Delivering bad news had never come easy to him, especially under so much pressure. "Ron Simons is dead." He blurted out. "They killed him last night."

"Who killed Blue?" Johnson's voice went up an octave in alarm. "What the hell is happening over there,

Kris?"

Garcia rubbed a hand over his face; his skin felt greasy, unwashed. "The Red River Gang jumped him on the way back from a hunting trip—we lost all six men in the party."

The radio fell silent, and Garcia slumped back in his chair. The Red River Gang had encircled the fort and had spent most of the early hours lighting fires against the outer walls and blasting at the gates. Suddenly thrust into the position of community leader, Garcia had rounded up the handful of men Blue Simons had designated as the fort's defense and had them take a look at what they were facing.

The report back was horrifying. They estimated at least a hundred of the Red River Gang were surrounding the fort. It was difficult to count them all as it was pitch black in the desert beyond the walls. Had it not been for the multitude of fires they'd started at strategic points around the periphery, it would have been an impossible task.

It was clear the gang were determined to get into the fort; Garcia had heard the nomad gangs were becoming increasingly desperate—food and fuel were dwindling resources, and the gangs had picked off most of the individual preppers holed up in their shelters. There had been an attack on another fort a couple hundred miles due west, and every man, woman, and child had been mercilessly slaughtered and left out in the sun for the buzzards to feast upon. Since there was no one left to confirm it had been the Red River Gang, it was impossible to pin it on them, but Garcia had been party to reports from the Simons' scouts that certainly pointed the finger in their direction.

And now it was his community's turn to fall under the attention of the brutal killers.

"They're burning their way through the walls—

they'll be through any minute. Can you help us, Joe?" Garcia spoke up; his mind was on his wife, Josephina and his children, Juan and Sofia. His daughter was less than a year away from her Quinceanera, and the thought she might not see that day come around killed him inside. "Can you send someone…?"

"You're an hour away, Kris." There was resigned sadness in the man's voice; Garcia's heart sank. "We wouldn't get to you in time… and I'm afraid we don't have the resources to spare to take on the Red River Gang."

"So, what are we supposed to do here?" Garcia snapped; his predicament wasn't Johnson's fault, but that didn't assuage the hollow feeling of abandonment in the pit of his stomach. The two communities had helped one another out over the past three years, especially in the recent eighteen months or so when the rains failed and the brutal Texas summers took their toll on the crops. The Little Alamo and Fort Simons had exchanged food, medicine, even skilled workers between one another and other neighboring compounds, but now they *really* needed help, Garcia had never felt so desperately alone.

"My advice," Johnson replied with a weary sigh. "Is to get as many people out of there as you can. Load up all your vehicles with as many supplies as possible and make a run for it—they'll be through your walls, and you don't want to be trapped inside."

"We can't outrun them, Joe," Garcia said. "We're low on fuel and many of our vehicles are on their last legs. We'll be sitting ducks out in there the desert—the Red River Gang will just hunt us down and…"

The walls shook and the sound of splintering wood had Garcia jump from his seat. A glance through the window of his hut saw the main square of the fort lit up by flames from its smashed wall and people—his people—running in terror.

The Red River Gang had broken through.

"Help us, Joe! *Please*!"

"Head north to the Little Alamo, Kris," Johnson said. His voice was shaking, as if he was on the verge of tears. "You'll be safe here."

Garcia caught another voice in the background and, although he couldn't make out the words, he knew they were frustrated, angry.

Then, Johnson said, "It's the least we can do for them, Tex—" and the connection went dead.

The square beyond Garcia's window filled with the Red River Gang as they drove through the gaping holes they'd burned and smashed through the fort's walls. The gang looked to be a ragtag bunch of long-haired savages, but Garcia knew they were far more than just another angry mob. They were organized, armed to the teeth, and determined to grab whatever they wanted from the compounds they attacked. In Garcia's mind, they were akin to a swarm of human locusts, creating death and mayhem and laying waste to everything in their path as they fought to survive in the cruel After Times.

Giving up on Joe Johnson and the Little Alamo for any form of help, Garcia snatched his shotgun and walkie-talkie off the desk and headed for the hut's back door. His one thought was to protect his family, no matter what it took, and do his best to save as many of his community as possible.

"Dan, you there?" Garcia held down the *talk* button of his walkie-talkie so hard his thumb ached. "Pick up, Dan!" He walked briskly down the narrow alleyway behind the row of huts, safely hidden by the dark shadows that lurked there.

"We're under attack, Kris!" Dan Christian's voice crackled through the speaker. Gunfire crackled and spat in the background.

"Get as many of the trucks ready to go as you can!" Garcia wasn't accustomed to barking orders at anyone, let alone the manager of the fort's modest fleet of vehicles. But, since the position of community leader had been thrust upon him as Deputy Leader upon Blue's death, Garcia had few other options.

"It's gonna take time," Christian protested.

"We don't *have* time!" Garcia snapped. "We have to get as many out as we can—head north! Spread the word, Dan."

"You got it."

Garcia slowed up and eased himself between two of the wooden buildings; the street beyond was quiet—the Red River Gang hadn't made it as far as his home.

Lights blazed in the windows of all the huts along the thin street; the commotion created by the fort's attackers had everyone awake and scared. At least there was some kind of plan for them to go with—even if it was leaving behind everything they'd worked so hard for and the one place they'd called home for three and a half years.

Garcia ran along his street, knocking on doors as he went. "*Get to the garage*!" he shouted as doors cracked open and worried faces peered out. "*We have to leave now!*"

Arriving at his own small house, Garcia burst through the door. Josephina was sitting on the couch with Juan and Sofia; her eyes widened at the sight of the gun in his hand—Kris Garcia never, *ever*, carried a weapon. "Grab what you can, we gotta get to the trucks." Garcia told her.

"Where are we going, Papa?" Sofia asked him.

"Away from here, at least for now. There are bad people who want to hurt us."

"Why?" Juan got up from the couch and ran to hug his father.

"They want what we have, and they'll do anything to get it." Garcia held his young son tight; Juan had only just turned eight, and his parents had done their best to keep the worst of the world outside from him.

Let the kid enjoy at least some of his childhood before telling him about the mess his generation would be inheriting.

"Go get your stuff," Garcia reiterated to his son. "As much as you can fit in your backpack—nothing more." Already, there was movement on his street as the neighbors hurried away toward the garage where he hoped Dan Christian would have getaway vehicles ready and waiting.

Garcia watched his wife and daughter scurry into the bedrooms at the back of the small ranch-style house; Josephina would remember to get the guns from beneath their bed, just as they'd rehearsed. Juan followed and ducked into his own bedroom to collect together the things that meant the most to him.

They had gone through the evacuation plan many times during their stay at Fort Simons, and always with the comfort of telling Josephina and the children it would never be required—Blue Simons had personally chosen the community's remote desert location and ensured the place was heavily armed, and they were all perfectly safe.

Only, not even the ever-prepared Blue could have anticipated the sheer force, or the number, of gangs such as the one that had accumulated over in Red River. What had started off as a straggly, disorganized bunch of displaced hippies and thugs in the early days following civilization's fall had built up into a small army several hundred strong.

They had looted all the small towns in a two-hundred-mile radius of Red River, then moved on to the preppers and smaller compounds. At first, they'd simply stolen food and supplies and only killed those foolish enough to try stopping them. They'd also absorb any of the communities' citizens who had grown disgruntled with compound life and the dwindling supplies into their collective, which helped swell the gang's numbers considerably.

But, as the fourth year of the After Times ground on and times became ever more desperate, the Red River Gang had garnered a reputation for being a vicious, murderous bunch who took great pleasure in killing innocent people.

The cacophonous sound of engines roared along the street. Through the window, Garcia saw high beams lighting up the people fleeing their homes. Three pickup trucks—each one sitting on huge wheels and lifted suspension like the Monster Trucks he used to love as a kid—raced side by side down the narrow street, their intention clear.

"We gotta go! *Now*!" Garcia shouted through the house as he looked on helplessly as friends and neighbors were crushed beneath the wheels of those God-awful trucks. In the rear bed of each one sat a handful of scruffy young men with long, greasy hair and wiry beards; they picked off the people who managed to evade the trucks' merciless rampage with silver revolvers and sawed-off shotguns.

One of the trucks stopped outside Garcia's house, while the other two continued on along their path of carnage. Its passengers disembarked and raced across to his front door and that of his next-door neighbors, Al and Meg. Garcia double-checked his gun—he still had the ten rounds he'd loaded into the extra-long magazine he'd had fitted to get around the government-mandated limit of three.

With a deep breath and trembling hands, he took aim.

The front door burst inward; wood splintered as hinges were ripped from the frame. A tall, scrawny guy rushed in, letting loose with random blasts of his shotgun; every shot missed Garcia by a mile.

Garcia returned fire, only less indiscriminately. The first shot knocked the scrawny guy clean off his feet as the full shell of buckshot punched a fat, ragged hole dead center of his chest. His body slammed into two raiders following in behind him, which slowed them down just enough for Josephina to hurry the kids to the back door of the house.

"*Kris*!" Josephina's cry distracted Garcia.

As he turned his head to reassure her he'd be right behind them, the pair of raiders found their feet and raced into his home, trampling over the corpse of their fallen comrade.

Acting on instinct, Garcia pulled his gun's trigger and felt the violent jolt of the recoil as it bucked wildly in his hands. As the second of the Red River Gang hit the wooden floor, Garcia saw movement outside his window: illuminated by his neighbors' burning homes across the street, he saw a whole bunch of guns pointed in his direction.

Kris Garcia swung his shotgun around to take them on, his finger already squeezing that trigger.

Chapter Fourteen

May 2032, Little Alamo, Texas

"Where are we going to put them all, Tex?" Lump asked.

"We'll figure it out." Tex's reply was filled with uncertainty; he studied the bedraggled column of refugees from Fort Simon as they made their weary way into the compound through the gates and felt guilty that he was pleased only a few dozen of them had survived the Red River Gang attack. "We always do."

"That's the problem," Lump said. "We can't keep taking in everyone displaced from their own forts like this—we don't have enough resources for our own people as it is."

Tex looked over at Victoria for at least a little moral support, but she remained silent; it had taken a long time, but somewhere within the three years since TJ's widow had lost her child, Tex and Victoria had gone some way toward rebuilding their relationship. Things were cordial between them, although Tex hoped for more, and he knew in his heart his willingness to take in other compounds' evacuees stemmed from a desire to show her he was capable of compassion.

There was no doubt bridges had been built between them, and Tex felt the spark of mutual attraction was still there, but there'd been no repeat of the kiss they'd shared that fateful night. Since that wonderful moment, Victoria had enjoyed the company of a handful of the compound's eligible men, which Tex had taken with a supportive smile when she came to visit. He'd succumbed to the insistent wiles of Rebecca Smithson, and had enjoyed the woman's company, but when things began to go south at the Little Alamo, his attention turned to that, and he and Rebecca drifted apart.

Lump was right, of course—the Little Alamo had taken in well over a hundred from surrounding compounds as the nomads, Red River Gang, and the forts own vanishing resources had wreaked havoc on the populations. In all, the refugees had swelled the Little Alamo's numbers to a touch over two-hundred fifty, almost double the initial number and considerably more than Tex and the founders had accounted for when they'd planned out the compound.

As a result, Tex and Lump had ordered the construction of more dwellings, plus the additions to some of the existing homes. It meant excursions into the forest to collect the lumber required for building projects, and that came with its own risks. It also meant the trees closest to the compound were being used up quicker than they could be replaced, which further exposed the Little Alamo and forced the firewood-gathering expeditions to go farther afield to feed the ever-hungry furnaces.

More and more families were being expected to share their homes, which most did with good Christian grace, and Tex had been grateful for that. But civility was eroding quickly, and tensions were rising. The overcrowding was causing unrest among the original population, and resentment was beginning to creep in.

"We can build more houses," Lump said as the three

of them watched the Fort Simons people milling around the main square looking lost and broken. "But how the hell do you expect us to feed all these extra people, Tex?"

"There's only thirty-odd of them, Lump," Tex argued, although he had no way of knowing that when he'd told Kris Garcia to have his people make their way to the Little Alamo; it could have been a hundred, which would have been a disaster.

"You had no right letting Joe Johnson offer them a place here." Lump sounded annoyed; it wasn't the first time he and Tex had crossed swords, and each time, the rift between the two friends had deepened considerably.

"What was he supposed to do, Lump?" Victoria broke the silence between the two men. "Turn them all away and leave them to the mercy of the nomads and the drought?"

Lump shrugged and frowned; he was definitely old-school and unaccustomed to being questioned by a woman—especially one with no authority at the Little Alamo. "What the Red River Gang did to them is terrible, I get that," Lump spoke hesitantly as if choosing his words very, very carefully. "But there has to come a time when we put our own citizens first."

As Victoria pursed her lips at Lump, Tex considered weighing in, but had no desire to be caught in the middle of the two. Lump was growing increasingly irritated by what he considered Victoria's *meddling* in the Little Alamo's affairs, especially when it came to its people. She wasn't one of the founders. Lump didn't see how Victoria thought she had a say in any of the policies and thought she used her close relationship with Tex to stick her nose in where he didn't want it.

"They have nowhere else to go," Victoria protested. "We're the only fort left standing for hundreds of miles now—if we didn't take these people in, they'd die."

"They may well die in here as it is," Lump growled. "Unless it's escaped your attention, Vic, we've been rationing food for eighteen months now—we've hunted down all the cows and sheep within a two-day drive, and there hasn't been a deer or wild hog seen anywhere near the compound for a hell of a long time." Pausing, he scratched at the stubble on his chin as if deep in thought. "We've even eaten all the damn ducks, Victoria." He added.

Naturally, Tex knew his friend and cofounder was making good sense; food rationing had become the tip of the iceberg for the Little Alamo as the brutal Texas heat had created the worse drought anyone at the compound could remember. The crops had withered and died, the animals succumbed to ill-health and stopped breeding, and the hunting parties had arrived home empty-handed more times than not.

Added to that, the gasoline and diesel reserves were depleted, the LPG was running low, and the solar panels and batteries had not lasted as long as expected; the Texas sunshine had certainly taken its toll on them. As a result, the compound's electricity supply was down to less than half capacity, which led to overnight blackouts so the vehicles could be charged up—they'd begun building a wood-burning generator to take advantage of the abundance of trees around the compound, in particular the ones they'd cleared away to improve the line of sight following the Nomads' raid. In all, it had led to an increasing reliance upon the horses, who were subject to hay rations as that, too, was running dangerously low.

Increasing the Little Alamo's population was not going to alleviate any of the increasing feeling of desperation at all; Tex knew that much for certain.

"I didn't realize you were so heartless, Lump." Victoria folded her arms across her chest and fixed him with an icy stare.

"Maybe a little heartlessness is what we need around here," Lump snarled back. "We keep on playing Mother Theresa, and we'll all be starving to death or too damn weak to fight off the nomads when they come around to pick off what little we've got left."

Since that first attack on the compound, there had been a handful of others—the Little Alamo was too well-hidden to be found other than by sheer dumb luck, and they'd made every effort not to broadcast its exact whereabouts.

"Look, I'm sorry, Lump." Tex lowered his eyes. "You're right, but I just can't turn people away to die out there."

Lump rested a hand on Tex's shoulder and gave him a conciliatory smile. "I get it, Tex, believe me, I do. You lost Krista, and in some way, you're trying to compensate for that."

Tex tried to speak, but the words caught in his tightened throat; Lump had hit the nail squarely on the head—he'd failed to save his beloved wife back in the Before Times and was attempting retribution for that.

"You can't save them all, my friend." Lump gave Tex's shoulder a squeeze. "We really have to put our own people first—I know it's hard. With things the way they are right now, there are hard decisions to be made.

Tex felt terribly deflated, especially so in front of Victoria. She'd understand, he knew that, but there was always the chance she'd see him as weak, and that just wouldn't do.

"I guess we'll have to draw a line under this batch." Tex regained his voice. "We'll do what needs to be done to accommodate them and, who knows, they might have brought supplies with them—or at least we can send a posse out to see what can be salvaged from Fort Simons.

"Tex, the Red River Gang raided it—there'll be nothing left but cinders by the time we get there," Lump stated the obvious. "And look at them—they were lucky to escape with their lives let alone any provisions." He nodded toward the pitiful sight of families on foot and in beat-up vehicles struggling to make it across the main square.

"Yeah, I guess you're right," Tex replied.

"You did a good thing, Tex." Victoria took his hand in hers; her fingers felt small, delicate, like one good squeeze would snap them like winter twigs. "All those people are alive because of you, they have hope because of the decision you made when you gave Joe the okay to invite them in. Wasn't the whole point of building this place to provide a refuge for people to rebuild their lives, to set about building a brand-new society that wasn't going to implode because of the greed of a few?"

"But it has to stop," Lump added.

"You created this place with compassion in your hearts," Victoria said. "Now is not the time to forget that—look what happened when we forgot the heart and soul of the Founding Fathers' constitution."

"Lump's right, Vic," Tex dared a squeeze of the small fingers nestled within his. "If we take in any more people, we risk those we already have. Until things improve here, I'm gonna have to take Lump's lead on this. He's right—I can't save them all."

Victoria's hand slipped from his, and Tex felt sad and alone.

"Tex Pemberton?" A petite, dark-haired woman dashed across the compound toward Tex, Lump, and Victoria. Behind her, trotting at a half-hearted, weary jog, trailed two children, the girl was around Lee's age.

"That's me," Tex helped the woman out; he had no idea who she was, and it was clear she didn't know what he looked like.

"I'm Josephina—my husband said I had to thank you for telling us we could come to you." The woman held out a hand for Tex to shake.

"Mrs. Garcia?" Tex recalled the last conversation he'd had with Kris Garcia and a lump formed in his throat.

"Papa is back at the fort." The young boy stepped forward before his mother could speak. "They're fighting off the bad guys, and then they'll fix it all up so we can go back home."

Josephina gave Tex a sad glance that told him what he already knew; Garcia had not made it out alive, and there'd be no rebuilding Fort Simons.

"That's really good to hear, young man," Tex said with a warm smile. "In the meantime, you and your mom and sister can make yourselves at home right here."

"Thank you so much," Josephina kept hold of Tex's hand, tears welling in her sad, brown eyes. "We had nowhere else to go…"

Lump turned to go, and Tex saw the tears in his eyes, too.

Josephina finally released Tex's hand and ushered her kids back toward the main square. There, her people were being allocated temporary accommodation by the Little Alamo's designated welcoming committee.

"Quit beating yourself up, Tex." Victoria looked up at Tex; the warm morning sun on her honey-tan skin made her look all the more beautiful. "You did the right thing for these people, and for the others we've taken in. Despite what Lump says, we *have* managed—it hasn't been an easy ride, but we've done it, and I know we'll be okay this time, too. Things *will* get better if we stick with it—just you wait and see." She turned to leave.

"Thank you, Vic." Choked with emotion, Tex struggled to get the words out. "I truly appreciate that." He wanted to say more to her, so much more, but those words simply refused to come out.

Instead, Tex watched Victoria walk away and harbored just a touch of hope in his heart that maybe, just maybe…

Chapter Fifteen

May 2032, 100 miles south of the Little Alamo, Texas

Tip Cain had agreed to head up the hunting party; after all, it was the least he could do to repay the kindness of the good folks at the Little Alamo. In the week or so since he, and what was left of the Fort Simons population, had descended upon the compound, Tip had picked up on just how difficult it had been for them to take in a whole bunch of refugees.

But even though he'd picked up on a little of the ill-feeling toward the extra people, Tip had yet to witness an ounce of outward aggression. The Little Alamo people were good people and were going out of their way to make everyone feel at home.

For his part, Tip had thrown himself into helping with the construction of the new homes around the fort, and when he mentioned there were still wild boar thirty miles and change from Fort Simons and he was an expert bowman, he'd been given the opportunity to take a hunting trip.

There were three in the party—Tip was used to a couple more, but happy to go along with the Little Alamo policy—a hunter with a crossbow accompanied by a pair of lookouts to keep a watchful eye out for nomads and scavengers. While the nomads had decreased in numbers across the years as pickings grew scarce, and the heat, drought, and rival gangs took their toll, those who remained were ever bolder in their desperation. Tip had heard of them attacking some of the smaller compounds and individual prepper families and leaving no survivors. And he, too, had heard the talk of nomads carrying off victims and consuming their flesh.

Of course, they were not audacious—or suicidal—enough to take on a fort the size of the Little Alamo with its formidable firepower and actively avoided the Red River Gang and bigger collectives, but Tip knew they'd be more than prepared to pick off a lone hunting party.

"We'll bivouac here," Tip told his companions, Sean Wopat and Don Woods.

He'd gotten to know them well during the two-hour drive to the edge of the overgrown woodland where they hoped to pick off a bunch of wild pigs to feed the folks back home, and they were good, solid guys. Wopat was an ex-Marine, and Woods came with plenty experience handling guns—although he shied away from letting on exactly what experience, Tip reckoned it had been something not entirely legal.

The three set up a couple two-man tents in a small clearing kissed by dappled sunlight; the broken light on the green canvas made the camp all but disappear into the trees and brush.

"We heading straight out?" Wopat asked. He cradled his rifle in his arms like it was a small child and looked kinda antsy to be getting on with the hunt.

"Yup," Tip told him and shouldered his bow. The hunts were done by bow and arrow—more sophisticated than those depicted in the old Western movies—not only to conserve ammunition, but to avoid scaring off other game and drawing attention to the party. He knew firing off even a couple rounds was likely to bring every nomad within earshot running with hopes of easy prey.

"Ready, Don?" Wopat asked.

Woods checked his rifle was fully loaded and gave a taciturn nod; the guy was a man of few words.

Tip led the way into the woods. Unlike the forests around the Little Alamo, it was filled almost exclusively with deciduous trees—mostly live oak, Texas ash, and cedar elm. Tip had hunted the area back in the day, when Blue Simons had delighted in taking hunting trips—the guy had been big on the sport in the Before Times and didn't want to lose his touch. It was a passion that, sadly, had resulted in the man's tragic undoing.

"There," Wopat whispered and stood stock-still. He pointed the end of his rifle at a dark section of the woods where a thicket of undergrowth clung to the base of a quartet of young elm trees.

Straining his eyes, it took Tip a second or two to see the wild hog snuffling around in the center of the thicket. It was a good ol' size. Tip guessed it to be two-and-a-half feet at the shoulder and maybe four feet long, although that was difficult to tell as it was mostly hidden by greenery. Oblivious to its audience, the pig dug enthusiastically at the soft ground with its snout and gobbled up whatever it came across.

Tip motioned for Wopat and Woods to remain still, and he readied his crossbow; the bolt was already in place, and all he had to do was wait for the shot and hope the wind didn't shift and give the pig a warning whiff of humans.

The wild hog pushed its way through the thick undergrowth and out into the open. Keeping its head down, all of the animal's focus remained upon rifling through the loose-leaf litter and rich soil beneath; most likely it was unearthing grubs and worms, and maybe even a truffle or two. Tip had heard rumors of the woods being a rich hunting ground for the delicacy, although he'd never understood the appeal of eating mold.

Tip held his breath and took careful aim as the hog turned its flank toward him and offered up a perfect shot of its heart.

The bolt tore straight through the hog's ribcage and embedded itself into the tree trunk behind it. The animal let out one shrill, strangled shriek and flopped limply onto its side in the damp leaves; Tip reckoned his target was dead the moment it hit the ground. He took a moment to be pleased with himself and with such a good, clean kill: there was no need to track a wounded hog through the woods, the creatures could do a man some serious harm, and the animal wouldn't be squealing in pain and frightening off any other game the hunting party hoped to encounter.

"We need to get it back to camp," Tip said quietly. "There's got to be more around here—don't want to scare 'em off."

Wopat helped Tip lift the hog, taking its front legs. Tip grabbed the rear legs and the two hefted the beast back the way they'd come while Woods maintained a watchful eye on the woods surrounding them.

Tip had the wild hog strung up, head down, from a tree branch a dozen yards from the camp; with expert ease, he slit the animal's throat to bleed it out, then removed its innards.

"We don't want these leaking on the drive back," he told his companions, who were both looking a little green about the gills at the sight of all the blood and guts. "This is your first time out hunting, eh?" He smiled at the two as they struggled to down the coffee he'd brewed up; they sat in the camp chairs by the small fire, staring at the flames.

Wopat shook his head. "We've guarded quite a few hunts now," he told Tip. "But this is the first time we've seen anything killed."

"Slim pickings out there?"

"Yeah, it's been a while since anyone caught anything in the forests around the compound," Woods added. "It's like we already ate everything there was."

"I've hunted here a lot," Tip scanned their verdant surroundings. "And it rarely disappoints." He was relieved to have made the kill as, in his mind at least, it helped make up for the added burden his people had placed on the Little Alamo. But he was realistic enough to know one wild hog was hopelessly inadequate.

"Ready to move out?" Tip asked the guys. "I think we should be able to bag us another couple before nightfall—the deer come out at dusk, and I'd like to go back with some venison."

Wopat and Woods got to their feet with a grunt; Wopat threw the dregs of his coffee into the fire and steam spiraled up into the air. He reached for his rifle.

"You'd better leave that where it is." Movement from the trees off to the left, and two thin, unkempt figures emerged from the undergrowth.

"You, too, buddy," the taller of the two men said to Woods; he aimed his own rifle at Woods, who raised his hands.

"You can take the hog," Tip said, scrutinizing the woods behind the two nomads—as far as he could see, they were alone.

"We fully intend to," the second nomad replied with menace. "We didn't wait here all this time to leave empty-handed." He advanced toward Tip, shotgun held at his hip, aimed up at Tip's chest.

"We don't want any trouble here," Tip said; guns made him nervous, especially in the hands of desperate, clearly starving, nomads. His guess was they'd been stomping around the woods like a pair of idiots trying to find something to shoot—he'd seen their kind before: no finesse, no stealth, and no food.

"Shut the fuck up," the tall man said. He marched up to the campfire and kicked over the water pot; the fire went out with a loud hiss. "You're gonna cut that pig up for us to carry." He prodded at Woods with his rifle. "And your friend here can sit the fuck back down and keep his hands where I can see 'em—otherwise I'm gonna start shooting."

Tip saw Woods pale at the notion of butchering the hog. "I'll do it," he said. "These guys don't know how."

"Then they can learn." The nomad jabbed Woods with the gun's muzzle, pushing him toward the pig hanging from the tree.

"He's going to need a knife." Tip plucked his trusty hunting knife from the holster on his belt.

"Take it easy, partner," the short nomad brought the shotgun up level with Tip's face.

"The guy needs something to carve up your pig." Tip kept his voice calm, his movements slow; one sudden move, one wrong word, and the nomad was likely to get trigger-happy.

"Toss it over to him." The nomad pointed his shotgun in Wood's direction for emphasis.

Seizing his chance, Tip thrust the knife's keen blade up into the soft part beneath the nomad's chin and threw his weight at the guy. The nomad's gun fired as the two crashed to the soft ground, the buckshot ripping harmlessly through the leaf canopy above.

The tall nomad reacted a fraction of a second too late. Twisting his head to see his companion squirming beneath Tip with blood gushing from his throat.

Woods made a grab for the tall nomad's rifle, but the guy held on, and the planned snatch turned into a vicious tussle. The nomad pulled the trigger, and the bullet tore through Woods' knee. His leg collapsed under him and as he hit the ground, the nomad swung the rifle toward his head.

Wopat was on the nomad before he had the chance to shoot. Jumping the man from behind, he took him down with an expert chokehold while simultaneously twisting his body to take the rifle's aim off Woods—a few seconds of pressure on the carotid artery, and the nomad fell limp.

"You okay?" Tip asked Wopat as Woods bandaged up his leg. His pants were drenched with blood, the bandages turning red the instant Woods rolled them around the wound.

"I reckon I'll live."

Tip saw Wopat was putting a macho façade—the shot had taken off most of his kneecap and must have hurt like hell. "We'll get you back to the Little Alamo as soon as we can," he assured.

"We can't go back with just one hog," Wopat protested.

Tip shook his head; stubbornness like that, although admirable, was what cost good men their limbs or their lives. "We can always head back in a few days," he said. "The woods aren't going anywhere."

"What about him?" Woods pointed over at the nomad he'd rendered unconscious; he was already beginning to stir. His partner in crime had bled out from the deep cut in his neck as efficiently as the wild hog Tip had strung up. He lay still, covered head to toe in congealing blood in the leaf litter, eyes staring up at the sky like he was searching for God.

Tip felt a pang of regret and pity; the nomad guy and his buddy had only been out looking to feed themselves—it was always possible they had families secreted away someplace safe, too. Sure, they'd chosen to steal food rather than hunt it for themselves, but they were all living in desperate times, and it really was the survival of the fittest.

Had it not been for the charity offered by Tex and the good people of the Little Alamo, Tip knew it might well have been him out to take from others just for a morsel of food; the nomads weren't the devils the hearsay made them out to be, they were only trying to survive by whatever means they could.

"I guess we leave him here," Tip offered. "Unless you guys want to take him back with us."

"Can't do that," Woods told him. "The policy is to neutralize all threats."

"How is he a threat?" Tip had a sinking feeling he knew where things were leading.

"He could have others to report back to, or he could be here waiting for us when we come back."

Tip shook his head. "We can't just kill him," he said.

"Sorry, brother." Woods picked up the nomad's rifle—they'd confiscated the nomads' weapons; even though they were in poor shape, they were still functional— and walked over to where the man was rubbing at his throat and struggling to sit up.

"No!" Tip's voice was drowned out by the rifle's report. Shocked by the cold suddenness of Woods' action, Tip could only look on in disgust as the nomad slumped back onto the soft ground, no longer a threat.

Chapter Sixteen

May 2032, Little Alamo, Texas

Jed Timothy looked a heck of a lot leaner than the last time Tex had seen him, and that had only been a few months before—the hard times were clearly taking their toll on the Timothy Clan as much as they were all the other communities the Little Alamo traded with.

"It's good to see you again, Jed," Tex greeted the man with a firm handshake, like he was an old friend. Timothy's hand felt small, frail in his. The guy was an inch or two taller than Tex and once sported a broad, muscular frame, but now his clothes hung off him like they were at least a couple sizes too small.

"Looks like you've been taking in waifs and strays again," Timothy looked around at the compound's busy main street.

Tex nodded as he walked along, weaving between the bustling people going about their business; Winnie ran ahead, scooting between feet and narrowly avoiding being stepped on—he knew where they were heading. The Fort Simons folk were integrating—helping build new accommodations—although tensions were running high in some places. "The Red River Gang destroyed Blue

Simon's place and we took 'em in."

"That's mighty charitable of you, Tex," Timothy said with a wry smile. "You look like you're straining at the seams here, though."

Tex hid his exasperated sigh and managed to avoid rolling his eyes—only just. Timothy was beginning to sound a lot like Lump, and he really didn't need it that morning. "We did what was right, Jed," he said. "Couldn't just turn all those good folk away."

"I guess you're right," Timothy replied with a disapproving look. "We'd have done the same if our place was big enough."

The Timothy Clan's fort was around a quarter of the size of the Little Alamo with a population of forty-some souls. They were blessed with surrounding land that had an underground stream and was incredibly fertile—even in the drought—which meant they always had food to trade; this trip it was potatoes and beans in the back of his truck in exchange for beeswax and honey.

Tex maneuvered himself and Timothy through a small crowd waiting outside the general store; it was a little late opening and a few in the line had annoyed impatience written all over their faces. Tex considered pausing to talk to them, try to nip any possible trouble in the bud, but he wasn't in the mood for chit-chat and wanted to get his guest sorted with what he came for and away—Tex had important business to attend to.

"Here we are," Tex guided Timothy through the small wildflower field, which housed the beehives—ten rows of five apiece—and led to the greenhouses. He was delighted to see Victoria pottering about among the tomatoes and greens in the unit closest to the hives—he'd been looking forward to having the excuse to cross her path again.

She spotted him and Timothy, gave a polite little

wave, and

"Where the magic happens," Timothy said as he dodged a low-flying bee. "What the heck do they know that we don't, Tex?"

Tex shrugged; damned if he knew. "No idea, Jed," he replied. "They just know where the pollen is, I suppose. It doesn't matter how hot it gets, or how dry the fields are out there, they just keep coming back and making their honey."

True, only a little over half of the hives were occupied and bee numbers were drastically down, but they still managed to provide the Little Alamo with plenty honey and wax, with a little surplus to trade, too.

"Hello again, Jed," Victoria wiped her hands on her jeans before offering one.

"Good to see you, Victoria," Timothy gave her a fond smile.

"What have you got for Jed this time?" Tex asked her.

Victoria laughed, and Tex saw a sparkle in her eyes he'd not seen in a long while. "Pretty much wax and honey, Tex," she giggled. "What else were you expecting from a bunch of bees?"

The three laughed together; it was a wonderful moment.

"Well, that's what I came all this way for," Timothy replied. "It never ceases to amaze me all the things they do back at the compound with beeswax. And your honey always tastes its very best in a nice malt whisky."

"It really does," Victoria agreed. "I think it's the clover they're finding out there—it gives the honey a sweet, smokey kind of taste."

Tex only half-listened, his attention taken by Victoria's beautiful face and bedazzling smile; she was stirring a whole host of feelings within him. As for the talk of honey and wax, Tex didn't find any of it engaging—the Little Alamo's craft group had discovered a whole raft of uses for the wax: candles, of course, wrap for food, crayons for the kids, and lip balm and body butter for the residents who liked just a touch of old-time luxury in the After Times.

They walked a little among the greenhouses and struggling flower beds, Tex a step or so behind Victoria and Timothy, Winnie scampering around his feet. And, while Vic's attention was very much taken up by the visitor, Tex was happy to be in her company—the strain between them had eased considerably over the past few months, and he was once again considering his feelings towards his old friend's widow. And, knowing he was more than likely to find her working the gardens that morning, Tex had readied himself to wear his heart on his sleeve and make his move.

"You seen much of the Red River Gang?" Timothy turned on a dime to face Tex. "I hear they've been running sorties in this neck of the woods."

The statement caught Tex off guard; he had no idea how talk of wax and honey could suddenly turn to the Red River Gang—he really hadn't been paying much attention.

"We haven't seen them here," Tex told him. "But after what happened to Blue Simons' place, we're on high alert. It's only a matter of time before they get desperate and crazy enough to take us on."

"I hope for your sakes they give you a wide berth." There was genuine concern etched on Timothy's face, his dark brown eyes lowered. "They're not just raiding compounds for food and fuel anymore, Tex, they're raping the women and taking young girls."

The thought appalled Tex; he'd heard the rumors bouncing between the compounds on the short wave, of course, but hearing the words from Jed's mouth brought a whole new, dreadful, realism to them. "We built a big fort for that very reason, Jed," Tex replied. "I don't believe even the Red River Gang will be dumb enough to take us on."

"They're growing their numbers," Timothy countered. "Those they don't kill during their raids, they take with them—I've heard talk about the Red River Gang being over a hundred fifty-strong now."

"Even so, they're nowhere near as well armed as we are, and that goes for all the bigger compounds, too. We designed the Little Alamo to give us every advantage if we came under attack, plus our ammunition stores very well stocked."

"Even the old Alamo fell at the end, Tex." Timothy's dour words hung in the warm air like a rotten stink; his face fell slack, expressionless. "You'd do well to remember that."

"Let's get you that honey," Victoria chimed in, obviously keen to interrupt the grim turn in the conversation. "I have that and your wax already boxed up for you." Turning toward the nearest greenhouse, she put a finger in each corner of her mouth and let out a loud, shrill whistle that physically hurt Tex's eardrums.

Winnie let out a delighted yelp and raced full pelt at Lee as he emerged from the greenhouse, his hands grimy with dirt. So wrapped up with thoughts of Victoria, Tex had forgotten it was his son's day to work the gardens. The boy had grown into a handsome, hard-working young man during his time at the Little Alamo, and he made Tex proud of him every single day.

"Hey, Dad," Lee shouted over.

Tex raised a hand in greeting.

"I swear that kid looks more like you every time I see him," Timothy said.

Tex didn't reply; he'd been thinking the exact opposite of late: Lee reminded him of Krista the more he grew, especially since he'd inherited his mother's eyes.

"Can you give Jed a hand with his boxes, please?" Victoria said to Lee, who was busy rubbing his dog's belly. Winnie was rolling around on his back in the dirt, lapping up the attention.

"Sure," Lee replied and beckoned for Timothy to follow him into the small, air-conditioned storage unit behind the greenhouses.

"That's my cue," Timothy said to Victoria. "I'll go help the boy." And, with that, he made his way between the greenhouses.

Finally alone with Victoria, Tex swallowed hard and figured it was time he took his chance. He'd waited long enough, he reckoned, and besides, what was the worst thing that could happen?

"Say, Vic," Tex fought hard to stop the quiver in his voice. "I was wondering…" He stalled.

Victoria looked up into Tex's face, her eyes meeting his. "What were you wondering, Tex?" She asked. "Are you going to share, or do I have to guess?"

Tex let out a nervous laugh and mentally admonished himself for the ridiculous noise he'd made. He was a grown-ass man, for Pete's sake, and there he was acting like some tongue-tied, lovestruck teenager.

"I was wondering if maybe you'd like to visit with me sometime soon." Tex finally spat out what had been on his mind for a long time.

With a puzzled expression on her face, Victoria replied, "I'm hardly a stranger, Tex."

"I know," Tex stammered. Victoria would often pop round to see Lee and drop off produce, "But, I mean, not in that way."

"Then in what way?" Tex spotted the flicker of a smile playing across Victoria's lips and he knew she was just teasing him; she knew darn well what he was wondering and was not going to make it easy on him.

"Visit with me." Tex summoned up the courage to blurt it out—it was shit-or-bust time for sure. "Let me cook you dinner, spend a little time together just the two of us."

The silence that followed played heavy on Tex's ears and soul. Was Victoria preparing her let-down speech or had he soured their relationship for the rest of time? The suspense was killing him.

"I'd love to," Victoria said after the longest pause Tex thought he'd ever had to endure. "Thank you for the sweet invitation."

"Is tomorrow evening good for you?" Tex spoke with a tad more conviction, his confidence boosted by Victoria's acceptance. "Lee is staying at his friend's, and we'll have the house to ourselves…"

Victoria took Tex's hand in hers. "That sounds perfect—I look forward to it."

"All good to go!" Jed Timothy's foghorn voice destroyed the moment. Victoria slipped her hand from Tex's, and he already missed it.

"I'd best walk him back to his truck," Tex said to Victoria by means of an apology. "See you tomorrow, then."

"For definite, Tex." Victoria headed back to the greenhouse as Timothy and Lee walked toward Tex, their arms laden with wooden boxes crammed with jars of golden liquid and rectangles of wax.

Tex took a box each from Timothy and Lee and led the way back to the main gates. And, rather than the heavy, anxious heart he'd had on his way there, Tex left the compound's gardens with a definite spring in his step.

Chapter Seventeen

Tex studied Lump, who stood in the lounge of his cabin alongside Rhino and Tip Cain. He'd sensed a cooler vibe from his old friend in recent weeks and, although he'd put it down to the stress everyone was feeling at the Little Alamo as life had grown tougher, Tex couldn't quite shift the notion there was more to it than that.

He made a mental note to address it with Lump upon his return.

Which brought Tex back to the purpose of that morning's early gathering. He'd summoned the three to his cabin, having first packed Lee off to go help squeeze what little milk they could from the weary cows, to share his concerns about the Red River Gang. After what happened to the Simon's fort, and what Jed Timothy had told him the day before, Tex reckoned he couldn't hide his head in the proverbial sand any longer.

"We need to build an alliance with Aaron Jones," Tex said as he nervously adjusted his hat.

"Are you *serious*, Tex?" Lump shot back. "The guy's a certifiable looney tune.

"Doesn't even have a proper compound to speak of," Rhino chipped in.

"He has *something*, at least," Tex replied. "And he

and his people are heavily armed."

That was putting it mildly; Aaron Jones and his loosely tied gang of cohorts had molded a collective between their individual bunkers and strongholds a half day or so due west of the Little Alamo. Jones was a renowned doomsday prepper long before the end of the Before Times; legend among his peers was he'd amassed enough weaponry and ammunition in his network of underground bunkers to arm a small country.

And with allegiances with his fellow looney tunes as Lump so eloquently called them, it meant Aaron Jones would make for one hell of a strong ally.

Certainly a more beneficial arrangement than having him as an enemy—it would be better to have Jones onside against the threat of the Red River Gang and their ilk than have him eying up the Little Alamo as fair game before supplies ran out and the crops and animals all died.

"We've only had little bits and pieces of communication with Jones," Lump threw in. "And practically zilch from any of his people. Not that I'd call 'em that; from what I understand, most of them aren't even on first-name terms."

"I think you might be surprised." Tip broke his silence. He'd turned out to be a man of few words, Tex had discovered, but he'd sure as hell proven himself on the last hunting trip out of the compound.

"You're familiar with Aaron Jones and his set-up?" Tex asked.

Tip nodded. "We sent out a scouting party from Fort Simons to go to his place back in the early days."

"Did you go?"

Nodding again, Tip said, "Aaron was welcoming enough, I guess. Though, he seemed none too keen on sharing what he'd got."

"The ammunition?" Rhino asked with a glint in his

eyes.

"Yeah," Tip said. "Lucky, we didn't need any back then—or at least, that's what we thought."

Tex caught the sadness in the newcomer's eyes; the poor guy and his family must have gone through hell when the Red River Gang ploughed through his compound like a gang of bloodthirsty Vikings laying waste to homes, taking what they wanted, and killing—or worse—anyone who crossed their murderous path.

"We could have used people like Aaron Jones when we were attacked," Tip continued. "I think it's a good idea to reach out to them right now and suggest we join forces."

"But what do we have to offer *them*?" Lump spoke up; he shifted from foot to foot as if antsy about something or anxious to get the meeting over and done with. "They have more ammo than we do, even if we have more weapons. They have vehicles, of course, and I can only imagine the mountains of canned goods Jones will have amassed in the Before Times."

"We have *this*." Tex pointed out through his lounge window. Outside, the morning bustle of the Little Alamo was just getting started. People went about their business in the hopes of getting done before the heat of the day set in and made most things impossible. Since they'd had to ration electricity for air conditioning to save fuel and avoid overburdening the generators and failing solar panels, large chunks of every summer's day had been rendered useless.

"We ran out of space when…" Lump cast a sideways glance at Tip. "No offence, Cain," he said.

"None taken," Tip replied with a wan smile. "I know me and my family have been a burden on the Little Alamo—as have the rest of the Fort Simon people you so graciously took in—which is why I'm more than happy to do what I can for you good folks."

"We have plenty of land to expand out into," Tex took off his hat and rubbed at his head a little. "I know that means going further afield for lumber, but that would be less dangerous with more manpower on our side."

It all made perfect sense: if it ever got to the point that they'd have to take in Aaron Jones's clan, then they'd be able to expand the compound—so, to Tex's reckoning, the problem would solve itself. And, following on from what Jed Timothy had told him, Tex knew he'd sleep a whole lot easier at night knowing Jones and his fellow crazies weren't planning anything stupid against the Little Alamo.

"I need you three to head out to Jones' compound, or whatever the hell it is he has going on out there, and talk to them. Grab a few of the guys to go with you as backup."

"Sounds good to me," Rhino said—the guy couldn't resist a little adventure and the chance of a scrap.

"Lump?" Tex prompted his old friend.

"If you think it's a good idea, Tex," Lump spoke slow and deliberately. "Then I guess it's a good idea."

Tex sat his hat back on top of his head; the hesitance in Lump's voice spoke volumes. Sadly, there wasn't time to sit and debate the decision and the thought processes behind it, and Tex was grateful Lump was happy enough to simply follow orders—just like back in the old days in the Iraqi desert.

"I appreciate it," Tex addressed all three men. "Again, I wish I was going out there with you guys. But there are things I have to work on back here—you know how it is."

Lump, Rhino, and Tip all nodded. Tex knew not one of the three would question his choice to remain at the Little Alamo: his perceived position as leader meant he had to remain safe and be available to deal with any domestic emergencies that could possibly arise—be it a failed generator or a full-blown invasion by the nomads or Red River Gang. Actually, Tex would have dearly loved nothing more than to set off into the unknown and barter with Aaron Jones and the other preppers—although Lump was, ironically, the far better diplomat between the two of them.

However, the truth was, it irked Tex to feel like he was hiding behind the relative comfort of the Little Alamo's fortified walls. To his mind, he'd become little more than a pencil-pusher and general nanny to his people, no matter how many times he reminded himself that a good general commanded from *behind* the lines.

As he watched the three men make their way out through the front door and off down the street, Tex felt that old, all-too familiar stab in the pit of his stomach; he wondered if he'd ever get used to giving orders with the knowledge he might well be sending good men out to die.

"Knock, knock," a familiar voice accompanied the light rapping of knuckles on Tex's door.

"Come in." Tex was delighted—if somewhat surprised—to have Victoria knocking on his door so early in the morning; the sun was barely peeking up over the horizon.

"I thought I'd wait for your guests to leave—I only brought enough breakfast for two," Victoria said as she let herself in. She held a covered basked in the crook of her arm.

"You must have read my mind." Tex smiled.

"No," Victoria returned the smile, "Lee told me you kicked him out early because you were having some important powwow with Lump—I guessed you'd have forgotten all about something as trivial as eating. So, I thought I'd come to the rescue."

Tex's stomach rumbled at the thought of food and the wonderful aroma of fresh-baked bread wafting from Victoria's basket. "Come through to the kitchen—it's lovely to see you again."

"Since yesterday, you mean?" Victoria teased as she plopped her basked down on Tex's countertop.

"Yeah," Tex replied sheepishly. He sat himself down at the small kitchen table and removed his hat.

"I have fresh honey to put on this." Victoria lifted a small, crusty loaf from her basket. "So fresh the bees only just finished making it."

"You had an early start at the hives this morning," Tex ventured. "Is everything okay over there? We didn't really get the chance to talk yesterday…"

"That Jed Timothy could talk the hind legs of a mule," Victoria laughed. "And yes, everything is as good as it can be given the circumstances. I like to get to the bees while they're still sleeping and before it gets too hot. This weather makes them extra pissy about me taking the hard-earned fruits of their labor—no matter how much smoke I give the poor things." From the wicker basket, she produced a small mason jar filled with honey the color of pure amber.

"Can't have you getting stung, now, can we?" Tex let out a light laugh he hoped didn't give away his nervousness.

"Toast?"

"What?" Tex looked at his guest, puzzled.

"Do you prefer your breakfast bread toasted or as it comes?"

"Oh," Tex stammered, "as it comes is perfect, thank you."

Victoria grabbed Tex's serrated bread knife from the block on the counter and set about cutting the loaf into inch-thick slices.

"Jed Timothy seemed downbeat yesterday—that's not like him at all." Victoria smeared a fat gobbet of honey onto the sliced bread. "He tried to hide it, but a woman's intuition *knows* these things."

“You do realize they’d have burned you at the stake for saying that back in the sixteen hundreds?” Tex laughed.

“And with good reason, too.” Victoria giggled along. “My mom always said I’d make a good witch.” She sat in the chair next to Tex’s, their knees touched, then placed a piled-high plate of honied bread on the table between them.

“Jed is worried about the Red River Gang,” Tex confided; he knew he could trust Victoria implicitly—that anything he told her would go no further was always.

“Has he had run-ins with them?”

“He’s *aware* of their presence,” Tex told her. “And, between them and the nomads, he’s getting nervous.”

“Al Mims says he’s hearing reports from all over that the nomads are venturing further out into the remote areas. The cities are either all plundered out or defended by those who took them over.”

“It won’t be too long before another bunch stumble upon the Little Alamo,” Tex said through a mouthful of bread; it was perhaps the sweetest, most delicious thing he’d tasted since the After Times began. “Which is why we’re seeking an allegiance with Aaron Jones.”

Victoria quit chewing, her mouth full; her eyes widened, her brow furrowed.

“Yeah, I know,” Tex sighed. “Lump gave me all the crazies spiel, and I’m all too aware of Jones’ reputation as some gun-crazy prepper, but his compound is the closest one to us left standing—what other options do we have?”

Victoria swallowed her mouthful. “Are you *that* worried about us getting attacked?”

As Tex met Victoria’s gaze—her eyes were stunningly beautiful—his mind spun back to some of the horrific stories he’d heard from Tip Cain and Josephina Garcia; he had to do everything within his power to ensure the same fate never befell the good citizens of the Little Alamo, no matter what it took.

"So long as an attack is a possibility, we have to be prepared," Tex said. "Things are getting a tad… *strained* here, and we're hearing of similar predicaments from forts and compounds across the country—this hot summer really is taking its toll on us all. That means the nomads will become increasingly desperate—and reckless—and with the Red River Gang moving further and further out of their territory, we can assume they are, too. And then there's the other groups—"

"Like Aaron Jones?" Victoria cut in.

"Like Aaron Jones," Tex agreed. "And any of the other compounds who run out of resources and decide they have nothing to lose by coming for ours."

Tex thought he saw Victoria shudder… just a little.

"Hey, I'm sorry," he placed a comforting hand on her arm; her skin felt so wonderfully warm and soft. "I shouldn't burden you with all my problems—it's my job to worry about those things, not yours."

Victoria slipped her hand over Tex's and gave a gentle squeeze with strong, slender fingers. "I'm glad you feel you can talk to me, Tex," she said. "I know how lonely it can be not having someone to share things with—especially when it does help to talk."

The breath caught in Tex's throat.

Completely caught in the moment, all he could think of was how beautiful Victoria was, how wonderful her hand felt upon his, how welcoming her lips seemed at that precise moment in time…

Unable to help himself, Tex leaned in toward Victoria, his eyes fixed on hers, his heart skipped as she leaned in to meet his lips with hers.

The kiss was long, lingering, and every bit as perfect as the last time; it held the promise of past pain forgotten and forgiven, the hope of a future… and the just the faintest hint of love.

Victoria's hand left Tex's to caress his stubbled cheek, her fingers soft and sensual against his skin; Tex slipped his hand around Victoria's back and pulled her gently toward him.

Victoria tasted so delicious, she had Tex's head spinning and passion stirring.

It was the taste of yearning and sweet, fresh honey.

Chapter Eighteen

Lump slowed up his steed as the first of the concrete bunkers came into view—he and Rhino had decided it would be a better idea to take the trip to Aaron Jones' place on horseback to not only conserve the dwindling fuel supplies and failing vehicles, but to present a more friendly front to the preppers. They'd also eschewed Tex's suggestion that they take along a few other men for the same reason. But Lump had made sure he, Rhino, and Tip were more than adequately armed just in case things turned unpleasant—Aaron Jones and his associates were very much an unknown quantity.

The chestnut mare pulled up amid a cloud of dry, red dust. Behind Lump, Rhino and Tip also brought their horses to a stop, and the three of them peered across the valley at the twelve bunker entrances set into the hillside.

"Is that it?" Rhino said. "It doesn't look much."

"I heard their bunkers go way back into the hill," Tip threw in. "And that they're connected by tunnels."

"Makes sense." Lump screwed up his eyes against the glaring late afternoon sun; there wasn't a single cloud to break up the blue skies overhead.

The sound of grating, heavy steel drifted across the dry valley, and the bunker door on the far right of the line slowly swung open.

"I guess that's our cue," Rhino said, his hand hovering close to the high-velocity rifle nestled in its holster on his saddle.

"Keep your weapons down." Lump didn't have to look around to know what Rhino was planning—he'd gotten to know the guy well over the years and, while he was irreplaceable to have around in the event of a fight, Lump knew the guy was just as capable of starting one.

With a soft click of his tongue and bump of his heels, Lump urged his horse into motion as a trio of armed, dark-clad figures stepped out through the bunker door. Behind him, Rhino and Tip followed suit, and the three set off toward the hillside with a thick red dust plume announcing their arrival.

"You come far?" Aaron Jones patted the chestnut mare's neck as Lump dismounted. He then stuck out a hand to shake.

"Just over half a day's ride," Lump said, not wanting to give away the Little Alamo's exact location too soon. "I'm John—the guys call me Lump—this here's Rhino, and that's Tip."

"You got some fine horses there—they look well-fed." Jones ignored the men and nodded at Tip's and Rhino's steeds. "You must me doing good at your fort… wherever the hell it is."

"We'll be happy to exchange information when—"

"When we don't kill y'all and cook you up for dinner?" Jones fixed Lump with an icy stare; for a brief moment, Lump regretted having not brought along reinforcements.

"I'm just messing with ya!" Jones let out a laugh and delivered a hearty slap to Lump's shoulder. The preppers on either side of him—a pair of tall, thick-set guys with bushy black beards covering at least half their faces—

chortled along at the supposedly hilarious joke.

Rhino laughed too, as did Tip, but Lump only managed a forced smile; there was just the slightest hint of menace in Jones's words that sent a prickle of gooseflesh down his back.

"Well, y'all had best come in," Jones said. "It's too darned hot to be standing out here, that's for sure."

"The horses…?" Tip ventured.

"Yup, them too," Jones replied with a wink. "We're not as primitive here as you might have been led to believe—don't think we haven't heard all the crazy stories going around out there."

Another laugh; a tad less good-natured.

"This is really impressive," Lump said—and genuinely meant it—as Jones led them through the small bunker and out through a wide barn-style door at the other end. His two sidekicks led the horses off to a corral housing a half dozen others; their hooves click-clacked on the hard stone ground.

Beyond the door stretched a cavernous space carved out of the hillside; its rough-hewn stone walls were almost two-stories high—it reminded Lump of the pictures he'd seen of the old salt mines that had hollowed out entire mountains then used for document storage.

Lump reckoned the almost perfectly square space was a good two and a half, maybe three, acres, complete with dead-straight walkways and white-painted Nissen huts lined up neatly to create small streets and alleyways. The whole place was pleasantly lit by rows upon rows of flickering gas lights, which cast a soothing dusk glow. As Lump scanned across the underground landscape, dozens of people went about their business, and children played in the expansive, Astroturf covered playgrounds.

"We had a hell of a long time to prepare," Jones told him. "While the rest of the world was busy ignoring what was staring them dead in the face—the Ruskies invading Ukraine was one hell of a red flag—and making fun of us good folks who *knew* what was coming, we were minding our own and building this place.

"How long did all this take?" Tip looked around in awe as Jones led them toward a larger building in the dead center of the cavern. It too, was painted stark white, and sported a tall spire and white cross at one end.

"Five, maybe six years in all," Jones told him. "Started out with just a handful of us in our own bunkers, but then we figured it best to join forces and work together."

It encouraged Lump to hear the guy say that: perhaps their trip out to the valley would be as fruitful as Tex had hoped. "That really is no time at all for… *this*." He swept his arm wide to indicate what appeared to be a thriving small town.

"I have to confess," Jones said. "A lot of the work was done for us—Mother Nature had made a whole system of caverns down here a long time ago. All we had to do was join 'em up and add the details. We even found a pocket of natural gas under the place—enough to keep the lights on for long after we've gone."

"You did good, Aaron," Tip said.

"For a bunch of looney tune, gun-toting hillbillies?" Jones grinned. "We're so civilized down here; I even surprise myself some days."

Arriving at the church, Jones pushed open the wide double doors and ushered his three visitors inside.

"Wow." Rhino's voice echoed within the place, carrying high into the rafters.

"There's a natural arch in the rock—about six stories up," Jones said, following Rhino's gaze up to the ceiling. "So, we built our church under it—glory be to God and all that. Actually, it's more than just a church—it doubles as our town hall, live music and dance hall… anything that involves getting the townsfolk together goes on here. Except for the drinking and whoreing, of course, because that just wouldn't be right in God's house."

Lump opened his mouth to say something, but really couldn't be sure if Jones was joking or not—his deadpan face certainly was giving away nothing either way.

"So, what brings you guys all the way out to the badlands?" Jones sat himself down at one of the two dozen circular tables that filled the church—the pews had been pushed against the side walls and a large space in front of the carved-stone font remained cleared. The place looked like they were getting ready for a formal dinner-dance.

Lump, Rhino, and Tip sat themselves around the table; their heads turned as footsteps echoed behind them.

Jones's bearded henchmen made their way through the church doors and with them walked a tall, dark-skinned, slim woman.

"Ahh, thank you for joining us, my darling." Jones stood up to greet the woman; she kissed him firmly on the lips. "Gentlemen, this is Angel, my good lady wife. Angel, this is Rhino, Tip, and John—*Lump*."

"Odd name," Angel said as she shook Lump's hand—her skin felt dry, rough; the woman was no stranger to hard work.

"Long story from my military days, thanks to Tex," Lump told her as she courteously shook hands with Rhino and Tip.

Then, formalities over, Angel sat herself down next to her husband.

The black-clad, bearded guys remained standing a handful of paces behind Lump and his comrades.

"Thank you for agreeing to see us," Lump began. "And for welcoming us into your home."

"It was either that or shoot you down before you got halfway across the valley," Jones said with a dry laugh.

"You're lucky you didn't come tearing down the riverbed in big trucks and four-by-fours and such."

"You'll have to forgive my husband." Angel leaned forward a little, and Lump saw what a true beauty she was. "He spends most of his days hoping for something to shoot at."

"It's all kinda dried up this past year or two," Jones lamented. "I can barely recall the last time we saw any kind of game down this way. There was a time you couldn't toss a rock without hitting a wild boar or a deer, or even a damned rabbit. Now, though…"

"It's the same where we are," Lump told him. "Out in the forest, there's not much left at all—the heat has driven them all away."

"You guys seem to be doing okay, though," Tip said to Angel. "I guess you stockpiled plenty of food."

Angel shook her head. "Not as much as you might think," she said. "We brought in a few more people than we'd planned for and taken in a few along the way—our supplies are running a little low."

"You still have plenty of ammunition, though?" Rhino chipped in; he looked uncomfortable in the hard, wooden chair.

Jones nodded. "Yeah, but you can't eat bullets."

"So, if it's supplies you're looking for, I'm afraid we have none to spare," Angel added with finality.

"It's not," Lump replied.

"So, why are you here?"

"Well, with the way things are out there, we want to propose an alliance."

"Do you now?" Jones leaned back in his chair and eyed his guests with some suspicion.

"What makes you think we'd want to form any sort of alliance with the Little Alamo?" Angel directed her question solely at Lump. "What do you have to offer that we don't already have here?"

"You said yourself supplies are running short." Lump figured it best to be direct—the woman clearly had no patience for wasting time. "And we saw what I'm guessing used to be farmland as we crossed the valley. Looks to me like those fields haven't yielded anything in a year or two."

"Almost three now," Jones corrected. "Once the creek dried up and it got too damn dangerous to set up any kind of irrigation out there, everything just died and turned to dust."

"You have trouble from the nomads?" Tip asked him.

"Yup," Jones snorted. "And the Red River Gang, and a couple of the compounds that used to be nearby."

"Used to be?"

"They came after what we had, so we went and took what they had," Jones said with a hardness in his tone that had Lump worried.

"You raided them?" Rhino asked the question forming on Lump's lips.

"We had no choice, John," Angel intertwined her fingers and rested them beneath her chin. "We did what we had to do to survive—I'm sure you would have done the same."

Lump wasn't sure Tex would ever sanction a raid on anyone else's compound no matter how much of a threat he considered them to be.

"These are different times, my friends," Jones added. "*Troubled* times, and it's kill or be killed, I'm sorry to say."

"We still have some functioning fields and livestock," Lump got back to the reason he was there. "And we are bigger, well-fortified, and have the manpower and weaponry to support you people—should you need it." He figured it wouldn't hurt to remind Jones and his good lady wife they'd be hopelessly outgunned should they decide to plan any kind of raid on the Little Alamo.

"We also have the capacity to expand our compound to accommodate more people, if necessary," Rhino said.

"For if we get tired of living like gophers?" Angel flashed a broad, white smile. "I think we're okay just where we are, thank you."

"It would take a lot of work for you guys to expand down here," Lump pushed. "I can't begin to imagine the logistics of dynamiting out more rock with people living here—I guess it was much easier when it was just caves?"

"We'll manage just fine." Jones appeared to be growing agitated.

"We have no plans to expand beyond our current capacity," Angel assured. "We will not take in any more outsiders, and we have an efficient planned parenthood system in place—we advocate effective birth control to *all* our citizens."

Lump cringed at the woman's inference but chose not to ask questions—how the Joneses and their people maintained a survivable population level really was none of his concern.

"And when your food supplies run out?" Tip asked Jones. "What then?"

Aaron Jones leaned forward in his chair and rested calloused, broad fingers upon the table. "There are always other compounds to go at, and then there's those folks holed up in the cities—I hear there's some rich pickings to be had for anyone with the willingness and ability to travel."

Angel stood up, her willowy frame towering over Lump, Tip, and Rhino. "Thank you for coming, guys," she addressed all three. "It's always nice to meet fellow survivors—we don't get too many visitors as you can imagine."

Lump got to his feet; he was totally deflated. The trip had been a waste of time, and the mission to make allies of Jones and his prepper commune was an absolute bust. All

Lump felt he'd achieved was to alert Aaron Jones of the Little Alamo's presence—he thanked God he hadn't divulged its exact whereabouts.

Although, that wasn't to mean Jones and his wife wouldn't have them followed on the way back…

"Thank you for talking to us." Lump shook hands with Angel and then Jones. "If you do change your mind, please give us a holler on the radio."

Angel ignored him, and so did her husband.

Instead, they shook hands with Tip and Rhino and made it clear to the visitors it was time for them to leave.

Chapter Nineteen

It was late afternoon the next day before Lump sought out Tex, who was just on his way from the veterinary clinic; he'd taken Winnie in for a checkup with Cory Mulgrew because he'd been limping a little on his back legs. Mulgrew had assured Tex the dog was just getting a little old and his joints weren't quite as supple as they used to be. He'd advised Tex to let the dog have a few more bones to chew on for extra calcium and sent him on his way.

As Tex walked along the street, Winnie trotted calmly by his feet.

"I was beginning to get worried about you, Lump," Tex said with a sardonic smile—if there was ever one person in the world he *didn't* have to worry about, it was Lump, even though his friend was tired, dusty, and stank of sour horse sweat.

"Rhino and me figured it'd be a good idea to camp overnight to rest the horses and make sure we weren't followed."

Tex grew concerned. "Followed? Why on earth would you be followed?"

"Our meeting with Aaron Jones didn't exactly go according to plan," Lump told him.

Tex's stomach sank; was Lump about to tell him Rhino and Tip were dead?

"Quit panicking, Tex," Lump read his mind. "Rhino and Tip are getting cleaned up and hitting the hay—I didn't want to keep you waiting for the debrief."

Relieved to hear that, Tex remained concerned about what he'd imagined to be a straightforward reach out to the Jones compound. He hoped his idea hadn't put the Little Alamo in any danger.

"Let's go grab a couple beers," Tex said and upped his pace in the direction of the John Wayne; Winnie scampered to keep up, his tongue lolling from the side of his mouth like a little pink worm.

Once there, with cold beers secured, Tex listened intently to Lump as he recounted the meeting he'd had with Aaron Jones and his statuesque wife.

"They had no interest in working with us at all?" Tex struggled to believe that had been the response to the Little Alamo's olive branch.

Lump shook his head and slurped at his beer. "If anything, I got the impression they were offended by the suggestion," he told Tex. "I guess they'd been preparing for all of this long before even we were. They're pretty much entrenched in their underground hideout, too, even though they're starting to run out of things like everybody else. I wish you could have seen what they've got there, Tex—it really is something."

"Maybe I will, someday," Tex said, although he doubted very much it would ever be the case; Lump and his posse's reception there strongly suggested they weren't welcome back.

"There is one thing…" Lump sounded hesitant. Taking a hearty chug of beer, he drained almost half the pint glass.

Tex narrowed his eyes; he knew when Lump had

something he needed to get off his chest, something his friend knew he wouldn't necessarily like hearing. "Come on, Lump, spit it out."

"Aaron Jones told us they raid other compounds." Lump spoke so fast it came out as almost one long word. "Smaller, less armed ones—he said that's how they've survived the past year or so."

Tex took a long drink of his own beer; the news was shocking, but not entirely unexpected—he'd known for some time it wasn't just the nomads and Red River Gang out there causing mayhem. "Are they a threat to us?" he asked.

"I don't think so," Lump replied. "I made sure to let them know we outmanned and outgunned them—just in case."

"Good call." Tex raised a hand at the barkeep—he needed another beer.

"It might not be a bad idea," Lump ventured, his voice hesitant.

"What's that?" Tex wasn't following; his mind was churning over the potential threat posed by Aaron Jones. Sure, Lump had been sure to let the preppers know the Little Alamo was more than prepared to repel any hostile action, but would that be enough to deter them if they got hungry enough?

"The smaller compounds," Lump lowered his voice as a pretty waitress brough over another two beers. "There are still some around—especially out west…"

Tex was taken aback by his friend's inference. He scratched his head beneath his hat as he thought. "You're not suggesting we mount raids on them, are you?"

Lump's silence spoke volumes.

Taking a moment to sip at his frosty beer, Tex studied his second-in-command. He'd definitely changed over the past year or so—he'd taken the hardships faced by the

Little Alamo to heart as if it was somehow his fault and had called into question Tex's decisions on more than one occasion. Especially when it came to allowing outsiders in.

But the two still remained good friends, and that was something Tex was determined to hold on to.

"We couldn't do that," Tex told Lump.

"Why not?" Lump played absently with the condensation on the side of his beer glass.

"Because it's… it's just *wrong*, Lump." Tex was surprised he even had to say it; there was a time when Lump and him were on exactly the same page. "Those folks have as much right to live their lives as we do—it's not our place to take that away from them."

"But it's our responsibility to take care of our own, Tex," Lump argued. "We're overcrowded, under resourced, and it's only going to get worse. What's gonna happen if we get another bad winter? On top of this hot summer we're having, it would be a disaster."

"We'll manage, Lump—we always do."

"The food is gonna run out, Tex," Lump was clearly fighting to keep his voice down; he knew better than to cause panic with loose words. "The forests are empty out there—where do you expect us to find more food?"

Tex took off his hat and ran a hand through his hair; it had seemed a lot thinner in recent months. "If we ration and pull as much from the fields as we can, we can make it. And there's always the option of sending hunting parties further afield—there are thousands of square miles of woodlands and prairies a few days west of here."

"There's also a whole bunch of smaller forts and compounds," Lump added. "Even if they're struggling, they'll have food, fuel, ammunition, medicine… all the stuff we're running dangerously low on. And, even if there's good hunting, that would only get us *food*, Tex, and we need more than wild boar meat right now."

Tex could only nod; Lump was speaking from the heart, and he was making some sense—no matter how abhorrent his suggestion. But there had to be an alternative means of securing what the Little Alamo required to see its people through until the weather changed and the crops and livestock thrived once more.

"We could send a posse out to Fort Worth, Dallas, maybe even San Antonio or Houston," Tex suggested. "We have the vehicles and fuel for that right now—especially if we use the LPG and hybrids."

Lump shook his head and downed a gulp of his beer. "We don't know for sure what's left in the cities, Tex. From what we're hearing in the few radio communiques getting through, survivors have built strongholds that would put the Little Alamo to shame. And they're protecting their supplies with deadly force—you're not the only one consider venturing into one of the cities to claim easy pickings."

"I wasn't suggesting it would be easy—"

Lump waved away Tex's protest with a flap of his hand. "It would be reckless, Tex, and you know it. And that's not to mention running across nomads and the Red River Gang out there—and that's not an *if*."

It pained Tex to admit it to himself, but Lump was making a good point. "We can't just mount raids on other compounds, Lump," he said. "That's not who we are here."

"It's not who we *were*, Tex." Lump said. "But times have changed since we planned the Little Alamo, and we have to adapt or…"

Lump didn't have to say it.

"Look, Tex," Lump leaned forward and rested his elbows on the table. "We've taken in a lot of strays since we settled here—far more than we even planned for. People are sharing their homes, and we can't get enough lumber fast enough to build more, let alone expand the boundary walls. Things are getting volatile between the original settlers and the newcomers, and it's only gonna get worse if we have to start rationing."

"We only reached out to Aaron Jones to form an alliance," Tex said. "I had no intentions of inviting them to come stay—unless they helped us to expand, of course."

"Jones doesn't *need* us," Lump replied. "They have everything they need and are far more secure in their underground bunker than we are in the forest. And, if they run low on something, they just go out and take it."

Tex shook his head; it was all so very wrong. He hadn't put all his time and energy into building the Little Alamo and creating a community to degenerate into a band of savage marauders no better than the Red River Gang. Then again, he had created the Little Alamo community with the primary objective of providing a safe haven for good folks in times when the rest of the world had gone to hell in a handbasket. And that meant ensuring their survival for when things returned to some semblance of normality out there and society needed rebuilding—even if that future might be several generations away.

"I'll give it some thought, Lump," Tex heard himself saying. "I promise. We'll always put the needs of our people first, you know that."

That appeared to appease Lump. Easing back in his chair with his beer glass clasped in both hands, he shot Tex a look that went way back to the early days of their friendship. "I know you'll do the right thing, Tex," he said and then took a long drink of his beer.

"I… er… I started seeing Victoria again," Tex ventured, as keen to change the subject from raiding possies as he was to share his good news.

"Seriously?" Lump's interest seemed piqued. "I thought you blew it with her?"

Tex shook his head. "Me too, but we'd been getting

closer over the past few months, and it looked to me like she'd put our past… *differences* behind her."

"So, you went in for the kill, you old horndog?!"

It was good to hear Lump laughing again. "No… nothing like that." Tex stammered—his old friend always did have the ability to get him tongue-tied.

"You mean to tell me you haven't sealed the deal yet?" Lump looked around to see if any of the bar's patrons had heard him.

"No," Tex hissed. "I'm taking it slow this time. Lee has gotten fond of her—she's kind of a mother figure to the kid now—and I don't intend to spoil that for him."

"Spoken like a wise man of the world, my friend," Lump said, tipping Tex a wink. "If it was me, I'd—"

"I know what you'd do, Lump, and you're an animal!" Tex's hearty guffaw resounded about the bar, and he and Lump got to talking about women and matters far less grim than attacking other compounds.

Chapter Twenty

The late-night air still held much of the day's heat but was nonetheless pleasant. The pond sat glassy still; the lone swan was asleep in the thick clump of reeds beneath the bridge.

"Thank you for coming out so late," Tex said to Victoria.

"Of course." She slipped her arm into the crook of Tex's elbow as they strolled across the compound's green toward the wooden bench at its far end. "How could I possibly resist the invitation of a midnight stroll with you?"

"Easily," Tex joked. "Especially with these little bastards bugging us—pardon my French." He flapped a hand at the handful of mosquitoes that darted and whined around his head; it was depressing to note there weren't as many of the blood-sucking insects around that summer—even they were feeling the pinch.

"I did offer a dab of tea tree oil," Victoria admonished. "But, oh, no, the mighty Tex Pemberton wouldn't hear of it—said he didn't want to smell funny."

Tex smiled as Victoria's soft, melodic laughter drifted out across the still water. It was good to hear something so beautiful after his grim conversation with Lump back at the John Wayne.

The hardest part for Tex to swallow, of course, was that Lump was correct in everything he'd said; the only way the Little Alamo was going to survive with its bloated population would be at the expense of other, more vulnerable compounds and forts. And, while it sickened Tex to remind himself, much of the blame for that rested firmly upon his shoulders: he was the one who'd insisted they take in the refugees from Fort Simons along with the other displaced folks who'd happened by.

As it was, Tex couldn't really see any other way around it, other than sit on his hands and wait for starvation, civil unrest, and even mutiny to take hold.

"Penny for your thoughts?" Victoria looked up into Tex's face as they neared the wooden bench—*their* bench; she was a good seven or eight inches shorter than him and had to strain to make eye contact.

"Huh?" Tex grunted, unaware he'd been miles away, caught up in his own reverie. "Just thinking about the first time I set eyes on this place," Tex lied. "When we first drove out here to scope it out, it took us an age to find it—which kinda sealed the deal, bearing in mind what we'd come all this way for. You could barely see what was left of the house—it was all overgrown and falling apart. I found out later it used to be called the Donkey Farm—maybe they bred mules or some such—and the old boy who owned it drowned in the pond trying to save some kid's life while waiting on his girlfriend to come live with him. His daughter moved across country to Maine after he passed and left the homestead to rot. We got the land dirt-cheap, she said she was glad to be rid of it. Only thing I kept was the old mailbox that sits outside the library—and this pond, of course."

"You're a liar, Tex," Victoria teased. "But thanks for the story anyways." She sat herself down on the bench, tugging gently upon Tex's arm.

"Sorry." Tex eased himself into the space next to Victoria and put his arm around her shoulders; the heady scent of the poppies surrounding the bench wafted up to greet him. "I just got a lot of Little Alamo business on my mind right now—nothing I want to spoil our evening with."

The honest truth was, Tex would have liked nothing more than to be able to discuss Lump's proposal with Victoria, to talk through the moral and logistical problems it faced, and to have her just listen as he got some of the burden off his chest.

But.

Tex knew he couldn't. At least not so early on in their rekindled relationship. He already dared hope it would blossom into something much, much more, and he knew in his heart Victoria wouldn't approve of him even considering such a plan. Tex really couldn't bear the thought of driving Victoria away again.

"You know you can talk to me about anything," Victoria told him, and Tex wished it was true.

"I do," he lied. "Thank you—that means a lot to me." His eyes met hers, which shone bright in the cold light of the half moon, and he leaned in to kiss her welcoming lips.

"Ouch!" Victoria jumped back aways on the bench as the brim of Tex's hat collided with her forehead. "Don't you know it's polite to take off your hat when you're kissing your best gal?" She gave him a playful poke in the chest and laughed.

"Well, pardon me, ma'am," Tex said in his very best, put-on Texan drawl. He then removed his hat, placed it across his knees, and kissed Victoria properly.

"I've been looking forward to that all day," Victoria said when, finally, she broke the kiss.

Tex nodded. "Me too," he said.

"Thank you for asking to see me again… like this." Victoria slipped her hand into Tex's; his fingers enveloped hers. “I’d been hoping you would ever since…”

“I am sorry about that,” Tex replied. “I was grateful you kept on seeing Lee—he really looks up to you, and you’ve helped him through some difficult times.”

“I could never turn my back on him—no matter what happened between you and me—Tex. But I’m happy we’re kinda back on track again.”

Tex nodded his agreement and gave Victoria’s hand a loving squeeze. It was wonderful, perfect, just being there by her side on their bench in the moonlight—it felt *right*. It had been a long, long time since Tex had experienced the emotions Victoria was stirring up in him—in fact, he hadn’t felt anything remotely similar since his early days with Krista, and it scared him.

Yes, there was no denying it, Tex was falling in love with Victoria; she’d been a part of his life for so long, they’d been through so much together in the years since Rusty died in the desert, and he’d done everything he could to maintain a distance between them after what happened all those years ago.

“Yeah,” Tex sighed. “I’m happy we’re back on track, too, Victoria. I’m thinking it was kind of meant to be, ya know.”

Victoria leaned her head against Tex’s broad chest and let out a soft sigh of her own. “Don’t you be getting all soft and sentimental on me, now, Tex,” she said quietly, “I’m doing alright on that score all by myself.”

Tex squeezed her shoulder gently and pulled her close, relishing the heat of her body next to his, and together, they watched the silver light playing upon the dark water of the duck pond.

Chapter Twenty-One

Tip slowed his horse at the edge of the forest clearing. Raising a hand, he motioned for the rest of the hunting party to do likewise. The three horses behind him pulled up and all four men peered into the tree-lined gloom, listening for any tell-tale sounds of game.

They'd set out an hour before daybreak to get some miles in before dawn broke and the heat of the Texas day drove any decent-sized animals into the shade and away from the hunters. There had been a time the forest was plagued by wild pigs; the things had bred uncontrollably all through the Texas forests and grasslands to the point of becoming a state-wide nuisance. Some counties had even placed a bounty on each hog killed in an attempt to get the numbers down.

But that had been a long time ago, in the Before Times, and Tip could count on one hand the number he'd seen in the past twelve months, including the one they'd bagged the week before.

"We going in?" Wopat asked, his voice a loud whisper. Tip had requested the guy accompany him because he was one of the best hunters he'd come across. Too bad, though, about Woods—he was still nursing his wounded leg and was likely to be out of action for some time.

They'd gone a few miles further than the previous hunt; Tip hoped to find pigs and deer in the undisturbed part of the forest—it was far enough from the Little Alamo and any other compound to be not hunted out.

Or so he'd thought.

The place was silent, save for the morning song of the birds—nothing big enough to waste a bullet on, though—and the gentle rustle of the leaves overhead.

"Yeah—there's got to be something in here," Tip replied, then urged his horse slowly forward into the trees; he'd spotted what looked to be a game trail and guided his mare toward that.

Fifteen minutes into the forest, and Tip began questioning his strategy. Even if they did happen across hogs or deer, it would be virtually impossible to see them until the horses practically stepped on the darned things. The trees were densely packed together, the scrub thick and high, and the sun all but blocked by the verdant canopy overhead.

A silent wave from Wopat.

Tip stopped his horse and twisted around in the saddle.

Wordlessly, Wopat indicated something off to the right where the trees were a little less dense, and the faint sound of a babbling creek wafted on the air. He pointed Tip's attention to a golden shaft of sunlight that pierced the gloom between a pair of lofty pines; a large, dark-brown shape made its way through the undergrowth.

It was a wild hog, and the thing was around the size of a small bear.

Tip waved at his fellow hunters to dismount and slid from his saddle without making a sound—years of hunting experience had taught him how to remain almost invisible when tracking his prey.

The four hunters tied their horses to a nearby tree and crept forward toward where the boar had forced its way through the thicket between the trees; it made so much noise crashing through shrubs and snapping twigs underfoot that Tip and the others didn't need eyes on it to know where their quarry was.

Slowly, carefully, silently, Tip and Wopat took the lead and inched their way toward the pig; Tip kept an especially watchful eye out on his periphery: wild hogs rarely ventured out alone, which meant it was possible there'd be others around. And, while that boded well for the cooking pot back home, it also spelled danger for him and his men; wild hogs had a famously nasty streak and could easily eviscerate a grown man with their razor-sharp tusks in one go.

There.

Tip held up a hand to halt the others, then slowly, carefully, eased his rifle from his shoulder and took aim; he'd decided against his usual bow because of the thick forest—it was far easier for a bullet to cut through leaves and twigs than an arow.

The pig was thirty, no more than forty, yards away and was one of the biggest he'd seen. He reckoned the animal would weigh in around the four-hundred-fifty-pound mark and was already mentally chopping it into quarters for the trip home. It would be a good kill and would feed a lot of hungry mouths that evening.

A whistle.

The pig let out a startled grunt and lifted its head; its tusks glinted bright in the shaft of sunlight.

Tip turned his head to silently question Wopat and the others; all three shook theirs.

Which meant they were not the only humans in the forest.

A shot rang out, followed by the sound of heavy

footsteps crunching through the dry leaves and sticks on the forest floor somewhere off to Tip's left. The hog sniffed the air with disdain and ran full pelt into the darkness.

"*Shit.*" Tip hissed. Lowering his gun, he stared hard into the gloom to see who had fired off the shot at *his* pig.

It took a few minutes but, eventually, a handful of men appeared from between the trees, followed by a half dozen more. Each of them wore shabby camo fatigues and carried a hunting rifle; they tromped through the forest like they couldn't care less what they scared away. Tip had them pegged as Red River Gang the second he laid eyes on them—there was just something unmistakable about those murderous bastards he could spot from a mile away.

"I told you it was too far away to take the shot, you asshole!" the guy second along in the ragtag line of hunters was saying. "No freakin' way you were gonna hit a hog from that far back."

"Shut your mouth, Malachi," the man at the front snapped. "Just because *you* couldn't hit it from there, don't mean I couldn't."

"But you *didn't*, Clayton," came the retort. "You missed the damned thing by a fuckin' mile."

Tip held his breath as Clayton, a short, skinny guy with mean eyes and a thin-lipped mouth, spun around and aimed his hunting rifle at his comrade's heart. "What did you say to me?" he demanded; his loud, angry voice resounded through the trees and, Tip reckoned, scared away anything worth hunting for miles.

Malachi held up his hands in the universal gesture of surrender and took a couple steps backward. The others in the hunting party stepped to either side of him—it was clear they fully expected their leader to put a high-velocity bullet through the guy's chest.

"I didn't mean nothin' by it, Clayton," Malachi said,

his Texas drawl slow, thick. "I was just sayin', is all."

"Well, *don't*," Clayton growled, and after a tense half minute, he lowered his gun. Then, squinting in the direction the wild pig had run, he said, "I reckon I winged the bastard anyways—but it'll have gone to ground by now. We'd best get back."

Tip studied the intruders, the men who'd spoiled any chance he'd had of taking back a fat hog to the Little Alamo, and weighed up his options. He and his men could stay where they were and wait for the Red River guys to head home—and hope their paths didn't cross elsewhere in the forest—or they could engage and reduce the number of the marauding savages terrorizing the area.

Sure, Tip's party were outnumbered three-to-one, but they had the element of surprise on their side. He was confident that he, Wopat, and the others could take out half of the Red River Gang hunters before they knew what was happening.

Sean Wopat's hand on his shoulder startled Tip. Snapping his head around, he shot the guy a quizzical glance.

Slowly, Wopat shook his head.

He was right, of course—they had no idea if the Red River Gang had other hunters in the forest, a legion of armed men who'd appear as if from nowhere at the first sound of a gun fight. Tip would be of no use to the Little Alamo dead in the forest.

And so, the four hunkered down and waited for their uninvited guests to leave until long after they could no longer hear the heavy, careless footsteps—just to be on the safe side.

Chapter Twenty-Two

"Are you sure they were Red River?" Tex was alarmed by Tip's debrief on that morning's disastrous hunt—he'd deliberately had them go further afield in the hopes of striking a rich vein of game. That way, he wouldn't have to contemplate Lump's proposal.

Tip's face fell, his mood darkened, and Tex regretted questioning him and dredging up what had to be painful memories of the fall of Fort Simons.

"Yeah," Tip said quietly. "I'd know those bastards anywhere—I could almost smell their foul stink."

"Then, they're closer to us than we thought," Tex said. "Even if it was just a hunting party you happened across, it shows the Red River Gang have the same ideas as us—stretch out into the forests in search of fresh hunting…"

"And new compounds to raid," Lump threw in.

"If they're that far east, the nearest one will be the Timothy clan." Tex rubbed at his chin and let out a snort. "We really ought to warn them."

"I'll have Al radio them," Lump said.

Tex shook his head no. "I think it'll be best to go see Jed, deliver the message in person." He fixed his eyes upon

Lump—his inference clear between the two of them. "It's a good opportunity to check things out over there, make sure they have enough security and firepower for if the Red River Gang decide to pay them a visit."

Lump nodded. "I'll take Tip and Rhino—we'll go in the LPG Hummer, if that's okay. That way, we can cover more ground and get there before nightfall."

"I'll have it filled up for you," Tex told him. "I'll call ahead so Jed's expecting you—I'm sure he won't mind putting you three up for the night."

Lump smiled; Jed's hospitality was legendary among those who'd ever stayed at the Timothy compound—they made their own vodka from potatoes they grew in small allotments around the place and distilled it in the trio of stills they'd fashioned by hand from scrap metal. Tex had partaken on more than one occasion and suffered hangovers bad enough to put any lesser drinking man off booze for life.

"Jed'll take good care of you," Tex told his friend. "Just be sure to keep your eyes and ears open when you're out in the open—if the Red River Gang are scouting about, they're not going to ignore you."

"I'll pack extra weapons and ammo," Lump said.

"I'd say we bring the semi-automatics," Tip added. "If we get surrounded out on the grassland, we're gonna need them to shoot our way out."

"I'm hoping it doesn't come to that." Tex was troubled by the thought of his recon team being waylaid by anyone, let alone the Red River Gang. A pack of wandering nomads would be easy enough to frighten away, but an organized, heavily armed gang of bandits would be another thing altogether. Thankfully, the dark-gray LPG Hummer was heavily reinforced with steel thick enough to stop most bullets and carried plenty of firepower; the vehicle wouldn't have looked too out of place in a Road

Warrior movie.

Of course, there was the ulterior motive for taking what amounted to a small, armored tank to Jed Timothy's compound: a show of strength on behalf of the Little Alamo. While Jed had seen for himself what Tex's fort had to offer by means of accommodation and security, he'd not had the opportunity to see what they had as a potential offensive force.

It hurt Tex's heart to be even contemplating attacking Jed and his people, and he sincerely hoped he wouldn't have to, but, as Lump had told him earlier, it certainly wouldn't do any harm to at least recce the place for if it did. After all, if the Red River Gang had the Timothy compound in its sights, then someone was going to be taking their supplies, and, by Tex's reckoning, it may as well be the Little Alamo.

"Keep communications open," Tex told Lump. "We'll be standing by with backup if you need it."

"I think you know me better than that, my friend." Lump flashed Tex the cocky smile of old. "Since when did either of us need backup?"

Tex tipped his hat back, exposing his forehead. "Good point, Lump," he said with a wry laugh—he couldn't think of a single time.

It took a couple hours to load up the Hummer and, when it was good to go, Tex made sure he was there to see it off. Again, the burden of his responsibility as community leader weighed heavily upon his shoulders—there had been a time he'd have been first in line to head up any kind of mission, no matter how dangerous, and it saddened him to know he couldn't.

But he did have his next soiree with Victoria to look forward to. They hadn't made arrangements as such the evening before, but she'd let slip to Tex the following day was her turn to help out at the small compound library—

so, he'd planned to drop in and take her for dinner once she closed up for the night.

Tex saluted Lump, Tip, and Rhino as the Hummer made its way out through the Little Alamo gates and, as they swung closed behind it, he once again wished to dear God he was going with them.

Chapter Twenty-Three

Jed Timothy was as welcoming as ever, although Lump thought he detected a hint of reticence when he, Tip, and Rhino trundled up to the compound gates in the armored Hummer.

"It's always good to see you," Timothy greeted the three with a warm smile and firm handshakes. "I was only over at the Little Alamo a few days ago—what brings you here?"

Lump liked the guy—he was pretty much no-nonsense and got straight to the point, traits Lump could easily identify with.

"Tex asked us to come see you," Lump said as they walked across the dry dirt square in the center of the Timothy compound. The whole place was less than a fourth of the size of the Little Alamo and housed around four dozen souls—but it still felt homely and comfortable.

"Why?" Timothy slowed his step a tad.

"We came across a Red River Gang hunting party yesterday—they weren't far from here, just the other side of the forest," Lump told him. "Tex wanted to warn you."

"Couldn't he have done that over the radio?" Timothy asked as he ushered his three guests toward the compound's one and only bar, which was packed with smiling, happy patrons.

The place was nowhere near as big or grand as the John Wayne, but it was a bar nonetheless with swinging saloon doors just like on the old western movies. A sign above the double doors read: BAR. It was as no-frills as Jed Timothy himself.

Lump had anticipated the question but, given his ulterior motive for visiting the Timothy compound, it still put him a touch on edge. "Tex thought it best we deliver the news in person," he wheeled out the reply he'd prepared. "You never know who might be listening in on the airwaves."

"Fair enough." Jed Timothy appeared placated by that. He pushed open the saloon's double doors and ushered his three guests inside. "So, why did Tex not come himself? He too high and mighty to take a road trip now?"

"There's too much to be done back at the Little Alamo," Lump told Timothy. "Tex gets himself bogged down in all the detail stuff that goes with running a compound. You know how it goes."

Timothy cracked a smile. "We have forty-seven citizens here, there's not that much detail to get bogged down in."

"Gotchya." Lump returned the smile.

Timothy leaned an elbow on the bar and waved over the barmaid; she looked to Lump to be early twenties. She wore a short, form-fitting red dress that perfectly complemented the fiery mane of copper-colored hair resting upon her slender shoulders. Spotting she had no band on her wedding ring finger, Lump gave the gal his best smile and made a mental note to get to know her as the evening wore on.

"I'm only yanking your chain." Timothy grinned as he ordered up four beers. "About Tex, I mean—although, it would have been nice to have him over for a few cold ones, you know?"

Lump nodded; it had been a long time since he and Tex had sunk a few beers and chilled out together, and he missed the days when it had been a regular thing. But, with the problems the Little Alamo faced and his friend's dalliance with Victoria Hyatt, Tex had made himself unavailable for anything but business conversations in the John Wayne bar.

"I'll be sure to drag him along the next time we come over," Lump said.

"Good call," Timothy replied as a foaming quartet of beers appeared on the countertop. He handed one each to his guests, then raised his in a toast. "To friendship and allegiances… cheers!"

As Lump clinked glasses with Timothy, Rhino, and Tip, he fought hard to shake off the gnawing sensation at the back of his mind—he reckoned it was his conscience pricking him, which was nothing a few more beers wouldn't solve.

Jed Timothy shepherded Lump and the others to a table at the end of the bar. It had been kindly vacated by a group of five young men, so their compound leader could sit down. "Much obliged, gentlemen," Timothy thanked the men as they made their way to stand at the bar with a respectful tip of their wide-brimmed hats.

More beers followed and then came the homemade vodka shots, by which time Lump was more than a little merry. He saw Tip and Rhino were well on their way to inebriation, and Rhino had caught the pretty barmaid's eye. Lump was disappointed by that, as he'd planned to make a move once the drinking let up—but he remained philosophical about missing out on some female company and inwardly wished his comrade well.

"You're gonna have to give us the recipe for this stuff," Tip slurred at Timothy and tapped a finger at the half empty vodka bottle in the center of the table. The clear liquid within rippled invitingly.

"I could," Timothy replied, his speech remarkably coherent—Lump figured the guy was used to downing his compound's self-brewed liquor and wondered what damage it was doing to the man's liver.

"But if I did, I'd have to kill you!" Timothy added and then let out a loud, raucous laugh that had everyone in the bar looking in his direction.

Lump, Tip, and Rhino laughed along—it seemed Jed Timothy was not quite as sober as he appeared to be.

"Nah, I'm just joking around." Timothy clapped Tip on the shoulder and topped up all four shot glasses. "It's the potatoes," he added.

"I kinda got that," Tip chuckled and downed his drink in one.

"Yeah, but it's the *type* of potatoes." Timothy leaned in and said in a conspiratorial whisper, "Maris Piper."

"Who?" Lump was struggling to keep up; the potent Timothy clan vodka had truly clouded his head.

"The potatoes," Timothy told him. "Maris Pipers—I got the original seeds from England back in the Before Times."

Lump nodded wisely as if he had an idea what the guy was taking about; horticulture was definitely not Lump's strongpoint.

"It's something to do with the high starch content… or sugar… or some such," Timothy said with a lopsided grin.

"Whatever it is, it works just fine," Tip said and wiggled his small glass for a refill.

A couple more rounds and Rhino stood up, excused himself, and walked across to the bar. The place had emptied some due to the late hour, and the redheaded barmaid was looking bored. Her face lit up as Rhino approached, though, and her beautiful green eyes sparkled when he offered to buy her a drink.

"So," Timothy leaned in once more, his voice lowered. "I got the impression all is not well at the Little Alamo on my last visit," he said. "The honey was as good as it always is—that gal your have taking care of the hives knows how to get the best from her bees."

"Victoria has a special way with most things," Lump replied; his mind conjured up his old friend, Tex. He was pleased he'd found happiness after so many years alone but could only hope the sentimental old fool wouldn't get complacent once he'd found love. He also hoped Tex wouldn't get his heart broken—it had taken him long enough to get over Krista's death to even contemplate dating another woman.

"We're doing okay," Lump said.

Timothy shook his head. "I saw what I saw," he replied. "We're going through a few trials and tribulations here—I think everyone is right now—so I know the signs, my friend."

The guy was either sharper than he appeared to be, or the situation back at the Little Alamo was worse than Lump had thought. Sure, Tex had confided in him things were getting tight when it came down to food and fuel, but they'd done their best to hide the fact from the people. Tex had said he didn't want to start a panic or any unrest, but Timothy's comment had Lump wondering if the guy was hiding something more from him.

"We've had better years," Lump admitted. "This hot summer sure as hell hasn't helped at all. It's the first time we've gotten nothing out of our fields."

"I hear that," Timothy said. "We're lucky we have plenty canned and dry goods to see us through a coupla bad harvests—and a whole bunch more Maris Piper seeds, of course." He pointed at the vodka bottle and tipped Lump a playful wink. "I guess having fewer mouths to feed than big forts like yours helps—and it means fewer folks breeding, too."

Lump thought back to Aaron Jones and the draconian birth control methods he'd alluded to, and wondered if Jed Timothy was enforcing something similar to keep his own population down to a manageable level. But, if it meant the survival of the community, who was Lump to judge?

"That makes good sense," Lump said.

"So, how long do you reckon you guys have got?" Timothy's pointed question took Lump by surprise. He glanced across at Tip in the hope of having him interject, but the guy was barely conscious. He just sat in his chair staring across the bar where Rhino was getting better acquainted with the barmaid—very much lights on, nobody home.

Lump shrugged. "Difficult to tell," he replied. "We have some livestock, canned and dried food, and fuel for the vchicles—although we're using horses when we can. Then there's the honey, of course, and we're surrounded by wood for the furnaces."

"So, how long?" Timothy pushed.

Lump eased back in his chair and glanced around. His alcohol-fogged brain lumbered along, its filters well and truly compromised. "Tex will deny it, but I'd say six months… a year if we *really* ration out the food."

Timothy sucked in air between his teeth; the thin gap there made a low whistling noise. "Then what?"

"The hope is, the weather will ease up and the crops will take hold next season," Lump told him.

"That's still eight, maybe twelve months away," Timothy stated the obvious. "How is Tex gonna keep all those people happy and fed while they wait for the corn to grow?"

It was Lump's turn to lean forward and lower his

slurred voice, tongue loosened by his host's vodka. "Tex and me have been talking about taking a leaf out of the Red River Gang's playbook," he said. "We reckon if we… *absorb* a few of the smaller compounds, we'd have enough to get by."

Jed Timothy's expression changed in a heartbeat. "You mean take in *more* people?"

The shake of Lump's head was barely perceptible. "Not necessarily," he said.

"Oh." Timothy sat back in his wooden bar chair and folded his arms across his chest. "I can't believe Tex would ever think that was a good idea—he's just not that kind of a man."

"Desperate times lead to desperate measures, my friend." Lump's tongue suddenly felt too fat for his mouth and his stomach churned wildly.

"Desperate enough to come take what we've got?" Timothy's words sounded cold, a far cry from the bonhomie he and Lump had been sharing over their drinks.

"No, no, *no*," Lump's reply felt forced. "We'd never, *ever* do anything like that—you have my word, Jed."

"That's comforting to know." Sarcasm dripped from the man's words.

Lump squinted across the table at Timothy—the guy's face was blurred, along with the rest of the bar—and knew he'd said too much. A jolt of nervous adrenaline sharpened Lump's mind just enough to let him know there was nothing he could say to backtrack on the inference he'd made: That the Little Alamo was planning to raid nearby, smaller compounds for their resources. And, although it was only something Lump had asked Tex to *think* about, Jed Timothy knew such a strategy would put his compound firmly within their sights.

Shit.

"We would never…" Lump began, but his tongue

failed him; Timothy's renowned vodka had won.

"I'd say it was time we turned in, don't you?" Timothy stood up. "There is a guest room set up for you and your colleagues upstairs." He nodded at the silent Tip and cast an icy glance across at Rhino, who had coaxed Redhead out from behind the bar and onto the bar stool next to his—they looked to be deep in conversation, and he had his arm around her trim waist.

Lump struggled to his feet, then helped Tip to his. "G'night, Jed," he managed to say.

"Goodnight, gentlemen," Timothy said as he walked away.

Shit.

Chapter Twenty-Four

It was still dark when the gray Hummer set off through the Timothy compound's gates; sunrise was an hour or so away and, even though Lump's head throbbed, he'd wanted to get an early start and avoid Jed Timothy.

Lump had told Tip and Rhino the reason for the ungodly hour was to put some ground between them and any Red River hunting parties that may be out and about and because he'd planned a different route home in order to scope out more of the wilderness.

He had no intention whatsoever of telling them how badly he'd put his foot in it with Timothy the night before.

Tip was badly hungover but at least awake and staying upright, and Rhino seemed barely affected by the previous night's revelry. That being said, he'd eased off the vodka with every intention of getting cozy with the redheaded barmaid. It was a strategy that had paid dividends, and Rhino had spent the night in the arms—and bed—of the gorgeous young gal. He'd also been less than delighted at being dragged away from her modest, wooden cabin while it was dark outside.

And, because Rhino had the clearest head of the three, Lump had insisted he drive.

"Why are we heading south?" Rhino demanded, his

mood not so jovial.

"We need to see what's down there," Lump told him; he hoped the guy would lighten up sometime soon, otherwise it was going to be a long, miserable journey for all three of them in the Hummer.

"No shit, Sherlock," Rhino sneered, and Tip chuckled from the back seat.

"Tex and me figured since we were out this way, we should recce the surrounding area," Lump lied—Tex had agreed to no such thing. "And with running into the Red River Gang yesterday, we could do with knowing where the hell they're hiding out here. They can't be too far from where we saw them, because they were either on foot or horseback."

"Makes sense to me," Tip chipped in from behind. "What do you say, Rhino?"

"What I say is you guys owe me big time—I was game on for a morning roll in the hay." Rhino groaned. "Shannon really was quite something in the sack."

"Thanks for sharing that with us, Rhino," Lump said, surprised at the tiny prick of jealousy he felt at the thought of the guy enjoying the redhead. Then, perhaps if he'd acted on his first instinct and approached the clearly accommodating barmaid, he wouldn't have let slip to Jed Timothy his and Tex's idea of raiding other compounds.

Now, that was a shitshow Lump hoped wouldn't bite him on the ass. If Timothy breathed one word to Tex, there'd be hell to pay.

"You're a lucky guy," Tip threw in. "She looked like a keeper."

"Hey, let's not get carried away here." Rhino forced out a strained laugh, and Lump was pleased to see the guy's mood was lifting a touch. "Shannon and me had a hot night of passion, is all. It's not as if I asked her to marry me or anything."

"So, you'd turn her down if we came back?" Tip was baiting him.

"Well..." Rhino mulled it over a beat or two. "That would be rude, wouldn't it?"

The three laughed together, the status quo once more balanced between them, and Lump was left to quietly contemplate what trouble he might have caused all thanks to Jed Timothy's damned Maris Piper vodka.

"What's that?" Tip broke the silence and disturbed Lump's thoughts.

"What?" Rhino peered through the windshield. The sun was just beginning to appear over the horizon; it cast an eerie, yellow-orange glow across the flat, dry landscape that spread out for as far as the eye could see.

Lump leaned forward in his seat, his brain suddenly alert, his eyes searching. "Slow up," he told Rhino.

As the Hummer slowed to a crawl, a collection of small triangular peaks came into view.

"Tents." Lump's quick estimate told him there was about sixty, maybe seventy, two-man tents along the gently sloping side of a dry river valley. There were red tents, blue, some khaki, others green—a veritable mishmash of sleeping quarters for what had to be up to 150 people.

"Red River," Tip growled with hatred in his voice.

"You sure?" Lump asked, although there was little doubt in his mind.

"It's one of their raiding gangs. I saw them before like this," Tip told him. "Just before..."

"You want me to get closer?" Rhino had eased off the gas completely; the Hummer rolled silently forward under its own momentum.

"No."

Rhino hit the brakes, and the vehicle came to a sudden stop. "What are we gonna do, Lump?"

"We should radio it in," Tip offered.

"We do that, and we tell all those sleeping beauties over there where we are and that we have eyeballs on them," Lump said. "The best we can do is make a note of the location and head back."

Lump gazed out across the small, distant, multicolored sea of canvas and wished he had the means—and firepower—to lay waste to every Red River Gang member while they slept. It would be a terrific coup and rid the wilderness of the thieving, murderous scum. And it would pave the way for the Little Alamo follow in their nefarious footsteps.

"Turn her around, Rhino." Lump heard the regret in his own voice; a good soldier never turned away from a fight.

"I say we skirt around the forest," Rhino offered. "That'll give us some cover until we get closer to home."

"Good call," Lump said as his comrade tapped the gas and maneuvered the Hummer in the opposite direction to the Red River Gang's encampment.

Even though Rhino drove as close to the shade afforded by tree line as possible, it was hot, unbearably so. The Hummer's air conditioning only worked at around half capacity because the refrigerant gas was running low and, of course, there was nothing to replace it with—it hadn't been deemed essential when the Little Alamo was being stocked up. In Lump's mind, that had been one hell of an oversight on Tex's behalf—they lived in the semi-arid region of Texas, for Christ's sakes!

Still, half capacity was better than nothing at all.

"How far?" Tip asked.

"Another three hours, maybe four." Rhino told him.

Tip let out an exasperated sigh, like some spoiled kid impatient to get to the rollercoasters.

"It'll give us time to scout around," Lump said. "See

what's out this way." His mind tormented him with the clumsy *faux pas* he'd made the night before and Jed Timothy's blunt reaction—at least Rhino and Tip hadn't asked why the compound's leader hadn't been there to see them off that morning. That would have made for some awkward explaining.

"What are we scouting *for*, exactly?" Tip wanted to know.

Lump shrugged his broad shoulders; his conversation with Tex regarding potentially raiding smaller compounds and forts was strictly on a need-to-know basis, and as far as Lump was concerned, only he and Tex needed to know until the plans were laid.

"Just whatever's out here," Lump said. "Any game that's still around, nomads, Red River Gang, small compounds we don't know about… you know the drill, Tip."

Tip nodded and peered out of the window.

The first crack of gunfire came from out of nowhere; not one of the three in the Hummer saw any sign of life, let alone someone using the vehicle for target practice.

"*Shit*!" Rhino growled as the bullet ricocheted off the reinforced passenger side door with a loud, metaling *ping*.

The next shot zipped through the Hummer's rear window, leaving a neat, round hole in the middle of the spider-webbed safety glass. Tip dropped down to the rear seat and, at first, Lump thought the guy had been hit; a quick glance told Lump that, thankfully, Tip was okay.

Startled, heart pumping, Lump stared out of each of the vehicle's windows in turn as Rhino steered it into the forest, crashing through the shrubs and dry undergrowth between the trees.

Another shot—it missed.

"Where the fuck are they?" Rhino snarled.

"No idea." Lump was forced to admit; the first shot

had come from their right flank, the second from behind, and he'd no clue about the origin of the third. "They could be anywhere."

"Or we could be surrounded," Tip offered from the back seat.

"Yeah," Lump agreed. "We need to be ready for if they close in." He hoped whoever was taking potshots at the Hummer was just trying to scare them off.

Rhino brought the vehicle to a juddering halt; the gaps between the towering pine trees had become too narrow to squeeze the Hummer through—the last thing they needed to do was get themselves stuck and become sitting ducks.

Lump grabbed his rifle from the back; Tip and Rhino followed suit. Rhino switched off the Hummer's engine, and the three sat in silence listening for anything to let them know if they'd been followed into the forest.

As it transpired, it didn't take too long for that question to be answered.

"Two o'clock!" Lump hissed as a trio of camo-clad figures appeared from the trees to his right.

"This side." Rhino grabbed for his door handle.

"We're surrounded," Tip threw in, peering out through the hole in the back window.

"I'm getting out," Rhino eased open his door and, using it as cover from the approaching men, crouched down on the forest floor.

Lump did the same—he knew that if they stayed in the Hummer, they really would be sitting ducks. At least out there among the trees, they'd have a good chance of fighting back or retreating, should they find themselves outgunned.

But Tip remained where he was; with the rear window cracked, it made for good cover—he could see out, but no one could see in. Lump figured the guy knew what he was doing and was grateful he'd volunteered to guard the vehicle.

Another shot rang out.

It zipped through the foliage above Lump's head to send a shower of shredded leaves and twigs down over his head.

A quick peek around the protective shield of the vehicle's door told Lump there were three men closing in on either side and three coming up from the rear. They were undoubtably Red River Gang—Lump could practically *smell* the thieving bastards.

Through the Hummer's open doors, Rhino indicated he was going to slip into the undergrowth at its front—there appeared to be no Red River guys coming in from that direction, and it would give Lump's team some advantage. And they certainly needed that being outnumbered three-to-one.

"Ya gonna come out an' make this easy on yourselves, fellas?" one of the Red River Gang shouted over, his voice muted by the thick forest. He was clearly the group's leader: he looked a little bit tidier than the rest, his gun was newer, and his camo gear less worn out. As Lump watched, he had his buddies all made their way toward the vehicle, rifles locked and loaded and aimed ready to kill.

Rhino made it to the undergrowth with a minimum amount of noise; not one of the surrounding men was alerted to the movement—the guy was a pro.

Another shot rang out, followed in rapid succession by three more, from all sides. Bullets bounced off the Hummer; Lump thanked God he and Tex had had the foresight to armor up the reconnaissance vehicles—and they'd decided not to visit Jed Timothy on horseback.

"*Hold yer fuckin' fire*!" The leader hollered above the loud reports. "Do you wanna fuck the car up?"

The gunshots ceased, but the Red River Gang continued on in Lump's direction.

Of course, it was the Hummer they wanted. And that meant they weren't about to give up until they got it—and Lump had a fight on his hands.

Holding his breath, Lump forced himself to stay patient as he waited for the Red River guys to be within easy range of the Hummer before opening fire. The knew the second he let fly the first shot he'd give away his position.

The three guys approaching Lump's side of the Hummer slowed their step twenty yards or so out. Treading through the dry leaf litter carefully, they held steady aim at the Hummer, no doubt watching for the slightest movement.

Lump knew he only had one chance to get his next move right, and he hoped Rhino and Tip were on the same page as him.

In a heartbeat, Lump ducked out from behind the open Hummer door, rifle at the ready, and let off a volley of fire at the Red River guys on his side. He heard shots from inside the vehicle and from where Rhino hunkered down among the trees.

Shouts filled the air along with return gunfire as Lump returned to safely behind the car's door. He'd seen two of the men on his side go down—one with a misty, red halo around his head as his skull exploded, the other with his right shoulder torn open.

Two down.

Lump hoped Rhino and Tip had been as fortunate.

Bullets punched into the Hummer's door. With a quarter inch of armor plating between them and Lump, the Red River guys were using some heavy-duty ammunition with a hell of a lot more penetrating power than they'd need for deer or wild boar. Lump cursed his own dumb luck: they hadn't run into hunters—it was a recon party out to hijack anyone they came across for anything they could get their hands on.

The stink of gunpowder filled the forest air and turned it into thick, cloying smoke that choked Lump's lungs. It was impossible to tell how many of the nine attackers were still standing, but the gunfire continued to come from all three directions.

A quick reload and Lump was ready to return fire. He made a recce of the scrub surrounding him and weighed the possibility of following Rhino's example and getting himself away from the Hummer. Since the vehicle was the focus of the enemy's attention, it might serve him well to get away from it and circle around to the rear of the Red River guys.

Lump poked his rifle's muzzle around the car door followed by his head. The gun bucked like a wild thing in his hands as he fired off shot after shot, ignoring the return fire that *thump-thump-thumped* into the Hummer's door and whizzed over his head like a swarm of angry gnats.

"Cover me!" Tip cried out, and Lump saw the rear door begin to swing open.

"*No*!" Rhino's disembodied voice rose above the cacophony of gunfire and the noise intensified as Tip opened the Hummer's door and threw himself out; bullets dug clods of dirt up around him.

Lump saw Rhino pop up from behind a thick tree trunk and let off four rounds at the two remaining Red River guys to the rear of the Hummer. One went down immediately with a surprised scream while the other spun around and fired in Rhino's direction.

There came the unmistakable cry of pain, a high arc of blood spray, and Rhino vanished behind the tree.

The Red River Gang closed in, and Lump knew his opportunity for taking cover in the forest was long gone—

they'd cut him down before he got so far as the nearest bush.

There was no other option but to shoot his way out

Chapter Twenty-Five

The Little Alamo

It was a pleasant enough afternoon. It was still oppressively hot, of course, and the citizens of the Little Alamo were either hunkered down doing indoors work or sticking to the shaded places around the wooden buildings. There were actually a handful of clouds up in the bright, blue sky, but they were thin and wispy with absolutely no chance delivering any rain; they'd burn off the second they moved across the unrelenting sun.

Nonetheless, Tex was happy enough to brave the heat and put up with his shirt sticking to his back if it meant getting to see Victoria again.

Since the night they'd walked to the bench by the pond and kissed with so much longing and passion, Tex had found it difficult to think of anything else. Naturally, he was still fulfilling his obligations as leader of the Little Alamo, only with the wonderful memories of that night and the happiness in his heart at being back with a chance of something meaningful with Victoria.

In keeping with the rest of the Little Alamo, the library was a modest, wooden building. It was situated at the opposite end of the main street to the John Wayne bar—a deliberate planning ploy to ensure library patrons got the peace and quiet they deserved to enjoy reading. Tex recalled with fondness planning and building the library back in the compound's construction days—he'd based the design upon the tiny, brick-built library he'd frequented back in his hometown growing up. The place had been his refuge, where he would escape his father's drunken rages among the pages of Hemmingway, Dickens, Salinger, Orwell, and so many more, and so Tex thought it a fitting tribute to recreate it within the safe walls of the Little Alamo.

He'd even instigated the same drop-off system as his childhood library, which consisted of the old mailbox he'd rescued from demolition when they'd leveled the old Donkey Farm to build the Little Alamo. The mailbox still had half its original address on the front—CR 1350—and Tex had resisted everyone's insistence he write a brand new one over it.

There was history embedded in what remained of that address, albeit a tragic one, and Tex didn't feel anyone had the right to paint over it.

As things worked out, the drop-off scheme had come in handy as the Little Alamo needed to conserve power. The library was open just four hours a day, four days a week in order for the kids to get some reading time in, so the mailbox idea was perfect for folks wanting to return books. Not that anyone got fined like in the good ol' days of Tex's town library, but it meant the limited number of books were kept in circulation.

"Hello," Tex said as he walked in; the rush of cool air on his face was most welcome.

A bunch of faces turned his way, and Tex was pleasantly surprised to see just how many people were taking advantage of the library. And to think Lump and the others had tried to talk him out of it—they argued the space, lumber, and manpower would be better off being utilized on something else.

Victoria, from behind her desk, looked up at Tex from over the book she'd been reading. For a split-second, he thought she was going to put a finger to her lips and *shush* him like the crusty old dragon librarians of old.

Instead, she smiled and said, "Hello, Tex. It's wonderful to see you." She placed her book face down upon the countertop. "Have you come in for something good to read?"

Tex blushed a tad; the truth was he'd barely set foot in the Little Alamo library since the day he'd arrived. He knew Lee was a frequent patron, as the boy always seemed to have a book on the go—he was a huge fan of science fiction and westerns. As for Tex, there just didn't seem to be enough time in the day to so much as pick up a book let alone immerse himself in one.

But that didn't mean he couldn't make the time.

"I came in to see you, actually," Tex told Victoria. "You said you'd be working here today so I figured…"

"You figured you'd stalk me?" Victoria said with a warm smile. "That's kinda cute, Tex."

Tex felt the color rise up in his cheeks some more and quickly changed the subject. "If you do have a book you could recommend…"

"I'd love to," Victoria reached out and, briefly, surreptitiously, squeezed his hand. "I think you'd like this one." She pointed at the book she'd been reading when he came in. It had a white cover with a sweet, artistic design that illustrated its title perfectly: *The Bridge*.

Tex's heart sank a little. "I'm not that big on romances," he said.

"I think you'll like this one," Victoria countered. "It's about an older widowed guy who falls hopelessly in love with a younger woman—I think they call them May-to-December romances.

Tex eyed the book with suspicion; the subject certainly resonated with him and how he was beginning to feel about Victoria, but could he *really* see himself reading some soppy romantic novel?

"It's kinda tragic, too," Victoria told him with a wink.

"Sold." Tex took the plunge; there was just something about the sweet expression on Victoria's face that tugged at his heartstrings. And besides, if it gave them a little common ground, something to talk about during what he hoped would be many more nighttime strolls, it would be well worth it.

"Perfect." Victoria took hold of Tex's hand again. Only, she didn't let go.

"You can pass it along to me when you finish it," Tex said.

"Oh, there's no need for that." Letting go of Tex's hand, Victoria bobbed down behind the counter, reappearing moments later with a pristine copy of *The Bridge* in her hand. "It seems there was some administrative screw-up, and a whole bunch of books got ordered twice," she slid the white-covered book across the counter to Tex. "And, lucky for you, this was one of them."

"Lucky me," Tex replied sheepishly.

"Give it a chance," Victoria said quietly. "I think you'll enjoy it. And… I promise I won't tell anyone you're reading a soppy romance story."

It was like the woman had read his mind.

"I can wait for you to catch up," she said. "Then we can discuss it together."

"Yeah," Tex was warming to the idea, "I'd really like that. Might you be free this evening?"

"That doesn't give you much time to dive into the book," Victoria teased. "But yeah, I think my social calendar is open this evening."

Tex was about to tell Victoria he was very much looking forward to it when the library's door crashed open and Josephina Garcia ran in, red-faced and very out of breath.

"Mr. Tex, you have to come!" she panted.

"Hey, what's going on?" Tex ushered Josephina to a nearby chair.

"It's Mr. Christie and the others—they came back and they are badly hurt…"

Tex's gut fell; just the thought of any of his people getting hurt sickened him, but Lump… he would never be able to forgive himself if his best friend was lost.

"Where are they?" He asked the distraught woman.

"The infirmary, with Dr. Barker."

All thoughts of books and reading with Victoria forgotten, Tex raced from the library like his boots were on fire—the only thing on his mind was losing more good people.

Chapter Twenty-Six

The Hummer was parked up outside the infirmary with all but one of its windows busted and deep pockmarks where countless bullets had hit along its full length.

As Tex ran by, he noticed blood smears on the passenger-side door and a thin trail leading into the infirmary. All he could do was pray he wouldn't be arranging funerals for the following day.

"Tex!" Hearing Lump's voice brought a huge wave of relief. Looking across the small vestibule, Tex saw his friend making his way over. Lump walked with a limp, his clothes darkened by drying blood, but otherwise he appeared to be okay—Tex figured if Lump had lost that much of his own blood, he wouldn't be walking, limp or otherwise.

Tex demanded. "Rhino? Tip?"

"Tip's gonna be okay—he got hit in the leg." Lump hesitated a beat. "Rhino took a couple in the chest and shoulder…"

"Oh shit," Tex groaned.

"Doc. Barker says we got him here just in time—his subclavian artery was hit, and he was close to bleeding out. He still won't give me a definite, but he said the next twenty-four hours will be critical."

Tex groaned again; it was the old, well-worn, clichéd doctor's reply for when a patient was at death's door—it wasn't the first time Tex had heard it. He figured it was their way of preparing people for the worst—next on the list was the "say your goodbyes, just in case" speech.

"What the hell happened out there, Lump?"

We came across the Red River Gang," Lump told him. "Looked like a scouting party to me—nine of the bastards."

"Looking for boar?"

Lump shook his head. "Looking for *people*," he said. "They were armed for raiding compounds and taking on the likes of us—we're lucky we got away with our lives. If Rhino hadn't driven us into the forest when he did, we'd have been picked off before the Hummer stopped."

"Where were they heading?"

"We came across a whole bunch of them camped out five, maybe ten miles from Jed Timothy's place," Lump said. "Must have been over a hundred-fifty of them. I reckon the guys we ran into were a recon team from there."

"Will they be reporting back about you?"

Lump shook his head. "We made sure all nine of them wouldn't be making it back to camp," he said. "As per orders."

"Good." It pained Tex to have to be the one to order the summary execution of anyone deemed to be a threat to the Little Alamo—life was precious, even if it was the Red River Gang—but when it came to the safety and security of his people, there really was no other choice he could make.

"My guess is they're on the way to Jed's," Lump added. "Another day, maybe two, and they'll be knocking on his door."

Tex ground his teeth. He'd sent Lump out to recce the Timothy compound with an agenda that would suit the

Little Alamo, but then the Red River Gang had popped up. It was inevitable they'd cross paths with the marauders at some point, but Tex hadn't wanted it to go down like that.

"We're gonna have to warn Jed," Tex told Lump, and thought he saw a glimmer of *something* cross his friend's face. "We can have them come here… and bring everything they can."

"That's another forty-seven people, Tex," Lump said. "Anything they bring will barely be enough to cover the extra bodies—they don't have the trucks to carry big loads."

Tex eyed Lump; the guy was telling him something he'd already worked out for himself, but what the hell was he supposed to do? The net gain of taking in Timothy's small population would definitely be in the negative.

Unless…

"We can send all our vehicles," he said. "We can more than triple what they can carry from their compound."

Lump looked at Tex as if he'd gone crazy, which Tex didn't much care for—surely he could see it would be better for the Little Alamo to take in Jed's people along with their provisions than have nothing at all. Sure, they could mount an attack straight away to take what the Timothy compound had and clash with the Red River Gang, but Tex didn't even want to think about what the cost of such action would be.

"I know what you're thinking, Lump," Tex said. "But there's really no other way around it. If we warn Jed now, we can get our vehicles over there by nightfall and have everyone back here by morning. If we send enough men, we could have everything we can carry loaded up and good to go. All that will be left for the Red River Gang will be empty buildings."

"I really don't think that's a good idea," Lump seemed adamant, which really wasn't like him. "We're already groaning at the seams here, Tex."

"You think I don't know that?" Tex snapped. "We already discussed expanding the walls here, Lump—with extra people to work, we can set to it straight away."

"And feed them what?"

"They'll come with food." Tex was growing exasperated. It seemed his old friend was hell-bent on simply raiding the Timothy compound and robbing them of everything they had.

Lump was about to reply when Andy Barker appeared as if out of nowhere. Fresh from the operating room, he still had on his pale blue scrubs, which were splashed with blood.

"How is he, Doc?" Tex asked.

The doctor gave him a nod, albeit a small one. "He's okay for now," he replied. "But, as I told Lump earlier, the next twenty-four hours will be make-or-break."

"He's gonna pull through, though?" Tex pushed.

Barker took in a deep breath as if attempting to hold back his exasperation. "If he makes it through to tomorrow, Mr. Rhino has a good chance."

Tex eyed the doctor and suddenly felt very small and very helpless; another of his people had been seriously hurt under his command and he was forcing the poor doctor to repeat himself, only in different words. "Sorry, Doc." Tex felt the apology was in order.

"He's lost a lot of blood, Tex," Doc. Barker told him. "And the blood bank's reserves are running low—we put as much as we dared into him."

"Rhino is a tough old bastard," Lump chipped in. "He'll pull through alright."

"I'm sure you're right, Lump." The doctor gave what was meant to be a reassuring smile—it came off as a grimace.

"Nobody care enough about me, then?" Tip hobbled into the waiting area from the treatment room, accompanied by his wife, Triss. One leg of Tip's pants had been cut away, his thigh wrapped in a neat, white bandage, and he supported himself by means of an aluminum crutch tucked under his left armpit. Triss walked slowly, patiently alongside her husband and shot Tex a withering look.

This is all your damn fault.

"Of course, I care," Tex strode over to give the wounded guy a hearty handshake. "Lump told me what happened out there—thank God you guys got out alive."

"How's Rhino?" Tip asked Doc. Barker.

"He's comfortable," Barker told him—Tex got the impression he was in no mood to go through the whole *next twenty-four hours* thing a third time.

"He's gonna be okay, Tip," Tex said, forcing a confident smile. "He's in good hands here." He nodded at the doctor and thanked his lucky stars they'd found the guy when they had.

"We're doing our very best," the doctor told them, managing expectations as well as he could. "I'll definitely keep you informed of Mr. Rhino's progress."

"I'm gonna head over to Communications," Tex said. "I need to let Jed know the Red River Gang are getting close."

"I could do that," Lump offered, and Tex thought he caught a hint of nervousness in the man's tone.

"No, you need to rest up," Tex said with firmness. "You've been through a lot, and I need you on your top game, my friend." He delivered a hearty slap on Lump's shoulder. "We'll talk later."

With that, Tex headed out of the infirmary.

Chapter Twenty-Seven

"Hey, Tex," Al Mims greeted him with a warm smile. "How are the guys?"

"They're all good," Tex lied—he wasn't about to get into details. "I need to speak with Jed Timothy. Can you try to patch me through?"

"Sure," Mims said. "He doesn't always have his shortwave manned, but we can give it a go."

As Al set about twiddling the dials on the radio, Tex's mind wandered: there was something not quite right about Lump—the guy had things on his mind he clearly didn't want to spill. That alone was most unlike Lump; he and Tex had always been able to talk about anything, and that's what worried Tex. Had something gone down when the Hummer had been attacked by the Red River Gang? Had they seen more than Lump was prepared to divulge? Or was Lump just tired, stressed, and concerned about Rhino?

Whatever the reason for his friend's out-of-sorts mood, Tex knew he'd have to get to the bottom of it before it drove him crazy.

"Hello?" Mims leaned in toward the microphone's fat head. "Fort Timothy, this is Davy Crockett—are you there?"

Tex snorted a tad; he'd never liked the radio handle

Mims had given the Little Alamo, even though it did fit. Kind of. That the original Alamo turned out to be Crockett's last stand seemed lost on Al Mims, but Tex didn't want to be the one to point that out; the guy spent eight hours a day in the small communications shack listening in on the chaos going on in the outside world, and he deserved a little levity in his life.

"This is Fort Timothy," a voice crackled out through the speaker. "Hearing you loud and clear, Davy Crockett."

"I have Tex Pemberton here for Jed Timothy," Mims said. "Is he there?"

"No, sir," the voice replied.

"That you Zack?" Mims smiled.

"Yessir."

"How are you and Marlene?"

"Still married." A laugh. "How are Susan and Petey and the new one?"

"All good, thank you—the new one is three this fall, so not so new."

"Jeez! Don't time fly when you're having fun?"

Mims laughed along with the ethereal voice. "So, you going to go get Jed or not?"

"Ten-four, good buddy," the voice replied.

"Zack used to drive big rigs across country," Mims told Tex as they waited—like he felt obliged to explain.

"He sounds like a hoot." Tex smiled.

"This is Jed Timothy," the familiar voice came through. "That you, Tex?"

Mims scooted his chair to one side to give Tex room enough to lean over the desk.

"Yes, sir," Tex replied.

"And to what do I owe this honor?"

"My three guys who visited with you yesterday came across a Red River Gang encampment on the way back here. It seems they're heading your way."

"We haven't seen anything this end."

Timothy sounded guarded, disbelieving.

"A recon group engaged my team—one is very badly hurt."

"Sorry to hear that—give him my best wishes."

"Will do," Tex pressed on. "Look, Jed, if the Red River Gang decide to attack your compound, they're going to level the place... and everyone in it. You've been hearing the reports as well as we have—they're nothing more than ruthless killers who won't let anyone get in the way of what they want."

"Why are you telling me this, Tex?" Timothy asked pointedly. "Are you offering to send in the troops?"

"I'm offering you and your people a place here," Tex told him. "Where you'll be safe. If you set to loading up now, I'll send all the trucks we have to help bring everything over. We can have you all here and settled before the Red River Gang can make their move."

A leaden pause filled the airwaves.

Then, "Thank you, Tex, but no."

Tex stood straight and looked quizzically at Mims, who shrugged his shoulders and pulled a face.

Leaning back into the mic, Tex said the only thing he could think of to say: "What?"

"I'm declining your kind offer, Tex." There was a hardness to Timothy's voice Tex had not heard before; it certainly didn't sound like the affable guy the Little Alamo had been trading with for more than three years.

"You're not safe where you are," Tex insisted. "You know what the Red River Gang are capable of—they'll kill all of you just for your supplies."

"Like I said, we haven't seen anything here," Timothy said.

"But we have."

"You *say* you have."

Tex recoiled at Timothy's thinly veiled accusation. "I know what my men saw, Jed," he said.

"And I know what we haven't seen," Timothy threw back. "For all we know, this is all a ruse for *you* to get your hands on what we have here. Who's to say you won't just load up what you can and lock us out of the Little Alamo… or worse?"

Tex could barely believe what he was hearing; he'd been on the best of terms with Timothy for years, and there'd never been as much as a hint of distrust between them—of course, the Little Alamo outmanned and outgunned Timothy's compound of just forty-seven souls, but Tex would have never dreamed of doing anything untoward.

Until recently, that was.

That was it.

Lump.

The guy had let something slip, most likely while drunk on Timothy's infamous vodka—what was to say he hadn't been plied with the stuff to get him to do just that? Had Jed Timothy been harboring some deep mistrust of Tex and the Little Alamo all those years?

Tex cussed beneath his breath and slipped his hat from his head; it suddenly felt clammy and uncomfortable in the comm's shack.

"I can assure you, Jed—"

"Save it, Tex," Timothy cut across him. "I can't—*won't*—put my people at risk."

"You're putting them at risk by staying put," Tex argued. "There's a hundred-fifty Red River Gang raiding party heading your way, and you know what that means."

"It means we're gonna have to hunker down and defend ourselves when—*if*—the time comes." Timothy sounded most defiant—Tex knew the guy wasn't going to be moved from his stubborn stance, no matter how much he tried to reassure him.

"It's your choice, Jed," Tex sighed. "But, *please*, think about the women and children you have there—is it your place to decide for them?"

A derisory snort. "Yes—it's totally my place to make that decision," Timothy replied. "As leader of the Timothy clan, I have an elected duty to keep everyone here safe and out of harm's way. And I don't think I could do that if I agreed to your suggestion. I'm sorry, Tex, but that's just the way it is."

Jed Timothy clicked off the air before Tex had a chance to reply. It was probably for the best, Tex thought, since he'd be wasting his breath trying to talk some sense into the man.

Tex knew it also meant he'd have to have an awkward conversation with Lump, and perhaps rekindle what they'd discussed before that fateful trip to the Timothy compound.

And that saddened Tex all the way down to his soul.

Chapter Twenty-Eight

In an attempt to shake off what he felt to be a personal insult from Jed Timothy, Tex made himself busy for the remainder of the day. First, he spent some time in the garage helping fix up the Hummer the Red River Gang had shot up—he said a quiet prayer of thanks for making the decision to armor-plate the thing. Had they not, he knew things would have been a whole lot worse out there; it was highly likely Lump, Rhino, and Tip wouldn't have made it back at all.

Washing the dried blood off the doors and seats was a sobering job—Lee helped out, along with Josephina Garcia and her daughter, Sofia. The gal was around Lee's age, and Tex caught the hint of something between the two: the occasional glance when they thought no one was looking, the private jokes and adolescent giggles between them, the way Lee looked at Sofia when he thought *she* wasn't looking—his boy sure was growing up fast.

Tex made a mental note to have *the talk* with his son—although, by the way Lee was acting like a besotted man around the Garcia girl, Tex kinda got the impression that might just be closing the stable door *long* after the horse had bolted.

The rest of the day was spent fixing up some of the

solar panels that were on their way out. For most of them, the wiring was at fault; it looked like mice or cockroaches—or both—had made a meal of the insulating sheath around the wires. Some had short-circuited, others merely yanked from their place—the latter being a relatively easy fix.

The short-circuited ones, sadly, were beyond repair.

"How are we doing for rodent killer?" Tex said into his walkie-talkie.

"There's some left," Phil Cross replied, his tinny voice crackling. "Want me to send some over?"

"Yeah," Tex growled. "I'm in the solar farm—we'd best do something before the vermin destroy every last panel out here."

"That bad?"

"Yup." Tex itched a spot just beneath the brim of his hat. "If it goes on like this, we'll have no choice but to cut power another couple hours."

There came the sound of breath being sucked in through teeth. "That's not good, Tex," Cross said.

"Tell me about it."

"Are the furnaces not working properly?"

"The furnaces are just fine, Phil," Tex told him. "It's the fuel that's the problem. There's about enough diesel to get us through the year—if we're frugal with it—and if we cut down much more of the forest, there'll be no damn trees left." It was an exaggeration, of course, but Tex knew it was becoming increasingly difficult to bring in good burning wood; it wouldn't be too long before that ran out as well.

"That reminds me," Cross said. "We need to talk supplies—tomorrow morning, okay?"

"Sure." Tex's heart sank; if Phil Cross wanted to talk about supplies, it wouldn't be to tell him they have more than plenty and everything was a-okay. Cross was highly protective of his supply store, and he'd not once requested a meeting with Tex.

Until now.

"Over and out." Cross clicked off and Tex's walkie-talkie fell silent.

Finishing up the panel he'd been working on—dusk was rapidly approaching, and the light was failing—Tex trudged wearily back home; what he wouldn't give for a little good news—was that really too much to ask?

His mind elsewhere, Tex almost stepped on the book that sat, propped up, against his front door. He recognized it immediately, of course: it was the romance novel Victoria had been pushing on him at the library before he was called away to the infirmary.

"Thanks a bunch," he mumbled beneath his breath as he plucked the book up off the doorstep. "Just what I need."

Once inside, Tex scratched Winnie behind the ears a little, took off his hat, grabbed a beer from the fridge, sat himself down in the faded leather armchair—his favorite seat in the house—and flicked on the light that perched on the wall above it. He'd always intended for it to be a reading chair, only neither he nor Lee had seemed to have much time for that since moving to the Little Alamo—there was usually too much to do, or they'd be too tired after the full days they put in. Of course, Lee had books to read for school, but that was never quite the same as reading for pleasure.

And, speaking of Lee, Tex recalled the boy had said something earlier about studying at a friend's house. By 'friend,' Tex assumed he'd meant the Garcia girl—he *really* was going to have to have that talk.

Tex took a slurp of his beer and opened up the white cover of *The Bridge*. Inside, in neat, girlish handwriting, Victoria had left him a note:

Thought you'd get away without reading this, eh? This is the duplicate copy—there'll be a pop quiz next time we meet! Enjoy reading, Tex. xxx

It brought a smile to Tex's lips and gladdened his heavy heart some; Victoria had a gift for doing that of late, and Tex was happy for the joy that gave him. He actually hadn't given the book a second thought since racing from the library to see Lump, Rhino, and Tip—a soppy romance novel was the furthest thing from his mind, even if it came with Victoria's recommendation and was tragic.

Tex was forced to admit to himself the book was probably just what he needed after the trying week he'd had, a welcome—albeit temporary—escape from the stress and worry of the responsibilities resting upon his shoulders; he wondered if Victoria had known that when she'd popped the book over.

Most likely.

But, with the little dog curled up by his feet and the cold beer balanced upon the arm of the chair, Tex leafed through to the beginning and began to read.

Chapter Twenty-Nine

Tex was at Phil Cross' supplies store bright and early. He'd slept through 'til dawn in the armchair, having fallen asleep reading *The Bridge*—he'd gotten a fair way into it, far enough to become emotionally invested in the book's hero, before his eyelids had become too heavy to continue. Exhausted, he hadn't even been awoken by Lee coming home; the kid had tiptoed up to bed—either he was being extra-thoughtful at not waking his sleeping father, or he'd taken full advantage because he'd come home after his curfew.

Either way, Tex was grateful for the sleep, even though it had left him with a stiff crick in his neck.

The Little Alamo's supplies store was the largest building in the compound and had been designed to house all the canned and dried goods, frozen meat, grain, light machinery, fertilizers for the crops, pest-control chemicals, and everything else required to keep the place running. Tex and Lump had drawn up the blueprints based upon extensive research on warehousing, and Tex was pleased with the outcome—it really was a warehouse for all occasions.

Only, it looked worryingly empty.

"I'm not sure rationing is going to solve this," Cross

was telling Tex. "We've been running prudently for seven months now, and this is what we have left." He swept an arm sideways to emphasize his point.

Tex surveyed the warehouse's vast interior; there were still pallets stacked high with cans, bags of grain, and the like, but they were dotted around the sides of the space—back in the early days, every square inch was filled with provisions. It had been a hard task to walk from one end to the other because of the amount of stuff in there—oftentimes it was necessary to clamber over the pallets to do so.

"If the crops hadn't failed this year, there'd be a lot more," Cross said. "More grain, more meat—the cows won't breed if they're on half-rations."

Tex nodded. "If we can just hold out until next season," he offered, "we should be able to restock."

"That's if the rain comes and the sun doesn't bake everything again," Cross replied. "I hate to sound negative, but it's something we can't just ignore, Tex."

The guy was stating the glaringly obvious, but it still irked Tex to hear him talk that way. "This kind of summer only comes around once every dozen years or so—even in Texas," he said.

"Kind makes you miss the days of TV weather forecasts—at least back then, we had a shot at preparing."

"Nothing much we could do to prepare for a drought like this one," Tex grumbled. "Even the irrigation quit working."

"Not much we can do when the water table drops," Cross frowned. "Except pray for enough rain to get it back up again."

Tex nodded. "So, what do we need to do to get us far enough for things to turn around, Phil?"

Cross rubbed at his chin, which was surprisingly baby's butt smooth. "Ration more, I guess," he said. "We could use more meat coming in—there's gotta be pigs and deer still out there somewhere—bears, too."

"Looks like those that weren't hunted out have headed for higher ground," Tex told him. "The pickings are better up there."

"Then why don't we follow them?"

"We've been trying to expand our hunting range, but it's getting too dangerous out there."

"I heard about Lump and the guys," Cross said. "How's Rhino doing? I was going to call in at the infirmary this afternoon…"

Doc Barker had called Tex first thing—had woken him up, actually—to let him know Rhino had made it through the night and was going to pull through; he'd been asking after some redheaded woman who didn't match the description of anyone Tex could place at the Little Alamo. "He's going to be just fine, Phil," Tex said. "I reckon he'd appreciate a visit from you."

"I'll take him fruit," Cross said with a wry smile and patted one of the plastic-wrapped food pallets. "Canned, of course."

Tex, doing his best to laugh along, began walking down the empty aisles. He felt some relief at Jed Timothy turning down the offer to relocate all the people in his compound to the Little Alamo, no matter what the reason. Another forty-seven mouths to feed would have meant the dwindling supplies would go down even quicker, even if they brought what they had at the Timothy compound; it would have been a huge strain on the Little Alamo—there was no ignoring that fact.

However, from what Tex had gleaned about the provisions Jed Timothy had stockpiled—he'd allowed for over double his contingent—he reckoned there would certainly be enough to see the Little Alamo through the rough patch, at least until the crops came back in and the hunting situation improved.

Which brought Tex back to Lump's proposal that they simply go get what Timothy had in the name of self-preservation.

In the Before Times, Tex would have been appalled at himself for even thinking such a thing. But, in the After Times, the world was so much different, and it was very much the survival of the fittest.

Or the most ruthless.

The way things were going, Tex could see a future in which the only residue of the human race were the vicious roaming gangs of nomads and the likes of the Red River Gang—he'd heard reports from all over the country of like-minded cutthroats pillaging and destroying everything from compounds ten times the size of the Little Alamo to individual preppers holed up in their tiny backyard bunkers. It was dog-eat-dog out there, alright, and Tex had the welfare and survival of almost a 150 souls resting on his shoulders.

Tex got around halfway down the length of the warehouse before turning on his heels to face Cross. "Do what you can to make all this last for as long as possible," he said. "I'm gonna talk to Lump and the others about bringing in more supplies."

Cross looked concerned; his voice hardened, "From where, Tex? You just said—"

"You leave that to me, Phil." Tex cut him off—the last thing he needed was a lecture in morality from the supplies manager. "Ration as much as you need to—just buy us time."

Cross looked as though he wanted to say more, but he kept his mouth firmly closed.

"Hello?" Victoria's voice echoed inside the warehouse. "You there, Phil?"

"In here!" Cross called over.

Tex watched Victoria as she walked across the warehouse to where Phil was standing; her eyes lit up when she saw Tex not twenty paces away. "Oh, hi, Tex." She smiled.

"Hi, Victoria." Tex returned the smile—was the woman stalking him?

He kinda hoped so.

"What can I do for you this morning?" Phil asked, his tone back to the friendly one everyone knew and loved.

"We need mouse traps and poison for the hives," Victoria said. "The critters have been getting in at night. I realize they're just hungry, but they tear the combs up and kill the poor bees. When they get the queen, the whole hive is done for."

"If it's either the mice or Victoria's delicious honey, I'm gonna side with the bees every time—what do you say, Tex?" Cross made his way to one of the locked storerooms near the front of the warehouse, fishing out his bundle of clinking keys as he walked.

"Amen to that," Tex replied and followed on.

"It's either them or us," Victoria chipped in with what looked to be an attempt at a fierce grimace—Tex thought it made her look all the more beautiful. "These are hard times, Phil," Victoria said. "We gotta do what we've gotta do."

The words resonated with Tex; Victoria understood what it took to survive, and it sounded like she was far less altruistic than he'd given her credit for. Okay, so she was only talking bees and mice, but the principle was the same: she'd definitely understand his stance should he and Lump decide to raid Jed Timothy's compound. And, somehow, that meant a hell of a lot to Tex. It was not simply the endorsement of his actions, but the comfort of knowing Victoria wouldn't look at him like he was some kind of monster should he authorize the attack.

Phil vanished into one of the storage rooms; Tex and Victoria waited outside.

"Thank you for the book," Tex said.

"My pleasure." Victoria smiled up at him. "You left the library in rather a hurry yesterday, and I knew how much you'd be disappointed at not having your copy of *The Bridge*."

A cheeky wink.

"Actually," Tex puffed out his chest. "I made a start on it last night."

Victoria appeared impressed, if somewhat surprised. "Well, good for you…"

A pause.

"What?" Tex was puzzled.

"What do you think?" Victoria prompted.

"So far, so good," Tex told her. "Why don't we discuss it later? Over dinner perhaps?"

"How about a nice supper under the stars?"

Tex nodded; that sounded wonderful. "Yeah," he said, "I'd like that."

"Then it's a date." Victoria beamed like the cat that got the canary. "Let's meet there—I'll bring a picnic."

"Then, I'll dig out the bottle of wine I've been saving for a special occasion."

"Sounds perfect," Victoria replied. "Oh and bring your guitar."

"Excuse me?"

"Your guitar… the one you keep propped up in the corner of your living room, Tex. Bring it with you tonight."

Tex was nonplussed: after making sure to load his beloved instrument into the Land Cruiser all those years ago, he hadn't so much as strummed a note since arriving at the Little Alamo. Krista's death at the hands of the baying, murderous mob had crushed his desire to play—she'd always loved it when he did that for her.

"Huh, yeah, sure." Tex knew Victoria heard the hesitance in his voice.

"And don't forget," she warned him playfully, "if you do, I'll send you straight back home to get it."

Phil Cross appeared from the storage room, arms full of ominous white boxes with death head skulls and warnings all over them.

"This ought to keep the little bastards at bay," he said. "Pardon my French."

"Nothing to pardon," Victoria replied. "Those little bastards are killing my bees."

With that, she took the poison from Cross and left the two men to their business in the dry warmth of the warehouse; Tex watched Victoria walk away and wished he was going with her.

"I'll incorporate a new ration structure from today," Cross picked up the conversation. "Folks are not gonna like it, though."

Tex snorted. "They'll understand," he said. "We can call a town hall meeting to explain things."

"Carefully, I hope."

"Of course," Tex took offense at the inference. "Don't worry, Phil, they're not going to resort to violence and come here mob-handed to take what you've got."

Cross shook his head. "They're all good people, Tex, I know that. But even good people can crack under too much pressure, when things start to crumble around them… just look at what happened in the Before Times."

Tex hardly needed reminding of that; he relived it most nights in dreams so vivid he could hear the shouts and screams of the mob, his wife crying out in agony as they tore her apart, the sheer terror of fleeing the family home before he and his son succumbed to the same fate.

Yeah, he knew all too well what good people were capable of when things got tough, and their own survival was at stake.

"It's all gonna be alright, Phil," Tex reassured the storesman. "We'll get through this, one way or another, and come out the other side stronger for it." He turned to leave.

"I hope you're right, Tex," Cross called after him.

And Tex sure hoped so, too.

Chapter Thirty

"You brought it." Victoria's smile was just what Tex needed to lift his spirits; it had been a rough day—rougher than usual—but at least he'd had their starlight picnic to look forward to.

"Just doing as instructed," Tex replied, lifting up his guitar with one hand, the bottle of red wine with the other."

"Thank you," Victoria said. "Sit yourself down and get the wine opened—I'm ready for a drink."

Tex let out a hefty sigh, took off his hat, and sat down beside Victoria with a low grunt. "Yeah, I hear that."

"I kinda got the impression things were getting heavy with Phil at the warehouse this morning," Victoria said as she busied herself picking bread, butter, cheese, and ham from the neatly prepared picnic basket she had on the tartan woolen blanket she'd spread out next to their bench. That done, she picked out a bottle opener and a pair of plastic wine glasses. She handed the opener over to Tex.

"I know that you, Lump, and Phil are trying hard to keep it quiet, but we're not that naïve." Victoria cut thick slices from the bread and set about preparing cheese and ham sandwiches for the two of them.

Tex popped the cork from the bottle and poured the wine into the glasses—the dark red liquid looked almost black in the moonlight. "We don't want people to panic," he told Victoria as he put one of the glasses in her hand.

Victoria took a sip. "Wow, this is *really* good, Tex—tell me you have more at home."

"A couple bottles." Tex took more than a sip from his glass and rolled it around in his mouth a second or two to savor the full-bodied, fruity flavor; say what you like about the Californians, but they do make a darn good wine. Swallowing it down, Tex only just stopped himself blurting out the wine was Krista's favorite—he didn't want to spoil such a perfect moment.

"Good to know." Victoria gave him *that* smile again, and his heart quickened just a little.

"Happy to share with you anytime," Tex told her. He shuffled his butt on the blanket to be closer, craving the touch of her thigh pressed against his; he *needed* to be close.

"You think people don't know how bad things are getting?" Victoria asked him, handing over a perfectly constructed sandwich. "The Little Alamo is a small, close-knit community, Tex, and word spreads like wildfire."

Tex gave a sage nod. "I get that. But we promised a safe, secure home for everyone who came here at the end of the Before Times, and now we can barely feed them."

Resting a hand on top of his, Victoria said, "None of us thought this was ever going to be easy, Tex. We all knew we were setting off on a journey together—a journey into the unknown. It's not every day the world order collapses and people have to flee into the wilderness to live like the early pioneers, so how could we ever be fully prepared?"

Tex had often thought of the Little Alamo citizens in terms of the settlers of old: Not just the fact they lived in a wooden fort in the middle of nowhere, but the community spirit that prevailed through all the hardships. Sure, it had taken folks some time to get used to life without all the electronic gadgets and gizmos they'd grown accustomed to—and being so far removed from what civilization used to be—especially the youngsters. But, over time, they'd adapted to the newer, simpler way of life, and in many ways, they were happier for it.

I still feel like I'm letting you all down," Tex said, his voice quiet. "Promises were made…"

"Look, Tex," Victoria said with a fond firmness. She squeezed his fingers with hers and looked him in the eyes. "We are all in this together. Sure, you're the leader, and you have Lump and the others around you, but we're all in the same boat. Most of us have lost someone, and we've all been through the hell of what happened when it all went bad out there. *All* of us are grateful for the home you provided—we feel safe here, and that goes a heck of a long way."

Tex struggled for words; emotion tightened his throat, and for an alarming minute or two, he thought his eyes might just tear up. Victoria's soothing words were just what he needed to hear, and they brought Tex more comfort than he thought he deserved. Even so, he didn't want their evening together to be mired in talk about the crisis facing their community—and certainly not in what he was seriously considering to alleviate it.

"I told you I'd made a start on the book you left for me." Tex's clumsy change of direction hung heavy in the air between he and Victoria for what felt like an age.

Her hand left his, she nibbled on the corner of her sandwich and took a delicate sip of wine. "You did," she said, finally. "I'm really impressed, Tex."

And then that smile again.

Tex gave an inward sigh of relief—for a moment or two, he thought he'd blown it, spoiled the evening by switching subjects like that. He wanted to tell her it wasn't that he didn't trust her by talking it through, nor did he see her as some lowly citizen unworthy of him taking into his confidence—he just didn't want to spoil their time together.

But seeing her beautiful, warm smile told Tex all was good between them.

"I'm impressed with myself." Tex reached for Victoria's hand and held it tight. "It's not really my kind of reading…"

Victoria chuckled, her laughter wafting out into the night. "I figured as much," she told him. "I also figured *The Bridge* would appeal to you—it's not your typical sappy young girl falls hopelessly in love with a mysterious billionaire romance."

"Thank you for that," Tex laughed. "I really can't imagine ploughing through something like that."

"Me either to be completely honest—give me gritty realism any day of the week."

"Yeah, I kinda get that the book's based on the author's own experiences." Tex was keen to show off what he'd already gleaned just a few chapters in—although his date with Victoria was beginning to feel a tad like a housewives' book club.

"I like how he's used his own name for the main character's," Victoria said. "Makes the whole thing feel more personal and… *intimate*."

Tex munched on the sandwich she'd put together for him—it was beyond delicious. "The guy's ex-military," he added. "And older, too. You don't really see that too much in books and movies—the romantic hero always seems to be some gorgeous, twenty-something dreamboat. It's refreshing to read about an older, experienced guy falling in love with a younger woman."

"I knew you'd relate." Victoria tipped him a cheeky wink and gave him a lingering peck on the cheek.

"Hey!" Tex laughed along. "I'm not *that* old—and I

haven't gotten that far yet, so—*spoiler alert*."

"My bad." Victoria smiled. "I was thinking you were further along. He *has* met Ana, though?"

Tex nodded and chugged at his wine. "He's at the stalking stage right now—going to the café where she works every opportunity he gets."

"That's kinda romantic, don't you think?"

Tex thought so—the guy in the book was besotted by the much younger woman in the café and really couldn't help himself. His common sense was telling him she was too young for an old ex-soldier like him, and the language barrier was definitely a problem—his German was practically nonexistent. But, despite that, Jesse found himself unable to stay away from the beautiful Ana.

After all, the heart wants what the heart wants.

Of course, it wasn't lost on Tex that Victoria had chosen *The Bridge* to share with him. Out of all the books in the Little Alamo library, she'd chosen the May-to-December romance, one with a story that mirrored her growing relationship with Tex. The age-gap wasn't so wide between him and Victoria, but Tex could see the parallels even early on in the book. So, maybe the book was a message from her to him? Was it a way for Victoria to gently let him know how she was feeling or a means by which he could express his feelings for her? Tex had always been one to hide his true emotions beneath macho bluster, especially when he found himself falling for someone.

Or could it be as simple as the fact that someone accidentally ordered two copies of the same book for the library?

Tex smiled at his own cynicism.

"What's so funny?" Victoria interrupted his thoughts.

"I was just thinking how the book could very easily take a sinister turn," Tex lied.

"That's what you get for only reading thrillers and westerns," Victoria teased. "I'm gonna have to get you reading more romances—soften you up a bit."

"You think I need softening up?" Tex feigned offence. "I'll have you know, I'm perfectly in touch with my emotions, Ma'am."

Victoria rested her head on Tex's shoulder and looked out over the dark water of the pond. "That may be so, Tex Pemberton, but you're not so good at sharing them."

She'd hit the nail on the head, of course. Tex had been brought up old-school: his father never showed any emotion he deemed to be unmasculine—he said it was a sign of weakness and literally beat it out of his son. It had taken Tex a long, long time to allow himself to open up, and it wasn't until he met Krista that he felt comfortable doing so.

And, *after* Krista… he just bottled them all back up again.

Maybe his father had been right all along, and it was a sign of weakness?

"I'm working on that," he told Victoria. "I really am."

Victoria sat up on the blanket, and Tex immediately missed her head on his shoulder. "So… are you going to play for me?"

"What, now?"

"I didn't ask you to bring that just to look at." She pointed at Tex's guitar that lay beside him on the blanket.

"Oh… yeah." Caught up in the moment with Victoria, Tex had completely forgotten about it.

"I used to hear you playing…" Victoria sighed. "Back then. Sometimes I'd stop what I was doing just to listen."

"I didn't know anyone could hear me," Tex felt a touch embarrassed.

"Your windows were single-glazed," Victoria said

with a fond smile.

“Ahh—we were always going to have them replaced, but never quite got around to it.”

“So…?” Victoria pointed at the guitar.

“I haven’t played in a long time,” Tex told her.

“That’s why I wanted you to bring it tonight.”

Tex picked the guitar up off the ground; it all of a sudden felt heavy in his hands, like something alien and strange. He couldn’t rightly recall the last time he’d played the thing—it had sat in the living room of the small, wooden house he’d built with his own hands like some haunting reminder of how life used to be. He’d thought many times about throwing it away, or at the very least sticking it up in the attic where he wouldn’t have to see it every damn day.

And yet, that reminder of the Before Times and of the wife he’d so cruelly lost, brought him a little comfort in his darkest times.

“Do you have any requests?” Tex asked Victoria.

“Nope,” she replied with a grin and, draining her wine glass, grabbed the bottle for a refill.

Tex strummed his fingers down the strings as he mentally ran through the songs he knew by heart—it was surprising how they flooded back to him after so long, and he knew he’d have no problem remembering the chords at all.

“Okay, I’ll warn you now, I pretty much only know country and western,” he said. “So, if that’s not your jam, you have time to escape now.”

“That’s perfect.” Victoria drew her knees up to her chest and hugged them with one arm.

“Here goes nothing…” Tex played the first chord of *When You Say Nothing at All*—he’d always been a huge Garth Brooks fan—and began to serenade Victoria.

Chapter Thirty-One

A couple days after that magical night, Tex was startled awake in the small hours by a thumping at his door. He'd been dreaming about sitting on the blanket by the pond, and Victoria's sweet face smiling at him while he played and sang, so he was not pleased by the interruption.

"What's going on, Dad?" Lee emerged from his bedroom across the hallway, rubbing his eyes.

"Go back to bed," Tex grumped. "I'll deal with it." He grabbed his revolver from the nightstand and set off down the stairs.

He pulled open the door.

"Sorry to wake you, Tex." It was Sean Wopat, and he looked like he'd not slept in a while; his face was a mask of worry.

"No problem at all," Tex said. He stepped aside to usher the guy in. "Come in, sit down—you need a drink?"

Wopat shook his head. He sat himself down on Tex's couch and wiped a hand down his grimy face. "We just got back from hunting out near the mountains," he told Tex.

"We?" Tex was puzzled; he knew nothing of any hunting parties going out.

"Me, Kenny Amberson, and Jimmy Bloodmountain.

We set out yesterday with Don Woods and a coupla Fort Simons guys I didn't know too well—Clancy Goedeke and Bri Farrell—and split up when we got to the tree line. We were supposed to meet back there this morning, but they never showed. Me, Kenny, and Jimmy spent a half day looking for them, but nothing. I figured we'd be best coming back to put a proper search party together."

Tex paced the room; his head spun while his temper seethed. He wasn't even aware Don Woods was healed well enough to return to hunting. "Did you hear anything?" he asked. "Gunshots?"

"We were hunting, of course we heard gunshots."

Tex shook his head at his own dumb question. "I mean. Anything that sounded like it could be something more than guys shooting at deer."

"No," Wopat said quietly. "It's like they just vanished into thin air, Tex."

"What the hell were you all doing out there in the first place?" Tex snapped. "Who's dumb idea was it to send out two hunting parties when we know damn well the Red River Gang are prowling around?"

"Lump said we needed to go find where the game is." Wopat lowered his eyes as if he was betraying a confidence. "He said you'd okayed it."

"I'd *never* have agreed to sending hunting parties out there," Tex growled; he knew that was the precise reason Lump had not mentioned his hare-brained scheme—likely he'd figured once the hunters came back with a haul of fresh meat, his indiscretion would be all forgiven.

Only, one of the parties hadn't come back at all.

Tex fought hard to keep his temper; it wouldn't be fair to take out his anger and frustration at his second-in-command on Wopat—the poor guy was beating himself up as it was. No, he'd take it up with Lump first thing in the morning—he'd been getting cockier over the past few months, like a teenager testing his parent's boundaries, but he'd gone and overstepped his authority a little too far.

"We're gonna have to go get them," Wopat said. "I can get a search party together right now."

Tex raised a hand to stop Wopat. "You need to get some sleep, Sean—you look like hell."

"Thanks." Wopat managed a feeble smile.

"We can wait 'til morning," Tex told him. "Grab yourself some shut-eye and tell Amberson and Bloodmountain to do the same—you three can head up the search party, show us where you last saw Don Woods and his guys."

"You're coming with us?"

Tex nodded. "This happened on my damn watch, Sean, so it's my job to bring those boys home."

Wopat slumped back on Tex's sofa; his were eyes half-closed. "I pray to God we find 'em, Tex." He spoke quietly. "That's no place to be left, not with the nomads and such on the lookout for easy meat. I heard they eat people—"

"I'm sure that's just hearsay," Tex told him, although he was beginning to doubt that; if the nomads, Red River Gang, and whoever else was out there beyond the Little Alamo's walls were getting as desperate as those inside, he reckoned it would only be a short step to eating anything they could gun down.

And that included people.

"Go, get some rest," Tex ordered Wopat. "We'll reconvene at first daylight and send a posse out."

Wopat stood up with reluctance—he looked like he could easily have slept on Tex's couch—and let himself out.

Tex watched him go, his mind reeling, planning just what the hell he was going to say to Lump when he caught up with him.

Chapter Thirty-Two

"You're not going, Lump," Tex said with as much calm as he could muster. "This is all down to you in the first place—what the hell were you thinking?"

Lump looked around; they were alone and standing toe-to-toe in the dirt courtyard behind the John Wayne bar.

Tex had asked Wopat to assemble the search party at the bar as soon as the sun rose, and then called Lump to meet with him. He'd also reckoned theirs was a conversation best held outside.

"People gotta eat, Tex," Lump protested. "You know how bad things are getting around here."

"Yeah, and we discussed what we could do about that, Lump." Tex wanted nothing more than to punch his old friend square in the jaw and the two of them fight it out, just like in their Army days. But both of them had their positions as community leaders to consider: it wouldn't look good if they started scrapping in the dirt like a couple of naughty schoolboys.

"I just thought if we could bring in some big game, we wouldn't have to raid Jed Timothy's compound," Lump said. "I saw how disgusted you were by the idea and wanted to spare you that. And… I didn't think you'd go through with it, even if it was our only option."

That accusation irked Tex: he and Lump had only just begun discussing mounting an offensive against the Timothy compound and suddenly he was being accused of going back on his word—one he hadn't even made yet.

To Tex, Lump's machinations had a definite ring of mutiny about them, and it was time to nip it in the bud.

"You had no right sending out hunting parties without consulting me first," Tex told his friend. "We agreed—"

"You're thinking with your wrong head, Tex," Lump snapped back with a nod downwards. "You need to focus more on the people who rely on you than trying to impress your bee-keeping girlfriend. If you had, I'd have been able to consult you."

Tex held back the response he wanted to make—his relationship with Victoria was none of anyone's business but theirs, and it sure as hell wasn't Lump's place to use it against him.

"You went against protocol and look what happened," Tex said with as much calm as he could muster. "We can only hope we're going out on a search and rescue mission and not to retrieve dead bodies, Lump. And by *we*, I don't mean you."

Lump narrowed his eyes and, for a split second, Tex thought they really were going to have that fight.

Instead, grudgingly, Lump backed down. "That's low, Tex," he grumbled. "That's really low."

Tex bit his tongue; he wanted nothing more than to shout in Lump's face, *So is sending men out to die, you irresponsible asshole!* It was better to take the moral high ground, though, Tex figured, especially since Lump appeared to know when he was beaten.

It saddened Tex to clash with his old friend in that way, especially given how much they'd been through together, but the safety of the Little Alamo and its citizens was paramount. It also niggled at Tex's mind that he'd have to keep a closer eye on Lump—he really couldn't allow the guy to go off script again—and he was going to find it difficult to trust him again.

"Stay by the radio," Tex instructed Lump—more to avoid completely alienating him than necessity; Al Mims was more than capable of providing comms support.

"Yeah," Lump backed down. "I can do that."

Tex watched Lump walk off toward Communications, then made his way back inside, where Wopat, Amberson, and Jimmy Bloodmountain waited patiently for him to finish up.

"We'll take the Cruiser and the Ram," he told them. "We're gonna be offroad for a lot of this, and it's obviously too dangerous to go on horseback." He reminded himself of the mess the Red River Gang had made of the Hummer; the Cruiser—*his* Land Cruiser—and the Ram 2500 pickup had both been armor-plated and converted to LPG, and they were the best 4-wheel drives the Little Alamo had at its disposal.

"We're taking two vehicles?" Wopat seemed surprised.

"It makes sense," Tex told him. "It'll be better for keeping eyes on the landscape, especially in the foothills and forest periphery—and it's a good idea for if we're attacked—all our eggs won't be in the one basket." He almost went on to say they may just need the extra room the truck and the Cruiser offered to bring home the bodies of Don Woods and his hunting party. But there was still some grain of hope; it was possible they'd simply walked too far and gone to ground to wait for daybreak, in which case, Tex's sortie would be an easy one.

He also didn't want to start off the trip on a negative—his crew already seemed apprehensive and more than a tad skittish.

"Are we loaded up?" Tex asked Amberson.

"Guns, ammo, food, and water," Amberson replied. "Plus, a little extra LPG for if we need it."

"Okay, I guess we're all good to go—let's go bring Don and his boys home." Tex tried to sound as upbeat as he could, even though his heart felt heavy in his chest—his spat with Lump had left him with an overriding sensation of dread, as if it was a portent for far worse things to come.

Chapter Thirty-Three

They found Don Woods, Clancy Goedeke, and Bri Farrell in the foothills of Couch Mountain, just a little way into the dense tree line, in a small clearing.

They'd all been shot in the back of the head, execution-style, stripped of everything including their underwear and boots. Their killers had left them where they'd fallen, face down in the leaf litter. Their vehicle, of course, was long gone.

"*Shit*," Tex growled as he surveyed the scene; other than the three corpses, there was nothing he could see that gave away what had happened.

"There were eight others," Bloodmountain told him; he'd spent the past half-hour scouting around the periphery and into the trees. "They brought them here from farther up the mountain to…"

Tex couldn't help but glance at the three bodies. Wopat and Amberson had covered each of them with a white sheet to preserve some of their dignity—it occurred to Tex that one of them had packed three sheets for the excursion as if they'd already known the fate of Woods and his Fort Simons guys.

"I guess we load 'em up and get them home," Tex said with a weary sigh.

He knew he was being naïve back at the compound when he thought they were going to find Woods's party safe, well, and hunkered around a campfire. In his heart, though, he'd prepared himself for the worse. Although, what he'd been confronted with had been far more than he'd expected—they'd even stolen their underwear!

What kind of sick animals did that?

"Red River Gang," Tex mumbled, and for a moment, he wished he was in Victoria's arms, his safe place.

"Most likely." Bloodmountain cocked an ear as if he's heard something. To Tex, the forest was silent. "We should be going."

"Get ready to roll out, guys," Tex told the others. He couldn't hear anything, but he trusted the tracker's senses and instincts.

Tex helped load the three bodies into the back of the RAM. Amberson strapped them down firmly with ratchet straps so they wouldn't bounce out over the rough terrain. It all brought back awful memories of his Military days, of helping get Rusty back to base camp, of suffering the loss of his friend in miserable silence, and Tex felt the all-too-familiar sick feeling creeping through his guts.

A gunshot split the tranquil forest air as Tex was climbing into the Cruiser. It zinged over his head and gouged a fat chunk of wood from the tree to his right.

Quickly, he hauled himself in beside Bloodmountain and slammed the door shut. A glance behind told him Wopat and Amberson were in the truck

"Where are they?" Tex asked Bloodmountain; there was no sign of movement anywhere to be seen.

The tracker pointed out through the passenger-side window with two fingers, like a kid playing guns. "They're coming from the east," he told Tex. "So the sun will be in our faces."

"Are they the same people who did… *that*?" Tex

pointed toward the rear of the RAM.

Bloodmountain shrugged his shoulders. "I can only guess at that, Tex, but I'd say it was more than possible. They left the bodies where we could easily find them—they've probably been watching us this whole time."

That thought sent shivers down Tex's spine; knowing that, at any time, he and his men could have been shot down was terrifying.

"We need to go now," Bloodmountain urged. "They're coming."

Instead of stepping on the gas, Tex clambered over to the Cruiser's back seat. "Give me a second," he said to his startled passenger.

Another shot rang out, followed by another. They bounced off the left-hand side of the Cruiser with a loud, metallic thump. More gunshots, and Tex knew the truck behind him was taking a hit.

He had to act fast.

Grabbing a gas canister, keeping his head low, Tex eased open the right rear door and heaved the canister out. It hit the ground with a dull, heavy *thud*.

Climbing back into the driver's seat, Tex gunned the Cruiser's engine and the vehicle lurched forward. "Let's go," he said, steering with skill between the trees in the opposite direction to the gunshots.

As they left the clearing, Tex saw his assailants in his rear-view mirror—all eight of them, just like Jimmy Bloodmountain had predicted. As he drove, the men ran into the clearing, rifles aimed, at took pot shots at the retreating vehicles.

Bullets pinged off the Cruiser as Tex maneuvered between the trees, and then, once he figured there was sufficient cover, he took a quick left. Behind him in the truck, Amberson followed on, no doubt wondering what the hell was going on.

The shots fell silent, which let Tex know they were out of sight of the Red River Gang. He pulled the Cruiser up to a sudden halt, so sudden, in fact, the RAM almost careened into its rear.

"What are you doing, Tex?" Bloodmountain sounded uncharacteristically scared—very little seemed to faze the guy.

Tex didn't reply. Instead, he grabbed his rifle from the back seat and climbed out of the car.

"We need to go…"

Tex shook his head and set off back in the direction they'd just come—using the flattened-down path through the undergrowth to move quickly, silently.

The eight Red River guys were still in the clearing. They appeared to be having some kind of argument—their voices carried, but not enough for Tex to be able to make out what they were saying, although they sounded pissed at one another and two of them kept pointing into the forest with their hunting rifles.

Slowly, carefully, keeping low to the ground, Tex eased himself forward until he came upon a rotted, fallen tree trunk he'd spotted minutes before from the safety of the Cruiser.

Crouching down behind it, Tex lifted his rifle and took aim.

His first shot punched a hole in the gas canister that lay two, maybe three strides away from the eight men. The second ricocheted off the metal carrying handle adjacent to the pressure gage to create a spark, and the canister blew apart with an ear-splitting *pop*.

Instinctively, Tex ducked down behind the log, the stink of decay assaulting his nostrils. He heard screams of surprise and pain as the resonance of the explosion died down and the crackle of flames amid the dry tree branches.

Footsteps behind him; Bloodmountain had followed

on.

"I couldn't just leave them." Tex felt like he owed some explanation. Of course, he should have simply carried on driving, gotten out of the forest, and headed back to the Little Alamo. But—"

"Not after what they did to Don and the others," Tex said.

Bloodmountain rested a reassuring hand upon Tex's shoulder. "You did the right thing," he said with a thin smile. "It's time to finish this."

The tracker was right—two of the eight in the clearing were still alive; their agonized moans drifted across the smoke-filled air like the cries of dying animals. The other six had been killed outright by Tex's makeshift bomb—their body parts and innards were splashed all across what remained of the clearing.

Tex broke cover and made his way across to the clearing. The brush smoldered, small fires spat and flickered around the trees, and tinder-dry branches burned overhead; it looked to Tex like some miniature, post-apocalyptic movie landscape.

Having Bloodmountain by his side gave Tex some comfort; the guy could hear everything—anyone—coming from a mile away. If the Red River Gang were not alone in the forest, the loud bang would bring them coming. Tex had to do what needed to be done and be out of there as fast as was possible.

The two survivors were in pretty bad shape—Tex figured delivering the coup de grace would be a mercy. There was no way on God's green earth they'd live through their injuries. One of the guys was missing an arm, one leg below the knee, and had a twisted chunk of metal shrapnel embedded in his eye, and the other had been all but disemboweled by whatever the blast had hurled his way.

Nonetheless, they were still alive, and capable of talking, should there be any others out there in the forest.

Tex took out his Colt .45 and dispatched the disemboweled man first. A well-aimed shot between the eyes—a quick, painless death, which was more than Tex thought he deserved. Had it not been for the risk of him telling other Red River folks what had happened and who to go after, Tex would have happily left him there to die in the dirt. His thoughts wandered to Victoria—she'd have been appalled at his actions—and he felt guilty at what he was doing.

Standing over the second survivor, Tex took aim.

"Tex Pemberton," the man struggled to say; tiny spumes of blood spat out from his mouth as he spoke.

"Do I know you?" Tex eased off the Colt's trigger.

"We met at the Little Alamo a year or so back."

Tex saw every word was agony for the man but was puzzled as to how they could have possibly met—he knew no one from the Red River Gang.

"I don't recall," Tex replied, although it would have been difficult to recognize anyone with their face so badly torn up.

"I visited you with Jed." The guy turned his head to one side and coughed up a thick, dark clot of blood.

"Jed Timothy?"

"Yup."

Tex could only stand and stare at the wounded man; he was from Jed Timothy's compound? "Are you all from Jed's?" he asked.

The man nodded the best he could. "We thought we had six, maybe twelve months before you raided us for everything we had," he said. "But after your folks came over, we figured not. Jed hoped he'd gotten it wrong, and it was just the vodka talking, but your deputy seemed quite certain. Maybe we should have given him the peach wine, eh?"

Tex finished the guy off with a bullet to the temple—he'd heard enough.

"We should leave, now," Bloodmountain said.

"Are there more coming?" Tex asked him—just how many men had Jed Timothy sent out there? And, had the eight he'd just killed been hunting game or Little Alamo hunters? One thing was for certain, though, they'd deliberately laid in wait for them to collect the bodies of the three they'd gunned down in cold blood—there could have been no doubt they were from the Little Alamo.

And that, as far as Tex was concerned, helped make up his mind on the next steps needing to be taken.

Chapter Thirty-Four

It was late afternoon when Tex and the others returned to the Little Alamo with the bodies of the hunters killed by Jed Timothy's men. And it was early evening by the time Tex had gotten through the awful job of breaking the news to each of the three families in turn; although delivering bad news was nothing new for Tex, it never became any easier, and he knew it never would.

What made things so much worse was that those families blamed him for their loved ones' death—Tex saw it in their tear-filled eyes. Since he was seen as the fort's leader, it would have been inappropriate for him to explain it had been Lump's idea to send out the hunting parties the morning before; even if he had, they'd still blame him for not keeping his deputy under control.

Such was the burden of accountability—it was always going to be his fault as leader that three men were going to be buried in the Little Alamo cemetery the following day.

Victoria had called him shortly after he'd returned home from the Woods' house. She wanted to know if he'd like to join her later that night and read a little together in the hope of taking his mind off things—for a while at least.

But Tex wasn't really up to reading another chapter

of *The Bridge*, although he did want to see Victoria. Instead of reading, he yearned to simply lay his head on her lap like a small child seeking comfort and have her run her fingers through his hair. Victoria had a way of soothing him even when his mind was crazy mess, and when it was just the two of them and the setting sun, he could forget all about the new world and just how hard it was to survive within it.

So, Tex told Victoria he'd do his darndest to spend the evening with her, and he meant it most sincerely.

But first, he had one more unpleasant duty to perform before he could even think about taking a well-earned rest.

###

"What the hell do you mean, *relieving me of my duties*?" Lump spat. "You can't do that, Tex!"

"I'm sorry, Lump," Tex said, his heart breaking at giving his best friend the decision he'd made out there in the Couch Mountain forest. "You've left me with no choice."

"We are *both* leaders of this community," Lump protested. He eyed Wopat and Tip, who Tex had brought along to his house for back up. "You have no place taking my rights away."

"You sent three men out to die, Lump." Tex spoke calmly—a raised voice might well escalate the already volatile situation. "That was irresponsible at best, reckless, even."

"Like you've never made a mistake that got people killed," Lump retaliated. "There's more blood on your hands than mine."

Tex ignored the jibe. It was irrelevant as far as he was concerned—this was all about Lump. "You also spilled your guts to Jed Timothy that we were planning to attack his compound," Tex said. "And that's *why* Don Woods and his part were killed!"

Lump fell silent.

"What were you thinking, Lump?" Tex stepped forward, his face inches from his friend's. "You got drunk and flapped your mouth, and now three men are dead. This is all your fault."

"It was just drunk talk, Tex," Lump offered by means of an explanation.

Tex snorted. "That doesn't excuse the fact you told Jed Timothy we were thinking about attacking his place—it was only a loose idea, you know that."

Lump shrugged and lowered his eyes; he knew he'd screwed up. "I was only trying to do what was best for everybody," he said. "I thought if the hunting parties brought something in, we wouldn't have to do anything we didn't have to."

"Three men are dead." The words grated on Tex; fresh memories of devastated families haunted his thoughts. "*Three*… and it looks like Jed Timothy is more than on the defensive—I still can't believe his people did that."

"I guess it gives us a reason to retaliate—we could overpower his compound in minutes."

"Don't try twisting this into a good thing." Tex was beginning to feel cornered; was it possible Lump had deliberately let the information slip to maneuver him into taking on the Timothy compound? As much as he didn't want to believe it of his friend, Tex knew it was a distinct possibility.

"I want you to work in the stores under Phil Cross," Tex said.

"What?" Lump glared at him. "Are you serious, Tex?"

Tex nodded. "You'll need to keep your head down until this whole fiasco dies down—there's enough unrest here as it is."

Lump looked as if he was about to protest, and Tex was ready with his rebuff, but the guy closed his mouth and fell silent.

Walking away from Lump with Tip and Wopat, Tex knew his friend was fuming beneath that quiet exterior. Even back in the day, in the desert, he'd had that chilling way of switching from volatile and enraged to suppressing his true anger, and that was when Lump was at his most dangerous.

All he could hope for was the guy would simmer himself down and not do anything else stupid that could get people killed. Tex asked Tip and Wopat to keep a discreet eye on Lump until the raw memory of the three deaths faded some and things returned to some semblance of normality.

Chapter Thirty-Five

Victoria was humming the Garth Brooks song to herself and emptying out one of the mouse traps when Tex turned up at the apiary. The dead mouse dangled limply from the wooden spring trap by its broken neck, and Tex felt a little sorry for it: all it had wanted was to fill its belly—just like everyone else in the Little Alamo.

"Looks like you're getting the rodent problem under control," Tex said.

Victoria jumped a little, startled by Tex's voice. "Oh, hey, Tex." she dropped the mouse into the trash bucket.

"I'm sorry," Tex said, fidgeting with the brim of his hat. "I didn't mean to scare you."

Victoria gave him a broad smile, put her arms around his neck, and kissed him firmly on the lips.

Tex savored Victoria's lips upon his. They felt warm, soft, and ever so much like *home*. Victoria's invitation to spend the evening with her had been his first thought after leaving Lump, and the kiss was so very much needed.

"If I'd known that was waiting for me, I'd have come sooner," Tex said when Victoria—finally—broke the kiss.

"You look like a guy who needed it." Victoria stepped back from him, mousetrap still in her hand.

"Boy howdy," Tex replied with a weary sigh. "Today

has not been a good day."

Victoria nodded her understanding and reset the trap—baiting it with a small chunk of honeycomb. "I'm almost finished up here," she told Tex. "If you're up to some company…"

Tex could think of nothing he'd like more than to escape the day in Victoria's arms. "That sounds good." He smiled. "I could cook, and we can read some more—if you'd like."

"I'd like that very much, Tex." Victoria popped the trap back in the beehive and closed the top; she'd subdued the bees with enough smoke to ensure they took her intrusion with good grace, and she had no need for the white beekeeper garb and net mask she typically wore.

"Then, I shall wait for you, ma'am," Tex told her. "Is there anything I can do to help?"

Victoria shook her head. "I'm all done for today, thank you. All I need now is for someone to cook me dinner."

###

They arrived at Tex's house at the same time as Lee.

"Hi, Dad. Hi, Victoria."

"You're home late," Tex said as he unlocked the front door. "Studying again?"

Lee flashed his father a sheepish grin, his face reddening a touch. "Yeah," he said. "Big test coming up."

"And how is Sofia?" Tex asked as the three made their way into the house.

"Tex! You're embarrassing the poor boy." Victoria admonished with a smile.

"I know." Tex squeezed his son's shoulder. "I'm his father—it's what we fathers are supposed to do."

Lee took Tex's joshing in good humor, and Tex

thanked his lucky stars they'd managed to forge a good relationship in spite of everything.

"I wanted to ask you something, Dad." Lee perched on the arm of the couch looking every inch the grown-up.

"If it's about the birds and the bees, I thought we already covered that," Tex joked.

Victoria play slapped his arm, Lee smiled, and at that moment, Tex felt like everything was as it was supposed to be. It was as if Victoria *belonged* right there in his home.

"I know it's probably not the best timing, but…" Lee took in a deep breath and Tex feared the worse—sixteen was far too young to be getting a gal in the family way, especially the Garcia girl. "I want to contribute more—to the Little Alamo, I mean—so I thought I'd volunteer for the hunting parties."

Tex's reply stuck in his throat; thoughts of somebody calling on him to deliver the news Lee had been found dead in the foothills of Couch Mountain made his blood run cold. Lee had been right: it really wasn't the best time to raise the subject.

"You taught me to shoot ages ago," Lee pressed. "And I'm a crack shot—all thanks to your expert training."

Tex couldn't resist a wry smile at the kid's attempt to butter him up; the two of them were more alike than even Tex liked to admit.

"And…" Lee softened his voice. "We are down some good hunting guys—I thought I could help fill in."

Tex looked to Victoria for support; she held his hand and gave it a squeeze. She said nothing, though, and Tex figured she didn't feel comfortable enough doing so.

"It's dangerous out there, Son," Tex said. "You know what happened to Don Woods and his men."

Lee nodded. "I'm sixteen now, Dad. I'm old enough to take on more responsibilities, and I'm a good hunter."

"I've never taken you anywhere out of sight of the

compound," Tex reminded his son. "When I was teaching you, we stayed where it was safe—and there were fewer threats out there back then."

With the addition of Jed Timothy's people to the nomads and Red River Gang, Tex knew things had never been more dangerous beyond the Little Alamo's walls.

"But you send other men out hunting," Lee protested.

Tex saw the kid was getting upset; he'd obviously set his mind to it and wasn't going to take no for an answer. Plus, Lee made a good point: if he was prepared to send other people's fathers, husbands, and sons hunting, then he had to be prepared to send out his own. If he didn't simply because Lee was his flesh and blood, that would make Tex Pemberton a hypocrite—and that was something he was not.

"Can you give me a few," Tex asked Lee. "I'd like to talk it through with Victoria, if that's okay."

"Sure," Lee stood up from the couch's arm and made his way to the stairs. "I'll get my rifle cleaned up."

Tex smiled as his son walked off; the scared little kid he'd uprooted to live at the Little Alamo had grown up into a fine young man indeed—and tall, too!

"Hope you don't mind," Tex said to Victoria. He sat himself down on the couch and invited her to join him with a gentle tug on her hand.

"Not at all." Victoria sat beside him. "I'm flattered you want to share this with me—I know how hard it must be for you right now."

Tex took off his hat and rubbed a hand over his scalp. "Yeah, the kid's timing could be better, that's for sure."

"He's mature enough to see we're three good hunters down," Victoria said. "I think that makes this perfect timing."

"We haven't even put them in the ground yet." Tex pushed the mental image of the three naked bodies lying face down in the forest to the back of his mind.

"So, Lee figured he'd strike while the iron's hot," Victoria ventured. "And before others stepped up and you had a good reason to not let him go."

"Am I that obvious?" Tex let out a sigh.

Victoria nodded. "You're Lee's dad, and you already lost his mother—it's understandable, Tex." She put both of her hands on his and looked him dead in the eye. "I'm sure there's a way you can give your son what he wants and keep him safe at the same time."

"I guess so. We do need to scout around the forest to the south of here—Jimmy Bloodmountain is saying he's seen signs of the wild boar coming back. It's certainly safer out there than Couch Mountain."

"Well, there you go!" Victoria declared with a clap of her hands.

"Thank you, Victoria." Tex was genuinely grateful—he'd forgotten just how good it was to have someone close to talk things through with. Since Krista died, he'd pretty much been winging it as far as raising Lee went, although he'd not done a bad job at it. She was right, of course, as was Lee, and Tex knew he couldn't block his son's desire to hunt. In many ways, as much as the thought scared Tex, it also made him immensely proud of the boy even though a big part of him wished he'd asked to volunteer to work in the library instead of the terrifying world beyond the compound.

"You have the wisdom of Solomon, Tex," Victoria said with a loving smile. "Which is why you make a good leader."

"Thank you for saying so." The truth was, Tex wasn't feeling that—not after the stunt Lump pulled. If anything, Tex was feeling a little out of control as if things were building up to something bigger and altogether more frightening.

"I'd like you to give him this… to help keep him safe." Victoria unclasped the silver chain that hung around her neck and put it into Tex's hand; he'd never seen Victoria without it on, and she looked strangely *naked.*

"You could give it to him yourself." Tex studied the chain and the small, silver cross it held. The cross was plain and smooth, nothing fancy at all, yet Tex knew it meant so much.

Victoria shook her head. "I wouldn't want to make Lee feel awkward," she told Tex. "And, besides, I think it'll mean a lot more coming from his father."

Tex closed his hand around the cross; it felt warm from Victoria, and yeah, it felt *safe*.

"So," Victoria broke the moment. "What's for dinner?"

Chapter Thirty-Six

It was so early that not even the roosters had woken up—Tex envied them, all tucked up in their coop surrounded by the hens.

"Quit worrying, we'll take good care of him," Tip Cane assured Tex.

"Your son is in good hands," Jimmy Bloodmountain added. "He is a good hunter—and I am sure we'll come back with something."

"I'm not worrying," Tex protested.

"You are his father. You will worry." Bloodmountain replied.

"I'll be okay, Dad," Lee chipped in; he had his camo gear on, and his hunting rifle slung over his shoulder by its strap—he'd sat up until the small hours cleaning the gun and it looked pristine.

The three stood by the compound gates waiting for them to open. Tip had opted to take one of the black, LPG Jeep Wranglers—they were good over rough terrain and more economical on fuel than the Cruiser or Hummer. The vehicle stood idling, its lights splitting the early morning darkness.

Slowly and without a sound, the gates eased open. Tip, Bloodmountain, and Lee made a move toward the

Jeep.

"Lee," Tex said.

Lee stopped in his tracks, turned around. By the look on his face, Tex reckoned the boy was thinking his old man had changed his mind and was about to tell him he wouldn't be going out hunting after all.

Instead, Tex walked over and placed the silver cross and chain Victoria had given him into his son's hand. "Take this—Victoria wanted me to give it to you."

Lee stared at the cross, glinting in the Jeep's high beams. "Tell her thank you," he said and slipped it into his pocket.

"Will do," Tex replied and took a step back—his way of saying, *off you go, son.*

The Jeep slipped out between the Little Alamo gates and into the darkness, and Tex watched it go until the gates closed. They'd be back before noon, in time for the memorial service for the three dead hunters, and Tex knew he'd be counting the minutes 'til then.

On his way back, Tex noticed Victoria's lights were on. He knew she was an early riser, so he figured she'd not mind too much if he called in to say hi.

Tex had barely rapped gently upon Victoria's door when it opened—it was almost as if she'd been expecting him and had lay in wait on the other side.

"Good morning, Tex," she greeted him warmly.

Tex struggled to get his words out; Victoria looked simply stunning standing there, framed in her doorway. She wore a long, ankle-length nightgown—it was black with tiny red roses; it fit her perfect, small frame like a glove and was just see-through enough to tantalize his senses. "I-I hope you don't mind my popping over…" he finally managed to say.

"Of course not." Victoria stood aside to invite him in. "It's always wonderful to see you, Tex—even at this ungodly hour of the morning."

Tex took that as a gentle admonishment; he *knew* he shouldn't have taken the chance. "I should go…"

"Don't you dare, Tex Pemberton." Victoria threw her arms around his neck and planted a soft kiss on his bristly cheek. She then nuzzled his neck, kissing, caressing with her lips as she did so.

Tex slipped his arms around Victoria's waist and pulled her close; the warmth of her body pressed against his was mesmerizing—he felt her breathing, the gentle swell of her breasts molding into his chest.

"I have a confession." Victoria's voice was muffled against Tex's neck.

"You do?"

"I knew you'd be walking by this morning," Victoria lifted her head to look Tex in the eyes; her beautiful face was so close, their noses touched. "So, I put on my lights and the nightgown."

"You knew I'd call in?"

"I know you better than you give me credit for—and the next time you want to kiss me, just go right ahead and do it." Victoria let out a laugh, her breath warm and sweet on Tex's face. "Although, you have resisted me for this long."

It surprised Tex to learn Victoria had cottoned on to his internal struggle—he thought he'd hidden it well. Of course, he'd wanted to take things slowly—even though he'd craved Victoria's touch for so long. He'd held back from attempting to seduce her through fear of scaring her away with too much, too soon, and also from the age-old fear of all men—rejection. For all he knew, she saw him only as a friend, although they had shared some romantic moments together in recent weeks.

"I wasn't resisting—"

Victoria silenced Tex's protest with a kiss. It was a

hard, urgent kiss; lips pressed to his, her tongue seeking Tex's.

Victoria pulled away—just slightly. "I'll warn you now, Tex," she purred. "After all this time waiting for you to make your move, I want more than a minute and twenty seconds."

Tex chuckled and assured her, "You'll be getting a lot more than a minute and twenty from me… a heck of a lot more."

They kissed again, and as Victoria skillfully led him to her bedroom, Tex felt the urgent stirrings down below and knew he might just be in trouble on that score.

As it was, they made love twice in quick succession; Victoria had been an incredibly understanding, considerate lover, and Tex simply couldn't get enough of her. After so long craving Victoria, it was almost like making up for lost time.

They rested awhile and, as the sun rose, they made love again.

Finally, when they were both sated and thoroughly exhausted, Victoria propped herself up on plump pillows against her headboard and Tex laid his head in her lap.

"Would you mind if I read to you a little?" she asked.

Tex shook his head, his eyes feeling too tired to remain open for long. "I'd like that."

Victoria plucked her copy of *The Bridge* from her nightstand and started to read—she backtracked a tad to where she knew Tex was so she didn't spoil any surprises.

Tex closed his eyes, just happy to be in the moment he'd longed for. And, for a moment, all the stress of the fight with Lump, the dwindling food supplies, and his son out hunting for the very first time melted away; the whole world was all just Tex and Victoria…

He could not have heard more than three words of Victoria's reading before exhaustion overtook him, and

Tex drifted away into a restful, mercifully dreamless sleep.

Chapter Thirty-Seven

The hunting party returned a little after ten, just as Tex was preparing himself for the memorial service; it was hard to find something to say when guilt was eating him up inside. Grateful for the distraction, Tex set off to the compound gates to welcome his son back from his first official hunting trip—he prayed the guys had been lucky out there.

"We were ambushed." The first words out of Jimmy Bloodmountain's mouth were blunt and unexpected.

Tex's first thought was of Lee.

"I'm okay, Dad," Lee said as he clambered out of the Jeep; the boy looked shaken but otherwise unharmed.

Tex let out the breath he'd held and hugged his son tight; what had he been thinking letting him out of the compound?

"You weren't supposed to go far out," Tex admonished Tip. "Where the hell did you get to?"

"Five, maybe six miles," Tip replied. "We found a bunch of pigs and followed them—bagged three of 'em, too."

A cursory glance at the Jeep told Tex there were no wild boar. "They took the pigs?"

Tip nodded. "And our weapons," he said. "I think we

were lucky that's all they did."

Tex shuddered at the thought of what could have been. "What are the Red River Gang doing this far?"

"They weren't Red River," Tip told him.

"No?" Tex was taken aback—he found it hard to believe the nomads had taken on a heavily armed vehicle.

"They were from the Timothy compound," Tip said quietly.

"Are you *sure*?"

Tip nodded. "I recognized a couple of them from when I visited with Lump and Rhino. They were drinking in Jed's bar."

"Shit," Tex growled. "How many jumped you?"

"There were five of them, Dad," Lee butted in.

"They told us they only wanted the pigs," Bloodmountain added. "But I saw death in their eyes—they were there to do more than rob us of our food."

Tex's mind raced—for all but the grace of God, he might well have been preparing a memorial service for his own son. Clearly, Jed Timothy was sending a message to the Little Alamo, although what he'd hoped to achieve by waylaying the hunting party like some olde-time highwayman, Tex couldn't be certain. Given that Timothy was paranoid about the Little Alamo mounting a raid on his compound, surely, he'd realize he was simply poking the bear by taking their food and guns

"I don't believe it," Tex grunted. "What the hell is he thinking? How did you guys manage to get away?"

Tip shrugged his shoulders. "They took the pigs and our rifles, loaded them up into their truck, and left."

"They just left?" Tex tried not to sound too much like he didn't believe Tip, but after what Timothy's men did to Don Woods and the others, it did seem like a stretch.

"For a moment, we thought they were going to kill us," Bloodmountain said. "They held us at gunpoint after they took everything…"

Hearing that, Tex wanted to hold Lee again—the kid must have been terrified. But he restrained himself, not wanting to embarrass his son who was being so very grown up about the whole ordeal.

"So, why didn't they take the Jeep?" Tex asked the obvious question. "And why not do to you what they did to Don?" He couldn't bring himself to say what was on the tip of his tongue: *why didn't they shoot the three of you and leave you naked in the forest?*

Tip stumbled over his words. "I honestly thought they were going to, but then they just… *left*."

"They planned to at first," Bloodmountain threw in, "when they ambushed us in the forest. But I think they didn't have the stomach for it…" He nodded toward Lee, who stood silently by Tex's side.

Tex rested a protective, fatherly hand on his son's shoulder, and even though he knew it was just an unrealistic reaction, he didn't want to let the boy out of his sight again.

If Bloodmountain's assessment of the situation was true, then Jed Timothy was sending more than a message—he'd pretty much declared war on the Little Alamo. Tex wondered how Jed had reacted when his men returned sans vehicle and having not killed the Little Alamo hunting party. Maybe his five men wouldn't admit to not finishing the job they'd been sent out to do and concocted some excuse about the Jeep?

If that was the case, Tex knew that gave the Little Alamo the upper hand: Jed Timothy wouldn't be expecting any reprisals. It was an advantage Tex had little option but to capitalize upon.

"Keep this between us for the time being," Tex said to Tip. "Meet me at my house after the memorial service—and bring Lump and Phil Cross with you."

“Will do,” Tip replied. “Anyone else?”

Tex shook his head; for a moment, he considered including Victoria—after their tryst earlier that morning, he figured she was going to become a bigger part of things. But Tex pushed the thought to the back of his mind; there’d be things to discuss with Tip and Lump he didn’t want Victoria to be party to—it was a side of him she didn’t need to see at that point in their relationship.

No, he’d tell her his plans after he’d firmed them up with his men.

Chapter Thirty-Eight

The memorial service had not left Tex in the best of moods for what he had to address. It had been a sedate affair, much as he'd expected, but the hard, accusatory glances he'd gotten from the families of the deceased had left him with a sick feeling in his stomach.

It also had him thirsting for revenge against the Timothy compound, which, while it helped him justify his next move against them, was not an emotion Tex was particularly proud of. He could only hope he was doing the right thing and that Victoria would understand he was doing what he thought he had to do.

"Okay, guys, this is not going to be an easy conversation." Tex studied Tip, Cross, and Lump—fresh from the service, they all looked somber in their black suits.

"You all know it was Jed Timothy's people who killed Woods, Goedeke, and Farrell…"

Nods all around.

"They also ambushed our hunting party this morning." Tex paused to let the enormity of his words sink in.

"The same men?" Lump asked.

"We don't know," Tex replied. Despite everything that had transpired with Lump, Tex was pleased to have him involved with the plan. For all the guy's faults, he was a good friend and one hell of a soldier. "What we do know is they were definitely from the Timothy compound."

"We saw them in Jed's bar," Tip told Lump. "No doubt at all."

"Dammit," Lump hissed. "Looks like old Jed has plans for the Little Alamo."

"I don't think he'd be stupid enough to attack us," Tip offered. "He knows he's no match for or manpower and weaponry—it'd be a suicide mission, even if it was totally unexpected."

"Well, now it's not unexpected," Tex said. "We can assume he's desperate enough to do something, especially since he's convinced we have plans against him."

Tex couldn't help but glance at Lump—Jed Timothy's paranoia and the attack on the hunting parties was entirely his fault. He held his tongue, though, it was not the time for finger-pointing.

"So, we're going to go after them before they come to us?" Tip shuffled his ass on Tex's couch as if he was uncomfortable with the notion; the guy was a hunter, not a soldier.

"We need to act fast," Tex said. "We use the element of surprise and mount an attack at sunset."

"*Today*?" Lump seemed shocked.

"Yes, today," Tex replied. "I'm assuming you can round up the vehicles and men in time?"

"It's a half-day drive," Tip added. "That gives us—"

"A couple hours," Tex interrupted and turned to Lump. "Can you get it done by then?"

Lump nodded. "It'll be a push, but yeah, it's definitely doable."

"Are you sure about this, Tex?" Phil Cross broke his silence. "There are women and children at the Timothy compound."

"There are women and children here, too, Phil," Tex

snapped back. "And they have to be our priority. We already offered Jed the chance to bring his people here to keep them safe from the Red River Clan—we can extend that to any of his people who want to come back after…"

"I'll make sure we have enough space in the trucks," Lump said. "I'm supposing this will be more than just a retaliatory mission.

Tex nodded; the weight of what they were strategizing was pressing down hard on his shoulders; he knew he had just one chance to get things right. "The objective is to bring back as many supplies as possible," he told Lump.

"Even at the expense of civilians?" Tip seemed to be taking in the role of Jiminy Cricket, and Tex was less than happy with it. The last thing he needed was anyone pricking his conscience—he knew what they were doing was morally wrong. But times were so very different, and it was definitely survival of the fittest.

"We have to prioritize the Little Alamo," Tex reiterated for Tip's benefit. "And if that means casualties or civilians left behind, then that's how it's gotta be. I need you in on this, Tip, you're a man I can trust and good with a rifle—but if you're not up to it…"

Tex's words hung heavy in the air.

All eyes turned to Tip Cane.

"Yeah, I'm in." Tip sounded less than convinced with his own words. "And I do understand, Tex—maybe more than you do."

Tip had never spoken much about his ordeal at Fort Simons, and Tex had never pushed him to. He'd seen enough of his fellow soldiers with chronic PTSD to know such things only came out when they were good and ready—if at all. Tip was a damned good man, and Tex valued the skills he'd brought to the Little Alamo even if he was turning into a bleeding heart.

"Look, guys," Tex addressed all three for Tip's benefit. "I know this isn't ideal, but Jed has backed us into a corner here. He's murdered Little Alamo people and attacked others." He held off adding, *including my son*—it wouldn't pay to make it personal.

"Two birds with one stone," Lump added.

"Precisely," Tex picked up. "We remove the threat the Timothy compound poses to us, and we give our own supplies a much-needed boost."

Tex knew just how mercenary that sounded; he'd have to figure out a different way of putting it for when he told Victoria.

"How many men?" Lump, ever the practical one, asked.

"Make it a two dozen," Tex told him. "With you, me, and Tip, that ought to be plenty—Jed only had forty-seven people in total, and we already took care of a bunch on trhem."

"And his walls are weak," Lump said. "I gave 'em a once-over the last time we were over there."

Tex bit his tongue.

"I'll have the trucks fueled up and good to go," Cross said. "All ten?"

"All ten," Tex agreed. "Plus, the Cruiser and three of the Jeeps."

"Roger that."

"Thanks, Phil," Tex said. "Now, if there's no other business, we need to get our asses into gear."

Taking the hint, Tip, Lump, and Cross made their way out of Tex's house to prepare for the raid on the Timothy compound.

Then, Tex took a walk to the library—Victoria's next volunteer day had come around quickly. She was busy slotting returned books to the shelves when Tex arrived, and she seemed pleasantly surprised to see him.

“Can we talk?” Tex asked her, the fond memories of their early morning together so fresh in his mind he could feel the touch of her skin against his.

A concerned look crossed Victoria’s face.

“It’s nothing to worry about,” Tex reassured her. “I could just use a friendly ear, is all.”

Visibly relieved, Victoria led Tex to the small office at the rear of the library.

There, Tex told her all about the plans to mount an offensive on Jed Timothy’s compound, along with the reasoning behind his decision—all he could hope for was she’d not think he was some kind of monster.

“I’m shocked at Jed,” Victoria said once Tex had finished. “I’d never in a thousand years believe he was capable of having anyone killed—no matter what he thinks they’re planning to do. Are you sure it was his people?”

“Without a doubt,” Tex told her. “And it was definitely Jed’s men who attacked Lee’s party this morning—Tip recognized them.”

“He must have been terrified.”

“The kid’s playing it cool,” Tex said. “You know how he is.”

Victoria nodded. “I do, and he’d have been terrified—he’ll hold it in for so long, and when it comes out, just be there for him, Tex.”

“Yes, ma’am.” Tex dipped his hat a little and smiled.

“Are you sure this is the only way, though?” Victoria ventured. “Have you tried talking to Jed?”

“He’s killed our people, Victoria, I think the time for talking is long gone.” It was not a conversation Tex wished to get into with her; the decision to attack had been made and there was no time for diplomacy. “Besides, when I suggested he bring his folk here to avoid the Red River Gang, Jed threw it straight back in my face. He accused us of only wanting to plunder his supplies.”

"I'm sure they'd do us a lot of good right now." Victoria hit the nail right on the head.

"Of course." Tex knew there was no point arguing otherwise. "We'll take what we need and offer Jed's people sanctuary here."

Victoria looked at Tex as if she barely knew him, and it made his heart ache; after finally making the huge leap in their relationship, he hoped he wasn't in the process of blowing it out of the water. He was doing what he knew he must, and he was doing his best to explain that to her—but Tex knew his words were coming across as cold and heartless.

"I get it, Tex," Victoria said after a too-long pause. "Honestly, I do, and I know it hasn't been an easy decision for you to make. I guess that's what happens when you're a leader, though. Everyone at the Little Alamo—especially me—owes you a big debt of gratitude for providing a safe home amid all the chaos going on out there, so it would be unfair to judge you for this. We all know you'll do whatever you feel is best for us all."

Tex took hold of Victoria's hands. "Thank you for that," he said. "I really needed to hear it."

"You're a good soul, Tex Pemberton," she replied. "And this will weigh on you for the rest of your life—I understand that much. Please look after yourself out there."

Although they parted with a fond kiss as Tex left the library, he had a niggling feeling Victoria had only said what he *wanted* to hear and saw him in a different light.

But there was no time for Tex to dwell upon matters of the heart; he'd pick up with Victoria when he returned from the Timothy compound and work his magic on her to show he wasn't some coldhearted warmonger.

Next, Tex stopped by the stores to see Phil Cross, who was busy loading up the first of the vehicles with ammunition, dynamite, and spare fuel.

"Got a minute, Phil?"

"Sure, Tex, what do you need?"

"While we're out, I need you to work on getting our defenses beefed up," Tex told him. "Shore up the back wall and the gates, have extra patrols set up around the fields and solar farm."

"There's not much in the fields to defend," Cross said with a weary sigh.

"Just the ones with something still growing, then," Tex said. "And especially those closest to the compound."

"What are you expecting, Tex?" Cross was growing apprehensive.

"Nothing, I hope, but it always pays to be prepared for the *un*expected." Tex fiddled with the brim of his hat. "And can you set up claymore mines around the perimeter, please?"

Tex had hoped not to have to use the homemade claymores, but it seemed as good a time as any to get them put into place. He and Lump had made the mines out of Tannerite, nails, nuts, and bolts to provide antipersonnel protection around the entire compound. Based upon the mines they'd worked with out in the desert, the claymores were designed to create a 360-degree blast radius of over a hundred-fifty feet; the shrapnel they threw out would kill anything within a thirty-foot radius outright.

"I'll get to it just as soon as I've got you guys set up and good to go," Cross said. "I hope we don't need it."

"Me too." Tex absently fiddled with the handle of his Colt. "Who the hell knows what's coming these days, Phil?"

And, with that, Tex headed off along the compound to prepare himself.

Chapter Thirty-Nine

They waited for the night to close in a couple miles north of the Timothy compound and away from where Lump and his crew had encountered the Red River Gang. Tex had the convoy of Little Alamo trucks and Jeeps hunker down in a shallow valley in the middle of what was pretty much nowhere. Tex knew it was unlikely any hunters would happen upon them as there wasn't so much as a living tree or blade of grass to be seen for miles; the whole area was dead, brown, and tinderbox dry.

But, on the off chance some stray hunters came across them, Tex had set up a half dozen men to patrol around the vehicles. Their orders were, quite simply, to silence anyone who may give away the convoy's position.

As the pitch darkness fell across the barren landscape, Tex gave the command to move out. He led the way in his trusty Cruiser, which Phil and the guys at the garage had patched up nicely; it felt like *home*.

"Kill the lights," Tex gave the order over the Cruiser's radio as the Timothy compound came into view, made visible in the blackness by the sparse smattering of twinkling lights from the dwellings within its walls. In synch, every vehicle behind Tex fell dark, and they navigated toward their target, homing in on those lights.

Tex took full advantage of the element of surprise; with no lights to give them away, his convoy was practically upon the compound before anyone heard the low rumble of engines and tires on the hardened ground.

Suddenly, floodlights lit up the landscape around the Timothy compound, exposing the would-be invaders. Gunfire followed mere seconds later.

The convoy split up into four groups, each one heading toward one of the compound's walls, with Tex's making its way to the main gates—he knew the armored Cruiser would be crucial in getting them past the pair of sentry towers Jed had protecting the compound's entrance.

Bullets pinged off the vehicle's bodywork as Tex pushed forward, his focus entirely on the double gates ahead. They were only half the height of the Little Alamo's and, in the floodlights, looked to be half the thickness and not reinforced with steel plates.

Nonetheless, Tex had a half-dozen sticks of dynamite at the ready to make splinters out of Jed Timothy's gates.

Doing his damndest to stay out of the line of fire, Tex floored the Cruiser's gas and sped up to the gates. "Light me up," he said to Lump, riding shotgun, who flicked his lighter and held it to the fuse of one of the explosive sticks.

Quickly, Tex rolled the window down just enough to drop the dynamite out and then raced off into the darkness beyond the floodlights. A volley of bullets followed, shattering the Cruiser's rear window.

The Timothy compound gates blew with a loud, dull *bang* and a bright flash of yellow light that lit up the darkness and filled the air with the thick reek of smoke.

Tex spun the Cruiser around on a dime and headed back toward the gates—the explosion had reduced them to little more than fragmented shards of charred wood. He saw that one of the sentry towers had toppled over; it lay on the ground inside the compound in shattered pieces.

As Tex maneuvered the Cruiser into the compound, he heard the resonating cracks of explosions from all of the other walls and knew his men were making their way inside.

"There!" Lump pointed at a small, squat, single-story building off to the left. "That's Jed's place."

Tex pulled on the steering wheel and the Cruiser swerved sharply, narrowly avoiding a pair of young men who ran out in front of it. Both were armed with what looked to be AK47s, but neither seemed keen on using them—Tex caught the look of terror in the men's eyes as he zipped by.

As the compound filled with Tex's invading force, chaos spilled out onto the narrow streets as Jed's people ran from their homes. Men, women, and children raced in all directions—some clutched armfuls of treasured possessions, some of the adults carried guns and headed toward the compound's ramparts. A few paused to take pot shots at the trucks and the black-clad soldiers who exited them.

Tex ground his teeth as the staccato sound of semi-automatic gunfire rang in his ears; his men had been ordered to engage only if there was a risk to their lives—Tex had hoped Timothy's people would simply lay down their arms and surrender once they realized they were outgunned.

But no, some of them had decided to fight back—at least enough to make things difficult for Tex and his soldiers.

Tex shot a fiery look at Lump, who sat beside him with his semi-automatic rested across his lap—the guy looked ready for combat as if he was actually looking forward to gunning down innocent civilians. It was thanks to him the Timothy compound were prepared for the invasion—Lump's loose tongue had given away the game plan and provided Jed enough time to put a defensive strategy into place, albeit a chaotic one. And, Tex figured, that tactic had included taking out the Little Alamo's hunting parties.

"I'm going in," Tex told his passenger as he pulled the Cruiser to a skidding halt outside Jed Timothy's door. "Cover me."

Lump pushed open his door and climbed out of the Cruiser, using its armored body as cover. He let loose with short bursts of fire as Tex jumped out and ran to Jed Timothy's small home.

Tex's head flooded with long-suppressed memories of his tours in Iraq: the jarring noise of gunshot, the metallic reek of gunpowder, the air thick with smoke from the burning wooden walls, the panicked screams of displaced people. He thanked his lucky stars he'd volunteered for counseling after his discharge; the PTSD that plagued so many of his comrades would surely have kicked in otherwise.

Acting on instinct and without a second thought, Tex shouldered the narrow, wooden door and burst into Jed Timothy's home.

"Don't do it, Jed!" Tex yelled and pointed his gun directly at Timothy's center mass.

The man stood motionless by a small writing desk at the side of the sparsely furnished living room. On the desk sat a short-wave radio, its tiny red light glaring like some small, malevolent eye.

Timothy had a sawed-off, double-barrel shotgun in one hand—it was pointed at the rough wood floor, but Tex had a good idea what the guy was thinking.

"We knew you'd come, Tex," Timothy said quietly. "I tried to get help, but nobody will come." He nodded at the radio.

"It didn't have to be like this, Jed." Tex kept his rifle aimed at Timothy's chest and hoped he wouldn't do anything stupid. "I offered to take you all in to keep you safe from the Red River Gang."

"And yet, you were the enemy all along."

Timothy's words stung Tex; it had only been a week or so since he'd been a welcome guest at the Little Alamo, visiting to trade potatoes and beans for jars of Victoria's delicious honey.

Victoria.

Tex wondered what she would think if she saw him in Timothy's house threatening the man with a gun and fully prepared to pull the trigger—she'd been married to Rusty long enough to know how soldiers were, but this was totally different to fighting terror in some faraway land.

She *knew* Jed Timothy.

And what if Jed was quicker with his shotgun than Tex was with his rifle? Would Victoria cope with losing *two* men she loved? Surely, that would be far too much for one lifetime. Tex had seen the look in Victoria's eyes when he'd told her about the planned raid on the Timothy compound, and it was not a look of approval. What would she think of what he'd become?

"Order your people to stand down, Jed," Tex said softly, calmly.

Timothy shook his head slowly; his knuckles whitened as he gripped his shotgun tightly. "Why? So you can plunder what you want without retaliation? My people are made of stronger stuff than that, Tex, you've underestimated us."

"No, Jed," Tex took a cautious step forward. "So we can avoid unnecessary bloodshed."

"Your people's, I assume?" Timothy sneered.

"Your people don't have to get hurt," Tex told him.

"Nobody does."

"It's too late for that," Timothy replied. "We'll defend what we have here until the last man."

"And what about the women and kids?"

"Those, too."

Tex caught a wild gleam in Timothy's eyes. It was the look of a man cornered, a dangerous man.

"Stand your people down, Jed," Tex repeated himself. "My offer of safe passage and accommodation at the Little Alamo still stands. It's been our plan all along."

"You don't want more people," Timothy said. "You only want our supplies."

"Then why would I have made the offer?"

"Who the hell knows, Tex." Timothy inched backward as Tex took another step toward him. "Maybe you'd kill us all in our beds the first night we got there and unloaded our stuff into your empty stores—I took the liberty of having a look around the last time I was there."

"We would never…" Tex protested. "We took in folks from Fort Simons, and we've always welcomed the waifs and strays who happened by."

"And where are they now? Buried out in your dead fields?"

"You're sounding crazy, Jed." Tex knew he wasn't getting through to the guy at all. "Have your people stand down and we'll talk about this like civilized—"

It all happened in a heartbeat: Jed swung his shotgun upward and Tex's training and reflexes kicked in—before he'd even had time to think, Tex's finger had squeezed his rifle's trigger.

The weapon jolted in Tex's hands, fire spat from its muzzle, and Jed Timothy flew backward like he'd been kicked by a mule. As he crumpled to the floor of his living room, Timothy's gun discharged and blasted a wide hole in the ceiling above him.

"Shit." Tex waited a beat or two, his gun still pointed at Timothy, even though the guy lay quite still. There was a line of neat holes diagonally across Timothy's chest, each one oozing red.

Then, Tex approached and kicked away the gun before checking for signs of life.

None.

"Dammit, Jed," Tex grumbled under his breath. "Why did you have to go and do that?" He thought of breaking the news of Timothy's demise to Victoria—she had grown quite fond of the man—and toyed with the notion of leaving out the fact he'd been the one who'd shot him dead in his own home.

The Timothy compound fell ten, fifteen minutes after the leader died. Overrun, out gunned, and their numbers depleted, they laid down their weapons and surrendered to Tex's men.

They'd put up a good, brave fight, though, which surprised Tex. He'd lost a handful of men, and a bunch of others were nursing wounds that would keep Doc. Baker busy for a few hours when they got back.

"We can take all of you back to the Little Alamo with us," Tex addressed the surviving Timothy clan—twenty-five in all; they'd lost over half their number. They were huddled together in the small compound square, lit up by floodlights and surrounded by a half dozen of Tex's soldiers.

"Why not just kill us here and save yourself the trouble?" a young woman spoke up. She was petite, with copper-red hair and a blood-smeared face. She had a rudimentary bandage wrapped around her left bicep.

"That was never our intention," Tex told her. "We can accommodate you in our compound."

"And make slaves of us?" The redheaded woman wasn't about to let up.

Tex shook his head as the Timothy people began chattering among themselves. Sure, it was difficult to play the Good Samaritan and plead altruism with his men loading up the trucks behind him with the Timothy compound's food and supplies.

"No," Tex said firmly. "I'm offering you a new home. A safe place away from the Red River Gang—they're on their way here."

"And you beat them to it." A middle-aged man shouted out.

"You're worse than they are," the redhead spat. "At least they're not *pretending* to be our friends."

Tex reeled at her harsh accusation; did they really think the Little Alamo had been pretending all those years, just waiting for the opportunity to take by force everything they wanted?

"At least let us take the women and children?" Tex tried his best to appeal to their sense of humanity.

"We'd rather take our chances here," the redhead said; a murmur of agreement rippled through the group.

"Yeah," the middle-aged man added. "We can defend ourselves here."

"Or go to one of the towns," a young man of no more than thirty said.

A sharp whistle silenced the chatter.

All eyes turned to the convoy as Lump whistled again, a finger in each side of his mouth.

It was time to go.

"This is your last chance," Tex said to the group.

The redhead stepped forward, her formidable chest puffed out, a look of determination on her face. She squared up to Tex.

"You're taking everything we have," she said. "Can you at least have the decency to leave us our weapons and enough vehicles and fuel to get to the nearest town? *That's* the chance we're prepared to take."

Tex could only nod; it hurt his heart to hear the people he'd offered to protect would rather fend for themselves in a ruined fort against the threat of the Red River Gang—just what kind of monster had he become?

All Tex could do was walk away from the defeated people—he ordered Lump to leave all the captured weapons and half the ammunition behind, along with five of the trucks and cans of spare fuel.

Like the woman said, it was the least he could do.

Climbing back into his Cruiser, Tex took one last look at the death and devastation he'd caused. The Timothy compound had ragged, gaping holes in its wooden walls, homes were alight, and corpses littered the narrow, dirt streets; the people he was leaving behind had no chance, he knew that much.

As Lump followed the convoy of trucks and Jeeps toward the compound's scorched gateway, Tex's radio crackled to life.

"Incoming!"

"Where?" he asked.

"Northside."

"Head south," Tex gave the order; he had a gut feeling the Red River Gang were on their way, no doubt attracted by the noise, fire, and smoke his attack on the Timothy compound had created. They likely wanted to get in on the action and grab what they could while there was something left to grab.

He spotted the first of the high beams coming through the hole his soldiers had blasted in the compound's rear wall. Tex twisted around to look through the Cruiser's shattered rear window and saw the people who'd just turned down sanctuary at the Little Alamo scramble to pick up the guns that had been left for them.

It had to be the Red River Gang, most likely the ones

Lump and Tip had reported seeing hiding in the dry river bed a few miles out. Knowing the fate that was heading their way, Tex fought the urge to have his men turn around and go back to pick up the Timothy compound survivors—by force if necessary.

Instead, all he could do was look on as the new marauders streamed in through the breaches his men had made in the Timothy compound's walls; they poured out of their vehicles and set about slaughtering the people Tex had left behind.

Vivid memories of Krista pulled down amid clamoring, clawing hands jolted Tex hard—he felt as helpless as he had back then, when all he could do was watch as his beloved wife died.

"Step on it, Lump," Tex ordered. "We gotta get back before they realize we have all the supplies and decide to come get it.

As he drove away with the sharp cracks of gunfire and screaming of innocent people ringing in his ears, Tex hoped Phil Cross had done a damn good job of bolstering the Little Alamo's defenses—seeing firsthand how ruthless the swarm of the Red River Gang were with Jed Timothy's people, there really was no margin for error.

And Tex would be damned if he was going to lose Victoria the same way he'd lost his wife.

Chapter Forty

Tex's convoy made it back to the Little Alamo shortly before noon; it had been a long, arduous drive across rough terrain in the pitch dark. And, because they'd taken the southern route in order to avoid the Red River Gang, it had added a couple hours onto the journey.

Weary, emotionally drained, Tex climbed from the Cruiser's passenger seat and made his way home, leaving Lump and Tip to supervise unloading the supplies they'd brought back with them.

Tex craved his bed, preferably with Victoria in it—he wanted to fall asleep on her lap again, to enjoy the comfort of her warm skin next to his, her soothing words as he succumbed to the fatigue eating into him.

But that was a luxury Tex knew he could ill afford. With the threat of the Red River Gang hanging over the compound, it fell to him to ensure everyone was fully prepared.

The house was empty—Lee was in school that morning and wouldn't be back until after one—which suited Tex because he didn't need any distractions.

First, he set the coffee maker to brewing an extra-strong pot of his favorite Columbian blend—he'd hidden a packet at the back of the pantry for just such an occasion—and then he phoned Phil Cross.

Cross picked up on the third ring. "Hey, Tex, you came back with a lot of stuff—well done."

"Meet me at the rear gates in an hour." Tex was in no mood to discuss the mission, not with Cross or anyone else.

"Oh… okay." Cross sounded a touch deflated.

Tex hung up before he could say anything else.

Next, Tex put a call into the comms room "Al, it's Tex. Can you have every adult assemble on the green at two? No exceptions."

"Will do," Mims replied. Tex was grateful he hadn't attempted to make conversation or ask questions.

Tex placed the receiver down on its cradle, but then picked it straight up again. He began dialing Victoria's number but stopped halfway through. He wanted to hear her voice, but she'd ask him about the Timothy compound—Jed in particular. And Tex wasn't ready to have that conversation with Victoria; he needed time to process his thoughts and emotions before he even attempted to articulate them to the woman he was falling in love with.

That realization stopped Tex dead in his tracks.

Standing there like some smitten teenager, the silent phone in his hand, Tex ran the thought through his head once more.

Yes, there was no doubt in his mind at all—he was falling in love with Victoria hook, line, and sinker.

Putting the phone back on the cradle, Tex made his way upstairs to shower off; the coffee would be brewed by then, and he'd down a mug of it to sharpen his senses before meeting with Phil Cross.

Then, *maybe*, he'd give Victoria a call.

###

"You've done good, Phil," Tex told the store man. The two of them walked around the outside perimeter of the Little Alamo—Tex cradled a rifle and had the reassuring weight of his Colt on his hip. On the wall above them, a pair of armed guards shadowed them from the walkway as they kept a watchful eye on the horizon for any sign of danger.

"I've used most of the claymores around the perimeter of the compound—and the solar farm, too," Cross told him.

"Then I guess we're pretty secure."

"As much as we can be," Cross replied. "We put them fifty yards out, so they don't take the walls down when they go off."

"Yeah," Tex said, thinking of the holes they'd made in Jed Timothy's walls and how helpless they'd left his compound. "What else?"

"We added extra sheet steel to the front gates, bolstered the west wall with lumber, and we're working on the east wall as we speak. As for the rear gates—you saw the additional steel we added. That's the last of the steel, though."

Tex nodded; Cross had done an exceptional job in a short period of time and with low resources—it *had* to be enough.

Making their way back into the compound through the rear gates, Tex scrutinized the waist-high row of sandbags either side.

"I'll organize extra security here," he told Cross.

"I was thinking we have someone on standby to weld them shut," Cross replied. "Hopefully we won't need to, but it's best to be prepared for the worst."

Tex nodded; it was a good idea, although he wasn't sure how long the gates would hold out under the onslaught of a determined Red River Gang. Still, if it bought them even a few minutes of time, it would be better than nothing.

"I need you to break out all the weapons we have in the stores, Phil," Tex said quietly—there were far too many people around. "But do it discreetly—I don't want to create panic."

"Everybody is on edge, Tex." Cross shot a worried glance across the Little Alamo's main square, where people were beginning to congregate on the compound's green in anticipation of Tex's address.

"Understandably so." Tex pulled the brim of his hat down slightly; the sun felt harsh in his eyes. Of course, folk were anxious—it was the first time in Little Alamo history they'd been asked to shore up the walls and prepare for possible attack. It was a day Tex knew—they *all* knew—would come around sooner or later, although everyone hoped and prayed it would not.

"I guess we can't afford to let them get complacent." Cross sounded a tad out of breath as he walked apace to keep up with Tex's long, purposeful strides. "How certain are you we're in trouble here?"

Tex snorted as his conscience jabbed at him with the sound of the blood-chilling screams that echoed from the Timothy compound as he drove away and the thought of all the innocent people he could have saved. But what was he supposed to have done? Force them all into his trucks at gunpoint?

Perhaps he should have done just that.

"The Red River Gang are less than a half day from here, Phil," Tex told him. "And they've been heading in our direction for some time now."

"They know we're here?"

Tex nodded. "It's safe to assume they've had scouts all over the area—they're far more organized than the nomads who attacked us a coupla years ago. And better armed, too. My guess is they planned to stock up on weapons and ammo at Jed Timothy's place before heading our way…"

"I guess it's a good thing we put a spanner in their works on that score, then." Phil offered a strained smile.

"It wasn't exactly how I'd wanted that to go down." It saddened Tex to have to admit that. "But yeah, if it means the Red River Gang are not quite as well armed and we have the benefit of Jed's armory, then it should give us the advantage."

"From what I've heard about the Red River folks," said Cross. "I reckon we're gonna need every advantage we can get."

"Don't get yourself in a state, Phil." Tex rested a comforting hand on the guy's shoulder. "If panic spreads before they even get here, we'll be more than vulnerable. The people need to know what they're gonna face, so we're all prepared, but we can't afford wholesale panic."

"That rests on your shoulders, Tex," Cross said. "I really don't envy you that."

The gathered citizens of the Little Alamo—every able-bodied man and woman, plus any kid over the age of sixteen and capable of handling a gun—parted to allow Tex through. Phil Cross had organized to have a large, wooden crate put into place from which Tex could address his people.

As Tex hauled himself up onto the crate with a loud grunt, he felt more than a little self-conscious. As practical as having a platform was, he couldn't help but feel like one of those crazy street-corner preachers yelling about fire, brimstone, and the End of Times.

Tex raised a hand to hush the crowd. "It's good to see you all gathered together," he began. "Although, I'd have wished for better circumstances—"

"Are the Red River Gang coming?" a voice broke the gathering's reverent silence.

Tex wanted to reassure them all that, no, the gang wasn't on its way, everyone was perfectly safe, and he was merely taking precautionary measures, but he couldn't. He had a sworn duty to protect everyone within the Little Alamo's fortified walls—even if it meant delivering bad news.

"Yes," he said with firmness. "We have good reason to believe the Red River Gang are on the way here with the intention of taking what we've got."

A murmur spread through the townspeople. Tex looked for a little moral support and saw Lump, Tip, Wopat, and even Rhino, who sat in one of the infirmary's wheelchairs.

Lee was there too, standing near the back of the crowd and, alongside him, Victoria.

Seeing Victoria there bolstered Tex's spirits: even though she *had* to be there, it meant the world to him. Tex promised himself he'd catch up with her once he was done.

"I don't need to stress how important it is to not only be fully prepared, but to remain calm." Looking at the small sea of faces before him, Tex knew the latter was a big ask; the majority looked terrified and on the verge of tears.

"We're reinforcing the walls and have laid mines the whole way around the outside periphery," Tex continued. "Every one of you will be fully armed and expected to patrol the upper walkway and interior—in shift, of course. When we've finished up here, make your way over to the stores, and Phil will issue all of you with weapons."

Small pockets of chatter broke out among the gathering; Tex knew most of them were proficient with a gun—it had been a prerequisite for Little Alamo citizenship—but he couldn't bank on everyone being prepared to actually fire one at another human being. Tex looked across the crowd at Victoria; their eyes met, and a warm smile lit up her worried face.

"When are they coming?" Another voice rose above the babble.

"We don't know," Tex admitted. "It could be today, it could be tomorrow, it could be in a week's time—the important thing is that we get ourselves prepared *now*. You've all seen what we've done to protect the compound, but none of that is of any use unless we all do our part. I can see many of you are scared right now, but we planned for this all those years ago when we were building our new home. We knew somebody would try to take what we have at some point and, with things only getting worse out there, it looks as if our time has come."

The crowd fell silent; Tex was beginning to feel like some warlord rallying his troops and wondered if the Red River Gang's leader was delivering a similar speech to his people.

Tex pointed toward Lump and the others. "We will train anyone who needs training in weapons use—I'm sure some of you have gotten a little rusty over the years." He attempted a smile. "Please make sure you're familiar with the guns given to you, and don't be embarrassed to ask for instruction if you need it." Looking over at Victoria, Tex saw her nodding; he wasn't even sure if she'd ever handled a gun before.

Done with his address—Tex didn't see much point in dragging it out with unnecessary detail and idle words—he made it clear anyone could ask anything about what was likely to happen, and stood down from his small, makeshift stage.

As he watched the crowd move en masse toward the warehouse to collect their arms, Tex muttered a little prayer for everyone's safety and hoped they wouldn't be burying more people in the days to come.

Tex headed home—he needed a little time alone—and then he had to see Victoria.

Chapter Forty-One

"I'd like you to have this," Tex said when Victoria opened her door to him. He held up his favorite Winchester Model 94 for her to see. In his other hand, he clutched a large box of ammunition. "It's one of the best lever-action rifles in the world—it's the gun that won the west, apparently."

"Oh, hello, Tex," she seemed surprised to see him. "Come in."

Tex stepped into Victoria's home and sat himself down on the couch; he leaned the gun against the wall.

"That's very kind of you," Victoria said as she settled herself down next to him. "But a kiss might have been a nicer greeting." She laughed, her face a picture of happiness.

So, Tex kissed his gal.

That done, Victoria took his hand in hers and smiled. "I can get a gun from Phil later," she told him. "There's no need for you to give yours away—you never know, you might just need it."

Tex shook his head. "I have plenty," he told her. "I have three other rifles, a semi-automatic, Lee has one, and I have my trusty Colt .45." He patted the revolver that sat reassuringly upon his hip. "I've had the Winchester a long time, and I'd really like you to have it—think of it as a good luck charm."

"Well, if it'll make you feel better, how could I possibly say no?"

"You can't." Tex returned the smile and leaned in for another kiss.

"But…" Victoria held a finger to Tex's lips, stopping him.

"But what?"

"I'm going to have to take you up on the kind offer you made out there for a little education," Victoria said. "I haven't fired a gun since… since before we came here."

"It would be my pleasure," Tex told her. "I can take you to the range right now if you're not doing anything."

Victoria shook her head. "I have no plans for the rest of the day," she said. "I got everything done early so I could be free for anything that needs to be done to help with the preparations."

Tex fought a wry smile; Victoria sounded more like they were planning for a July 4th cookout than a Red River Gang invasion.

###

"You surprised me today," Tex said as he sat on the wooden bench by the pond with his arm around Victoria's shoulders and watching the lonely swan paddle around in the murky water; dusk was beginning to creep in, the shadows long upon the ground, the compound quiet after the day's hectic activity. "At the range—anyone would have thought you'd grown up around guns."

"I surprised myself, if I'm honest," Victoria admitted. "The last time I fired a gun was when Rusty taught me how to shoot."

A sudden lump in Tex's throat stifled his words; it

was the first time Victoria had mentioned her late husband's name—she always stopped short of saying it. The word sounded strange coming from her lips, it kind of brought his old friend back into the present.

"I'm going to volunteer to man the walls," Victoria filled the awkward silence between them, and Tex reckoned she'd felt the moment, too. "Or should that be *woman* the walls?"

Tex chuckled along with her, and the tension lifted. "I think the days of worrying about offending people with that bullcrap are long behind us."

"That's something I'll never miss about the Before Times," Victoria snuggled into Tex's body, even though the late evening air was hot and humid; she seemed to fit just perfectly.

Tex squeezed Victoria's shoulder. "Are you sure about that? Manning the walls, I mean."

Victoria tensed. "Because I'm a woman?"

"No… *no…*" Tex felt his face heat up. "Because you haven't fired a gun in so long."

"I did good at the range—you said so yourself." Victoria argued. "I'd like to do my duty and defend our home, Tex."

Tex just wanted to blurt out that the *real* reason he wanted Victoria to reconsider was he couldn't bear the thought of losing her; she seemed to have a romantic notion of defending her home against the marauders, but Tex knew all too well the brutal realities of war.

People got hurt, people got killed.

Losing Victoria would destroy him, Tex knew that deep in his heart and soul. And not simply because he'd experienced the unbearable pain of losing Krista, it was because…

"I love you, Victoria." Tex had planned out how he was going to tell her, how he was going to make it the most romantic gesture ever—there was, after all, only ever the one first time he'd get to tell her how he truly felt.

Instead, he'd just blurted it out like an idiot.

"And I love you, too, Tex," Victoria said softly as she lay her head upon his shoulder.

"I've been meaning to tell you for some time, now."

"I know."

"You did? So why didn't you say something?" Tex asked.

"And spoil this moment?" Victoria sighed. "Why on earth would I want to do that?"

Tex let out a small, relieved laugh. "Kinda reminds me of how Jesse felt about revealing his true feelings for Ana in *The Bridge*," he said. "It's a scary point in any relationship for a guy."

"In case it's not reciprocated?" Victoria ventured. "I suppose I get that."

"Every guy, like *ever*, is terrified of rejection," Tex told her.

Victoria lifted her head from Tex's shoulder and looked at him, her face close to his. "And you thought I'd reject you? Why would I do that, Tex? Do you have no idea how I feel about you?"

Tex smiled sheepishly; he'd had a good idea, of course, but he'd never been one to make assumptions or shoot from the hip when it came to matters of the heart—it was a trait Krista used to tease him made him appear *cold*. "I hoped you felt the same way," he told her, "but you women can be difficult to read at times."

With that, Victoria gently caressed Tex's lips with hers, then followed with a long, passionate kiss that took his breath away.

The first of the explosions from beyond the Little Alamo wall split the tranquility and broke Tex and Victoria's kiss.

Then came the second and third blasts in close succession.

Startled, Tex and Victoria looked across the green to where a thick column of white smoke rose high up into the darkening sky; someone had triggered one of the claymore mines Phil Cross had so carefully laid out. Tex felt tiny dewdrops of wetness tickle his cheeks and realized it was blood from the mines' hapless victims.

As Tex stood up from the bench and headed for home, his hand gripping Victoria's, the Little Alamo became a hive of activity once again as people ran from their houses with guns in their hands.

Victoria slipped her hand from his and raced in the direction of her house—Tex watched her go with a heavy heart.

Reaching his own place, Tex burst in to find Lee already loading the rifles.

Chapter Forty-Two

Tex got to his place on the compound's wall above the west wall—it was one of the weak points he and Lump had identified, and Phil Cross had worked hard to reinforce it. He'd left Lee back home to defend the place should the Red River Gang manage to break through—Tex hoped his son would be safe there.

Looking out into the night at the intimidating gathering of would-be invaders driving trucks and modified 4x4 off-roaders—some were even horseback—Tex's thoughts turned to Victoria. She was up on the rampart by the rear gates. Tex offered up a prayer that his trusty old Winchester would indeed keep her safe, and he'd get to tell Victoria he loved her again once everything was over.

Suddenly, the wall shook, and a loud, dull *clang* reverberated through the night. It was followed by gunshots as the soldiers closest to the gates fired down at the attackers.

Tex's walkie-talkie crackled to life. It was Lump. "Shit! They got battering rams!" There was panic in his voice.

Tex ran along the wooden walkway to where Lump was busy shooting through a narrow gap in the wall.

He heard the revving of an engine, then the gates clanged, and the wall shook once more.

"We gotta stop them!" Lump shouted above the cacophony of gunfire. "Tip says they're doing the same at the back, too."

Victoria.

Chancing a look over the parapet, Tex saw a black, hulking F-650 reversing away from the front gate. The front of the truck was armor-plated all the way down to the wheels, with just a narrow slit over the windshield and had been fitted with a thick steel construction beam by means of a battering ram. Behind the giant truck a flotilla of smaller trucks sat in the darkness just out of effective gunfire reach.

Tex's heart sank; there was no way they'd be able to stop the thing, and the gates and walls could only take so much hammering—it was inevitable the Red River Gang was going to break through.

"We need to get as many guns down around the gates as we can," Tex told Lump. "We're useless up here—those bastards are coming in, and we have to be ready for them!"

Lump nodded his agreement and pulled out his walkie-talkie to give orders to the deputies, Tip, Wopat, and Rhino, the latter of which had been tasked with defending the infirmary—from his damn sick bed if necessary.

As Tex made his way from his post to support the people on the ground, a whole bunch of claymores let rip. They lit up the darkness and filled the air with an acid reek of gunpowder; Tex hoped they'd taken out a good number of the Red River Gang with them.

Tex made his way to the rear of the compound with his thoughts on Victoria—if the Red River Gang were focusing on the rear gates, she'd be in the direct line of fire.

An explosion rocked the Little Alamo wall to Tex's

left—a scorched hole the size of a small child appeared in the thick timber and splinters of burning wood rained down inside the compound.

The blast had not come from one of the claymores—it was too close to the wall and sounded entirely different from the dull, muffled *whoomph* of Phil Cross's mines.

The Red River Gang had dynamite!

"Shit," Tex growled under his breath and broke into a full-on run by the John Wayne bar and down the main street.

"*Tex! Come in Tex*!" The walkie-talkie burst to life with Lump's voice and the grating *crack-crack-crack* of gunfire—the guy was panicking, which concerned Tex greatly: he'd never once seen his old friend be anything other than ice-cool.

"Speak to me, Lump!" Tex was out of breath from running; he was beginning to feel his age.

"They got dynamite! They're trying to blast through the gates here!"

"Hold tight, Lump, I'm on my way!" Tex panted and, the second Lump signed off, he hit the button again. "Tip? Wopat? Get as many reinforcements to the south gates as you can spare—the bastards are coming through!"

Tex rounded the corner of the short chunk of road that led to the compound's rear gates to be confronted by chaos: Lump was up on the walkway above the double gates with seven heavily-armed guys—all firing down at the would-be pillagers as dynamite blasts jarred the heavy, reinforced gates. Tex counted fifteen, maybe more, men and women darting around in front of the gate and hunkering down behind huge, wooden equipment crates that had been strategically placed to hinder the progress of any vehicles that managed to get into the compound.

"Victoria!" Tex shouted over; she was crouched down low behind one of the crates, the Winchester cradled across her knees.

Twisting around, she looked over her shoulder toward Tex and, just as their eyes met, the twin gates blew open with a forceful blast so strong it knocked Tex flat on his ass.

Even before the smoke and debris settled, the Red River Gang rushed in through the ruined gates in their trucks and 4x4s; and behind them, foot soldiers and a bunch of feral-looking men on horseback.

Tex picked up his hat from the dirt, slung his semi-automatic over his shoulder, and crawled across to where Victoria was hunkered down. Looking across at the shattered gateway, Tex saw the walkway had collapsed completely, and the Red River vehicles and horses were running over the bodies on the ground. Lump and a couple of his men had managed to escape the blast—Tex saw them circling around behind the small sentry building to take pot shots at the invaders.

"We can't stay here!" Tex shouted to Victoria above the cacophony of growling engines, gunfire—and dynamite explosions from every direction; their attackers were clearly hell-bent on destroying as much of the Little Alamo's walls as they could.

"I'm not leaving!" Victoria was defiant. She swung her rifle around, popped around the side of the crate, and fired off a trio of shots at the advancing Red River vehicles.

"It's not safe, Victoria," Tex insisted; he'd been in enough combat situations to realize when retreat was the best—and only—option.

"You go, Tex," Victoria said. "I'm not gonna let them take our home!"

Tex began to argue just as an F-650 plowed into one of the crates ahead and to the right of where he and Victoria were hiding. The steel beam battering ram welded to the truck smashed through the crate like it was matchwood and the wheels crushed the two young men cowering behind it.

With no time to argue, Tex grabbed Victoria's arm.

"What the hell, Tex?" Victoria turned on him, and Tex saw something hostile in her eyes.

Ignoring that, Tex darted out from behind the crate dragging Victoria along with him.

Bullets whizzed and zinged around them as Tex raced toward the barn—it was less than a hundred yards away but felt like a hundred miles. Victoria struggled against Tex right up until the moment they saw the crate they'd just left behind disintegrate in a loud bang and ball of yellow-orange flame.

And, when they got to the barn, Victoria sat herself down on the straw-strewn ground to gather herself and reload the Winchester. The cows mooed anxiously around them, the handful of sheep restless in their stalls.

"*Tex, are you there*?" It was Lump.

"Lump, you okay?" Fumbling with the walkie-talkie, Tex realized his hands were shaking.

"Yeah, I'll live."

"We have to get everyone in and around the center," Tex said. "Now the bastards are inside, we gotta fight them head-on before…" A glance at Victoria, and Tex knew the rest didn't have to be said. He also knew things were pretty bad out there—he'd hoped against hope the walls had been made secure enough to withstand even the most determined attacks, but anything other than thick plate steel wasn't going to be impervious to dynamite.

Now you know how the Timothy compound folks felt, Tex's conscience pricked him.

"I'm going back out there," Tex told Victoria. "You stay here, catch your breath."

"Damned if I'm going to do that, Tex Pemberton," Victoria snapped. "We're in this together, come hell or highwater."

With that, Victoria kicked open the barn's door and stepped outside, her gun at the ready.

The citizens of the Little Alamo met the invading Red River Gang at the green with a show of force. They'd secreted themselves in the buildings around the green, taking the best advantage of being on their home territory.

Tex and Victoria got to her house via the back alleyways and positioned themselves in the front window in time for the Red River convoy to appear.

"You ready for this?" Tex asked Victoria, concerned; he recognized the early signs of PTSD and was worried she'd crumble or do something reckless

Victoria nodded. "I got this," she said, but her determined voice was obviously faked.

Tex pulled out his walkie-talkie and thumbed the button. "Okay, *fire*!"

In an instant, the entire green was lit up by floodlights and bright flashes from guns surrounding the Little Alamo's uninvited guests—then came the succession of small explosions, which took their toll on their vehicles and had the horses galloping around with terror in their eyes.

Tex was grateful they hadn't used up all their own dynamite raiding Jed Timothy's place.

The Red River foot soldiers were mowed down first, followed by the horsemen—most of whom had been thrown from their mounts and left on the ground at the mercy of the defending gunfire. The vehicles stopped and a horde of armed men clambered out; they ran in all directions across the green, not knowing which way to return fire as they were under intense attack from all directions.

Tex fired out through Victoria's window, easily picking out the men beneath the harsh lights out on the green that offered no cover whatsoever. Beside him, Victoria followed suit, and Tex was impressed to see what a good shot she was—she was handling the Winchester like a pro.

It took the Red River Gang twenty minutes—a half hour at the most—to realize they were beaten: a good proportion of them lay dead and wounded on the green, their blood staining the dry grass a dark, reddish brown, and at least half of their vehicles had been rendered useless by the relentless gunfire aimed at the wheels and engines.

"They're retreating," Tex said as he eased off his trigger.

Victoria let off another couple of shots—a man hit the ground by the duck pond and lay still.

"Hold your fire," Tex barked into his walkie-talkie.

Outside, what remained of the Red River Gang had quit shooting back at the buildings around them. They couldn't see who to aim at and had no chance of getting off the green to get into the houses and stores to put a stop to the gunfire that pinned them down. So, they scurried back to the trucks that were still functional and scrambled back inside them.

Victoria finally put down her gun and watched with Tex as the marauders' ruined convoy rumbled off the green and headed toward a gaping hole they'd blasted in the compound's side wall.

"Make sure they all leave," Tex said into his walkie-talkie.

"*Roger that*," Lump replied.

"*You got it*," Wopat added.

"You got that, Tip?" Tex asked.

Silence.

"Tip? Where the hell are you?"

"*He was at the front gate when they blew it*," Lump replied, and Tex's heart sank.

Chapter Forty-Three

Tip Cane was dead, the Little Alamo was a mess—its walls peppered with holes from fist size to big enough to drive a truck through; it was going to take a long time to fix them up again to be strong enough to withstand another attack. Tex knew it was a job the whole compound would need to pitch in on to secure their home as quickly as possible: there was every possibility the Red River Gang would regroup, replace their dead, add to their numbers, and make a return visit to finish what they'd started. And, if the Little Alamo was still vulnerable then, Tex reckoned they wouldn't be so lucky the second time around.

Walking through the night-darkened streets, Tex took in the devastation the Red River Gang had left in their wake: homes were ruined—most riddled with bullet holes, some with their fronts completely blasted away—and many of the small stores had been shot up, a couple were on fire. The John Wayne had all of its windows blown out, and even the library had not survived unscathed—its wooden façade was scorched, the door blasted to smithereens, and Tex's mailbox had been crushed beneath the onslaught of heavy vehicles.

And, of course, people had lost their lives.

The first count had come in at fourteen with almost twice that number injured to some degree—Lump had taken a bunch of shrapnel in the back but still counted himself lucky. Lee had come through the fight in one piece—Tex had checked in on him the second the last of the Red River Gang had left the compound. He'd left Victoria at her house and raced home to find his son taking it easy on the couch.

But, despite the losses, the citizens of the Little Alamo appeared to be in a jubilant mood; they'd fought off the brutal Red River Gang, the boogeyman they'd feared for so long, and lived to tell the tale.

As cynical as the notion was, Tex thought the attack had been just what the people needed to boost their flagging morale—the moment they'd cleared the Red River bodies off the green, impromptu barbecues and small bonfires appeared in the main square, along with a whole bunch of chairs. Phil Cross had broken out a dozen kegs of beer and several crates of Timothy Compound vodka from the stores, and a couple people brought along guitars, bongo drums—Tex even heard the sweet strains of a violin.

"We need to make a start on the walls and gates." Lump appeared alongside Tex as he walked back toward his house.

"Post some extra men," Tex told him. "We can get to fixing them first thing—the Red River Gang won't be back tonight, and I think we need to give the townsfolk time to celebrate their victory."

Lump winced as he shrugged his shoulders. He ran a hand over his shiny pate. "I guess you're right—but we can't afford to get complacent."

"I hear you, Lump," Tex said with a reassuring smile. "I'll take my turn on guard duty at the second shift—make sure everyone gets to have a little fun."

"You included?"

Tex nodded. "I reckon we leaders ought to show our faces," he said. "So, I'll see you there, my friend."

Lump said nothing, but the knowing nod he gave Tex spoke volumes; he was almost moved to tears at being forgiven and accepted into Tex's leadership.

"You're not going?"

"Of course, I am," Tex replied. "I just need to go grab my guitar from home."

"Seriously?"

"Yeah, it's been far too long," Tex told him. "I reckon it's about time I treated the good people of the Little Alamo to my talents."

"About time, too," Lump agreed. "I guess we have the lovely Victoria to thank for this change of heart. You haven't played a note since you got here."

Tex snorted a little and let that be his reply. "See ya later, Lump," he said and headed for home.

###

Tex took his guitar and made his way to the wooden bench by the duck pond; he wanted to spend a little time alone with his thoughts and welcomed the solitude—everyone was over in the square, and the pond was completely deserted.

The death and destruction with which he'd been faced that night would stay with him a long time—he knew that much from his bitter experience in Iraq. Only, this time, there was no Army psychologist to talk it all out with—but there was Victoria.

She'd come into his life just when he needed her the most, and in just the right way. More than a friend, more than his friend's widow, and hopefully more than just a lover. Tex knew in his heart he wanted to spend the rest of his days in Victoria's arms and longed to be with her again.

"Hello, Tex." Victoria's voice startled him, and, for a moment, he thought she'd stepped straight out of his thoughts.

"Hey," Tex said, turning around. "What…?"

The words wouldn't come; Victoria stood there behind him with an icy expression on her beautiful face and the Winchester pointed directly at him.

"I hate you, Tex Pemberton," she said, matter-of-factly. "I want you to know that before…" She wiggled the rifle for emphasis.

"What are you saying, Victoria?" Tex struggled to believe his ears—had she succumbed to PTSD from fighting the Red River Gang?

"I'm saying I hate you for Rusty's death—you sent your best friend to die—and I hate you for making me lose my baby," Victoria said. "She was yours, Tex, did you know that?"

Tex shook his head.

"She died, and when I lost her, I was so messed up inside I couldn't have any more. So, I lost everything because of you."

"Victoria…" Holding out his hands toward her—the guitar still clutched in one—Tex ignored the Colt at his side. He struggled to equate the loving woman he'd shared a wonderful kiss with as the sun went down only hours before. "You've been through a lot tonight—you don't know what you're saying."

"Spare me the PTSD speech, Tex," Victoria snapped. "I could have just shot you in the back, but I wanted you to die with a broken heart—just like you broke mine and left me to die inside all those years ago."

"I thought we were past that." Tex said. "You told me you loved me."

"I told you a lot of things," Victoria hissed. "Except

how much I resent you for what you did and who you are."

"Please, Victoria—"

Tex's plea was punctuated by the sharp retort of his own rifle. The guitar broke apart in his hand, and he felt the unmistakable kick of a bullet punching deep into his stomach.

Placing the Winchester carefully on the ground, Victoria turned her back on Tex and walked away from him.

Chapter Forty-Four

She'd left the book on the bench—*their* bench, *their* book—and Tex laid his hand on its white, glossy cover. He'd never get to finish it, he knew that, and that made him sad—was it possible Ana was also going through the façade of loving her would-be suitor for some nefarious reason? The thought hurt Tex to his core; he'd opened his heart to Victoria without realizing she harbored such a deep hatred for him—everything they'd shared had been a sham from the very beginning.

His heart broken; Tex was more than happy to embrace death.

"We gotta get you to the infirmary," Doc Barker said as Lump escorted him to the bench overlooking the pond.

Tex waved him away. "I'm done, Doc," he said. "It'd be a waste of good resources to haul me in—there are a lot more deserving cases than me in there tonight."

"Don't be stupid, Tex." The doctor tried lifting him from the bench.

"Leave me alone," Tex said. "I don't want to die looking at white walls and tubes—I want to look at the community I helped build and defend. I'm happy just being here."

Tex saw Doc Barker exchange a look with Lump—

the guy clearly knew when he was beaten.

Lump sat down beside Tex and, together, they watched the doctor amble away. In the background, the happy sounds of merrymaking, of jubilance in the face of adversity drifted across the stillness of the pond

"Why did this happen, Tex?" Lump asked as his friend rested his head upon his shoulder.

"Who the hell knows, Lump," Tex sighed. He pulled his trusty old Colt from its holster and handed it over. "Can you make sure Lee gets this—and tell him his old man loves him."

Lump took the revolver from Tex. He glanced down at the book in Tex's hand as he did so and spent the last moments of his friend's life in silence.

EPILOGUE

Victoria confessed to Tex's murder at the cursory trial Lump called the day after they laid him to rest alongside those killed by the Red River Gang. She offered no defense, no reason, other than she'd shot him dead with his own rifle.

It had been the first murder at the Little Alamo, so Lump, as the new leader, wasn't sure what to do by way of punishment. In the end, he resorted to Texas law and decreed Victoria must face execution.

That didn't bother her one bit—in fact, Victoria welcomed the prospect of an end to the bitterness that had eaten her up for so long she'd forgotten how her life felt without it.

The date was set for a week from the brief trial, and Victoria was to be placed under house arrest.

It was Lee who spoke out in her defense. He told Lump that his father would not have wanted it to end like that. Despite everything, he'd loved her, and she had made him happy.

And so, Victoria was given the choice to leave the Little Alamo and take her chances in the outside world that had changed so much since the Before Times. She'd taken the opportunity, of course, and left that night under cover of darkness for her own safety—not one single person in the compound would have hesitated to do her harm had they seen her in the street.

Victoria cast a sorrowful glance behind her as the Little Alamo's hastily repaired gates swung closed. The place she'd called home looked peaceful, quiet, happy, and she knew she'd never find anything like it ever again.

END

About the Author

Jesse Myrow is a US Army veteran who always dreamed of writing a novel.

In doing so, his goal is to share some of the sights he experienced during his years of traveling as well as add a little love and a drop of drama to create *The Bridge* and *A Shot of Love* that links everything together.

Born and raised in Texas, Jesse always enjoyed the outdoors and loved adventures; his mind would run wild as he could only imagine places he'd never been and people he never knew.

But, all that changed when Jesse joined the Army—he realized dreams do come true and life really is one great big adventure.

Also by Jesse Myrow

The Bridge

Fifty-year-old Army veteran, Jesse, walks aimlessly around the streets of Germany longing for companionship and—maybe, just maybe—love.

After his beloved wife died, Jesse neglected his need for love and focused solely on his daughters' happiness. But they grew up so quickly and all too soon had families of their own. Now, Jesse's only respite from the soul-crushing loneliness is his penchant for wandering through the European cities in which he works…

Which is how Jesse accidentally stumbles upon a small, quaint café in an secluded back street. And how he meets Ana.

A stunning beauty, Ana is refined, intelligent, cultured—and, at just thirty-two, almost twenty years younger than Jesse—so it's no surprise she catches his eye the very first moment he sees her. Jesse and Ana create a burgeoning relationship from that first meeting, which blossoms into the love Jesse craves so much.

Despite their age gap and the obstacles created by families and occupations, the two lovers navigate the often-difficult consequences of being both together and apart, and remain blissfully unaware that tragedy lurks just around the corner.

www.ingramcontent.com/pod-product-compliance
Lightning Source LLC
Chambersburg PA
CBHW070832020826
48982CB00019B/1042/J

* 9 7 9 8 2 1 8 1 1 5 1 2 8 *